SILVER NAILS

ROSANNA SIGHED. 'I'll have to scry him,' she said, reluctantly. 'The name must be uppermost in his mind. He's been trying to write it.'

Harald knew why she was unhappy. Sharing what was in Stieglitz's skull – the pain, the suffering, the hatred – would be a filthy business, like fishing for a jewel in a cesspit.

Rosanna took the prisoner's hand, and shut her eyes.

From the window, the trusty screamed, and fell out of the way. Harald turned, his Magnin suddenly in his hand.

The bird came into the office, its huge wings beating, and moved as fast as water on an incline. Van Zandt covered his head and dived behind a desk.

A beak sliced down, across the trusty's chest, loosing a bright red trail of blood. Then, the creature went for Rosanna.

More Warhammer from the Black Library

· THE VAMPIRE GENEVIEVE NOVELS ·

DRACHENFELS by Jack Yeovil
GENEVIEVE UNDEAD by Jack Yeovil
BEASTS IN VELVET by Jack Yeovil

· GOTREK & FELIX ·

TROLLSLAYER by William King
SKAVENSLAYER by William King
DAEMONSLAYER by William King
DRAGONSLAYER by William King
BEASTSLAYER by William King
VAMPIRESLAYER by William King

· THE KONRAD TRILOGY ·

KONRAD by David Ferring
SHADOWBREED by David Ferring
WARBLADE by David Ferring

· THE TALES OF ORFEO ·

ZARAGOZ by Brian Craig
PLAGUE DAEMON by Brian Craig

· WARHAMMER NOVELS ·

CLAWS OF CHAOS by Gavin Thorpe
ZAVANT by Gordon Rennie
HAMMERS OF ULRIC by Dan Abnett,
Nik Vincent & James Wallis
GILEAD'S BLOOD by Dan Abnett & Nik Vincent
THE WINE OF DREAMS by Brian Craig

A WARHAMMER NOVEL

SILVER NAILS

Kim Newman
writing as Jack Yeovil

To Maura and Martin, a wedding present

A BLACK LIBRARY PUBLICATION

First published in Great Britain in 2002 by
Games Workshop Publishing
Willow Road, Lenton, Nottingham, NG7 2WS, UK

The Ignorant Armies was first published in the anthology *Ignorant
Armies*, copyright © GW Books, 1989. *Red Thirst* was first published
in the anthology *Red Thirst*. *No Gold in the Grey Mountains* was first
published in the anthology *Wolf Riders*, both copyright © GW Books,
1990. *The Warhawk* and *The Ibby the Fish Factor* are
previously unpublished.

10 9 8 7 6 5 4 3 2 1

Cover illustration by Clint Langley

A CIP record for this book is available from the British Library

ISBN 1 84154 258 X

Set in ITC Giovanni

Printed and bound in Great Britain by
Cox & Wyman Ltd, Cardiff Rd, Reading, Berkshire RG1 8EX, UK

See the Black Library on the Internet at
www.blacklibrary.com

Find out more about Games Workshop
and the world of Warhammer at
www.games-workshop.com

CONTENTS

Red Thirst   7

No Gold in the Grey Mountains   65

The Ignorant Armies   89

The Warhawk   135

The Ibby the Fish Factor   191

RED THIRST

EVENTUALLY, VUKOTICH WAS awoken by the steady rumbling of the wheels and the clatter of the chains. It was dark inside the closed wagon, but he could tell from the bumpy ride that they weren't in Zhufbar any more. A paved road within the walls of the city wouldn't be as bumpy as this. They were being taken up into the mountains.

He smelled his travelling companions well before his eyes got used enough to the gloom to make out their shapes. There were too many of them to be comfortably confined in the space available, and, despite the mountain cool outside, it was uncomfortably hot. Nobody said anything, but the chains clanked as the wagon lurched over obstacles or swayed from side to side. Someone started wailing, but someone else cuffed him soundly and he shut up.

Vukotich could still feel the blow that had knocked him out. An acolyte of the Moral Crusade had bludgeoned him with his blessed iron during the arrest and he supposed from the pains in his chest and legs that the Guardians of Purity had taken the opportunity to kick him thoroughly when he was unconscious. Glinka's blackhood bastards might not be much when it came to knocking back the juice or groping the girls, but they were certainly unequalled champions of unnecessary violence. He only wished he'd been awake when the Company of Killjoys reached for their skullbreakers. He'd been through enough campaigns to learn a little about self-defence.

Like everyone else, Vukotich hadn't at first taken Claes Glinka seriously. He had been hearing a lot lately about this cleric who adhered to no particular god, but called himself the Guardian of Morality, and preached fiery sermons in rural town squares against lasciviousness, in favour of the sanctity of marriage and lamenting the decline of the Empire's moral values. For Glinka, all the things a man might take pleasure in were steps on the Road to Chaos and Damnation. Then, so swiftly that most people barely had time to react, Claes Glinka had won some measure of Imperial approval and was the figurehead of a sizeable movement.

His crusade swept through the Old World from town to town, from city to city. In Nuln, he had managed to get the university authorities to close down the Beloved of Verena, a brothel that had been serving the students and lecturers of the city since the days of Empress Agnetha. In the Sudenland, he had supervised the destruction of the fabulously-stocked wine cellars of the Order of Ranald, and seen to the burning of that region's famous vineyards. His agitators worked in the councils of the rulers to change the laws, to enforce prohibitions against strong drink, public and private licentiousness, even sweetmeats and tobacco. Many resisted, but a surprising number, frequently those most known for their own personal laxity, caved in and let Glinka have his way.

Vukotich tested his shackles. His feet were chained to a bar that ran the length of the wagon, inset into the floor. His hands were in manacles, stringing him between the prisoners either side of him. He felt like a trinket on a memento bracelet. The smell got worse as the journey progressed. The wagon made no latrine stops and some of the prisoners didn't have Vukotich's self-control.

He had come to the fortress-city in search of work. His last employment had ended with the rout of Vastarien's Vanquishers by the bandits of Averland. Upon the death of Prince Vastarien, he became free to pledge his sword-arm to another employer and he had hoped to find a suitable position with one of the warrior aristocrats attending the Festival of Ulric in Zhufbar. The festival, dedicated to the God of Battle, Wolves and Winter, took place each autumn to celebrate the onset of winter, and was held in a different city every year. This was where the campaigns against the creatures of darkness were planned, where the arrangements for the defence of the Empire were made and where the disposition of Emperor Luitpold's forces was decided. It was also the best place for a masterless mercenary to come by a position.

The boards of the wagon's roof were ill-fitting, and shafts of sunlight sliced down into the dark, allowing him to see something of his companions. Everyone was in chains, their feet shackled to the central bar. Most of them had obvious bludgeon wounds. To his left, stretching the chain between their wrists to its utmost, was a fellow with the oiled ringlets of a nobleman of Kislev, dressed only in britches that had been put on back to front. He was in a silent rage and couldn't stop trembling. Vukotich guessed he would rather have remained in whoever's bed he had been hauled from. An old woman in well-worn but clean clothes wept into her hands. She was repeating something, over and over, in a steady whine. 'I've been selling herbs for years, it's not against the law.' Several others were long-term boozers, still snoring drunkenly. He wondered how they'd react when they found out they were about to take the Cure in a penal colony. All human misery was here. And the misery of several of the other higher races too. Opposite were three dwarfs, roped together and complaining. They poked at each other's eyes and grumbled in a language Vukotich didn't know.

Zhufbar had been different this time. Claes Glinka was in town, and had gained the ear of the fortress-city's Lord Marshal, Wladislaw Blasko. There were posters up all over the streets, announcing strict laws against gambling, drinking, brawling, dancing, 'immodest' music, prostitution, smoking in public and the sale of prohibited stimulants. Vukotich had laughed at the pompously-phrased edicts and assumed they were all for show. You couldn't hold a festival for the God of Battle and expect a cityload of off-duty soldiers not to spend their time dicing, getting drunk, fighting, partying, chasing whores or chewing weirdroot. It was just ridiculous. But the black-robed acolytes were everywhere. In theory, they were unarmed, but the symbol Glinka had chosen for the crusade was a two-foot length of straight iron carved with the Seven Edicts of Purity, and those were well in evidence whenever the Guardians attempted to enforce the new laws.

On his first morning in the city, Vukotich saw three hooded bullyboys set upon a street singer and batter the lad senseless with their iron bars. They trampled his mandolin to pieces and dragged him off to the newly-dedicated Temple of Purity. Where before there had been ale-holes and tap-rooms, there were now crusade-sanctioned coffee houses, with in-house preachers replacing the musicians and cold-faced charity collectors rather than welcoming women. On his last visit, Vukotich had found it impossible to walk down the city's Main Gate Road without being propositioned by five different whores, offered a chew of weirdroot for five coppers, and hearing twelve different types of street singer and musician competing for his attention. Now all he found were tiresome clerics droning on about sin and Moral Crusaders rattling collection tins under his nose.

The prisoner shackled to his right hand was a woman. He could distinguish her perfume amid the viler odours of the other convicts. She sat primly, knees together, back straight, looking more fed up than desperate. She was young and dressed in immodestly thin silks. Her hair was elaborately styled, she wore a deal of cheap jewellery and her face was painted. Something about the set of her features struck him as predatory, tenacious, hungry. A whore, Vukotich supposed. At least a third of the convicts in the wagon were obvious prostitutes. Glinka's Crusade was especially hard on them.

The first day of the festival had been fine. He had attended the grand opening ceremony and listened to the speeches of the visiting dignitaries. The Emperor was represented by no less a hero than Maximilian von Konigswald, the Grand Prince of Ostland, whose young son Oswald had recently distinguished himself by vanquishing the Great Enchanter, Constant Drachenfels. After the ceremony, he had found himself at a loose end. Later in the week, he would learn which generals were hiring. But now, everyone was busy renewing old friendships and looking for some entertainment. Vukotich had fallen in with Snorri, a half-Norse cleric of Ulric he had served with during his time defending Erengrad from the trolls, and they had toured the hostelries. The first few houses they visited were deadly dull, with apologetic innkeepers explaining that they were forbidden by law to serve anything other than beer and watered-down wine and then only for an absurdly brief given period each evening. There were always hooded acolytes sitting in the corner to make sure the taverners obeyed Glinka's edicts.

As they stormed out of the third such place, a small fellow with a black feather in his cap sidled up to them and offered, for a fee, to guide them to an establishment that cared little for the crusade and its restrictions. They haggled for a while, and finally handed over the coin, whereupon Blackfeather led them through a maze of alleyways in the oldest part of the city and down into some disused defence tunnels. Zhufbar had been a dwarf city originally, and the Norseman had to bend over double to get through the labyrinth. They heard noisy music and laughter up ahead, and their hearts warmed a little. Apart from anything else, they'd be able to stand up straight. It turned out to be a 'Flying Inn,' a revelry that moved from place to place, two steps ahead of the crusade. Tonight, it was in an abandoned underground armoury. A band of elf minstrels were playing something good and loud and raucous, while their admirers chewed weirdroot to better appreciate the music. Blackfeather offered them dried lumps of the dream-drug, and Snorri shoved one into his mouth, surrendering to the vividly-coloured dreams, but Vukotich declined, preferring to sample the strong black ale of the city. Girls wearing very little were dancing upon a makeshift stage while coloured lanterns revolved and different varieties of scented smoke whirled. Huge casks were being tapped and the wine was flowing freely, dicers and card-players were staking pouches of coins and a dwarf jester was making a series of well-appreciated lewd jokes about Glinka, Blasko and various other leading lights of the Moral Crusade. Someone somewhere was making a lot of money from the 'Flying Inn'. Of course, Vukotich had barely drained his first tankard and started looking around for a spare woman when the raid started...

And here he was, in chains, bound for some convict settlement in the mountains. He knew they'd put him to work in some hell-hole of a mine or a quarry and that he'd probably be dead within five years. He cursed all Guardians of Morality and rattled his chains.

For once, he had a stroke of luck. His left manacle was bent out of shape, its rivets popped. He slipped his hand free.

Now, when the wagon stopped, he would have a chance.

ONCE THEY WERE out of the city, Dien Ch'ing felt free to pull off his black steeple-hood. This far to the west, the people of Cathay were uncommon enough to attract attention, and so the Order's face-covering headgear was a convenient way of walking about unquestioned. The round-eyed, big-nosed, abnormally-bearded natives of this barbarous region were superstitious savages, ignorant enough to suppose that his oriental features were marks of Chaos and toss him into the nearest bonfire. Of course, in his case, they wouldn't have been entirely unjustified. All who ascended the Pagoda of Tsien-Tsin, Lord of the Fifteen Devils, Master of the Five Elements, had more than a trace of the warpstone in their blood.

A few too many clashes with the Monkey-King's warrior monks had forced him to leave the land of his birth, and now he was a wanderer across the face of the world, a servant of Tsien-Tsin, an unaltered acolyte of Chaos, a Master of the Mystic Martial Arts. He had been shepherded through the Dark Lands by the goblins, and conveyed across the World's Edge Mountains to the shores of the Blackwater. There was an Invisible Empire in the Known World, an empire that superseded the petty earthly dominions of the Monkey-King, the Tsarina of Kislev or the Emperor Luitpold. This was the empire of the Chaos Powers, of Khorne and Nurgle in the west and north, and of Great Gojira and the Catsidhe Daemons in the east. Tsien-Tsin, the Dark Lord to whom he pledged his service, was known here as Tzeentch. The Proscribed Cults of Chaos flourished, and the warp-altered horde grew in strength with each cycle of the moons. The kingdoms of men squabbled, and the Invisible Empire grew ever more powerful.

They made slow progress up into the mountains. Ch'ing sat on his padded seat beside the driver of the second wagon. He was impatient to get this coffle to the slave-pits, and be back about his business in Zhufbar. He had made this run many times and it was becoming boring. Once they reached the secret caves where the goblins waited, the convicts would be separated into three groups. The young men would be taken off to work in the warpstone mines of the Dark Lands, the young women sold to the slave markets of Araby, and the remainder slaughtered for food. It was a simple business and it served the Powers of Chaos well. Always, he allowed the goblins to pick out a woman or two, or perhaps a comely youth, and watched them at their sport. Claes Glinka would be shocked at the ultimate fate of those whose sins he abhorred. Ch'ing laughed musically. It was most amusing.

But this was not the time for amusements. There was important business to be transacted at the Festival of Ulric. There were many high-ranking servants of Chaos in the city, and they too were plotting strategy. When Ch'ing had been visited in the Dark Lands by Yefimovich, the Kislevite High Priest of Tzeentch, he had been told that the dread one wished him to take a position within the Moral Crusade and do his best to turn Glinka's followers into an army for the advancement of Chaos. Thus far, his subtle strategies had worked well. The crusade hoods could conceal more than slanted eyes and Ch'ing knew that many an iron-carrying acolyte bore the marks of the warpstone under his mask. Glinka was a blind fanatic and easily duped. Sometimes, Ch'ing wondered whether the Guardian of Morality had not made his own dark bargain with the Invisible Empire. No one could put aside so many pleasures without a good reason. However, Glinka was just as likely sincere in his passions. All western barbarians were mad to some extent. Ch'ing wondered what it must be like to fear one's own appetites so much that one sought to suppress the pleasures of all the world. To him, thirsts existed to be slaked, lusts to be satiated, desires to be fulfilled.

The sun was full in the sky now. The coffle had been on the road all night. Most of the convicts would still be asleep or nursing their hangovers. There were three wagons in all, and although the drivers were used to the mountain roads, progress was still frustratingly snail-like. Just now, they were on a narrow ledge cut into a steep, thickly forested incline. Tall evergreens rose beside the path, their lowest branches continually striking the sides of the wagons.

There were bandits in the mountains, and worse things: altered monstrosities, renegade dwarf bands, black orcs, skaven and beastmen. But he took comfort; there was unlikely to be anything worse out there than himself. His position on the Pagoda gave him the power to summon and bind daemons, to tumble through the air in combat, and to fight for a day and a night without breaking a sweat.

The first wagon halted and Ch'ing nudged the driver beside him to rein in the horses. The animals settled. Ch'ing waved to the third wagon, which also creaked to a stop.

'Tree down ahead, master,' shouted the acolyte on the first wagon. Ch'ing sighed with irritation. He could use a simple spell to remove the obstacle, but that would drain him, and he knew the Blessings of Tsien-Tsin would be required soon for other purposes. There was nothing for it but to use the available tools.

Holding his robes about him, he stepped down to the road. He had to be careful of his footing. It would be easy to take a fall and wind up bent around a tree hundreds of feet below. The mightiest of warrior magicians always met their deaths through such small missteps. It was the gods' way of keeping their servants humble.

He walked round to the back of the wagon and unlocked the door. The foul stench of the prisoners wafted out and he held his nose. Westerners always smelled vile, but this crew were worse than usual.

The convicts cringed away from the light. He knew some of them would be startled by his Celestial face. So be it. They were in no position to be offended.

'Attention,' he said. 'Those of you who do not assist us in the removal of the tree that blocks our path will have their ears severed. Volunteers?'

The driver yanked at the chain threaded around the central bar of the wagon and took out the keys. Guards with whips and swords clustered around the wagon. Ch'ing stood back. The central bar was raised and the convicts were hauled out, their ankle-shackles pulling off the bar like beads from a string. Their feet were free, but they would still be chained wrist to wrist.

First out was the fragile girl he had been warned against. She didn't like the strong sunlight, and covered her eyes. After her was a sturdy young man with more than a few battle scars. Vukotich, he knew. One of the mercenaries. Then, there was a pause as the half-naked Pavel Alexei hesitated on the lip of the wagon.

Something was wrong.

The whore and the mercenary were shackled together, and the man held his arm up awkwardly, as if chained to the degenerate. But the Kislevite was pressing his hand to his forehead, an empty manacle dangling from his wrist.

Two of the prisoners were loose from the chain.

The mercenary looked him in the eyes, and Ch'ing saw defiance and hatred reflected at him.

He had his hand on his scimitar-handle, but the mercenary was fast.

Vukotich embraced the girl, lifting her up into his arms and threw himself off the road. The two of them became a ball and bounced into the woods. Their cries of pain sounded out as they vanished between the trees.

Pavel Alexei, bewildered, tried to follow them, but he was still chained to the next prisoner, and he slipped, dangling from the wagon by his manacled left wrist.

Ch'ing sliced with his scimitar and the Kislevite fell at his feet, leaving his neatly-severed hand in its iron cuff at the end of the chain.

'Anyone else?' he asked mildly. 'No? Good.'

The cries had stopped. The whore and the mercenary were probably dead down there, but Ch'ing could take no risks.

'You, you and you,' he indicated three guards. 'Find them and bring them back.'

They stepped off the road and began to edge their way downwards.

'And take off those hoods,' Ch'ing added. 'You'll only slip and break your necks.'

The guards pulled their hoods back and followed the path of broken bushes and scraped trees that marked the escapees' route down the mountain. Soon, they were gone.

The Kislevite was whimpering, pressing fingers over his leaking stump.

'Perhaps next time you won't be so keen to share the bed of another man's wife, Pavel Alexei,' Ch'ing said.

The Kislevite spat at his shoes.

Ch'ing shrugged, and the driver killed Pavel Alexei with his iron bar. The goblins expected a certain wastage along the road.

Ch'ing pulled out his clay pipe and tamped in some opium from his pouch. He would travel to the Pagoda for a few moments, in search of further enlightenment.

Then, when the guards brought back the whore and the mercenary, he would make sure they were dead, and then the coffle could be on its way again.

THANK THE GODS, he had not broken any bones in the tumble down the mountainside. But his clothes were ragged, and great patches of skin were scraped from his back and shins. The girl didn't seem greatly hurt either. Too bad. It would have been easier if she were dead. Her silks were torn, her long hair was loose, and she had a few bruises, but she wasn't bleeding.

He hauled her to her feet, pulling on the chain between them, and dragged her through the trees, away from the flattened bush that had broken their roll. It was important to get away from any trail that could be followed. They had gained some time on the guards by their dangerous, headlong descent, but there would be acolytes after them. A brief exchange of glances with the Celestial in charge of the coffle had convinced Vukotich this was not a man to expect much from in the way of mercy.

'Keep quiet,' he told the girl. 'Do what I say. You understand?'

She didn't look as panicked as he had expected. She simply nodded her head. He thought she was even smiling slightly. She was probably a weirdroot-chewer. A lot of whores were. They sold you their body, but kept their dreams for themselves. It was much the same with swords-for-hire, he supposed.

He picked their way through the trees, taking care with his footing. It was hard to keep a balance with their wrists chained together. The girl was agile and unfussy, and kept up with him easily. She had a lot of control. She was probably very good at what she did. He wondered whether she were more than a street harlot. More than one great assassin had found a career as a courtesan an efficient way to get close to their targets.

They would be expected to keep going down, so Vukotich took them up, hoping to strike the roadledge a few miles behind the wagons. The Celestial was unlikely to send men back after them, and it would be impossible to turn the coffle round. They should be able to get away if they made it too much trouble to bring them in. Somewhere, there were slave-pits waiting for the convicts, and the Moral Guardians wouldn't want to have three wagonloads of prisoners stranded half-way up a mountain just to bring in a couple of

minor carousers. Of course, you could never tell with fanat-
ics...

The girl grabbed his wrist. Their chain rattled. She tugged.

'That way,' she said. 'There are three men coming.'

She was sharp. At first he couldn't hear anything, but then
her words were confirmed by clumping feet and huffing
breaths.

'They've split up,' she said. 'One will be here soon.'

She looked around.

'Can you climb that tree?' she asked, indicating a thick
trunk.

Vukotich snorted. 'Of course.'

He must be staring at her.

'Now,' she said. 'Quickly.'

He snapped to and obeyed her as if she were a sergeant-at-
arms. It was awkward, but there was a stout branch within
reach, and he was able to chin himself one-handed. She
dangled from the chain, and swung herself up like an acrobat, then hauled him onto the branch. They were both
securely perched. He was breathing hard, but she kept her
wind.

'Don't be amazed,' she said. 'I've done this sort of thing
before. Lots of times.'

He had been staring at her again. She pulled a branch, and
they were hidden behind the thick leaves.

'Now,' she said. 'Be quiet.'

They could hear the acolyte now, blundering around
below. He wasn't tracking them properly, just looking at random. They must have found the bush where their tumble
ended, and split up in three directions. These bullies were
city boys, unused to following people through trails of broken twigs and trampled grass.

Vukotich and the girl both had their hands against the
trunk, steadying themselves. He saw the chain hanging
between their wrists, and noticed something odd about
their shackles. His manacle was plain iron, flecked with odd
lumps of some other stuff that sparkled. Hers was different,
a padded ring of leather sewn around the metal. He had
never seen that before. It looked as if their captors wanted to

spare her the discomfort of a chafed wrist, but he couldn't believe Glinka would wish to treat a whore so lightly. More likely, the cuff was designed to prevent her slipping free by dislocating her thumb and pulling her slender hand out of the metal grip.

He guessed her age at sixteen or seventeen. She was slim, but not delicate. She was perfectly balanced on the branch, with an almost catlike ease. In the sunlight, her harlot's paint made her look like a child's doll: white face, red lips, blue-shadowed eyes. She had spoken Old Worlder with a slight accent. Bretonnian, he thought. Like him, she was far from home.

It was a shame, but he would have to get rid of her at the first opportunity. No matter how competent she seemed, chained to him as she was she was as useful to him as an anvil.

The unhooded acolyte was directly below them now, robes swishing as he looked about. He had a wicked curved sword in one hand, and his bar in the other. He didn't seem to be guarding anyone's purity. He let loose a very un-moral stream of blasphemous oaths. Vukotich could have sworn that the lumps on the acolyte's forehead were the buds of daemon horns.

Not for the first time, Vukotich wondered if there was something extremely sinister behind Glinka's crusade.

The girl laid her hand over his and nodded sharply. He was a beat behind her thinking, but caught up.

Together, they leaped from the branch and onto the acolyte. He cried out, but she got her free right hand over his mouth and stifled him. Vukotich looped their chain around his throat and they both pulled. The acolyte struggled, but he had dropped his weapons. His hand groped for Vukotich's face, but he pushed it away. All three fell to the sloping ground and the acolyte was pressed beneath them into the mulchy soil.

Vukotich's wrist hurt, but he kept up the pressure. The girl was pulling equally hard. The chain bit into the acolyte's neck and his face was red with blood. Noises gargled in his throat. The whore took her hand away from the man's mouth and Vukotich saw the teeth-bruises in the heel of her palm. She made a fist and punched the guard's face.

The acolyte's tongue had expanded to fill his mouth. Blood gushed from his nose. His eyes rolled upwards and showed only white.

The girl drew her forefinger across her throat. Vukotich nodded. The acolyte was dead.

They disentangled their chain from his throat and stood up. Vukotich gave a silent prayer to his family totem. *Let the blood I have spilled be not innocent.* He looked around and picked up the curved sword. It felt natural in his hand. He had been naked without a weapon.

As he admired the blade, he felt the tug of the manacle, and stuck out his arm, directed by the girl. The swordpoint sank into the chest of the acolyte who was rushing at them. His was the force behind the killing stroke, but she had provided the aim. He should not have been distracted in the first place. He should have been ready himself to react.

Their hands were entwined around the swordhilt now. They withdrew it from the dying acolyte and stood over the bodies. The first had latent horns, the second wolfish teeth. Under the hoods, things were not so pure.

'One more,' she said. 'No. He's sensed what's happened, and is running away, back up to the road. He'll get help.'

Vukotich had to agree with her.

'Downwards,' she said. 'If there's no pass in the crotch of this valley, there must be a stream. We can follow it.'

Vukotich had another priority. He took the sword into his left hand and looked around. There was a fallen tree. That would do for a chopping block.

He dragged her over, and laid the chain on the wood.

'That's useless,' she said. 'The chain is tempered iron. You'll just blunt the sword.'

Nevertheless, he chopped down. The blade turned aside, kinked where it had met the iron links. The chain showed a scratch of clean metal, but wasn't broken.

It was a shame, but...

He pulled her hand and slipped her sleeve away from her wrist. He looked her in her face.

'I'm a swordsman and you're a whore,' he said. 'You can practise your trade without your left hand, but I need my right...'

Red rage sparked in her eyes.

'That won't...'

He struck the blow and felt a shock that jarred his arm from wrist to elbow. The sword bounced and scraped against her padded manacle.

'...work.'

Incredulous, he looked at her wrist. There was a purple bruise where he had struck, but the skin wasn't even broken. He should have sheared her hand clean off.

She sighed, as if with impatience.

'I told you. You should have listened, fool swordsman.'

His left hand felt as if it had been struck with a stone. She took the bent sword out of it as if she were taking a toy from a child, and threw it away. She shook her left hand, trying to get the pain out of her wrist.

Vukotich noticed he had torn the leather around her shackle. The exposed metal core caught the light and shone silver.

Silver!

Her eyes were almost completely red now. She smiled, revealing sharp white teeth, needle canines delicately scraping her lower lip.

Iron for him, silver for her. Their captors had known what they were about.

The leech thing took his throat with an unbreakable grip and leaned across to kiss him.

GENEVIEVE KNEW SHE should kill Vukotich, wrench his arm off, and have done with it.

But, vampire or not, she wasn't that sort of girl.

In six hundred and thirty-nine years of more-or-less life, she had been and done a lot of things. Including plenty she wasn't proud of. But she had never been, and wasn't now, a casual murderess.

She'd killed for sustenance, she'd assassinated several people without whom the world was a better place, and she'd killed in combat – the two dead acolytes lying back there beneath the trees bore witness to that – but she'd never just slaughtered someone because it was the easiest course to take.

Not that she hadn't been severely tempted on many occasions.

Her grip on Vukotich's neck relaxed and she pushed him away.

'Come on,' she told the startled mercenary, her eyeteeth receding into their gumsheaths. 'We have to move quickly.'

The anger subsided and her eyes cleared. She still felt the red thirst. But there was no time to bleed the fallen. Drinking from the newly dead wasn't pleasant, but she had done it before. She would have been more worried that there would be warpstone in the acolytes' blood. She was immune to most diseases, but the caress of Chaos wasn't like plague or the fevers. Her natural defences might not be enough to keep her whole with that stuff inside her.

She jerked him to his feet and led him downwards. Unlike the traditional melodrama heroine, she was highly unlikely to twist her ankle and become a nuisance for her big, brave protector. She was able to sense the root-holes and low shrubs that might trip them up.

She had been right. They came to a shallow stream that ran fast downwards. It must eventually feed into the Blackwater. If they followed it, they would find a settlement. She hoped it would be one with a blacksmith who held a very low opinion of Claes Glinka's Moral Crusade. If not, it would mean resorting to force and terror, and she was tired of that. She had come to Zhufbar to get away from her reputation for great deeds and she did not relish another brush with the makings of songs and folktales.

She tugged the chain and her padded manacle shifted. She felt a sharp sting as the exposed silver pressed against her flesh and let out a pained hiss. She twisted the manacle and the burning stopped, but the metal still gleamed white.

She took a handful of mud from the stream and gave it to Vukotich.

'Smear this on the tear,' she said. 'Please.'

He took the mud and, without questioning her, applied it to the manacle like a healer putting a poultice on a wound.

'Thank you,' she said. She took a large leaf and stuck it over the mud, tightening it around the leather. It would dry and fall off eventually, but for now it would protect her.

'Don't worry,' she told him. 'I'm not going to drain you dry at a draught. Not that I wouldn't be justified after your amateur attempt at surgery.'

She rubbed her wrist. The bruise was already fading. He had nothing to say. He wasn't even sheepish.

'Come on,' she tugged again. They jogged along the stream, feet splashing in the water. He was wearing heavy marauder's boots, while she only had dancer's slippers.

'But...' he began.

She was ahead of him. 'Yes, I know. Running water. Vampires aren't supposed to be able to cross it.'

He nodded, exerting himself to keep apace with her.

'That holds true only for the Truly Dead. They're the ones who can't stand religious symbols or garlic or direct sunlight. I'm not one of those. I never got around to dying.'

He wasn't the only one who didn't know much about vampires. Glinka's vigilante squad had come for her with wreaths of garlic around their necks, bearing enough medals of Shallya and Verena to slow them down considerably. One of her 'clients' must have informed on her. They came to her room in the East Wall Hostelry just after sunup, when she would normally be sinking into her daytime doze, and found her with Molotov, an official from the Kislevite delegation to the Festival of Ulric, delicately tapping his throat. They had silver scythes and hawthorn switches, and soon had her bound and helpless. She had expected to feel the prick of a stake against her ribs, and for it all to be over.

Six hundred and thirty-nine years wasn't a bad run for her coin – it was more than Chandagnac, her father-in-darkness, had managed – and she had at least the feeling, since the death of Drachenfels, that she had done something worthwhile with the length of her life. But they had just chained her and kept her.

Vukotich was coughing and spluttering now, his human lungs exhausted by their pace, and she slowed down. She could not help but be amused at seeing the warrior so help-less, so easily outstripped by someone who must seem to him like a little girl. This would pay him back for her wrist, and prompt him to go less by appearances in the future. He was in his thirties, she supposed, solidly built and with a good crop of battle-scars. There was a simple strength to him. She could feel it in his aura. If there was time, she would like to bleed him, to take some of his strength.

The tsarina's man had been dissolute, his blood too sauced with stinging vodka and weirdroot juice. Molotov had been a poor lover too, a disappointment all round. She had been working the festival, paid by Wulfric, Master of the Temple of Ulric, to go with visiting dignitaries the cult wished to sweeten up. She was being paid a little extra for any sensitive military information she might happen upon in the course of her duties, but so far the diplomats and generals from out-side the Empire had been more interested in boasting of their achievements on the battlefield or in the boudoir than in talking about fortifications and siege engines. Whore-cum-spy wasn't the most noble of her many professions, but it was better than being a barmaid. Or a heroine.

The stream was rushing swift about their feet now. They would have to watch out for waterfalls. They had descended to the foothills. As far as she could tell, there were no acolytes on their track. She hoped that Dien Ch'ing had given up on them, but somehow she knew that was too much to ask the gods.

She had seen the Celestial before. At the opening cere-mony of the festival, when the acolytes of the Moral Crusade doffed their hoods for the singing of the sacred songs of Ulric. She had travelled in the Orient, spending a century sailing between Great Cathay and the islands of Nippon, and knew more about the East than most of the inward-looking citizens of the Old World. Yellow faces were unusual in the Empire, and Ch'ing's must be unique among the followers of Glinka. She had planned to mention him to Wulfric when next she gave her report. She could sense

powerful magics about him. Not the familiar enchantments
of the Empire's wizards, but the subtler, more insidious
spells she had learned to fear in the East. Master Po, with
whom she had shared three decades, had taught her a little
of the magic of Cathay. She barely had her foot on the
Pagoda, but she could recognise one advanced many levels
towards the apex. Ch'ing was a dangerous man – and he
was no Moral Crusader.

Vukotich stumbled and fell. She dragged him a few yards
then pulled him out of the water. He lay exhausted, breathing heavily. Impatient, she sat beside him and tried to feel
her way back into the woods. No one was following them.

For the moment, they could afford to rest.

THE BLOODSUCKER TOLD him her name. All of it. Genevieve
Sandrine du Pointe du Lac Dieudonné.

'Yes,' she said at his involuntary start of recognition, 'that
one.'

'The vampire in the songs of Brave Oswald?'

She nodded in irritated confirmation.

'You killed Drachenfels.'

'No. I was there, though. Unconscious. I missed the big
battle.'

Vukotich couldn't understand. Being this near to the
unhallowed creature appalled him, made him want to puke
his guts, but he was as curious as he was disgusted.

'But what are you doing–'

'As a whore? It's nothing. I've been a pit fighter in my time,
and you wouldn't want to give that as your profession to a
census taker. I've swept stables. And I've been a slave... in
Araby and the Dark Lands. That's one thing about living forever. You get to try everything.'

Vukotich found it difficult to reconcile this bedraggled,
street-fighting little girl with the glamorous immortal in the
songs. She seemed distracted, annoyed about something. She
could stand him trying to chop off her hand, but she didn't
like being forced to tell him who she was. She wasn't what he
expected of the undead. Those he had met before had been
foul-smelling monstrosities, vermin to be captured, staked,

beheaded and forgotten. He mustn't let this one's almost human appearance fool him. Appealing or not, this was a woman-shaped piece of filth. In this world, there were natural things and there were monsters. Genevieve was a monster.

Biting down on the words, he asked, 'But... well, you must be a heroine of the Empire?'

She spat in the stream. Her phlegm was threaded with blood.

'Yes, but sometimes heroines are embarassing, you know? Especially if they live forever and drink blood. I got fed up with being surrounded by politely terrified officials who thought I was going to go for their throats at any moment.'

'And Prince Oswald?'

'He's not like the songs, either. No one ever is. I met Magnus the Pious once, and he tried to put his hand up my dress.'

She was distracted, thinking of her prince. He supposed the man must have used her and bested her. She was fetching, but she was a dead thing, an instrument of evil. Vukotich had killed several of her like in his campaigns.

But she could have her uses. Vampires, as he had seen, were unnaturally strong. With a crafty grin, he held up his manacled hand.

'Did you think I hadn't thought of that?' she said. 'I tried back in the wagon. Look.'

She held up her left hand. The fingertips were burned.

There was something mixed with the iron of his shackles. 'Silver,' she said. 'Not enough to weaken the links, but enough to be uncomfortable for me.'

'So,' he sneered, 'your powers haven't done us any good at all really.'

Her eyes fired again. 'Not much, they haven't. How do you suppose your other manacle, the all-iron one, got broken?'

She made a fist, and Vukotich imagined the iron cracking in her grip.

They still had shackles around their right feet, dangling the chains that had been threaded to the bar in the wagon. Fortunately, one silver cuff had been enough expense for the

Guardians of Morality. She prised her own anklet apart and dropped it in the stream.

'I should just let you drag that thing, shouldn't I?'

Vukotich didn't ask for help. With a gesture of exasperation, Genevieve bent over and freed him. The crack of breaking metal was as loud as a pistol shot.

By now, the hammering inside Vukotich's chest had died down.

'Can you go on? I can carry you if you can't, although, as I'm sure you'll understand, I'd rather not...'

'I can walk,' he told her, his cheeks reddening. She pulled him upright. By the sun overhead, he judged it to be nearly noontime, and he was getting hungry. And thirsty.

With a chill, he wondered if Genevieve were feeling the same.

ALTHOUGH DIRECT SUNLIGHT didn't affect her as it would one of the Truly Dead, Genevieve felt a growing lassitude. It was a clear autumn afternoon and unclouded sunlight filtered down through the tall, straight trees, and fell heavily upon her. Her eyes were watering and she wished she had the smoked glasses she usually wore by day. They were left with the rest of her things in the East Wall. Her exertions had tired her and she could no longer outstrip Vukotich with ease. The mercenary was tiring too, and they had continually to lean on each other for support. Their chain was a nuisance.

Vukotich was an intolerant man and instinctively disliked vampirekind. That was not uncommon. Master Wulfric, who was only too pleased to make use of her to further the ends of the Empire, was much the same: have her risk her life for the Greater Glory of Ulric, but don't invite her to sit at your table, don't let her go to a coffee house with your son, don't encourage her to worship at your temple. She'd had over six hundred years of wandering from place to place, leaving stake-waving, garlic-smeared, silver-scythed would-be monster killers behind her. Almost all of them were dead now, left behind by the years. But she took scant comfort from that.

The trees were thinning, and afternoon turned to
evening. She could feel her senses sharpening and now she
was propping up Vukotich, pulling him onwards, her full
strength returning. And with the strength came the red
thirst. Her teeth hurt as they shifted in her jaw and her
mouth filled with blood-threaded saliva. Soon, she must
feed.

She heard Vukotich's strong heartbeat and felt the steady,
even circulation of his blood. His distaste for the act might
add some spice to it... But she wasn't desperate enough yet
to bleed an unwilling partner.

For a few miles, the woods had been different. There were
treestumps bearing the marks of axe and saw, well-trampled
pathways, old bones and discarded food wrappings. Above
the trees, the smoke of several chimneys combined into a
spectral twister which dispelled into the sky.

'There's a village up ahead,' she said.

They stopped and tried to do something about their
chain. Vukotich was wearing a long-sleeved leather jerkin
and was able to wrap most of the chain around his forearm
then pull the sleeve down over it. They had to hold hands
like young lovers, their fingers entwined.

'Now, this is going to be uncomfortable,' she said, 'but if I
put my arm around your waist, under your jerkin, and you
twist your arm backwards...'

Vukotich winced. Genevieve wondered if he wasn't hurt
inside from the fall or the fight.

'There.'

Together, they strolled towards the village, not exactly con-
vincing as a woodsman and his girlfriend out for an evening
in the forest, but not exactly obvious as runaway convicts
either.

It was a small settlement, a few peasant dwellings clustered around a hillock, upon which stood a nobleman's
hunting lodge. There were fires in a few of the houses, but
the lodge was dark. It must be between seasons.

Genevieve guessed they might be in luck. Where there
were huntsmen, there would have to be a good ostler's and
a good smithy.

It was full night now and her blood was racing. But she would have to restrain herself. They couldn't deal with a blacksmith at night. They would have to sound out the villagers first, win the smith over by stealth, and make sure that they weren't in a nest of Glinka's moralists.

'Let's find a woodshed,' Vukotich said. 'Maybe there'll be tools.'

Genevieve hadn't thought of that. Vukotich could probably swing a hammer as well as any smith.

She felt a chill. She was alerted to some danger. She put her forefinger over Vukotich's mouth.

There were people coming out of the woods. Genevieve heard armour creaking. Armed men.

They saw lanterns approach and heard people talking. The acolytes must be searching the area.

But surely they weren't important enough to warrant this much time and these many men?

The lanterns came out of the woods, and a small group of men-at-arms emerged, trudging into the village. They were being directed by a sergeant on horseback. He bore a familiar crest on his helmet, that of the Blasko family, and his breastplate was decorated with the mailed fist symbol of Zhufbar. Genevieve had seen soldiers dressed like this in the city. They were with the Lord Marshal's elite personal guard.

Escaped felons or not, Wladislaw Blasko was unlikely to be concerned about a couple of offenders against public morals.

The soldiers were conducting a house-to-house search. Doors were pulled open and the peasants quietly stood aside to let the men look around. Blasko's guards were efficient and polite. They were careful not to break anything. They didn't seem to be searching for anyone or anything in particular. From the way the soldiers and the villagers acted, she guessed that this was a familiar procedure. The sergeant even took the time to sweet-talk a middle-aged woman who brought him a goblet of wine.

The wine was a good omen. None of Claes Glinka's foul coffee for these men. The crusade had not taken hold here.

Genevieve pulled Vukotich into an alley between buildings, not too quietly. She felt his body tense, and knew he was expecting a fight.

'Relax,' she told him. 'They're not here for us.'

But they had been noticed.

'Who's over there?' shouted the sergeant. A soldier fast-walked across the roadway to investigate, his lantern jogging.

Genevieve put her free hand up to Vukotich's face and kissed him. He squirmed and tried to protest, but then realised what she was trying to do. He went limp in her embrace, not resisting, not reciprocating.

Tasting him, she felt the need for blood.

The lantern was shone at them and they looked, blinking, at the soldier.

The man-at-arms laughed, and turned away. 'It's all right, sir,' he shouted. 'Courting couple.'

'Lucky devils,' said the sergeant. 'Leave them alone. We've plenty more forest to sweep.'

The lantern was taken away. Vukotich went tense again and Genevieve put her hand on his chest, restraining him. She felt his heart beating fast, and realised her nails were growing longer, turning to claws.

She regained control and her fingerknives dwindled.

Vukotich was bleeding slightly, from the mouth. She had cut him when they kissed. A shudder of pleasure ran through her as she rolled the traces of his blood around her mouth. She swallowed and felt warm.

The mercenary wiped his mouth with the back of his hand and looked at her in disgust.

Soon, she must feed. It was more than a physical need. It was a spiritual desire. The red thirst wasn't much like the simple need men and women felt for water. It had more in common with the acute craving of the far-gone weirdroot addict, or the lusts of the libertine.

The soldiers had gone now.

'We must find somewhere for the night,' he said.

She was irritated, but saw the sense. She was off her best in the day, but could still keep moving. He needed to sleep.

They would have to proceed to his advantage for the moment.

'The lodge. No one's using it.'

Slowly, their bodies pressed together, they made their way up to the hunting lodge. It wasn't especially large or luxurious, but it was better than a floor of pine needles, a roof of sky and a quilt of leaves.

They didn't even need to break in. There was an unfastened window at the rear. Inside, the lodge was one large room, carpeted with furs, with a sleeping gallery running around the ceiling. Hunting trophies hung on the walls.

Vukotich found a bottle of wine and unstoppered it, drinking deep. He offered it to her, but she declined.

With some awkwardness, they climbed the ladder to the gallery and found a corner where, under some furs, Vukotich could sleep. He finished the bottle and passed out.

Genevieve sat, her arm outstretched as Vukotich curled into a protective position, and let the night go to waste.

VUKOTICH DREAMED OF the Battle at the Top of the World. He had had these nightmares since childhood, and the strega of his village tried many times to read in them intimations of his future. In these dreams, his body was unfamiliarly heavy and hurt, not with the wounds of combat but with the weight of years. On a vast plain, where his breath turned to ice in the air, he found himself amid a conflict in which all the races of the Known World fought apparently at random. Hideously altered creatures clashed in purposeless jousts, many shades of blood darkening the ground. They were all knee-deep in the bones of the fallen. In the darkness, Vukotich fought...

Then, he was awake. The vampire was close, her hand over his mouth. Annoyed, he made fists. Did she think he was a child who cried out in the night?

There was light in the lodge, and he could hear voices.

Genevieve's face loomed over his. With her eyes, she directed his attention.

There were people in the lodge, standing around a blazing fire.

'He will be here soon?' asked a tall, completely bald man in ceremonial armour edged with purple silks and wolf's fur.

A robed and hooded figure nodded.

The bald man paced impatiently, a goblet clutched in his hand. From his bearing, Vukotich could tell that this was a man unused to being kept waiting, a man of power. Vukotich was sure he had seen the man before, perhaps at the opening ceremony of the Festival of Ulric, along with all the other generals and barons and Imperial heroes.

Genevieve mouthed a name and Vukotich caught it: *Blasko.*

Vukotich looked again. Yes, it was Wladislaw Blasko, the Lord Marshal of the fortress-city. Also, the man who had allowed Claes Glinka's crusade to take hold, who had let Zhufbar's famously riotous wine palaces be turned into glum coffee houses with religious tracts on every table and cold ashes in the hearths.

Blasko drained his goblet at a gulp and held it out for an attendant to refill. The glowing purple liquid certainly wasn't Glinka's coffee.

As Blasko paced, the robed figure stood as still as a devotional statue. He wore the hood of a Moral Crusader, but there was something strange, almost inhuman, about his bearing. Although his head was bowed, he stood a full hand's breadth taller than the Lord Marshal, and his elbows seemed to bend the wrong way. Vukotich guessed that whoever was underneath the hood had a touch of the warpstone.

Morality and mutation. These were strange partners.

Vukotich understood now why there had been soldiers in the village. The Lord Marshal was the commander of Zhufbar, and Zhufbar was a key link in the chain of fortresses that stretched from Karak Ungor in the icy north down the World's Edge Mountains to Karak Azgal in the volcano-blighted south. These were the only line of defence against the Dark Lands, where the goblin hordes still ruled, where daemons raged, where schemes were laid against humanity. Such an important man does not go anywhere without making sure no assassins lie in wait. If they survived this escapade, Vukotich would suggest that Blasko engage some new elite guards. His current crop had been easily fooled. Were he and the vampire bitch out to win favour with the Proscribed Cults, they could easily kill the Lord Marshal from their hiding place, and maybe an Empire would totter a little.

A group of newcomers arrived, bringing with them a chill blast of night air and a few traces of mist. Blasko was pleased that his wait was over.

'Hah,' he said, 'good! Comrade, some wine?'

The chief of the newcomers, robed like the tall figure, shook his head. Blasko had his own goblet refilled again.

The two robed men exchanged bows and gestures, communicating in ways Vukotich did not understand.

The newcomer, whose black robes were edged with discreet scarlet, broke off his silent conversation and turned to Blasko.

'I am Yefimovich,' he said, pulling off his hood.

Blasko spluttered his drink and stepped back. Vukotich felt a rush of terror, as Yefimovich's inner fires spread red light up into the gallery.

He was like a living statue of transparent glass, perfect in every detail, filled with fire. Eyes like black marble peered out of his infernal face and he smiled.

His robes fell away from his blazing hands and he clapped Blasko on the shoulder. Vukotich expected the Lord Marshal to burst into flames, but although he flinched he was unharmed. With fascination, he gingerly laid his hand over Yefimovich's, and suffered no hurt.

'Our dark masters demand strange sacrifices, Wladislaw,' the fiery man said.

Yefimovich spoke Old Worlder with a Kislevite rasp.

'Will I…?'

Blasko was unable to finish his question.

'Undoubtedly,' Yefimovich replied. 'Something will be required of you. You must learn to leave your preconceptions about physical form behind. This might seem quite a startling condition, but it is surprisingly pleasant. With the changes of the warpstone come certain improvements. With strange sacrifices come strange rewards. It is different for each soul, Wladislaw. Who knows what is locked within your heart?'

Blasko turned away. His goblet was empty again.

Yefimovich's still-masked lieutenant walked across the room, swaying slightly. Underneath his robes, his limbs moved the wrong way. He must have more elbows and knees than was natural. Vukotich was thankful that this horror was decorously covered.

Always, the marks of Chaos had filled him with a fear that made him detest himself. He had killed many of these warp-spawn, but he could never kill his dreams. The Battle at the Top of the World still waited for him each night.

'Things are well, I trust?' Yefimovich asked.

Blasko didn't look at the fiery man, but he replied, 'Yes. I have made the arrangements for the closing ceremony of the festival.'

'Glinka will speak?'

'He will preach. On the shores of the Blackwater, there will be a gathering of all the representatives. Glinka will call for the Emperor to embrace his Moral Crusade...'

Yefimovich laughed, nastily. 'Then he will die?'

'Yes. The man you sent me will carry out the assassination. Glinka's wizard advisers are interested only in orthodox magic. The Celestial has methods unfamiliar to them.'

'Excellent, excellent. You are well placed to succeed to the position of power within the crusade?'

Blasko gulped more wine. 'Of course, of course. My trusted aides already outnumber Glinka's people on the inner councils of the Temple of Purity. I shall be appointed in his stead.'

Yefimovich's face flared into a grin. 'And as the power of the crusade grows, so shall the influence of our Invisible Empire. There is an amusing irony, don't you think, in our taking advantage of a campaign against sin?'

Blasko didn't say anything. He was sweating. Vukotich noticed that the attendant who brought him his wine was bone-white with terror. They weren't all monsters. Yet.

Genevieve was intent on the conversation, her brows knitted. Vukotich wondered where her sympathies would lie. As

a monster, she must have some affinity with Yefimovich and
his like. But she had campaigned against Drachenfels, the
Great Enchanter. She wasn't like the other creatures of darkness he had encountered.

Yefimovich embraced the quivering Blasko and kissed him
on the mouth, obviously enjoying the Lord Marshal's discomfort. Vukotich remembered how he had felt in
Genevieve's cold embrace, feeling her razor teeth against his
lips.

'Tzeentch willing, we shall meet again in three days,
Wladislaw,' said the monster, 'after the ceremony. I shall
look forward to your elevation. As our friend from the east
might say, you are to climb the Pagoda...'

With his robed comrades, Yefimovich left. Blasko turned
to his attendant and wiped his lips. Vukotich remembered
the sweet taste of Genevieve, the shameful moment when he
had felt aroused by her, felt a desire for her to continue the
dark kiss...

The attendant was crying now, almost gibbering with fear.

Blasko was in a cold fury, trying to purge himself of his
rage. He looked around for something to hurt.

'Stop that whimpering, Meyyes,' he snarled.

The attendant, no more than a lad, fell to his knees, and
began to pray to Shallya for forgiveness.

Blasko threw the dregs of his goblet into the fire, and
looked for a long moment into the flames. The attendant
kept praying, his pleas to the goddess interrupted by sobs.

The Lord Marshal turned round, a dagger in his hand, and
shut Meyyes up.

He kicked the corpse, and left the lodge.

As HE DID each morning, Dien Ch'ing cast the yarrow sticks.
Something about the configuration disturbed him. This
close to the assassination, he was liable to fuss over details,
to take additional precautions. He was still in an ill humour
over the pair who had escaped from the coffle yesterday.
They weren't important, but they were a flaw in the tapestry
of his life, and if he were to neglect such things the whole
fabric would come apart.

He uncrossed his legs and stood up. His cell in the Temple of Purity was bare of all decoration, but there was an exquisitely carved trunk under his cot. It was the only thing he had brought with him from Cathay, and it had been blessed by a High Priest of Tsien-Tsin with a blood sacrifice.

Reciting the words of restraint, he opened the trunk. If he were to stray by so much as a syllable from the ancient ritual, he knew his heart would burst in his chest. Tsien-Tsin demanded perfection.

From among the other magical implements, Ch'ing drew out a shallow, unpatterned bowl. He set it on the flagstone floor and filled it with water from the jug by his cot. Then he added three drops of jaguar oil from a phial he found in its slot in the trunk. He slipped a thumb into his mouth and sank his teeth into the fleshy part, piercing the skin. He squeezed out precisely three drops of his blood, and set the bowl spinning.

The oil and the blood swirled in the water, clouding it over. Ch'ing focused his mind, trying to see the Pagoda in the water, its lower levels strewn with lotus and chrysanthemum, its upper levels decorated with the bones of those who had failed Tsien-Tsin.

Music was forbidden within the temple by order of Claes Glinka, who claimed that even the most devotional air was an invitation to lewd behaviour. But Ch'ing heard the orchestra of the Fifteen Devils playing on the Pagoda. For a moment, he was melancholy for the land of his birth.

He gave the bowl another spin, and it revolved as if on an axis like a potter's wheel. The impurities in the water collected around the rim, and the bowl became a window.

Ch'ing saw a hunting lodge in the forests, first from the outside, then from within. He nodded to himself. This was where Wladislaw Blasko and High Priest Yefimovich should have met last night, to discuss the work of the Proscribed Cults. The window was high up in the lodge, and Ch'ing saw Blasko and Yefimovich talking silently below.

What was wrong with this picture?

The conspirators were not alone. Ch'ing cursed Blasko's western wizards and their lack of true vision. The Lord

Marshal should not have, need not have, allowed his business to be overheard.

There were two of them, in the gallery, listening attentively to things that were not their concern.

The window sank towards the eavesdroppers, and Ch'ing recognised them. The vampire and the mercenary. He included himself in his curses. This would not have happened had he not been careless.

The bowl slowed and the window closed. He was simply staring at a bowl of water.

The Celestial thought things through. He could not admit his mistake to Blasko, lest he be replaced as assassin. It was important to Tsien-Tsin that he, and not some feeble initiate necromancer of Nurgle, deliver the Moral Crusade into the hands of the Dark Gods. If he were to step aside, his bones would adorn the Pagoda.

Genevieve and Vukotich must be found, and silenced.

He took a bamboo flute and blew a silent note, conjuring the spirit of a humble ancestor who had been buried under the tree which provided the wood for the instrument. Ancestor Xhou formed in the air, and he despatched the spirit at once to harry the pair.

Then he set out to perform his devotions for the crusade.

THEY HAD STOLEN an ox-cart, and were on the road to the Blackwater. It was as good a direction as any, considering that to the east were the Dark Lands, to the south the Blood River and the Badlands, and to the west the Black Mountains. What they had learned last night troubled Vukotich a little, but it was really none of his concern. Like Genevieve, he had no especial cause to wish to protect Claes Glinka from his enemies. He was not a citizen of the Empire, and he was not currently sworn to serve anyone. If the Crusade of Purity were to be infiltrated completely by the Proscribed Cults, then it could hardly inflict any more damage than it was already wreaking in its intended form. Until someone paid him, this was not his fight. And Genevieve, he suspected, stood to profit from the encroachments of Chaos. Surely, her filthy kind would be more

likely to be tolerated if the likes of Yefimovich were to rule
over the Old World.

Their best plan was still to find a smithy and go their separate ways. Vukotich could certainly breathe easier without
the leech girl as an anchor.

They had found some rag blankets in the cart and
wrapped them around themselves. Genevieve was dozing
now, her head against his shoulder, the blanket tight over
their shackles. He held the reins in his left hand and let the
ox do the work. They were supposed to be an old peasant
couple. They had met no one on the road worth lying to.

If Blasko's followers were to come to power in the fortress
cities, they would be able to betray the World's Edge
defences to the goblin hordes. There would be wars. Noble
houses would be set against each other. The Empire's armies
would clash with the forces of Chaos. Kislev, Bretonnia and
Estalia would have to pitch in. Everyone would have to take
sides. There would be plenty of work for a mercenary. A war
would be good for business.

But still Vukotich remembered his dreams. There was little honour, glory or profit in his nightmare of battle.

Cloaked in the robes of Purity, the inhumans could get
close to the Emperor himself, could all but take over the
Empire. Maybe there would be no great fields of combat,
only a series of treacheries, betrayals and ignoble victories.

The cart trundled across a crossroads. There was a sturdy
gallows built there. A dead dwarf hung from the rope, flies
swarming on his face.

They were getting near civilisation again.

Genevieve was awake, her fingers digging into his side.

'There's something dead here.'

'Just a sheep thief,' he told her.

'No. His spirit is gone. Someone else remains. A foreign
spirit, from a very great distance...'

There was a miniature explosion in the air and something
took shape. It was indistinct and it flew as fast as a hum-
mingbird. It danced above the ox's head.

Genevieve threw back the blanket and made some passes
in the air with her hands.

Vukotich's right hand had gone to sleep. It dangled under hers from their chain.

'I'm not very good at this. I've never been much of a spell-slinger.'

The spirit settled and became a small old man in patterned golden robes, sitting cross-legged in the air over the ox. He had long fingernails and stringy moustaches like the Celestial's.

'Greetings, honoured ones,' he said, in a tiny voice. 'I bring you the multiple blessings of my most worshipful descendant, Master Dien Ch'ing, who has attained the exalted position on the Fifth Tier of the Pagoda of Tsien-Tsin. I am Xhou Ch'ing, unworthy dog of a servant, and I request your kind permission to convey to you a proposition upon which I hope you will look with merciful favour.'

Genevieve managed to get a charm to work and violet fire sprung from her nails. Xhou waved the bolts aside as if a light breeze had disarranged his moustaches, and continued.

'My descendant bears you no ill-will, and promises that he intends to do you no further harm. All he requires is that you remain within these forests for three days, and not attempt to communicate any information you may have come by at the hunting lodge last night to anyone in the city of Zhufbar. Thereafter, he will reward you with anything you desire... riches, a position, spiritual guidance, arcane knowledge. All these can be yours if you simply refrain from taking action...'

Xhou had floated nearer and was now holding steady an arm's length away from them. He kept his position in the air relative to the cart even as it moved forwards. Vukotich's reins passed through Xhou, remaining visible inside the transparent spirit.

Genevieve was working frantically, but she had very little magic. Xhou kept absorbing her blows with ease. He purred suavely, making more and more offers. Vukotich had the feeling that they were in trouble.

'It pains me to raise the possibility,' Xhou said, his face an exaggerated tragic mask, 'but were you not to give your assent to my descendant's honourable and equitable proposition, I would suspect that he intends to do you considerable injury. As a favoured associate of the Lord of the Fifteen Devils, he can summon up considerable enchantments, against which you would have no chance at all of prevailing. Indeed, I am privileged to be familiar with the exquisite torments to which you are likely to be subject if, regrettably, you do not hold your worthy tongues, and I can assure you that the pains you will experience will be extensive, varied, unmerciful and...'

Suddenly, Genevieve lashed out with her right hand, dragging Vukotich's arm away from his body. Her hand sank into Xhou's form, and she dipped her arm into the spirit to the elbow.

Xhou flew to pieces, and was gone.

Vukotich was astonished. Genevieve smiled, a little smugly. 'Vampires aren't the only things that don't like silver.'

'Of course.'

'There'll be other attacks. The Celestial won't stop at sending messengers.'

Vukotich knew she was right.

'If we change our direction, we might appease him. If we went to the Black Mountains that would show we have no intention of interfering in his business.'

The vampire looked shocked. 'You'd let them get away with it?'

Vukotich shrugged. 'Why not? I don't give a lashworm's tooth for Glinka.'

'But what of the Old World?'

'It's not my master. I have no master. If I'm paid, I'll fight. If not, then the Emperor and the Chaos cultists can tear each other to scraps for all I care.'

The vampire was quiet for a moment. Vukotich pulled the reins and halted the ox.

'Do we turn around?' he asked.

Genevieve's face was unreadable. She had scraped off her whore's paint and looked very much like a child.

'Well?'

'No,' she said. 'We'll go to Zhufbar and save that damned killjoy. We have no choice.'

'You may not, but I do.'

Genevieve smiled, teeth gleaming. She rattled the chain. 'Vukotich, where I go, you go. Remember that.'

'We should part soon. You can be about your business, and I shall follow my own course.'

The vampire was exasperated. 'You really are an Iron Man, aren't you? You've nothing but your calling.'

Vukotich almost remembered something, but it was from his long-vanished, never-again-thought-of past. It passed.

'Pay me, and I'll fight.'

'Very well. I'll become your mistress. You may not like it.'

Vukotich looked at her. 'You have nothing, bloodsucker. You have no gold to buy me.'

Genevieve laughed bitterly. 'No, but I have a little silver.'

BY NIGHTFALL, THEY were in Chloesti, a medium-sized town. They arrived during some ceremony. There was a huge bonfire in the town square and the familiar robed figures were approaching in a procession, throwing fuel into the blaze. It was a solemn occasion, without any music or dancing. Genevieve supposed it might be some kind of funeral rite. The old practices died hard in the outlying settlements of the Empire. Once, hundreds of years ago, she'd been thrown into a fire just like this in a Black Mountain village. It had taken ten years to grow all her skin back. She was surprised that the Moral Crusade had established itself even out here in the wilds. It lent an added urgency to her sense of mission. Blasko must be stopped.

Since they made their bargain, Vukotich had been quiet. Genevieve wasn't certain how they could get past whatever barriers the Celestial was erecting to stop them, but she knew if she could get to Temple Master Wulfric, she could do something. If they were lucky, this affair would discredit Glinka as well as Blasko, and the Empire could get back to its comfortable mix of vice and virtue. It was strange how fate came around. Here she was, pretending to be a heroine again. When this was over, she would go back to being a barmaid, or perhaps seek out the Convent of the Order of Eternal Night and Solace and retreat from the messes of humankind. She was tired of great deeds, of songs and chap-books.

They found the path of the cart blocked by townsfolk, standing in silence as the Moral Crusaders marched up to the fire.

'What's going on?' Genevieve asked.

A dejected-looking young man cursed and spat. 'Glinka's Goodbodies just took over the Burgomeister's offices.'

'What's in the fire?'

A respectable-looking woman shushed them. She had a noticeable moustache.

The young man, who had obviously been drinking something not coffee, ignored her.

'Immoral books, they say, the meddling morons. They can't read and they can't write, but they know which books aren't good for you.'

Genevieve was intrigued. What could Chloesti harbour capable of outraging the crusade? Was there perhaps a secret cache in the area, containing the Proscribed Grimoires of Slaanesh, as famously illustrated by the perverse woodcutter Khuff, or Berthe Manneheim's long-forbidden *Arts of a Courtesan*?

'Immoral, hah!' the young man spat again. 'Children's picture books, and the plays of Tarradasch. Images offend the gods, they say, and words are worse. Words are the worst thing of all, because they make people think, make people want for things outside the narrow range of their experience. Things like freedom. The freedom to think, to love, to question. The freedom to breathe.'

Two acolytes struggled by with a huge painting depicting the sister goddesses Shallya and Myrmidia at play. The technique was crude, but there was a certain naive charm to the interpretation. It was tossed into the flames and consumed in an instant.

Acolytes on horseback dashed into the square, dragging broken statues behind them with ropes. Stone and plaster limbs and heads shattered against the cobbles. A head rolled under the ox's hooves. Painted marble, it looked unpleasantly realistic.

The fires burned fiercely. Firefly sparks spiralled up into the air like daemon ticks.

'It must be hard for them,' the young man said, 'to be confined to burning poems, when what they'd really like to do is burn poets.'

The complainer's hands, Genevieve noticed, were liberally stained with ink, and his hair was a fingerlength longer than customary in this region. There was a large, floppy blossom in the lapel of his waistcoat, and his sleeves were loose and embroidered. She deduced his profession.

'Barbarous fools,' the poet shouted, waving a fist. 'You'll never silence the voice of Art!'

The woman with the moustache was deeply offended now. She had a child with her, a plump boy who was looking up at the angry poet with obvious admiration. Anyone capable of so upsetting his mama must have something worth watching. Burning pages floated above the square, crumbling to black ash.

The poet had attracted the acolytes and a few of them were converging on him. Genevieve shrank against Vukotich, trying to seem like an innocent bystander.

'He's the trouble-maker,' said the woman, pointing. 'The long-haired disgrace.'

The child was pulling at her skirts. She swatted him and dragged him away.

The acolytes took hold of the poet and wrestled him out of the crowd.

The woman was fighting her son now. 'Come, come, Detlef,' she said, 'you don't want to be with these nasty people. Poets and playwrights and actors and harlots. You're to be a vegetable merchant, like your papa, and keep us comfy in our old age.'

Genevieve felt sorry for the little boy. She looked at him. He couldn't have been more than six or seven.

The acolytes had their iron bars out now and were giving the poet a pummelling. He was still shouting about Art living forever. There was blood on his face.

'And she's in it too,' the vegetable merchant's wife screeched, pointing at Genevieve. 'She's with the scribbling swine!'

The acolytes' hoods bobbed as they looked up at the cart. Vukotich shook his head. He must seem massive from below, and definitely presented a more threatening appearance than the reedy poet.

'Well,' said the woman, 'aren't you going to chastise them as sinners?'

Genevieve and little Detlef stared at each other. There was something about his chubby face. He seemed fascinated with her. That happened sometimes, especially with children. Vampires were supposed to have that power, and some she had known – certainly including her father-in-darkness Chandagnac – had indeed been possessed of it. With her, it was a random, unselective, rare thing. And it worked both ways.

The acolytes thought better of picking on Vukotich and dragged the poet away. The mercenary glowered at the vegetable merchant's wife. She was shoved forwards by the crowd and Vukotich put out a hand to fend her off. She backhanded his arm out of the way, and he fell in the seat, his hand flailing down by the woman's skirts. Genevieve wondered what he was doing. He righted himself. The woman forced her way away from the wagon, tugging on her son's arm. Little Detlef smiled at Genevieve, and was gone.

The moment was over, the *frisson* passed.

A wheelbarrowload of books went into the fire and the acolytes pitched the barrow itself after them. There were no roars of approval, just a blank silence. Someone on a raised platform was preaching a sermon against wine, sensational literature, dancing and licentiousness.

'Her,' someone shouted, pointing at a young woman standing near them, 'she makes up to all the men, leads good husbands astray...'

The woman cringed, and turned to run, her long braids falling from her headscarf.

'And Ralphus Mariposo,' shouted another voice, 'he is always singing, always dancing...'

The accusations flew. Townsfolk turned on each other, branding their neighbours as degenerates, lechers, drunkards, gluttons, slackworkers, weirdroot-chewers, inverts, daemon worshippers, adulterers, rumour-mongers, body snatchers, abusers of the livestock, lycanthropes, changelings, subversive elements, free-thinkers, hobgoblins-in-disguise, traitors to the Empire. Some were hauled out by the acolytes and beaten. Others fled, or were turned upon by the crowds.

Genevieve nudged Vukotich and tried to get him to back the cart out of the crowd, but it was impossible. The people were packed in too tight, and the animal couldn't move. It strained in its harness.

There was a near-riot now. Cobblestones had been pulled up and were flying through the air. One struck Genevieve in the head, doing no harm. The ox was down on its knees now, people fighting around it.

'...perverter of children... imbiber of foul liquors... oblater at unclean altars... strangler of young goats... sourer of cream... giver of short measures...'

'We have to get out of this,' she told Vukotich.

The ox's hide was bloody now. Someone had stabbed the animal. Two men were fighting with knives, each accusing the other of molesting a girl called Hilde Goetz. Someone was pushed into the fire, and ran screaming through the crowd. It was an immensely fat dwarf, and his oiled hair was burning like a lantern.

Vukotich put his arm around her, wrapping the chain about her back, and got a good grip. He stepped down from the cart, helping her as if she were an invalid.

'Out of my way,' he said. 'My wife is going to have a baby.'

The brawlers separated, and they were able to make their way out of the crowd. She was surprised at his presence of mind in coming up with a reasonable excuse for their behaviour.

'You,' he said to one of the knifemen. 'Where's the nearest hostelry?'

Vukotich towered over the man. His opponent stood off while he answered the mercenary.

'Th-the Easeful Rest,' he said. 'It's on the Karak Varn road, to the north.'

'Thank you, friend. My regards to Hilde Goetz.'

They walked away from the crowd, Vukotich supporting her as if her time were near. She moaned and groaned.

The brawlers got back to their fight, knives flashing in the firelight.

'We'll take refuge for the night,' he said, 'and be on our way early tomorrow.'

'We've no money, Vukotich.'

He grinned and produced a pouch of coins.

'The goodwife with the moustache won't miss it.'

THE EASEFUL REST was the type of hostelry where all the previous customers appear to have been couples named either Schmidt or Braun. The night man was snoring, balanced against the wall in his chair, when Vukotich and Genevieve arrived, their blanket around their shoulders as if it were raining outside. With his left hand, which he was getting used to favouring, Vukotich rang the bell, and the night man fell out of his chair.

'A room for the night,' Vukotich said.

The night man ambled over, and pulled out the great, leatherbound ledger and a quill. He opened its pages as if handling a sacred grimoire containing the secret whereabouts of Sigmar Heldenhammer, and wrote in the date.

'Your name?' he asked.

'Schmidt,' Vukotich said. 'Johann and Maria Schmidt.'

The night man's throat apple bobbed up and down.

'We've stayed here before,' Vukotich insisted.

'Yes,' the night man agreed, 'before... before was, I'm afraid, a different matter. The Moral Crusade, you understand...'

Vukotich glowered, trying to look as intimidating as possible.

'...without a certificate of marriage, I'm sorry, but we have no rooms available...'

With his left hand, Vukotich reached out and grasped a handful of the night man's shirt.

'We're good customers. Mrs Schmidt and I have always enjoyed the hospitality of the Easeful Rest.'

'Um... er... certainly. It's a pleasure to see you again, Mr Schmidt... I hope you and your lovely wife enjoy your stay with us.'

Vukotich grunted. The night man held out the quill, and Vukotich reached for it.

Genevieve grabbed his wrist and kept his right hand by his side, and took the quill herself.

'I'll sign, shall I, dear?' she said. 'Johann has hurt his hand.'

Embarrassed at having nearly made such a blunder, Vukotich kept quiet as Genevieve neatly scribbled their aliases in the register.

The night man found a candle and a key, and gave them instructions to find their room. It was off the first floor landing, with a commanding view of the pigpens and, alas, the fragrance to go with it.

'I could do with a bath,' Genevieve said.

'No chance in a filth-hole like this,' Vukotich replied, stamping on a many-legged creature that scuttled out from under the large bed. 'Besides, we'd have to cut ourselves out of our clothes.'

'You could do with a bath, too. A couple of days in that outfit hasn't perfumed you too much.'

She wandered around the room, looking in the drawers of the chests and opening the cupboards, and he, of necessity, trailed with her. Finally satisfied she had the measure of the room – a mixture of curiosity and caution, she tugged him over to the bed, sat down, and unlaced her torn and grimy slippers.

He was ready to drop on the bed and die, but Genevieve, the night creature, was more awake than ever.

Her clothes had stood up even less well than his to the exertions of the last few days. Flimsy in the first place, they were now indecent enough to give Claes Glinka apoplexy. She slipped the blanket off and dropped it on a floor, then stretched like a cat. Almost playfully, she pulled their chain, and raised her sharp nails to brush his cheek.

Vukotich would never understand women, much less vampire women.

'How old…?' he asked.

She pouted slightly. 'Very.'

They were both on the bed now, their chain curled daintily between them. Vukotich wasn't tired any more.

Genevieve unfastened her chemise, and exposed her slim white body to the light of two moons. Her chest rose and fell. She still breathed.

That was important to Vukotich, to know she was not really dead, just different. He'd been with women who were different before, and never caught a trace of the warpstone.

He rolled over and kissed her harshly. She didn't struggle, but he could tell she thought he tasted bad. With both hands, her arm and the chain in the way, he unfastened his britches.

She didn't fight him. She held him patiently and responded pleasantly, but he could tell she wasn't caught up in their love-making. A lesser whore would have counterfeited a reaction, cajoled and flattered him. The chain got caught between them and left red link-marks on their bodies.

It was over quickly.

Exhausted, sweat-damp, Vukotich pulled himself from her, and crawled under the coverlet. A chain's-length away, he lapsed into sleep.

Her touch came on his face, cool and pointed.

'Satisfied?' she asked. It was a traditional whore's question.

He breathed a 'yes,' hoping he would not dream of the Battle tonight.

'Good.' She kissed him gently, and slipped beside him, curving her body against his.

She kissed him again. Half-asleep, he could not respond.

She kissed his shoulder, and his neck.

He felt a brief prick of pain as her mouthknives parted his skin, and then drifted into a daze.

He was emptying, slowly, deliciously…

* * *

THE WATERBOWL SHOWED a town across the Blackwater. Chloesti. Dien Ch'ing had never been there, but he knew where it was. There was a hostelry. The Easeful Rest. A most apt name. Most apt.

Venerable Xhou had proved a disappointment, and would be bound by Tsien-Tsin in the Netherhells beneath the Pagoda for a century or so as a punishment for failure. The vampire and the mercenary would require a sterner lesson.

On the flagstones, warmed by the light of the early morning sun, Ch'ing laid out scraps from his trunk. A dried piece of bamboo from the Forbidden Fields of Wu-Fan-Xu. An empty ivory vessel from Jackal Province. A phial of soil from the Eternal Gardens of the Monkey-King. A sealed bauble of water from the Great River of Cathay. A smear of eternally-burning sulphur from the Dragon's Tongue Slopes.

Wood. Air. Earth. Water. Fire.

Ch'ing conjured up the Five Element Masters, the chief subject daemons of Tsien-Tsin.

The Masters would bar the interlopers' path.

Ch'ing pulled on his robes. He must meditate for a day and a night. For tomorrow, his magic would be needed in the service of Tsien-Tsin.

Tomorrow, Claes Glinka would die.

VUKOTICH WOKE UP to an intense awareness of his hurts. He felt every wound he had ever sustained, as if they were open and bleeding again. His limbs were anvil-heavy. The sunlight was a hammerblow.

'Don't worry,' she said. 'It'll wear off.'

He sat up and lunged for her. The sudden movement triggered a series of hitherto-unnoticed pains, and, seized up, he sank gently back onto the pillow. His rage still burned.

'You bled me, you bitch!'

She was fully dressed, some of the bedclothes converted into a practical skirt and shawl.

She looked at him, unreadably.

'It was only fair. You took your pleasure of me.'

He fingered the wounds on his throat. They still itched.

'What have you done to me? The light hurts.'

She took a physician's look into his eyes.

'You'll be a little sensitive for a few days. Nothing more. You won't be my get. Not that you'd have any right to complain if you did. How many girls have you left pregnant on your campaigns, eh?'

'That's...'

'Not the same? I know. Come on, get up. We've a day and a night to get to Zhufbar.'

Vukotich remembered it all. The assassination. His bargain with the leech. He'd had some unsavoury masters and mistresses in his years as a sword-for-hire, but this one was the crowning glory of a murky career. No one was ever going to sing songs about him.

She helped him dress. It was humiliating, but his movements were slow, as if he had all the physical symptoms of drunkenness without the exhilaration, and hers were deft. They were getting used to managing the chain, and it vanished without much fuss up his sleeve and under her new shawl.

Downstairs, the night man was still on duty. At least, he was still there. And there were others waiting for them. A couple of local bullyboys with the symbols of the Moral Crusade pinned to their sleeves, a steeple-hooded acolyte of Purity, and a timid, spinsterish cleric of Verena.

The night man pointed at them. 'That's Mr and Mrs Schmidt,' he said, trembling.

Vukotich's heart slumped in his chest.

'Made quite a night of it, by the looks of them,' said the acolyte.

Vukotich wished he had thought last night to steal a weapon.

'Married, are you, then?' asked the acolyte.

'For three years, now,' replied Genevieve. 'We've two children, left with their grandmother in Zhufbar.'

The acolyte laughed nastily. 'Pull the other one, it's got Taal's antlers on it.'

'Marriage,' began the cleric, 'is a sacred thing. Its name should not be abused and sullied for the furtherance of base carnal lusts.'

Vukotich thought the Worshipper of Learning and Wisdom would have been truly upset to learn what had actually happened in their room last night. His blood, what little of it was left, started to race again.

'If you're married,' said the acolyte, 'then you won't mind taking a few vows before the Goddess of Truth, would you?'

The cleric pulled out a sacred text from under her cloak, and started looking through it for the marriage ceremony. There must be a condensed version for urgent occasions.

The bullies were smirking. Vukotich knew this charade had more to do with the universal desire to poke into everybody's business than with any notion of spiritual purity. He remembered that Claes Glinka's idea of just punishment for fornication was a thorough stoning.

'Do you, Johann Schmidt, take this woman...'

Suddenly, every scrap of furniture in the room burst into splinters. The chairs, the desks, the low table loaded with religious tracts, even the beams in the ceiling. Everything made of wood. One of the bullies had false teeth, which leaped out of his mouth. The staircase beneath Vukotich and Genevieve collapsed.

Instinctively, he covered her with his body, and his back was lashed by innumerable needles.

The wooden fragments danced in the air.

The acolyte dropped to his knees, a chairleg protruding from his heart. He tore at his hood, pulling it away from an open, ordinary face. One of the bullies was bleeding and moaning on the floor, the other had been thrown out of the hostelry.

The night man made a dash for the window, but the sill and the crossbars reached out for him. The cleric looked for the rite of exorcism.

This must be some cursed Celestial magic.

The wooden whirlwind was assembling into a manshape.

Vukotich dragged Genevieve out of the Easeful Rest through a new-made hole in the wall. She was lucky not to have suffered the acolyte's fate. A length of oak or ash through her heart would have ended her eternity.

The wood daemon erupted from the ruins of the inn, pursued by the chanting priestess. It had a face, and its face looked angry. The streets were full of panicking people.

The Moral Crusaders had come in a carriage, which stood waiting at the kerb. Vukotich hauled Genevieve, who was picking bits and pieces out of her clothes, up onto the seat, and grabbed the reins.

'Hang on tight.'

He whipped the horses and the carriage tottered away from the Easeful Rest. People got out of the way, fast. The wooden creature loped after them, but it wasn't used yet to physical form, and they outdistanced it. It was hampered by its size and the buildings in its way, but it kept steady on their trail, smashing whatever got in its way.

'What was that?' Vukotich asked as they cleared Chloesti, and followed the beaten-earth Blackwater Road. The horses had had enough of a fright to give them added speed. The carriage rattled as it jumped in and out of the wheelruts.

'A Cathayan Wood Master,' Genevieve breathed. 'I hoped I'd never see one of those things again. It's an elemental.'

'Wood? That's not an element.'

'It is in Cathay. Along with the usual ones... Air...'

A wind blew up, knocking the horses over, tilting the carriage. Two of the wheels spun backwards in mid-air. Vukotich hauled on the reins, but felt himself slipping...

'...Earth...'

The road in front of them erupted like a volcano, spewing muddy soil into the sky...

'...Water...'

A small pond rose out of the ground, shaping itself as it twisted. The carriage was on its side now, and they were sprawled, feeling the movements in the road as the elementals formed.

'...and Fire!'

There was a terrific explosion.

GENEVIEVE TRIED TO remember the tales Master Po had told her in Cathay. One of them had some relevance to their current situation. The Monkey-King, when he was a

Monkey-Prince, had faced all five Masters, and bested them through trickery.

They were under the carriage now, with the Masters standing over them, more or less in oversize human form. The Wood Master exchanged a ferocious look with the Fire Master, and Genevieve remembered the fable.

It was ridiculous, but it was the only thing she had that might work. 'It's like the dragon swallowing its tail,' she muttered, 'or the scissors-paper-stone game.'

She crawled out from under the wrecked vehicle, dragging Vukotich on his chain.

She bowed in the Cathayan fashion, and addressed the elementals in their own language.

'Masters, I recognise that my time has come to pass beyond the gates of life. I grant you an honourable victory. However, in view of my many years I would request that my death be solely the responsibility of the mightiest of the mighty. May I enquire which of you is the most powerful, the most terrible, the most feared?'

She thought she had the Monkey-Prince's speech down to the last word.

The Tales of Master Po were evidently prohibited on the Pagoda, for the five giants looked, bewildered, at one another.

'Come now, one of you must be mightier than the others. It is to him I would offer my surrender.'

The Fire Master roared. The Air Master blew a hurricane. The Earth Master rumbled like a tremor. The Wood Master creaked like an aged tree. The Water Master showered them with rain.

'Surely, all of you cannot be the mightiest? One of you must be Lord of all Others. Each must have his place on the Pagoda.'

Vukotich was open-mouthed, unable to understand.

The Masters clamoured again, each insisting on his superiority over all the others.

'This, I do not believe,' Genevieve said. 'Five Masters, all of equal mightiness. Truly, my death will be quintuply honoured.'

The Fire Master lashed out a tentacle of flame, and Genevieve flinched. But she need not have, the Water Master had knocked the flame aside. The Fire Master shrank away from the Water Master, causing the Wood Master to take a few steps backwards to avoid the Fire Master's burning body.

The elementals argued among themselves.

Finally, arguments were not enough. The Masters turned on each other, and the area was devastated.

Vukotich and Genevieve, spared in the fight because they were the prize, stood in an island of calm amid the chaos.

'While the Monkey-Prince laughed,' Master Po had said, 'the Fire Master burned up the Wood Master, the Wood Master broke the hurricanes of the Air Master, the Air Master blew away into dust the Earth Master, the Earth Master absorbed the moisture of the Water Master, and the Water Master doused the flames of the Fire Master. Eventually, Lord Tsien-Tsin transported all the Masters back to the Pagoda, and subjected them to his wrath.'

In the fable, it sounded a lot neater and cleaner than it was. Mud rained down on them, and charred chunks of wood. The elementals merged into one body, and that body tore itself apart. They were deafened by the shrieks of the suffering daemons.

'Thank you, Master Po,' Genevieve said, bowing her head.

Finally, calm fell. The area was littered with burned wood and splatters of mud. The air was still. Boiling pools hissed.

Vukotich gave thanks to his gods in a tongue Genevieve didn't know.

'What did you say?' he asked.

'I told them a story.'

He was satisfied.

Their carriage was useless. One of the horses was lamed, the other dead.

'So,' she said. 'We walk to the Blackwater, and then to Zhufbar.'

They trudged through the mud, and left the remains of the Element Masters behind them.

* * *

THEY REACHED THE shores of the Blackwater by nightfall. Vukotich felt strange as the sun set, the weakness that had nagged at him all day fading with the light. Evidently, there were compensations to being bled by a vampire. The day's journey had been hard on them both and they had abandoned all pretence of hiding their chain. If they were taken now, they could at least tell their story and pass on their responsibility. But they met no one on the road save a party of dwarfs who vanished into the forests at the first sight of them.

Genevieve had been quiet since she convinced the elementals to destroy themselves, and Vukotich had saved his lungs for walking. Something invisible hung between them, a communion of blood that linked them as surely as their chain of silver and iron. Weary under the sun, Vukotich had tasted the vampire's dreams. There was nothing coherent, just a set of impressions, of tastes, of images.

Last night, taking her into his bed, he had felt a certain shame mixed in with his desire. Although he could not deny his attraction to the girlshape, he had still felt almost a disgust at himself for so wanting the monster. Now, he had changed his opinion. Genevieve Dieudonné was a creature of the night, but she was no thing of Chaos. Her flesh might be cool, but she was more truly human than many he had known. Feelings he had never allowed himself danced just beyond his thoughts, waiting to move into his mind just as the forces of Chaos wait forever to overwhelm the world.

The Blackwater was still, two moons reflected in its dark, glassy surface. All the harbours and jetties for pleasure boats and fisherfolk were on the other side, at Zhufbar and Karak Varn. This was the further shore, where the forests stood at the edge of the inland sea and the mad wolves drank the salt water.

It would take too long to travel around the Blackwater. They must find a boat and cross.

The moons were high and Vukotich's blood was singing. He could hardly contain his energies, and found himself fidgeting with the chain.

'Stop that,' Genevieve said. 'It'll wear off in a few days. You've a trace of my blood in you. With Ulric's blessing, it will give you the strength to get us across the sea.'

Vukotich wanted her again. Here, where the dark waters lapped the stony shore, he wanted to make a bed and force himself upon her. He was dizzy with lust. But more than he wanted her, more than he needed a release for his desires, he wanted her to open the wounds on his neck, and bleed him. If she drank from him again, he felt sure that the vague impressions she had left him with would become glass-clear in his mind. Knowledge would be his. He would be stronger, better, purer. He pulled his shirt away from his bites. They were bleeding.

Delicately, like a clean-minded cat, she licked his throat. A thrill coursed through his body. He could taste the spices in the night air. His hearing was as acute as hers. He waited for the prick of her teeth.

'Come on,' she said, yanking his chain, 'we've no time for that. Stop mooning like a lovestruck poet and help me find a boat.'

Her words were like slaps across the face. She turned and pulled, and he stumbled along after her.

He thought of the silver he was being paid and he was ashamed of himself. He thought of her flat, closed, understanding face as he made love to her, and he hated himself. He thought of her sharp-furred tongue cleaning away the blood seeping from his wounds... and he made himself pick up his feet and trail after her.

They found an old rowing boat tied up at a disused quay. Genevieve thanked the gods, and Vukotich examined it closely.

'It's rotten,' he said. 'The bottom will give way. It's a miracle it hasn't sunk at its mooring.'

'But it will get us across the Blackwater,' said Genevieve, the bloodfire in her eyes. 'Because it must.'

EMERGING AT DAWN from his trance of preparation, Dien Ch'ing pulled on his acolyte's robes. He would join the others of the Temple of Purity outside the city walls, on the shores of the Blackwater. This small inland sea, one hundred miles in length, fifty miles across, was famous for the impenetrability of its depths. A fabulous monster was rumoured to inhabit it, and the fishermen were always competing with tall tales of the creature's size, ferocity and mysteriousness. After today, there would be other stories told about the Blackwater. The story of Claes Glinka's death on its shores.

Ch'ing joined the procession as it left the temple, and bowed his hooded head. Under his robe, he carried the magical blade that could strike from afar.

Wladislaw Blasko would have his speech of vengeance rehearsed. And his confederates in the conspiracy would have an especially hideous mutant – a dog-headed retard – ready to take the blame and be promptly put to death by the militia. Then, quietly, he would be able to depart the city for Kislev, where Lord Tsien-Tsin and High Priest Yefimovich would have other missions for him. The Invisible Empire rewarded its faithful servants.

The sun shone down on the inky black waters, and the delegates to the Festival of Ulric were waiting in the especially erected stands. It had been a hard week of ceremony, secret negotiation, planning, bargaining, speech-making and decorous feasting. Glinka's coffee houses had been overflowing with officers searching in vain for entertainment.

Glinka was at the head of the procession of purity, his hood thrown back. Ch'ing was a few acolytes behind him, focusing his attention on the small of the Moral Crusader's back, where the shadowblade would strike.

Everyone was quiet. Glinka would have no music for this parade. Ch'ing had read the speech the Crusader intended to deliver and mused to himself that even the staunchest defender of the Empire would secretly bless him for cutting it short.

There was a stage put up on the beach, the shimmering black waters lapping at its foundations. Blasko stood upon it, with several of his men-at-arms, and with some heroes of the Empire. Maximilian von Konigswald looked bored and

sullen. A week without strong drink or a pretty girl does that
to a soldier.

Blasko was calm, collected, prepared. There would be no
trouble there. He was perfectly schooled in his part.

Blasko shook Glinka's hand as the crusader took the
lectern, and was brushed off. He smiled at the slight. Ch'ing
kept well away from Glinka, but felt the magical buzz building up in the knife. Without removing it from his robe, he
could thrust into the Moralist's vitals...

Glinka began his address, and the distinguished audience
grew restless.

Ch'ing called for the strength of Tsien-Tsin to do the bidding of the Invisible Empire of Chaos.

Glinka got worked up about the sorry state of the Empire's
morals, and pointedly looked from face to face as he listed
the sins even the most exalted were prone to: lechery, drunkenness, dishonesty, gluttony, questioning of authority and
sacrilege.

Ch'ing's fist grew hot as the magic charge grew.

Suddenly, from behind, there was a commotion. Glinka
paused, and everyone turned...

There was a small boat on the water, near the stage. Two
people were climbing out of it, hauling themselves up the
support beams. A man and a girl, chained together at the
wrist.

Ch'ing pulled out the knife and pointed. A bolt of blue
flame squirted across the stage. The vampire twisted out of
the way.

Maximilian's sword came into his hand and Ch'ing had to
give him a jolt. He couldn't waste the magic. Glinka had to
die.

The Moralist was white with terror. He turned to run, and
Ch'ing discharged the killing fire in his direction.

Someone got in the way – an unlucky acolyte – and burst
into flames. Robes streaming fire, he leaped into the waters.

Vukotich and Genevieve were on him now, and he was
using the magical implement as a simple dagger.

The mercenary was heavy, but would be an experienced
hand-to-hand fighter. The vampire seemed frail, but he

knew that must be an illusion. He would not underestimate these foes.

He stabbed and slashed, but there was a coil of rope under him and he lost his footing. The gods were being unkind to him, punishing him for his arrogance. So be it.

The devil-dagger clattered across the stage. He threw off his assailants, and leaped upright, balancing perfectly. He called for the strength of Lord Tsien-Tsin.

He was alone among his enemies. Very well. It was time to demonstrate his own mastery.

It was time these big-nosed westerners learned the meaning of the Mystic Martial Arts.

THE CELESTIAL TOOK up an unfamiliar fighting stance, standing lightly on his feet, his arms casually outstretched, his hands like chopping blades. Vukotich had heard something of the combat techniques of Cathay and Nippon. Now, he supposed, he was going to get a taste of them.

Dien Ch'ing leaped, feet out. Vukotich knew he was going to take a terrific blow on the chest, and probably lose his ribs. But Genevieve was fast, and yanked him out of the way, launching a fast blow of her own.

She punched Ch'ing in the side, and brought him down.

Blasko had a knife out and was panicking. He stabbed at the girl, ordering his men to follow suit.

Genevieve avoided the daggerthrust, and kicked Blasko's weapon from his grip. Ch'ing launched a toe-point kick at the vampire's head, and struck the empty air where it had been.

Blasko's men had their halberds up, but Maximilian put up his hand, and overruled their master. Of course, as Prince Oswald's father, he must know who she was.

'Treachery!' shouted the Grand Prince.

Blasko reached for Vukotich's neck. The mercenary grabbed the Lord Marshal's wrists and squeezed. Blasko sank to his knees, but as Vukotich bent over him, he pulled the chain, and Genevieve was off-balanced.

Ch'ing chopped at her face with his hands. Another girl would have been killed, but she was just pushed backwards.

The Celestial was unbalanced and launched himself into the air. Twisting like a daemon acrobat, he sailed over the halberdiers and landed rightside-up behind Genevieve, landing a snake-swift punch on her shoulder as she turned to face him.

Someone started screaming in a loud, high-pitched voice. It was Claes Glinka, howling for help while people fought for his life.

Blasko struggled out of Vukotich's grip and made a dash for safety, careering through his own men. His nerve had gone completely. He came to the edge of the stage, and tottered over. There was a splash.

Vukotich and Genevieve stood up, their chain taut between them. Dien Ch'ing smiled at them, bowed, and launched his last attack.

His hands took on a golden glow as he passed them through the air, and his eyes shone. He muttered in his own language, calling down unholy powers. Lightning crackled around him and a wind came up from nowhere.

He levitated off the stage and floated towards them, gesturing wildly.

'Sorcery!' shouted someone. A couple of mages tried working spells of their own. Maximilian ordered everyone to stand back.

The Celestial rose slowly, wisps of white matter emerging from his mouth and taking a shadowform around him. He was floating in the middle of a phantom creature, his eyes glaring out through the horned sockets of a snarling dragon, his outstretched arms the leading edges of ragged spectre wings.

A pike was flung at his heart. It turned aside, and clattered to the stage, the force of the throw spent. A mage, the symbols of power standing out on his cloak, strode forwards, his hands up, chanting wildly. Dien Ch'ing let rip with a laugh that literally froze the blood, and the mage was struck with the full impact of it, frost sparkling on the surface of his eyeballs, white droplets of iced sweat starting out on his exposed face. He tumbled like a broken statue, and cracked against the stage.

Everybody stood back.

Vukotich looked at Genevieve, who was staring up at the Celestial, her face set, her body tense.

Ch'ing grew a foggy grey claw from his chest and it drifted out at the end of an arm, reaching for Glinka. The Moralist shrieked and sobbed, and clutched at the robes of an acolyte who was trying to flee. The ghost hand settled upon Glinka's head and closed into a fist. Glinka's screams shut off, but his twisted features were dimly discernible through the thickening murk.

The Celestial's wings were spreading, casting an expanding shadow over the crowd below. The rope of ectoplasm that linked him to Glinka pulsed and thickened. A flower opened in his chest, and bubbles of purple erupted into the ghost arm, drifting through the grey fog towards Glinka's head. Vukotich sensed that if the purple touched the man's face, he would be dead.

'Silver and iron,' said Genevieve, raising her left arm, dragging Vukotich's right up with it. 'Silver and iron.'

The links touched the spectral arm and jerked up into it, cutting like a heated wire through hardened cheese.

In their attempt to bind them, their captors had given them two of the most magical elements known to alchemy. Silver, anathema to vampires, shapeshifters and spirits. And iron, the scourge of daemonkind.

The chain emerged from the top of the ectoplasmic tube, and the spectral limb came apart, a light dew falling from the air where it had been. Glinka was screaming again and pleading with someone for help. Maximilian slapped him with the pommel of his sword and shut him up.

Vukotich and Genevieve, their chain stretched between them, looked up at the Celestial. Ch'ing beat his wings and rose into the sky.

Maximilian ordered the archers to bring him down, but their shafts snapped in two as they neared the mage. He was still protected by powerful daemons.

Before he vanished into the clouds, Dien Ch'ing waved a cloaklike wing in mocking farewell. To Genevieve, he said, 'We'll meet again, my lady,' and then he was gone. Vukotich

felt a spurt of anger. Why did the Celestial see Genevieve as
his chosen foe? Was he so insignificant as to be ignored?
Then, a bone-deep tiredness hit him, and his head was as
heavy as lead. He watched the mage blend with the grey
clouds, and sank to his knees, pulling at Genevieve.

'Blasko's gone,' Maximilian said. 'All that armour has
taken him to the bottom. He'll be food for the Blackwater
Beastie.'

'Grand Prince,' said Genevieve, between breaths, 'there
was a plot. The Lord Marshal was in league with the
Proscribed Cults.'

Maximilian snorted. 'I thought as much. Never cared for
the fellow. Wouldn't put an egg in his broth. No taste.'

Vukotich tried to get up, but his limbs were too much for
him. His aches were beginning to tell. And he hadn't eaten
for days.

'Sir,' said one of the men-at-arms to Maximilian. 'Look.'

The Grand Prince strolled over. Genevieve followed, and
Vukotich had to crawl after her on his elbows like a dog.

Attendants were trying to calm down Glinka, whose robe
had fallen open.

'Glinka's an altered,' said the guard.

It was true. There were spindly extra arms descending
from the Moralist's armpits.

'Not so pure, after all, eh?' Maximilian was trying not to
gloat. Vukotich knew this revelation would mean the end of
the Moral Crusade. The Grand Prince turned to an attendant. 'Get me a drink,' he said. 'Get us all a drink. And I
don't mean blood-and-damned coffee!'

A blacksmith was found, and their shackles sawn off.
Genevieve was quiet, surrounded by officials asking her
questions. She was polite in her answers, but distant.
Vukotich rubbed his wrist. It felt strange to be free. It was
amazing what you could get used to if you had to. Then, he
collapsed again.

HE WOKE UP to find Maximilian von Konigswald by his bed,
with a bottle of *Alte Geheerentode* rum.

He had slept for two days.

During that time, mobs had torn down the Temple of Purity, and Claes Glinka had been imprisoned for his own protection. Since his exposure as an altered, he had been a raving madman. His coffee houses closed down, and mainly reopened as the taverns they had once been. The second-hand bookstalls in the market were burdened with unsaleable tracts of moral improvement. Wladislaw Blasko's body had not been found, and a new Lord Marshal had been appointed from among the ranks of the city's best men. Dien Ch'ing had disappeared completely, spirited away by daemons. According to Celestial lore, any follower of the dread Tsien-Tsin who failed in the accomplishment of a mission could expect and long and painful afterlife in the Netherhells, and so Ch'ing was not thought to have escaped justice by his disappearance. The Courtesans' Guild had declared that its members would work one evening for free in celebration at the downfall of the Moral Crusade, and the largest city-wide festival ever to be seen in Zhufbar had taken place. And Vukotich had missed it.

'Where's...'

'The girl?' Maximilian looked puzzled. 'Gone. She slipped away before all the celebrations started. A pity. She'd have been a heroine all over again. It's her way, though. She did the same thing after she and my son... well, you know the story.'

Vukotich sat up in bed. His wounds didn't pain him so much now, although his throat was still tender.

Genevieve! Gone!

'She said something about a retreat. Some convent or other. In Kislev. You'd best leave her be, lad. Heroine or not, she's still... well... not quite like us, you know. No, not quite like us.'

Maximilian poured him a goblet of the dangerous spirit, and he scalded his throat with it.

'She left you something, though. She said you'd know what it was for.'

Vukotich took another fiery swallow. Hot tears came to his eyes. It was the strong spirit. *Alte Geheerentode* would make any man's eyes water.

The Grand Prince threw the padded ring, shining silver where it was sawn through, onto the bed.

'Genevieve said you'd understand. Do you?'

Fingering the marks on his neck, Vukotich wasn't sure. Inside him, the last sparks of her were fading. The wounds he would wear forever, but the link he had had with the vampire was shattered with their chain.

He picked up the silver, and gave it to Maximilian. 'Give it to the temple,' he said, 'for the poor.'

'Which temple?' asked the Grand Prince.

Weariness crept up Vukotich's body again. Inside him something was dying.

'Any one,' he replied. 'Any one.'

NO GOLD IN THE
GREY MOUNTAINS

ON THE OPPOSITE crag, the seven towers of the Fortress of
Drachenfels thrust skyward like the taloned fingers of a
deformed hand. The sunset bloodied the castle as Constant
Drachenfels, the Great Enchanter, had done in life. Joh
Lamprecht had heard all the stories, all the songs. He knew
of the long-lived monster's numberless crimes and of his
eventual downfall and defeat. Brave Prince Oswald and Fair
Genevieve, his vampire ladylove, had ended the horror, and
now the castle was untenanted, all but the most earthbound
ghosts flown to the beyond. However, it was still shunned.
No peasant of this mountain region would dare set his boot
upon the path to Drachenfels while the stories were told in
whispers, the songs remembered by ill-favoured minstrels.
And that was what made the place ideal for Joh's purposes.

Big, slow Freder was too lackwitted to be concerned with
superstition, and dark, quiet Rotwang too wrapped up in his
own skills to take any notice of the rumoured creatures in
the darkness. Which left only young Yann Groeteschele to
be frightened by the old legends, the shadows and the night
winds. Joh could count on the young bandit's unswerving

loyalty for as long as Groeteschele's fear of him outweighed
his fear of the name of a dead sorcerer. That should be a considerable time.

Groeteschele had only heard the songs about
Drachenfels's Poison Feast and the Sack of Gisoreux, but he
had been present when Joh broke the back of Warden Fanck
and led the mass escape from the penal quarrypits of the
Vaults, to the south, and the fringes of Loren Forest he had
held down the writhing body of Guido Czerepy, the silk
merchant, while Joh tortured out of him the location of his
hidden cache of gold.

In the still air, the rattle of the coach was audible from several miles away. Joh keened like a crow and Rotwang
answered from his position of concealment down by the
road. Joh tapped Groeteschele and indicated the youth's
crossbow. The lamps of the coach became visible in the
evening haze. Joh felt the old excitement in his vitals and
gripped the hilt of his curved sword. He had taken the scimitar from the corpse of a slain envoy of Araby, shortly after
relieving the man of the jewelled tokens of esteem he was
bearing to the Imperial court, and found it a more satisfac-
tory item of killing steel than the common straight sword of
the Old World.

Groeteschele slipped a quarrel into his crossbow and
steadied it against his cheek. Joh kept his eyes on the coach.
As robberies went, this was simple. Three times last year, he
had held up the same coach – carrying gold from the
Kautner seam down from the mountains and through the
Reikwald Forest to Altdorf – and the trick had been easier
each time. Once the miners had paid their tax tribute to the
Emperor's collectors they were hardly disposed to buy
guards to escort it to Karl-Franz's coffers and so it was placed
on the regular mail and passenger run.

Tonight's plunder would serve to equip Joh and his band
for a more daring, more profitable exploit. Joh had a nice little Tilean princedom marked down, its vaults ripe for
plundering, but he would need to hire specialists, to buy
equipment that could not be stolen, and to make arrangements with a slightly dishonourable banking house to

dispose of the accrued funds. A chest of Kautner gold should set the job up perfectly.

The coach was near enough for Joh to see the horses' breath frosting. The coachman sat alone on the box, draped in a cloak. He would be wearing a breastplate under his garments, but killing the coachman never stopped anything anyway.

There was a long, creaking sound and a crash. A tree fell on the road just as the coach had passed. Good. Freder had done his part well. Joh nodded and Groeteschele stood up, firing and reloading. His first quarrel took the lead horse of the four-strong team in the side of the neck and it tripped. A figure darted into the road, sword flashing. Rotwang drove his blade deep into the animal and it fell. He leaped aside, and the team continued, dragging its dying comrade a few yards.

Joh made his way down from the rocky mountainside towards the road, Groeteschele following. He had complete confidence in Rotwang's expertise with this manoeuvre. It was tricky. Many bandits were crippled or worse when they got tangled up with the horse they were trying to immobilise. But Rotwang was the best killer Joh had ever seen, trained to it from birth.

When he came out of the trees, all was well. The coach was halted, and Rotwang stood a little way away from it, red sword dripping. Freder held the still-standing horses and glowered up at the coachman. His height, broad shoulders and apish appearance helped to deter many a solid citizen from interfering in the band's business. Joh nodded to Groeteschele and the young man climbed up beside the quivering coachman and sorted through the luggage, throwing parcels and packages to the dirt road. Someone inside the coach was complaining loudly.

'It's not here,' Groeteschele said.

'What!' snapped Joh. 'Idiot, it must be. Look harder.'

It should be in a small chest with the Imperial crest and a fine Bretonnian lock. It usually was. Groeteschele rooted among the remaining cargo.

'No, nothing,' he said.

Joh signed to Rotwang, who walked towards the coach.
The coachman was trembling, praying to all the gods.
Groeteschele climbed down and Rotwang pulled himself up
to the top of the coach. He moved like a big cat, with strong
but apparently lazy gestures, and he could strike like a daemon. He sat beside the coachman, plucking and throwing
away the man's whip, and then did something to the man
with his hands. The coachman screamed, and Joh knew
Rotwang's inexpressive face would be wearing a slight smile.
Rotwang whispered, passed his hands over the coachman's
body again and there were more screams.

Little knives flashed red in Rotwang's hands, and he paid
some attention to the coachman's face. Finally, the bandit
spat into the road and pushed the coachman off his seat.
The man sprawled, dead, beside his vehicle.

Joh looked up at Rotwang.

'No gold,' the killer told him. 'The Kautner seam petered
out three months ago. No more gold in the Grey
Mountains.'

Joh swore, calling down the wrath of Morr on this venture.
He had blundered badly, and would have to redeem himself
or lose position. Groeteschele was young and Freder was a
clod, but Rotwang – who had so far displayed no taste for
leading the band – could easily take his place.

'What is the meaning of this?'

The coach door opened and a well-dressed man stepped
out. His elegantly booted foot landed on the coachman's
body and he cringed away. He looked at Joh and
Groeteschele and drew a long, fine duellist's sword. He
assumed a fighting stance and looked at Joh, waiting for the
bandit to strike the first blow. Groeteschele shot him in the
head and he staggered back, shaking from the blow. Freder
pulled his purse away from his belt and threw it to Joh. It
was heavy, but not heavy enough to make this job worth its
while. The ill-advised hero slid down the coach and sat,
dead, in the road beside the coachman, eyes staring either
side of Groeteschele's bolt.

Joh went to the open door and looked into the coach.

'Hello,' said a musical female voice, 'are you a bandit?'

She had golden curls, and was dressed fit for the Imperial court in a brocaded dress with pearls worked into the bodice. She was not ostentatiously bejewelled, but her fingers and ears yielded more gold than many a small miner's claim would in a year. Her pale oval face was lovely, delicate and lightly painted.

She sat on the plush seat of the coach like a dressed-up doll, her feet not touching the floor. Joh judged her to be about twelve years old.

'Is there anything worth stealing?' Groeteschele asked.

Joh smiled at the girl, who smiled back.

'I think so.'

HER NAME, SHE told them, was Lady Melissa d'Acques, and she was distantly related to both the royal family of Bretonnia and the Imperial House of the Second Wilhelm. She had insisted the bandits bring her luggage to Drachenfels when they took her there, and from the number, quality and expense of the dresses in her travelling wardrobe, Joh knew her family would be capable of paying a substantial ransom for her return. So far as he could make out, the girl was somewhat simple for her age. She treated her captors as if they were servants pretending to be bandits and this whole episode a game to while away a dull afternoon in the gardens. So far, this had worked to Joh's advantage – she had ridden on Freder's saddle and given them no trouble – but he dreaded the inevitable moment when she tired of play and wanted to be taken home. Typically, she seemed to have found a soulmate in Freder, with whom she was laughing and joking, exchanging nonsense rhymes. If only she knew how many men and women the rough-faced giant had killed with his hands alone.

She didn't complain at the quality of the food they gave her at their camp, which was pitched in one of the courtyards of the fortress, and she tried cheerfully to answer all his questions. His problem was that, in order to convert his stroke of luck into gold crowns, he needed to know more about Melissa's family. How he could get in touch with her father, for instance. But Melissa, although only too willing to expound at childishly tedious length about the minutiae of her family life, was unwilling or unable to give an address where her family could be contacted, and only had the vaguest awareness of anything outside the cloisters of her aristocratic circle. Joh gathered her family maintained households in Parravon, Marienburg and Altdorf, and that several of her male relations could be found in the courts of Bretonnia and the Empire.

As Melissa spoke, Freder squatted by her, grinning, enraptured by her stories about playthings, pets and servants. Everyone and everything in the d'Acques circle had a nickname. She experimented with several unflattering nicknames for Freder, and tried to extend the practice to Joh and Groeteschele. The wolf-faced Rotwang she was – wisely – a little afraid of, and so Joh had him see to business elsewhere, settling down the horses. It was vital that he learn more...

'Tell me, Melissa, where is your father now? Were you travelling to him?'

Melissa cocked her head to one side and then the other. 'That depends, Mr Joh. Sometimes, he's in his castle, sometimes he's in his palace. Now, he's probably in his palace.'

'And where is his palace?'

'He's a count, you know, and a baron. It gets so confusing remembering. The servants have a terrible time. In Bretonnia, he's a count, and in the Empire, he's a baron, and there are fearful penalties for getting them mixed up. We travel between Bretonnia and the Empire quite a bit.'

Melissa yawned, forgetting to cover her mouth, and stretched. She didn't appear to be very comfortable in her starched and formal clothes. That might mean she was being sent on a short journey, that she had people nearby. She hadn't known the man in the coach at all before setting out, and hadn't formed a good opinion of him. 'He pinched my cheeks and patted my hair too much. He deserved to be killed.'

Lady Melissa was quite a startling little girl. The aristocracy bred its young bloodthirsty, Joh guessed. Certainly the duke's son he had had to kill all those years ago, after the fop had run through Joh's father from behind on a minor

quarrel, had been a death-happy fool. That had been the
first step on the road to outlawry. There was a song about
Joh Lamprecht, telling of how he was driven to the bandit
life by injustice and tyranny, but Joh knew he would never
have been content to be a copper miner like his father and
grandfather. He would have been a bandit even if he had
been born on the estates of Benedict the Benevolent, rather
than the iron-fisted Duke of Diijah-Montaigne.

'I'm tired,' she said. 'Can I go to bed now?'

Joh nodded to Freder, who took the child up in his arms
like a fond father, and bore her away. Joh had had Rotwang
air out one of the bedrooms in the castle, and do his best to
clean the cobwebs away. They had chosen a room with a
still-functioning lock and an available key. It had no exterior
windows and would serve as a comparatively luxurious cell.

Freder came back, grinning, to the campfire.

'Well?' Groeteschele asked Joh.

Rotwang came out of the shadows suddenly.

'We could do very well out of the lady,' Joh said. 'But we'll
have to take it slowly. She's rich. They aren't like you and me,
Groeteschele. They have strange ways. I think we'll be able to
find out about her family, and then we'll bargain for a ransom.'

'What if they don't want her back?' Rotwang asked. He was
a foundling, sold for a pit-fighter before he could walk, and
had no ideas about his real family. Joh sometimes wondered
if Rotwang were entirely human.

'Of course they'll want her back, Rotwang. She's a precious
package.'

Freder tried to say something. It took him a long time to
get a sentence out, and usually it wasn't worth the wait.
Because they were all tired, Joh, Rotwang and Groeteschele
sat back and let him speak.

'Cuh-cuh-cuh-couldn't w-we cuh-cuh-cuh-keep her?'

Rotwang spat in the embers. They hissed. The shadows
closed in.

IN THE DARKNESS of the Fortress of Drachenfels, the Old
Woman crept, her fingers curved like claws, her still-sharp

mind reaching before her. She had no need of her eyes after all these centuries. As a creature of the night, the cursed stones were comfortable to her. There were intruders now, and she would have to see them off or be destroyed. Her veins were thinned and her sharp teeth slid in and out of their gumsheaths. It was too long since she had slaked her red thirst.

Drachenfels was gone, but he had left something of himself behind. She could taste the residue in the foul air. The spirits writhed deep in the shadows. But the living beings stood out like beacons. She latched onto them all, sipping their thoughts – although she would rather have been sipping their blood – and fixing them in her ancient mind.

The bandits and their prisoner. It was an interesting situation. She found human relationships endlessly fascinating. There were so many ways they could be broken down, set aside and tampered with. For her, there was pleasure in the panic and fear she could whip up in the bandits before the feeding frenzy fell upon her, just as an epicure would prepare his palate for the main course with a selection of *aperitifs* or a great amorist postpone lovemaking with extensive foreplay.

She was pleased that the strongest physically of the living men was the weakest in mind. That made things so much easier. His strength would nourish her, help her get through the long night, and deal with the more dangerous of the intruders.

Her eyes filled with blood.

JOH WAS STARTLED awake, as if by a mailed fist clenching around his heart. He was sure he had cried out. Groeteschele was shaken out of sleep at the same moment. They bumped heads. Blinking in the afterlight of the fire, they looked at each other. Something was wrong, but they couldn't tell what it was. Joh had been dreaming, he knew, but the dream vanished from his head as he was jolted out of the fug of sleep. It had been a bad one and he was sweating.

Rotwang was up, daggers in both hands. He kicked something and it rolled towards the light.

Groeteschele let out an involuntary oath, his voice womanish and shrill. Freder's head lay at his feet.

'The rest of the oaf is here,' Rotwang said.

Joh stabbed a pitch-covered torch at the embers. It caught, and he held it up.

Rotwang stood over Freder's bulky body. The head had been taken off neatly and there was almost no blood. This was not a natural killing.

'It's this place,' Groeteschele said. 'It stinks of that devil Drachenfels.'

'The Great Enchanter is dead and gone,' Joh said.

'So is Fat Fool Freder,' said Rotwang.

'There's someone else here with us.' Groeteschele was shivering, but not with the cold. In his nightshirt, with his long, milky-white face, he looked himself like a cheap engraving of a ghost.

'That's obvious. It's a big place.'

'The girl?'

Joh had a moment of concern for the Lady Melissa. He did not want her dying in any manner he could not profit from.

The three bandits pulled on jackets and boots over nightclothes. Joh swore as he cut his palm open on the silver spur he had forgotten to remove from his rough riding boots. There was no time now. Weapons in their hands, they entered the wing of the castle where the captive's room was. Rotwang lead them through the dark. The sharpness of his eyes in shadow was among his most valuable attributes.

Joh knew how serious their trouble was when he noticed that Rotwang wasn't sure about the path he was taking. The fortress was legendary for its labyrinthine and contradictory byways. That was one of the reasons Joh had chosen to pitch camp in the courtyard.

After a moment of near panic, they found the room. 'Look,' said Rotwang.

The wood around the handle was deeply scored, as if a knife-fingered hand had tried the door.

It was still locked. Rotwang fumbled with the key, and opened the door.

'What are you doing?' Melissa said, sitting up in bed, her hair loose. 'Am I to be murdered in my bed?'

AS SOON AS he saw Freder's bodiless head, Rotwang knew that Joh Lamprecht's time as a King of Banditti was over. It only remained for Rotwang to live out this night in the castle, and leave. Perhaps he would turn to the mercenary life again and enlist in one of the many armies of the Old World. There were always opportunities for people with his skills, and many employers uninterested in the legalities of his previous adventures. He was not profligate in the deployment of his abilities, and liked to see gold from each of his killings. So far, the coachman had not been worth the effort. The little girl would never bring more than her jewellery. Kidnapping was a fool's crime, and had Joh proposed it outright Rotwang would have left there and then. The business of the bungled coach hold-up had been bad enough, but the kidnapping – and now the death of one of their number – told him that the days of easy plunder were at an end.

Currently, Joh was trying to talk to the Lady Melissa, to no great purpose. The girl knew nothing. Groeteschele was sitting in a chair, hugging himself. The youth was badly scared. He had been as courageous as any in the band's previous exploits, but had only faced cold steel and human muscle. Whatever it was that walked this castle was no natural thing, Rotwang knew.

Prince Oswald should have had the place razed to the ground once the Great Enchanter was dead.

'We stay here and protect the girl,' Joh ordered.

Rotwang didn't know if his chief fully meant what he said. He had not hitherto been noted for his sense of chivalry. Still, a farmer would guard from wolves a calf he fully intended to butcher on the morrow.

Groeteschele was too deeply frightened to answer. Joh looked to Rotwang.

This was as good a position as any to defend.

He nodded.

Joh sat on the Lady Melissa's bed, and told the child to lie back and go to sleep. He stroked her hair, almost tenderly.

'Good night, Mr Joh.'

The little girl smiled, shrugged, and pulled the covers up over her head.

'Shut the door and wait, Rotwang,' Joh said. 'It'll come to us.'

'I know.'

JOH WONDERED IF the only dangers in the castle were outside the room. Groeteschele was nearly mad with fear, and the mad can be dangerous to those who mean them no harm. The lad was gripping his sword with both hands, holding it vertical in his lap, his forehead pressed against the flat of the blade. His eyes were active, looking at every corner of the room, but empty of intelligence. Joh had never bothered to find out what Groeteschele had been before Warden Fanck shackled them together in the quarries. They had shared days and nights ever since, but Joh still knew nothing of Groeteschele's antecedents, his former life, his original crime. Somehow, he knew it was too late now.

And Rotwang was slow to respond to his orders, taking a second to think things through. Obedience was no longer automatic. The killer was out for himself, and would not hesitate to leave the others to a ghastly death if he thought he could survive the better for it. After all, the man had lasted so long in his profession precisely because he was dangerous, treacherous, conscienceless. Often, Joh had wondered what the result would be if he were to duel with the killer. Rotwang would have the edge in training, experience and simple skill, but Joh thought the other man was dead inside. He killed without passion, without interest, and Joh suspected – hoped – his own brand of hot-blooded combat would prove superior to Rotwang's chilly discipline. It was a question he had never felt the need to put to a practical test.

The torch burned in its sconce, filling the room with red shadows. The Lady Melissa slept, or seemed to, the covers rising and falling as she breathed.

Joh had to turn the situation around to his advantage. He had to extort a suitable ransom from the d'Acques clan. He had to proceed to his Tilean pickings and make his name as a strategist. There would be more songs about Joh Lamprecht. More odes to his glories.

Outside, in the bulk of the castle, there were sounds. Joh knew the same winds that had blown the night before were setting shutters to rattle and old furniture to creak. But amid the thousand tiny natural sounds of night, there were silences that betokened huge and malevolent presences. Drachenfels was dead. There was no question of that. But the dead could still be dangerous. Perhaps something of the Great Enchanter remained behind in his fortress, waiting, watching, hungry...

Like Groeteschele, he clutched his weapon as a cleric does the symbol of his deity.

He could only wait.

THE OLD WOMAN was glutted with the first of her victims. Freder's blood had proved rich, and with it came a rush of the memories of his body. She felt his pains and his pleasures as she drained him lustily. She had absorbed his life, and freed his tethered, childish spirit from its cage of meat. As an afterthought, she left him for the others to find. She found it easy to pass through the castle. Locked doors, walled-up passages, and trap-laden corridors posed no problems for her. Like a mist, she could pass where she willed.

From Freder's dull memories, she learned about the others. It was easy to see how to proceed against them. So easy. People never changed, never learned. They were always easy.

In the warm darkness she made and unmade fists, extending and retracting her hard, sharp nails.

Her thirst was quenched. The rest of the night's work would be for the pleasure of it.

Considering who her prey were and their intentions towards their captive, the Old Woman believed she served the cause of Justice as surely as any Imperial man-at-arms or thrice-blessed servant of Verena.

She could still taste the blood in her mouth.

She reached out for the weakest of the minds against her, and forced herself in.

* * *

AFTER SITTING STILL for over an hour, Groeteschele screamed. His sword leaped slightly in his hands and blood trickled down his forehead. He stood up, the blade scraping his skin. Joh was startled out of a half-sleep by his friend's cry and pushed himself off Melissa's bed. The child miraculously stayed asleep. Rotwang took an apparently casual interest.

Groeteschele dropped his sword. He was bleeding profusely, but his self-inflicted wound looked comparatively minor. His scream died away, but he kept whimpering.

'Calm yourself,' Joh ordered.

Groeteschele didn't take any notice. He was gabbling to himself, his meaning impossible to gauge. Blood dropped from his cheeks and chin onto his nightshirt. He shook his head and wrung his hands. He could have been posing for a statue of the muse of fear.

Joh reached out to take hold of Groeteschele's shoulder, but the younger man dodged back, his terror increased by the prospect of human contact.

Rotwang stood aside, impassive.

Groeteschele began to chant something in a language Joh didn't recognise. It was the unknown tongue the bandit used when he sometimes talked in his sleep, the tongue Joh assumed was that of the never-mentioned land of his birth. As he chanted, he made signs in the air with his fingers. Droplets of blood detached from his face and fell to the floor.

Groeteschele hit the door and passed through. Joh heard him blundering down the corridor, still chanting.

The bedclothes rose in a hump, and the Lady Melissa burrowed her way sleepily to the surface.

'What's going on?' she asked.

Joh's face was wet. Groeteschele had splashed him with his own blood.

'Watch the girl,' he told Rotwang. 'I'm going after him.'

Rotwang nodded. Melissa smiled and rubbed her eyes.

Lantern in one hand, scimitar in the other, Joh stepped outside. He could still hear Groeteschele babbling.

He walked slowly, towards the noise.

* * *

JOH LAMPRECHT WAS a sentimental old fool, Rotwang thought.
The boy, Groeteschele, was dead, and Joh should have left
him to rot. But Joh had formed an attachment to the youth-
ful Yann, and would not be dissuaded from plunging into
the darkness to face whatever horrors lay dormant in
Drachenfels, waiting for him with claws, pincers and hot
coals.

He paced the bedroom, struggling with unfamiliar feelings. Hitherto, he had faced death with a cool reserve born
of a knowledge that those who let their emotions take
over in a crisis were those least likely to walk away whole.
In combat, he was as dispassionate as a surgeon, and he
still lived, while all the berserkers he had faced were
wormshit.

Now, he felt fear. Not just the healthy quickening that kept
you cautious in the pit, that reminded you to keep your
body away from your foeman's blade, but a deep-down fear
that whispered to him, incessantly compelling him to throw
down his sword and run like Groeteschele, run until he was
free of Drachenfels, free of the Grey Mountains...

He knew that was the way to die, but the temptation was
still there.

The little girl was sitting up in bed now, playing with her
long, fine hair.

Although roused in the middle of the night, her curls
seemed naturally composed rather than tangled. Joh was
right; the rich were different.

He had pledged his sword for the rich all his life. In the
pits as a child, he had been wagered on by aristocratic
sportsmen who prided themselves in picking a winner.
Later, he had fought for the Elector of Middenland when his
tenant farmers tried to resist a raise in the tithe. So much
blood spilled, so much profit made, and so little of it, in the
end, for his own benefit.

'Mr Rotwang?' the girl asked. He didn't reply, but she continued. 'Mr Rotwang, are you a really brave and ferocious
bandit, like Blaque Jacques in the songs?'

He ignored her. Brave and ferocious. That is what he had
been earlier in the evening, before the accursed Joh

Lamprecht led him to this doom-laden castle and exposed him to the terrors of the dark.

Brave and ferocious. Now, he was not so sure about that.

HE COULD STILL hear Groeteschele chanting. The monotone had changed now and the young man seemed to be singing. He was breathing badly, interrupting the song in the wrong places and Joh assumed he was near the end of his strength. Good. He didn't want to have to fight his comrade to bring him back.

He had never realised before how much the young man meant to him. Freder had been a cretin, and Rotwang was beyond conversation, which meant Groeteschele was the only person in the band Joh could talk to, could hand down the benefit of his experience to. Unconsciously, he had been training the lad to be his successor on the outlaw path. Without him, Joh's nights would be long and empty. All the passed-on wisdom would go to waste.

If Yann Groeteschele died here in Drachenfels, there would be nobody left. When Joh himself passed on, there would be nobody left alive who knew the workings of the Three Gold Crowns Scam, the mechanics of the Vault-Piercing Screw, the profit to be had from the Joh Lamprecht Stagecoach Switch Manoeuvre. Without Groeteschele, Joh's life would be a waste.

In the back of his mind, Joh knew these thoughts weren't like him. Groeteschele was another crossbowman, no more nor less. Warden Fanck and sheer chance, not a bond of affection, had shackled them together. And yet, here in the dark of Drachenfels, something was coming out of him. He thought he was being worked on, and tried to resist.

Joh found Groeteschele backed up in a blind corridor, squeezed into a corner, still chanting. His eyes were shut tight, crusted over with his scabbing blood, and he was tracing symbols in the dust. Joh recognised a few gods' names – Shallya, Verena, Ulric – in Groeteschele's litany, and the scrawl on the floor included approximations of several sacred signs.

'Come, lad, there's nothing to fear,' Joh lied.

Groeteschele kept up his mad prayer. Joh set down his lantern and went to his comrade, and bent over, hoping to help him to his feet, to guide him back to Melissa's room to await the dawn.

Groeteschele's right hand was still tracing signs, but his left was at the belt he had drawn around his nightshirt, gripping something tightly. As he touched the young man's right upper arm, Joh realised what Groeteschele was holding.

He kept his quarrels strung on his belt.

Joh tried to pull back, but Groeteschele was fast. His eyes flicked open and his left hand shot upwards. He spat a curse, and lodged the point of the crossbow bolt between Joh's chest and shoulder.

Joh felt the the weapon scrape his upper ribs and sink through the joint. Pain flowed up and down his arm and he dropped his scimitar. Groeteschele was standing up now, working the quarrel deeper, his right hand caught in Joh's hair.

They struggled together. The lantern was knocked over under their feet and a small spill of burning oil spread in the dirt. Joh saw red shadows dancing on the walls as he wrestled with Groeteschele. He punched the young man in the belly with his left hand and knocked the wind out of him. Groeteschele broke the clinch and staggered away. He let go of the quarrel with a final yank that shot another bolt of pain into Joh's torso.

Groeteschele was going for Joh's dropped sword. Joh kicked him in the side and tipped him over. He fell into the burning pool, and his flimsy cotton nightshirt caught in an instant, flaming up to his legs.

Screeching curses, Groeteschele came at Joh, the flames spreading over his entire body.

Joh stepped back and there was a wall where one hadn't been before. He struck the stone with his wounded shoulder, and screamed out loud, nearly fainting with the agony. He held up his left arm like a shield as the fiery Groeteschele lurched forwards. The bandit's smooth face was on fire now, the features running like wax, and the enclosed space was thick with the stench of burning flesh.

Joh's scimitar was ten yards away, and Groeteschele stood between him and it. He only had one weapon available.

Clenching his teeth against what he was about to do to himself, he got a proper grip on the barbed bolt in his shoulder. He hoped to be able to pull it out as easily as one draws a dagger from a sheath, but the arrowhead tip tore muscle as he extracted the spike. He invoked the name of Khorne and held up the dripping quarrel like an offering.

A great scream was building up inside Groeteschele's chest, and emerged through an enlarged and ravaged mouth as he leaped at Joh, his flame-tipped hands reaching out to throttle.

With his left hand, Joh stabbed, aiming for the cut on Groeteschele's forehead. He struck home and, thumb over the end of the quarrel, forced the steel into his friend's brain.

Groeteschele's eyes died, and Joh pushed the dead man away from him. His left sleeve was alight. He tried to reach for it with his right hand, but as his elbow bent a crippling wave of pain made him sink to his knees. He scraped his burning sleeve against the wall, and the fires went out.

He felt like curling up and going to sleep, letting his pains fade away. But he knew that would be fatal.

At least his legs were uninjured. Unsteadily, using the wall as a brace for his back, he got to his feet.

Now, he realised how little notice he had taken of the path to this place. He had no idea how to get back to Rotwang and Melissa.

The fires died down and he was in total darkness, alone with his pain.

Trusting to instinct, he pushed himself away from the wall and followed the corridor.

THE OLD WOMAN'S brain buzzed with the emotional discharge from the clash between the former friends. Their pain and fear was so much the greater for the bond between them broken by their fight. Her mouth was dry, but jolts of pleasure coursed through her human-seeming body.

Over a thousand years ago, when she was truly young, her coach had been stopped by a bandit. Not a gold-seeking thug such as these, but a wild-haired monster of the blood-line of Belada the Melancholy, an unlettered savage who could live for an eternity but who lacked the refinement to make such an existence bearable.

She was that vampire's get, his daughter-in-darkness, and she had birthed many a blood herself. The lady Genevieve, whose finest moment had come in this castle, was her granddaughter-in-darkness, the get of her get. It had been a proud, productive life...

Freder's blood flowed through her veins, mingling with her own ichor. It was time she killed again, took more sustenance.

Two bandits and their little captive. They were alone in Drachenfels. The configuration was amusing.

In the morning they would all be dead. But the Old Woman's death would be like life. The others would be gone, used-up husks thrown away to rot.

Her eyeteeth extended and grew sharper and she ran her velvety tongue over them.

THE LITTLE GIRL smiled innocently at Rotwang. A few minutes ago, he had realised he was nervously walking up and down the carpet and resolved to calm himself. Now he stood stock still, barely breathing, swordhilt in his hand. He didn't have too tight a grip – that made you too inflexible when it came to responding to an attack – and he was visualising a stylised wolf's head in his mind. It was the symbol he had worn as a pit fighter, and it always helped him relax before a battle to dwell upon its shape. Maybe the wolf was his personal talisman. He had always favoured Ulric, God of Battle, Wolves and Winter, over the more obvious Khaine, Lord of Murder, as the protector of his profession.

Sometimes, he dreamed that he *was* a wolf. He had been thickly-pelted as a child, although he was not abnormally hairy now, and he wondered if his unknown parents had lycanthrope blood in them. He had never shapeshifted, but he was not like other men in many ways.

The girl was singing to herself, a Bretonnian lullaby he didn't recognise.

'Mr Rotwang?'

'Yes, my lady?' He hated himself suddenly, for lapsing into the servile form of address. But it was only natural to him. 'What is it?'

'Tomorrow, when the sun comes up, will we be here?'

He had no answer.

Melissa scrambled out of bed. She wore a long, gold-embroidered nightdress that could almost pass for a ball gown. Her bare white feet were silent on the thick carpet. She danced around the room to her lullaby, holding her skirts out and curtseying to an imagined courtly admirer.

When Rotwang was her age, he had been killing for seven years. He resented the Lady Melissa for her family, her wealth, her childhood. All these things had been denied him. He hated his possibly wolfish parents for abandoning him among men. He should have been suckled on the steppes, raised with the pack, and taught the trick, the trick of shaking aside human form.

The door was hanging open now. Since Groeteschele and Joh had pushed through it, he hadn't bothered to pull it shut. Anything that could so neatly decapitate Freder wouldn't be bothered by a lock. Rotwang preferred to see what was coming at him.

Outside in the gloom, he could make out a bare stone wall, interrupted by niches containing long-unlit lamps. Constant Drachenfels was rumoured to favour human oil in his lamps. It would not have been out of character for the Great Enchanter, whose reign stretched back to the time of Sigmar and beyond.

'Mr Rotwang,' asked the child, 'when are you going to try and kill me?'

Rotwang turned and looked at the open face of the child, feeling her words like the slap of an armoured gauntlet across his cheek. He held up his sword, out in the open. He hoped she could see it was no immediate threat to her.

But again, he had no answer for her. Something foul-smelling came out of the darkness behind him, and a claw-gripped hand fastened on his shoulder...

* * *

THE OLD WOMAN fastened on Rotwang's mind, and burrowed deep. She found the wolf, and she turned it loose.

ROTWANG WAS RAISING his sword to the Lady Melissa. Joh assumed he had gone mad, and laid a hand on the bandit's shoulder, spinning him around.

Rotwang's eyes were yellow, and his nose was reassembling as a snout. The creature opened its mouth and disclosed pointed, discoloured teeth. It was still Rotwang – his front tooth was still chipped – but a beast was rising inside him.

The little girl backed away and climbed up onto her canopied bed. She held onto a bedpost and watched.

Joh leaned against the doorjamb, a dreadful numbness seeping from his swollen shoulder through his entire body.

Rotwang lashed out and he ducked aside. Still, the creature's claws brushed his head, tearing lines in his scalp.

The Rotwang-thing had thrown its sword away. The bandit didn't need the knives sheathed on his belt. He had knives in his fingers.

It was strange that you could ride with someone for five years and never know certain things about them.

Joh's knees felt weak. His arm was useless. He was going to die soon, and he thought the easiest thing to do would be to offer his throat to Rotwang's teeth and nails. But he had been surviving too long to take the easy way out.

His scimitar was gone, and his knives. But he still had his boots. And his silver spurs.

Silver. If Rotwang were a true werewolf, he would be averse to silver.

Rotwang lunged at him, coming on all fours. Joh reached up with his left hand for the top of the door and got a grip, hauling himself into the air. His left shoulder felt lanced, but he managed to get himself aloft.

Rotwang, his charge started, passed under him. He jabbed down with his heels, and dug in as deep as he could.

The creature howled like a wounded wolf and reared up. Joh was pushed against the lintel and lost his grip. His head smashed against the stone and he felt something break inside.

He was falling, and he was face-down on the floor. The howling thing was on his back. He kicked upwards, hoping to slice with his spurs.

The weight was gone and he tried to roll over.

Melissa was still watching, as she might do a puppetshow at court. She was giggling and clapping. There was something seriously wrong with the way the little girl had been brought up.

He reached for his heel and twisted one of his spurs off. The spiked star spun as he sliced the air with it.

Rotwang was suffering. His clothes were torn, and his thickly-furred body was bleeding.

Man and monster got shakily to their feet.

Rotwang breathed noisily, blood and saliva dripping from his twisted snout. His shoulders were huge, and his claws extended.

Joh held up the spur.

Rotwang rushed at him, and he chopped into the monster's face, drawing the spur through his eye into his snout.

Claws sunk into the meat of his belly, and he broke away, leaving his weapon lodged in the werewolf's face.

He pressed the flaps of skin on his stomach, holding his insides in. He could feel almost nothing.

That was bad.

Rotwang was leaning against the bed, shaking and twitching as he changed back into human form. Blood streamed from his wounded head.

Melissa reached out and patted his shoulder, smoothing the thinning fur. She could have been looking after a family pet.

The rich. They were barely human.

Melissa's expression changed. She looked almost sad as Rotwang's wolfish growls faded into the human sounds of painful sobs. The spur was still stuck into his head. She opened her pretty little mouth, and Joh saw the unnaturally sharp teeth flash as she fastened on Rotwang's neck, tearing through to the vein.

A gusher of blood came out of the bandit, and Melissa suckled greedily.

THE OLD WOMAN drank the bandit's wolf-spiced blood, feeling his spirit depart as she stole his life from him.

He had killed others. Many times, he had killed without mercy. She did only what was right.

When it was done, when Rotwang was empty, she wrestled his head off and turned her attention to the wounded man in the corner.

'Hello Mr Joh,' she said, 'does that hurt?'

MELISSA, THE OLD woman who seemed to be a child, knelt by him and watched as he died.

'You were my favourite bandit, you know,' she said.

He couldn't feel pain any more, but from the writhing wetness he couldn't contain in his gutwound, he knew it was bad.

'How... old...?'

Melissa daintily pushed her hair aside. Her eyes were remarkable. Joh should have noticed them before. Eyes of experience in a face of innocence.

'Very old,' she said. 'Over eleven hundred years. I never grew up.'

The cold was settling in now. Joh felt it travelling up his body.

'Your... family...?'

She was wistful, almost melancholy. 'Dead and dust, I'm afraid. My human family, at least. I have sons-in-darkness, but none who would have paid you a ransom.'

He was shivering now. Seconds lasted for an age. The final grains of sand of his life took an eternity to drip through the glass waist. Was this death? A slowing curve that forever dragged out the pain, but never really ended. Or was that life for Lady Melissa d'Acques?

He had one last chance. Silver. Vampires like the stuff no more than werewolves. He scrabbled for his other heel, but his fingers seemed swollen, awkward, and wouldn't respond. He cut himself. Melissa took one of Rotwang's dropped knives and deftly cut away the spur, flipping it to the other side of the room without touching it. She smiled at him, the sympathy of a victor. There was nothing more to do but die.

She took a dainty kerchief and dabbed the smears away from her bee-stung lips. At once a child and an ancient, she was beautiful but beyond his understanding.

'Kiss me,' he said.

She tipped his head away from his throat, and granted him his wish.

THE NEXT MORNING, the sun rose over the Fortress of Drachenfels, and a small human figure made its way down the mountain towards the road.

Lady Melissa left the bodies were they were. Those she had drained were decapitated. The bandits would not be her get. She was more responsible than some undead fools who let loose a plague of thoughtless offspring.

She hauled her bulky but light trunks down to the road and made a canopied chair of them.

Sunlight hurt her eyes a little, but she was not one of the Truly Dead bloodsuckers who burst into flames after cock's crow.

As the sun climbed, she settled down to wait. The road below Drachenfels was ill-travelled, but someone would come along eventually.

Under her makeshift sunshade, she closed her eyes and slept.

THE IGNORANT ARMIES

And we are here as on a darkling plain
Swept with confused alarms of struggle and flight,
Where ignorant armies clash by night.

– Matthew Arnold, 'Dover Beach'

SETTLING TSARINA DOWN, he saw the frozen blood around her
hooves. The last blacksmith's nails had gone too deep. The
horse's ankles weren't good, and the last three weeks' ride
had been hard on her. She'd barely been worth the price
they'd paid for her when she was fresh. Now, she was a
dependent. And they couldn't use dependents.

'There, Tsarina, there,' he said, smoothing the horse's
mane, feeling her fragile warmth through thick hair. Her
flesh wouldn't be warm much longer. Not through another
snow, another skirmish, or another day's ride.

As always, Vukotich had been right. When they had bar-
gained successfully with the trader months ago, Johann had
suggested calling the pair Tsar and Tsarina in honour of the
ruling house of Kislev. The Iron Man, face unreadable under

his scars, had snorted and said, 'Johann, you don't give a name to something you may have to *eat*.'

Vukotich had been in the northern forests of Kislev before, as a mercenary in the service of Tsar Radii Bokha, subduing an insubordinate boyar, fending off minor incursions from the Wastes. He had known what he was talking about. This wasn't the Old World, this was a cruel country. You could see it in the faces of the people, in the iron-hard ground and the slate-coloured sky. In the forests, you could see it in the gallows-trees and the looted graves. Everything had been hacked and scarred into misery. In the hostelries, the songs had been brutal or gloomy, the food was like spiced leather, and all the jokes referred to filthy practices involving the livestock.

In the dusk, Johann saw Vukotich, a spiky shadow in furs, emerging from the trees with an armload of firewood. Stripped of the ice-threaded bark, the wood would burn smokily, but it would burn the night through. Vukotich dumped his load in the centre of the dark brown circle from which he had cleared the snow. What little light was left in the sky had to fight its way down through four-hundred foot trees. They should have made camp an hour ago to be relatively secure by nightfall, but they had been pushing on, Tsarina had been limping, and – just maybe, without consciously working at it – they had wanted to be a temptation to Cicatrice's tail-draggers. Sigmar knows, Johann thought, it would be sweet to be done with this business.

The horse whinnied, and Johann felt her hot breath on his wrist. He loosened a drawstring and pulled off his glove, making a fist against the cold. Then he stroked the horse again, twining his fingers in her mane. The beast knew, he could tell. He could see the panic in her clouded eye, but she was too tired, too resigned, to fight back. Tsarina would welcome death. Vukotich stood over man and horse, his hand on his knifehilt.

'Do you want me to do it?'

'No,' said Johann, drawing one of his own knives – a hunter's pride, one edge honed to razor sharpness, the other serrated like a joiner's saw. 'I named her, I'll finish her...'

He breathed into Tsarina's nostrils, soothing the horse with his naked left hand, his gauntleted right bringing up the knife. He looked into her eyes, and felt – imagined he felt – the animal willing him to be swift. He got a good grip, and drove into Tsarina's neck, puncturing the major artery. He sawed through muscle and gristle to make sure the job was well done, and then shuffled back on his knees to avoid the spray. He felt the frozen earth through his padded knee-protectors. His britches would be speckled with Tsarina's red tomorrow. The horse kicked and emptied fast, the spirit flown forever. Johann made silent prayer to Taal, the God of Nature and Wild Places, one of the few gods he bothered to appease these days. He stood up and brushed bloody snow from his clothes.

Vukotich knelt and put his hand in the flow of blood as one might put one's hand in a mountain stream. Johann had seen him do the like before. It was some superstition of his native land. He knew what the man would say now, 'innocent blood'. It was like a little prayer. One of Vukotich's sayings was 'never underestimate the power of innocent blood.' If pressed, the old soldier would invoke the blessed name of Sigmar, and trace the sign of the hammer in the dust. Johann shied away from magic – he had had some bad experiences – but all knew of Sigmar's harsh benevolence. If there were miracles to be had, only he could be even half-counted upon. But Sigmar's mercy, Sigmar's hammer and Sigmar's muttered name had done nothing for the horse. She was still now. Tsarina was gone, and they had meat for two weeks' journey in this forest.

Vukotich wiped his hand clean, flexed the fingers as if invigorated, and produced his flint. Johann turned, and saw his companion had constructed a simple pyramid fire, building a tent of logs over a nest of twigs. Dry grass was hard to come by here, but Vukotich could root out mosses and combustible fungi to start a blaze. Vukotich struck his flint, the fire took, and Johann smelled the fresh smell of woodsmoke. His eyes watered as a cloud of smoke wrapped his head, but he kept his place. Best to ignore the discomfort. The smoke column passed, twisting around to reach for

the other man. It was an infallible rule of the fire, that it
would have to smoke in someone's face.

'So it's horse tonight?' asked Vukotich.

'Yes, we'll have to cure the meat tomorrow if we're to carry
on.'

'Is there any question of that?'

'No,' Johann said, as he always had.

'You wouldn't lose any honour if you were to return to
your estates. They must have gone to ruin since we left. I'll
continue the tracking. I'm too old to change. But you
needn't keep up with it. You could make a life for yourself.
You're the baron now.'

He had heard the speech before and many variations on
it, almost from the beginning. Never had he seriously considered returning to his ruined home, and never – Johann
thought – had Vukotich expected him to. It was part of the
game they played, master and servant, pupil and tutor, man
of iron and man of meat. In some circumstances, Johann
knew, meat breaks less easily than iron.

'Very well.'

Johann set to butchering the horse. It was one of the many
skills he wouldn't have acquired had he been a better shot at
sixteen. If his shaft hadn't missed the deer and pierced
Wolf's shoulder... If Cicatrice's band hadn't chosen to lay
waste the von Mecklenberg estate... If the old baron had
employed more men like Vukotich, and less like Schunzel,
his then-steward... If...

But young Johann had been fumble-fingered with a longbow, Cicatrice had realised too well the weakness of the
Empire's outlying fiefdoms, and Schunzel had fussed more
over wall-hangings and Bretonnian chefs than battlements
and men-at-arms. And now, when he would ordinarily have
been currying favour for his family at Karl-Franz's court in
Altdorf, Baron Johann von Mecklenberg was gutting a nag in
a clearing dangerously near the frozen top of the world. *The
Arts of a Nobleman*. If he were ever to write a book, that's the
title he would want to use.

Together, they pulled strips off the carcass and hung them
on a longsword supported over the fire by two cleft

branches. It was black from many previous services, stained
by dried-in grease, and could never be used in a polite
engagement. Throughout his education, Johann had been
taught that weapons were the jewels of a nobleman, and
should be treated as a master musician would his instrument, a sorcerer his spells and spices, or a courtesan her face
and figure. Now, he knew a sword was a tool for keeping you
alive, and that meant filling your insides far more often than
it did exposing someone else's.

'You saw the tracks today?' asked Vukotich.

'Four, more-or-less human, travelling slowly, left behind
for us.'

Vukotich nodded. Johann sensed his teacher's rough pride
in him, but knew the old man would never admit it. The
schooling was over, this was life...

'They'll turn soon. If not tonight, then the next night. Two
of them are weak. They've been on foot from three days into
the forest. The skaven is lamed. Pus in his bootprints. If he
lives, he'll lose a foot to the gangrene. They'll all be tired.
They'll want to get it over with while they still have an
advantage.'

'We're on foot too, now.'

'Yes, but they don't know that.' In the firelight, Vukotich's
face was a dancing mass of red and black shadows. 'Two of
them will be broken, given this duty because Cicatrice wants
to get rid of them. But since the Middle Mountains, he will
have stopped underestimating us. He lost enough raiders in
that pass to make him think us more than a nuisance. So,
two of them will be good. One of them will be a champion,
or something very like. It'll be altered. Twisted, but not crippled. It's something big, something enhanced. Something
they think will take care of us.'

His eyes shone with flame. 'I'll watch first.'

Johann was aware of the aching in his back, his legs, the
cold that had settled into his bones when they crossed the
snowline and would never – he dreaded – depart. How
much more would Vukotich, with his many past wounds,
with the increasing weight of his years, feel the aches and the
chills? The Iron Man never complained, never flagged, but

that didn't mean he had no feeling, no pain. Johann had
seen him when he felt unobserved, seen him sag in his saddle, or massage his much-broken left arm. After all, the man
couldn't go on forever. Then what?

What of Cicatrice? What of Wolf?

They ate, chewing the tough meat slowly, and Vukotich
mulled some spiced wine. Warm inside at least, Johann
climbed into his bedroll in his clothes, pulling the furs
about him. He slept with his knife in his hand, and
dreamed...

THE BARON OF Sudenland had two sons, Johann and Wolf.
They were fine boys and would be fine young men. Johann,
the older by three years, would be baron after his father, and
an elector of the Empire. He would be a warrior, a diplomat
and a scholar. Wolf, who would be his regent when the business of the Empire took him to Altdorf, would be Johann's
strong right hand. He would be a jurist, a master huntsman
and an engineer. Joachim, the old baron, was proud to have
two such sons, who would, upon his death, preserve his
lands and bear his responsibilities. And the people of the
barony were pleased they would not have to live under the
whims and woes of petty tyrants, as did so many others
throughout the Empire. The old baron was much loved, and
his sons would do him honour. New words were made up
for old songs, celebrating each achievement of the growing
boys.

The old baron engaged many tutors for his sons; tutors in
history and geography, in the sciences, in the ways of the
gods, in etiquette and the finer accomplishments, in music
and literature, in the skills of war and the demands of peace,
even in the rudiments of magic. Among these was a warrior
who had served throughout the Old World and beyond. The
survivor of numberless campaigns, he never talked of his
origins, his upbringing, even of his native land, and he had
but one name: Vukotich. The baron had first met Vukotich
on the field of combat, during a border dispute with an
unruly neighbour, and had personally captured the mercenary. Neither man spoke of it, but after the battle, Vukotich

put aside his profession and swore allegiance only to the House of von Mecklenberg.

The baron had many homes, many estates, many castles. One summer, he and his retinue chose to spend time in an isolated stronghold at the edge of the barony. There, in the greenwood, his sons would learn how to hunt game, and win their trophies. This Joachim had done when he was a youth, and this his sons would now do. With pride, the old baron watched from the towers of his castle as Vukotich took his sons off into the woods, accompanied by Corin the Fletcher, his arms master. Whatever Johann and Wolf killed would grace the baron's table that evening.

Wolf was a born huntsman and was blooded his first day in the woods, bringing down a quail with a single quarrel. He soon became proficient with the longbow, the crossbow, the throwing lance, and all manner of traps and snares. Wolf, it was said partly in jest, was well-named, for he could stalk any beast of the forest. From birds, he progressed to boar and elk. He was equal to them all, and it was said that Wolf might be the first von Mecklenberg in generations to bring home a unicorn, a jabberwock or a manticore as trophies of his prowess in the woods. Corin had discovered that Andreas, one of the stable boys, had once been apprenticed to a taxidermist, and soon had the boy assigned to the preparing and mounting of Wolf's trophies. Within a month, there were more than enough to fill his corner of the great hall of the von Mecklenbergs.

But Johann found the chase not to his taste. Early, he had developed an interest in the animals of the wood, but he couldn't see them through a hunter's eyes. Shooting at straw targets, he could best his brother with any weapon; but with a living, breathing creature before him, his hand faltered and his eye was off. He was too moved by the magnificence of a full-grown stag to want to see it dead, beheaded and stuffed, with glass eyes and dusty antlers. Everyone understood, which made it much worse for Johann, who was foolish enough to think compassion a womanish weakness. The old baron, seeing in Wolf his younger self, nevertheless recognised in Johann the makings of a better man than

either of the huntsmen could be. To Vukotich, he confided
'Wolf's delight in the hunt will make him a good regent, but
Johann's instinctive turning-away from killing will make
him a *great* elector.' But Johann tried to overcome his quirk
of the mind. He would not give up eating meat, and he
believed he could not honourably eat if he could not hunt
in good conscience, so he applied himself.

Still, one day, while out with Wolf, Corin and Vukotich,
Johann missed a deer he had a clear shot at, and his arrow
slipped through the trees, lodging in his brother's shoulder.
It was a clean, shallow wound and Corin dressed it quickly,
but Vukotich was sufficiently cautious to send the boy back
to the castle. Johann had felt bad enough then, but later this
incident would come to haunt his nights. If his life had a
turning point, that careless shaft was it. Afterwards, nothing
was as it was supposed to be.

There had always been outlaws, of course. Always been
evil men, always been the altered ones. Especially in the
forests. There had been raids and battles and bloodshed.
There were many areas of the Empire where the servants of
the Law dared not venture. And there had been many campaigns against the dark. But there had never been a
Champion of evil like Cicatrice. So named for the livid red
weal scratched across his face by the claw of a daemon in the
service of Khorne, Lord of Blood, Cicatrice had come out of
the Wastes transformed beyond humanity. With his so-
called Chaos Knights, Cicatrice had terrorised the
Southlands, unfettered in his bloodlust in victory, eluding
capture even in defeat. Emperor Karl-Franz himself had
placed 50,000 gold crowns upon his head, but – though
many had tried, and failed to survive the attempt – none
had claimed the reward. The songs of his crimes were dark
and dramatic, full of blood and fire, and just barely tainted
with fascination. For the people of the Empire, used now to
the comforts and pettiness of civilisation, Cicatrice was an
important figure. He was the outcast, a monster to remind
them of the things waiting beyond the circle of light.

Cicatrice had seen a weakness in the summer home of the
von Mecklenbergs and mounted a raid that had shocked the

Empire. An elector murdered, his household put to the sword, his castle razed to the ground, his child – and the children of his retinue – stolen away. Never had there been such an atrocity, and rarely since did the other electors travel anywhere remote without a force of men capable of besting a small army. Hitherto, stealth, poison and treachery had been the favoured weapons of the night. Cicatrice had changed that. Truly, he was a Chaos Champion, and even the warlords of the Empire credited him as a brilliant strategist. If only because he was still alive and at the head of his Knights twenty years after his first raids, Cicatrice was unique among the servants of evil.

In his dreams, Johann kept being pulled back to that burning castle. He saw his father again, hanging in pieces from trees twenty feet apart. He saw poor, fat, silly Schunzel, the fires in his face and belly still alight. He saw Vukotich, in a rage he had never shown before or since, hacking at a wounded beastman, screaming questions for which there would be no answers. Then there were the slaughtered horses, the violated servant girls, the unidentifiable corpses. Absurdly, he remembered the tennis lawns – not a scrap of green among the red – with its pile of eyeless heads. A skaven had been left behind, a rat-faced mutant he found among the carcasses of his tutors, sawing off fingers for rings. For the first time, Johann had killed without effort. He had never since hesitated to kill, higher race or beast. He had learned his last lesson.

There was another elector now, a cousin who called himself baron, and claimed that Johann had given up his rights to the title by deserting the remnants of the House of von Mecklenberg and setting off on his travels. Johann would not have argued with him. The business of Empire had to continue, and he had other business.

Even with his shoulder wounded, Wolf would have fought. But he was not among the dead. He was among the missing. At thirteen years of age, he would have interested Cicatrice.

That had been ten years, and inconceivable miles, ago. They had followed Cicatrice's band in ragged circles around

the Empire; up through the Grey Mountains to the borders
of Bretonnia, surviving ambushes on the waterfront of
Marienburg, then through the Wasteland into the Drak
Wald Forest – where Johann and Vukotich had been
enslaved for a spell by a mad dwarf with a magic mine – and
up through the Middle Mountains – where they had fought
off a concerted attack, and lost Corin the Fletcher to a goat-
headed monstrosity – into the Forest of Shadows. Then,
down into the Great Forest and east through Stirland
towards the World's Edge Mountains where the powers of
darkness are paramount, and where they struggled against
phantoms that were sent against their minds by powerful
enchanters.

The seasons came and went, and the slow progress continued. Johann knew they had been close more times than
he could count, but always something had intervened. He
had forgotten how many ravaged settlements they had
passed through, seeing themselves mirrored in the numb
rage of the survivors. Cicatrice's band was unstable, and they
had met deserters, cast-offs or defeated would-be champions. Vukotich had more scars now, and Johann wasn't the
youth he had been.

Back and forth, up and down, the wandering had progressed across the land, constantly at the edges of the Old
World, constantly at the extremes of experience. Johann had
seen horrors beyond the imagining of his tutors, had
learned not to concern himself with the caprices of the gods,
and had survived so far. He had given up expecting to see
each day's dawn, he had almost given up expecting to see
Wolf at the end of it.

But still, even to the top of the world, they kept on
Cicatrice's tracks. By day, Johann tried not to think about the
past, or the future; by night, he could think of nothing else.
He had long since become used to sleeping badly.

THE HAND ON his shoulder shook him awake. He opened his
eyes, but didn't say anything.

'They've turned,' said Vukotich, his voice low and urgent,
'their stink is in the air.'

Johann slipped out of his bedding and stood up. The forests were quiet, save for the drip of snow, and the laboured breathing of Vukotich's horse. The fire had burned to ash, but was still casting a glow. The chill had not left his bones. Ice daggers hung like lanterns from the lower branches of the trees, mysteriously lit from within.

They rolled furs into man-sized humps, covered them with bedding and arranged them near the fire. In the dark, they would pass. Vukotich took his crossbow from his saddle and selected a quarrel. He checked the sleeping horse Johann couldn't help but think of as Would-Have-Been-Tsar. Then, they withdrew into the forest.

The wait wasn't long. Johann's sense of smell wasn't as acute as Vukotich's, but he eventually heard them. His tutor had been right: there were four, and one was limping. The noises stopped. Johann pressed close to a treetrunk, shrouding himself in its shadow.

There was a sound like the tearing of silk, and the bedding rolls shuddered. Each was pierced with a crossbow bolt where the head would be. They glowed green, and emitted little puffs of fire and smoke. Johann held his lungs. He didn't want to breathe even a trace of whatever poison that was.

The flares died and nothing moved in the clearing. Johann gripped the hilt of his sword, while Vukotich brought up his crossbow. He didn't favour poison, but with his eye he didn't need to.

Johann heard his heart beating too loud, and fought against all the imagined sounds in his head. Finally, the real sounds came.

A human shape detached itself from the darkness and ventured into the clearing. It limped badly, and its head was elongated, with shining eyes and sharp little teeth. It was the skaven. Piebald, with tatters of clothing over oddments of armour, the ratman was distorted in the emberlight. It stood over the murdered bedrolls, its back to them. It wore the eye-in-the-point-down-pyramid symbol of the Clan Eshin on its ripped blackhide jacket, and the stylised scarface worn by all the followers of Cicatrice. Vukotich put his bolt through its eye. The skaven breathed in sharply, and half-turned. Vukotich's arrowhead stuck out bloody a few inches from its chest. The ratman went down.

Johann and Vukotich circled away from their spot, until they faced the direction from which the thing had come. There were eyes in the darkness. Vukotich held up three fingers, then two. Three against two. It had been worse before.

Fire exploded above them, as arrows pinned balls of burning rag to trees. The balls exploded and rained streamers of flame around them. Three figures came into the clearing, tall but shambling. Johann could smell them now. One of them wasn't alive.

Vukotich put a quarrel through the throat of the creature in the centre, but it still kept walking. It walked to the fire, and Johann saw a rotted ruin of a face. It was leaking dust from its split neck. It had been female, once. Now, it wasn't a person, it was a puppet. One of the others must have raised it, or been given the reins by the magician who had. Like many of Cicatrice's Knights, it had a line of red warpaint across its face, echoing its leader's scar. It moved awkwardly because of its mortal wounds, but that wouldn't stop it from being deadly.

'We'd better do something about that,' said Vukotich, 'before it gives us the Tomb Rot.'

Together, Johann and Vukotich ran forward and counted coup on the undead woman, whipping it with their swords, taking care not to touch the diseased thing. Johann felt brittle bones breaking inside it. The thing staggered from side to side as it was struck, and stepped onto the embers of the fire. Its tattered shroud caught light and so did its desiccated shins. When the flame reached its pockets of rancid flesh, they cooked through with a foul hiss. With an awful keening, the creature became a writhing mass of fire. Johann and Vukotich stepped back, prodding it with swordpoints, staying out of its burning reach.

Its companions came forward now, faces flickering in its dying light. Johann parried a blow and felt its force ringing throughout his entire body. His opponent was taller by a head, and heavily armoured, but its reactions were slower, and its helmet was distorted by a head that seemed to have expanded inside it. It was an altered of some sort, a human being under the influence of the warpstone, that unclassifiable substance so many Servants of the Night had about them, turning into the physical image of whatever dark desires or fears it had harboured. The changes were part of the bargain made with whatever forces they owed allegiance, Johann knew. He had seen too many barely human things left in Cicatrice's wake. This thing was plainly in the throes of some fresh alteration. Under its helm, it would be some new monstrosity.

Johann stepped back and slashed across the creature's chest, denting its breastplate, caving in the scarface symbol etched into the metal. Suddenly, he felt arms around him and pain at his back. The burning thing had hugged him. He shook free, smelling his scorched clothing, ignoring the pain, and ducked away from a blow that could have sheared his head from his shoulders. The undead got in the way again, and the Knight reached out with a huge hand. The giant got a grip on its flame-haloed head and with a grunt crushed it to dust. It fell, useless now, and the Knight returned its attentions to Johann.

Vukotich was grappling close with a toad-faced altered with too many limbs and green ichor was sizzling in the snow around them as his knife went in and out of the thing's bloated stomach. It didn't seem slowed by its many wounds. Vukotich had an arm around its neck, pressing down its inflating ruff.

Johann faced the Knight and made a few tentative passes at its legs. It was already slow; a few bone-deep cuts would make it slower. He realised that the thing was roaring. Johann wasn't sure, but it sounded unpleasantly like the laughter of the heroically insane. The altered's dented breastplate sprung outwards, spiked from within by hard eruptions springing from its mutating body. Whoever it had once been, it was under the warpstone now, progressing far beyond humanity. The Knight screamed its poison mirth, and tugged at its armour. The breastplate came free and Johann saw the growing spines and plates on its skin.

Cicatrice's face was tattooed on its chest. The helmet
stretched outward, cracks appearing in the beaten steel,
horns pushing through above the eyeholes like bulbshoots
emerging from fertile soil. Johann thrust at the altered's
chest, but his sword was turned aside by the creature's
armoured hide. The Knight wasn't even bothering to fight
back. Johann struck at its neck and his sword lodged deep.
It still laughed at him and his sword wouldn't come free. He
pulled two knives from his belt and sunk them into the
altered's body, aiming for the kidneys. The laughter continued and the Knight began to peel away the ruined sections
of his helmet.

Eyes peered at Johann from bone-ridged cavities. There
were seven of them, arranged across the Knight's forehead.
Two were real, five were polished glass set in living flesh.
Johann prayed to the gods he'd ignored for years. The Knight
dislodged Johann's sword from its neck and threw it away.

'Hello, Master Johann,' it said, its voice piping and childish, almost charming. 'How you've grown.'

It was – it had been – Andreas, the von Mecklenberg stable boy, the mounter of trophies. He had found other tutors
since Johann had seen him last.

The great hands reached for him, and Johann felt weights
on his shoulders. The fingers gripped like blacksmith's
tongs. There was no longer ground under his feet. Johann
smelled Andreas's foul breath, and looked up into his former servant's mask of expanded flesh. He pulled the knives
from the altered's sides and sawed away at its stomach and
groin with them. He merely cut through altered flesh that
grew back as he ravaged it. Andreas pushed him and he flew
twenty feet through the air. He hit a tree, for a moment
dreading that his back was broken, then fell. The earth was
hard and he took the fall badly.

Vukotich's opponent was downed, and the tutor strode
towards the Knight, two-handed sword raised. Andreas put
out an arm to stop him and brushed aside the swinging
blow. He grabbed Vukotich's wrists with one hand and
forced the Iron Man to his knees. The altered was still laughing. Daemons screeched in his laughter and murdered

children wailed. Andreas pushed Vukotich back, bending him double, shoving his head towards the still-burning remains of the undead, forcing his own sword towards his face. Vukotich struggled back, and Andreas's huge shoulders heaved as he exerted pressure on the dwarfed human. The sword was fixed between their faces, shuddering as they threw their full strength at each other. The Knight shrugged off his back armour, which fell from him, and Johann saw a streak of white down the creature's mottled and encrusted back.

Ignoring the pain, he ran across the clearing, stepping in the mess Vukotich had made of his toadman, and hurled himself onto Andreas's back. There, the alterations were not quite complete. He drove his knives in between the Knight's horny shoulderblades, where a patch of boyish skin remained between the bony plates, and sawed down the line of his spine, going as deep as he could, cutting through ribs. Blood gushed into his face, and at last he felt his thrusts sink into the real, unaltered Andreas, doing some damage.

The laughter stopped and the altered stood up, trying to shake Johann from his back. Johann gripped Andreas's waist with his knees, and continued his sawing. His hands were inside now, and he was hacking at random, hoping to puncture what left of the heart. Something big in Andreas' torso burst and he fell writhing to the ground. Johann kept riding him, his hands free now, stabbing where he could. Andreas rolled over, and Johann disengaged himself from the dying Knight. He stood up and wiped blood out of his eyes.

Andreas lay face-up, red froth on his lips, the light fast going from his face. Johann knelt and took his head in his hands.

'Andreas,' he said, trying to reach through the Knight of Darkness to the stable lad, 'what of Wolf?'

The Knight gathered phlegm in his throat, but let it drip bloodily from his mouth. In the two living eyes, Johann saw something still human. He plucked the glass eyes from the face and threw them away.

'Andreas, we were friends once. This wasn't your fault. Wolf. Where's Wolf? Is he still alive? Where is Cicatrice taking him?'

The dying man smiled crooked. 'North,' he gasped, broken bones kniving inside his flesh as he spoke, 'to the Wastes, to the Battle. Not far now. The Battle.'

'What battle? Andreas, it's important. What battle?'

The ghost of the laughter came again. 'Baron,' Andreas said, 'we were never friends.'

The stable boy was dead.

VUKOTICH WAS HURT. The toadman had lost his dagger early in their struggle and his barbed hands hadn't proved a threat. But, when cut, he bled poison. The green stuff ate through clothing, discoloured skin, and seeped dangerously into the body. Vukotich had spilled a lot of it on himself. When the morning light penetrated to the clearing, Johann saw the irregular holes in Vukotich's leggings, and realised his tutor was having trouble standing. He tottered and fell.

'Leave me,' Vukotich said through clenched teeth. 'I'll slow you down.'

That was what Johann had been taught to do, but he had never been a model pupil. With handfuls of snow, he rubbed at Vukotich's wounds, working away until most of the poison was gone. He had no idea how deep the blight had sunk into his flesh, and also didn't know anything about the properties of the toadman's blood. But if it were fatal, Vukotich would have told him so, in an attempt to get Johann to leave him. He tore a spare shirt into rags, and bandaged where he could. Vukotich was quiet, but winced throughout. Johann didn't ask him if he were in pain.

With branches, and strips of leather from their fallen enemies' clothes, Johann made a stretcher which he fixed to Would-Have-Been-Tsar's halter. It was rough, but padded with furs it sufficed. He helped the unprotesting Vukotich onto the stretcher and wrapped him warmly. The old soldier lay still, gripping a sword as a child grips a favoured toy, his face still stained green in patches.

'We're going north,' Johann said. 'We'll be out of this forest by night. There'll be some settlement before the steppes.'

That was true, but didn't necessarily imply a welcome, a healer and a warm bed. There was a saying: 'In the forests, there is no law; on the steppe, there are no gods.' This was still Kislev, but no tsar reigned here. Beyond the steppes were the Wastes, where the warpstone was the only rule, changing men's minds and bodies, distorting souls, working its evil on all. It was Cicatrice's spiritual homeland, and the only surprise was that his trail hadn't brought them there earlier.

They travelled slowly, and Johann was proved wrong. By nightfall, they were still in the forest. Vukotich slept fitfully as he was dragged, voicing the pains he would never admit to when awake. Would-Have-Been-Tsar plodded on like a machine, but Johann knew the horse wouldn't outlive the moon. They'd need fresh horses on the steppes if they were to keep up with Cicatrice, and Vukotich would need healing.

The next day, after an undisturbed night's camp, the trees began thinning and the gloom lifted. There was even a trace of sun in the dead sky. Johann had seen tracks, had found the spot where Cicatrice had camped – the gutted corpse hanging by its feet from a tree was an obvious signpost – and knew they continued on the right trail. Beneath the corpse, someone had scrawled TURN BACK NOW in the snow in fresh blood. Johann spat at the message.

It took a while to realise how strange this country was. There was no birdsong, and he had long since ceased to notice any animals. At first, he was so relieved not to be constantly on guard against wolf and bear – he had three rakemarks on his back to remind him of an old encounter – that it didn't occur to him quite how ominous the lack of life was.

The forest finally died. Johann passed through a thick stretch where tree corpses leaned against each other, or rotted where they lay, and emerged onto the barren steppe. It was like passing from night into day. Looking back, he saw the edge of the forest like a wall extending to the horizon on either side. The trees were packed together like the fortifications of a castle, and didn't seem to fall outward.

If the forest was dead, the steppe was deader. There were
scraggy clumps of grass and areas of naked, frozen earth. The
snows had been thin, but still remained here and there. In a
hundred years, this would be desert.

In the distance, a trail of grey smoke spiralled up into the
empty sky, and something large and ungainly with wings
flapped slowly through the air.

'There's a village ahead, Vukotich.'

They rested a while, and Johann dripped some water –
they had been reduced to melting snow – into his tutor's
mouth, then fed the horse. It had been over a month since
they'd seen another creature who'd not tried to kill them.
Perhaps, by some miracle, there would be some hospitality
to be bought at the village. Johann wasn't too hopeful, but
hadn't developed Vukotich's automatic distrust. Men still
had to earn his enmity.

Vukotich wasn't speaking, conserving his strength, but
Johann could tell his tutor was mending. In him, life was
like a seed that lives through the arctic winter to sprout
when spring brings a trace of warmth. Twice, Johann had
thought him dead and been proved wrong. Cicatrice's bandits had given him the name Iron Man.

Johann chewed a long strip of Tsarina as he rode towards
the smoke, and tried not to think about Andreas, not to
think about Wolf. He remembered the stable lad as a cheer-
ful youth, and could not see in him the beginnings of the
Chaos Knight. But they had been there. Perhaps it had
always rankled with Andreas that he was born to serve, while
Johann and Wolf were born to the barony. The ways of the
warpstone were subtle. They could steal into a man's heart –
a child's heart – and find the resentments, the petty injuries,
the flaws, then work on them until the heart was rotten as a
worm-holed apple. Then, the outer changes began. In
Andreas, in the toad-thing, in the many others they had seen
over the years. The goat-headed altered that had killed Corin
the Fletcher had once been a simple cleric of Verena,
Goddess of Learning and Justice, lured into evil by a desire
to glance at the Forbidden Books. Cicatrice himself had
been a distant relative of the Prince-Elector of Ostland,

posted to the Wastes by a jealous rival during a family feud, changed now beyond recognition.

What could warpstone have done to Wolf? Would his brother remember the unlucky arrow in his shoulder, and greet his rescuers with a murderous attack? Would he even recognise Johann? With each year, the likelihood of his putting up any resistance diminished. Now, most probably, he would have to be rescued against his will. And even then, he might prove too far gone in the ways of darkness to help.

Johann and Vukotich had not discussed the end of their search. It had always been assumed between them that Wolf would be rescued. But just lately, Johann had begun to wonder. He knew that he could never bring himself to raise an arm against his brother, but what of Vukotich? Did the Iron Man feel it would be his duty, if Wolf could not be saved, to put an end to him by the sword? Vukotich had mercy-killed before, in his wars, even along their trail. Would it be so different? And would Johann try to stop him? He suspected that, even wounded, Vukotich was the better duellist.

Something crunched under Would-Have-Been-Tsar's hooves, jolting Johann out of his unhappy reverie. He looked down. The animal was standing on a clean skeleton, his right foreleg buried in a ribcage that gripped his ankle like a trap. Johann dismounted, and pulled the old bones away. The skeleton was nearly human, but for the horns on the skull and the extra rows of teeth.

They were in the middle of a sea of bones, stretching as far as the horizon. This must be the site of some ancient plague, or some calamitous conflict...

Andreas had spoken of a battle.

Johann got up on the horse, and continued, proceeding slowly. The stretcher dragged through long-undisturbed bones. Some of the skeletons were barely recognizable. Johann shuddered and kept his eyes on the smoke. He could see now that it was coming from a group of low buildings, more an outpost than a village. But there would be people. What kind of people would live among the detritus of massacre?

When Vukotich awoke, Johann would ask him about the battle. He would know who had fought here, and why. As if it mattered. Some of the skeletons were hundreds of years old, he thought. Their armour and weapons long since stolen away, only their useless bones remained.

Then the smell hit him. The smell he'd become used to. The smell of the zombie that had been with Andreas, the smell of all recently-dead things. The stench of decay.

The quality of the dead had changed. These skeletons were clothed with rags of flesh. They were more recently dead, or else preserved by the cold. They didn't crumble under the horse's hooves or the trailing edge of Vukotich's stretcher.

It was a bumpy ride. Johann half-turned in the saddle, and saw Vukotich waking up. The stretcher rose over a huddled corpse, dragging it a few feet before leaving it behind. Empty eye sockets looked up, and a second mouth gaped in its throat. One of its arms was a man-length clump of tentacles, now withered like dry seaweed. It had been stripped naked.

'The Battlefield,' said Vukotich.

'What is this place?'

'Evil. We're close to Cicatrice. This is what he's come for.'

Vukotich was in pain again. Talking hurt him, Johann knew. The tutor slumped back on his stretcher, breathing hard.

The dead were around them in heaps. Some were obviously fresh-killed. There were birds now. Unclean carrion-pickers, tearing at exposed flesh, pecking out eyes, fighting over scraps. Johann hated the carrion birds. There was nothing worse than living off the slaughtered.

Armies had passed this way, less than a day ago by the looks of some of their leavings. And yet they had been following a band of raiders, not an army. Cicatrice could command only a hundred Knights at his best, and his band was well below strength since their exploits in the Troll Country.

'The gathering,' Vukotich got out, 'is here. Cicatrice will be one among many.'

A pack of rats, close together like a writhing carpet, swarmed over a skeleton horse, and swept towards the stretcher. They skittered up over the branches and fastened on Vukotich's legs. He waved his sword and sent them flying away. The cutting edge was red. Johann could see his tutor had been bitten.

'Damn. The plague'll get me yet.'

'Easy. We're nearly at the village.'

Vukotich coughed, and shook on his stretcher. He spat pink froth. 'By nightfall,' he gasped. 'We must be there by nightfall.'

THE SKIES WERE reddening when they reached the village. It consisted of a scattering of shacks around a central long, low hall. The buildings were all sunken, little more than roofed cellars with slit windows and fortifications. Johann was reminded of the shelters he had seen in lands afflicted by tornadoes and hurricanes.

There were no dead among the buildings. Indeed, the corpses seemed to have been cleared away from a rough circle around the village. There was a hitching rail by the hall. Johann dismounted and tied Would-Have-Been-Tsar to it.

'Yo,' he shouted, 'is anyone here?'

Vukotich was awake again, shivering in his wrappings.

Johann shouted again, and a door opened. There was a depression in the earth beside the hall, and the entrance was in it, surrounded by bags of dirt. Two men came out of the hall. Johann touched his swordhilt until they were in full view. Neither was significantly altered. One, who stayed back near the door, was a beefy, middle-aged man with a leather apron and a gleaming bald pate. The other, who came forward, was scarecrow thin, a wild-haired individual with a tatty mitre perched on his head. He was weighed down with amulets, badges, medals and tokens.

Johann recognised the icons of Ulric, Manann, Myrmidia, Taal, Verena and Ranald. Also, of the Chaos Powers, including the dreaded Khorne; the Gods of Law, Alluminas, Solkan; Grungni, Dwarf God of Mining; Liadriel, Elven God of Song and Wine. The hammer of Sigmar Heldenhammer,

Patron Deity of the Empire, was there. No priest could truly bear the talismans of so many disparate, mutually hostile gods. This was a madman, not a cleric.

Still, it is best to treat the mad with courtesy.

'Johann,' he said, extending his empty hand, 'Baron von Mecklenberg.'

The man approached sideways, his gods tinkling as he did, smiling the smile of an imbecile.

'I'm Mischa, the priest.'

They shook hands. Mischa darted away, cautious. Johann noticed he wore the dagger of Khaine, Lord of Murder, as well as the dove of Shallya, Goddess of Healing and Mercy.

'We mean no harm. My friend has been injured.'

'Bring them inside,' barked the bald man. 'Now, before nightfall.'

Vukotich had mentioned nightfall. Johann had a bad feeling about that. He had had an unrelishable experience with a certain vampire family in the Black Mountains.

'Come, come,' said Mischa, gesturing to Johann to come inside the hall. He danced a little on one foot and waved a loose-wristed hand in the air. Johann saw the blood in his eyes, and held back.

He turned to Vukotich, who was struggling to sit up, and helped his friend. The Iron Man was unsteady on his feet, but could stumble towards the hall. Johann supported him. The bald man came out of his hole in the ground and lifted Vukotich's other shoulder. Johann sensed strength in him. Between them, while Mischa darted around uselessly, they got Vukotich through the door.

When Mischa was in, the bald man slammed the door behind him and slid fast a series of heavy bolts. It took Johann a few moments to get used to the semi-darkness inside the hall, but he gathered immediately that there were others inside.

'Darvi,' asked someone, 'who are they?'

The bald man let Vukotich sag against Johann, and stepped forward to reply. The interrogator was a dwarf who held himself oddly.

'This one calls himself a baron. Johann von Mecklenberg. The other hasn't spoken...'

'Vukotich,' said the Iron Man.

'Vukotich,' said the dwarf, 'a good name. And von Mecklenberg. An elector unless I miss my guess, and I never miss my guess.'

'I've abdicated that responsibility, sir,' said Johann. 'Who might I be addressing?'

The dwarf came out of the shadows, and Johann saw why his movements were strange.

'Who might you be addressing?' The dwarf chortled, and bowed very carefully, the hilt of the sword shoved through his chest scraping the beaten earth floor. 'Why, the mayor of this nameless township. I'm Kleinzack... the Giant.'

Kleinzack's sword was held in place by a complicated arrangement of leather straps and buckles. It stuck out a full foot from his back, and seemed honed to razor sharpness. Johann was reminded of the apparatus used by actors to simulate death, two pieces fixed to a body to look like one speared through it.

'I know just what you're thinking, your excellency. No, this isn't a trick. It goes all the way through. A miracle I wasn't killed, of course. The blade passed through without puncturing anything vital, and now I daren't have it removed for fear the miracle won't be repeated. You can learn to live with anything, you know.'

'I can believe it, Mr Mayor.'

'You've met Mischa, our spiritual adviser. And Darvi, who is the keeper of this inn. Come share our meagre fare, and be introduced to the rest of us. Dirt, take his cloak.'

A hunched young man with limbs that bent the wrong way shuffled out of the shadow at Kleinzack's order, and took Johann's cloak from his shoulders, carefully wrapping it as he crept away.

A madman, a cripple, a dwarf... This was truly a peculiar community.

Kleinzack took a lantern and twisted up the flame. The interior of the hall became visible now. There was a long table, with benches either side.

A young woman in the remnants of a dress that mightn't
have been out of place at one of the tsar's famous balls
passed by the diners, doling out a stew into their bowls.
They were as tattered a collection of outcasts as Johann had
ever broken bread with.

Kleinzack climbed a throne-shaped chair at the end of the
table, and settled his sword into a well-worn notch in the
back.

'Sit by me, your excellency. Eat with us.'

Johann took his place, and found himself looking across
the table at an incredibly ancient creature – perhaps a
woman – who was enthusiastically sawing at a hunk of raw
meat with a large knife.

'Katinka doesn't favour civilised cuisine,' said Kleinzack.
'She's a native of this region, and only eats her meat raw. At
least it's helped her keep her teeth.'

The crone grinned, and Johann saw teeth filed to nasty
points. She raised a chunk of flesh to her mouth, and tore
into it. Her cheeks were tattooed, the designs crumpled by
her wrinkles.

'She's a healer,' said the dwarf, 'later, she will tend to your
friend. She can do all manner of things with herbs and the
insides of small animals.'

The young woman splashed stew into Johann's bowl. He
smelled spices, and saw vegetables floating in the gravy.

'This is Anna,' the woman curtsied with surprising dainti-
ness, balancing the pot of stew on her generous hip. 'She
was travelling with a fine gentleman of Praag when he tired
of her, and left her for our village as repayment for our hospitality.'

Anna's eyes shone dully. She had red hair, and would have
been quite pretty cleaned up. Of course, Johann realised, he
wasn't himself much used to baths and scents and etiquette.
That part of his life was long gone.

'Naturally,' laughed Kleinzack, 'we don't expect such grat-
itude from all our guests.'

Various diners joined in, and banged their fists on the
table as they guffawed. Johann didn't find the hilarity pleasant, although the stew was excellent. The food was the best

he'd tasted in some months, certainly better than smoked horse.

The meal passed without incident. No one asked Johann what his business was, and he refrained from asking anyone how this village came to be in the middle of a battlefield. The villagers were too busy eating, and Mischa the priest made the most conversation, invoking the blessings of a grab-bag of gods upon the night. Again, Johann felt uneasy about that.

Katinka took a look at Vukotich, and produced some herb balms which, when applied, soothed his wounds a little. The Iron Man was asleep again, now, and didn't seem to be suffering much.

The hall was sub-divided into sleeping chambers. Several of the villagers scuttled off to them when the eating was done, and Johann heard bolts being drawn. Kleinzack produced some foul roots and proceeded to smoke them. Johann refused his kind offer of a pipe. Anna – who didn't speak – fussed with the dishes and cutlery, while Darvi drew ale from casks. Dirt shuffled around, keeping out of the way.

'You're far from home, Baron von Mecklenberg,' announced Kleinzack, puffing a cloud of vile smoke.

'Yes. I'm searching for my brother.'

'A-ha,' mused the dwarf, sucking at his pipe, 'run away from home, has he?'

'Kidnapped by bandits.'

'I see. Bad things, bandits.' He found something funny, and laughed at it. Dirt joined in, but was silenced by a cuff around the head. 'How long have you been after these bandits?'

'A long time.'

'Long, eh? That's bad. You have my sympathy. All the troubled peoples of the world have my sympathy.'

He stroked Dirt's tangled hair, and the bent boy huddled close to him like a dog to his master.

Something fell out of Dirt's clothing, and glinted on the floor. Kleinzack's face clouded, and Johann noticed how quiet everyone else was.

With elaborate off-handedness, Kleinzack downed his
pipe and picked up his goblet. He drank. 'Dirt,' he said,
suavely, 'you've dropped a bauble. Pick it up and bring it to
me.'

The boy froze for a moment, then scuttled to the object.
His fingers wouldn't work, but he finally managed to
squeeze the thing between thumb and forefinger. He laid it
on the table in front of Kleinzack. It was a ring with a red
stone.

'Hmmn. A nice piece. Silver, I do believe. And a ruby,
carved into a skull. Very nice.'

He tossed it to Johann.

'What do you think?'

Johann could hardly bear to handle the thing. It was
somehow unpleasant to the touch. Perhaps he had been seeing too many skulls lately. This one was slashed diagonally.
It was a familiar scar. Cicatrice was nearby.

'Crude workmanship, but it has a certain vitality, eh? Your
excellency doubtless has many finer jewels than this.'

Johann put it down on the table. Kleinzack snapped his
fingers, and Anna brought the ring to him. He gazed into its
jewel.

'Dirt.' The boy looked up. 'Dirt, you evidently want this
trinket for your own.' The boy was doubtful. A rope of spittle dangled from his lips. 'Very well, you shall have it. Come
here.'

Dirt shambled forwards on his knees and elbows, advanc-
ing like an insect. He held out his hand, and Kleinzack took
it.

'Which finger, I wonder...'

The dwarf jammed the ring onto Dirt's little finger, then
bent it savagely back. Johann heard the snap as the bone
went. Dirt looked at his hand, with its finger sticking out at
an unfamiliar angle. There was blood on the ruby. He smiled.

Then the din started outside.

JOHANN HAD BEEN in enough battles to recognise the noise.
The clash of steel on steel, the cries and screams of men in
the heat of combat, the unforgettable sound of rent flesh.

Outside the village hall, a full-scale war was being fought. It was as if armies had appeared out of the air, and set at each other with the ferocity of wild animals. Johann heard horses neighing in agony, arrows thudding home in wood or meat, shouted commands, oaths. The hall shuddered, as heavy bodies slammed into it. A little dust was dislodged from the beams.

Kleinzack was unperturbed, and continued to drink and smoke with an elaborate pretence of casualness. Anna kept efficiently refilling the dwarf's goblet, but was white under her filth, shaking with barely suppressed terror. Dirt tried to cram himself under a chair, hands pressed over his ears, eyes screwed shut as clams. Darvi glumly stood by his bar, eyes down, peering into his pint-pot. Katinka bared her teeth, apparently giggling, but Johann couldn't hear her over the cacophony of war. Mischa was in his corner, kneeling before a composite altar to all his gods, begging at random for his own skin.

Outside, one faction charged another. Hooves thundered, cannons boomed, men went down in the mud and died. Johann's ears hurt.

He noticed that Darvi, Katinka and a few of the others had padded wads of rag into their ears. Kleinzack, however, did without; evidently, he was far gone enough to last a night of this.

They were all mad, Johann realised, maddened by this ghost of battle. Could it be like this every night?

He went to Vukotich, and found his friend awake but rigid, staring in the dark. The Iron Man took his hand and held it tight.

Eventually, incredibly, Johann slept.

HE AWOKE TO silence. Rather, to the absence of clamour. His head still rung with the memory of the battle sounds, but outside the hall it was quiet. He felt hung-over, and unrested by his sleep. His teeth were furred and his muscles ached from sleeping sitting up.

He was alone in the hall with Vukotich. Light streamed in through slit windows. His tutor was still in deep sleep, and

Johann had to work hard to slip his hand out of the Iron Man's grip. His fingers were white, bloodless, and tingled as his circulation crept back.

Puzzled, he went to the door, and found it hanging open. He put a head round it and saw nothing threatening. Hand on sword, he went outside, and climbed up the steps cut into the earth. The air was still and smelled of death.

The village stood in the middle of a field of the dead and dying. There were fires burning, carrying on the wind the stink of scorching flesh, and weak voices cried out in unknown tongues. Their meaning was clear, though. Johann had heard the like after many a combat. The wounded, calling for succour, or for a merciful blade.

At the hitching post, he found what was left of Would-Have-Been-Tsar. An intact head still in its bridle, hanging loose from the wood. The rest of the horse was a blasted, blackened and trampled mess, frosted with icy dew. It was mixed in with the limbless remnant of something small. A dwarf or a goblin. It was hard to tell, the head being mashed to a paste in the hardened mud. From now on, Johann would walk.

Ghosts or not, the armies of night left corpses behind. He scanned the flat landscape, finding nothing but the remains of war. Where did they come from? Where did they go? All the dead bore the marks of the warpstone. He could sense no pattern to the battle, as if a multitude of individuals had fought each other for no reason, each striving to kill as many of the others as possible.

That made as much sense as many of the wars he had seen on his travels.

Dirt came from the other side of the hall, his body strapped into the semblance of straightness by leather and metal appliances. He was still a puppet with too many broken strings, but he was upright, even if his head did loll like a hanged man's, and he was walking as normally as he ever would. Johann noticed his broken finger splinted and bandaged, and wondered if he'd come by his other twisted bones in the same manner. He was carrying a double armful of swords, wrapped in bloody cloth. He smiled, revealing surprisingly white and even teeth, and dropped his burden onto the earth by the hall. The cloth came apart, and Johann saw red on the blades. He had learned about weapons – formally and by experience – and recognised a diversity of killing tools: Tilean duelling *epees*, Cathay dragon swords, two-handed Norse battle blades, curved scimitars of Araby. Dirt grinned again, proud of his findings, and fussed with the swords, arranging them on the ground, wiping the blood off, bringing out the shine.

Johann left him to his business and went among the dead.

The villagers were on them like carrion birds, stripping armour and weapons, throwing their booty into large wheelbarrows. He examined one catch, and found rings, a silver flask of some sweet liqueur, an unbloodied silk shirt, a bag of gold crowns, a jewel-pommelled axe, a leather breastplate of Elven manufacture, a good pair of Bretonnian boots. Anna was filling this barrow. She worked delicately with the corpses, robbing them as if she were a nurse applying a poultice. As he watched, she slipped the rings from the stiff fingers of a dandified altered, then progressed to his filigreed armour. Without pausing to appreciate the workmanship, she loosed the leather ties on his arm-plates, and pulled them free. His skin was rotten beneath, and had been even before the battle. She eased his dragon-masked helmet from his head, and a knotted rope of silky hair came loose with it. His features were powdered and rouged, but had decaying holes in them. His eyes opened, and his limbs spasmed. With a small, ladylike move, Anna passed a knife under his chin, and he slipped back, blood trickling onto his chest. He sighed away his life, and Anna worked his body armour loose.

Sickened, he turned away, and saw Kleinzack. The dwarf was bundled up in furs and wore a ridiculous hat. In daylight, the sword through him looked more bizarre than ever.

'Good morning, excellency. I trust you slept well.'

He didn't reply.

'Ah, but it's fine to be alive on such a morning.'

Mischa appeared, laden down with more religious tokens – some still wet – and bent low to whisper in Kleinzack's ear.

The mayor laughed nastily, and slapped the mad priest. Mischa scurried off yelping.

'The gods have made him mad,' said Kleinzack, 'that's why they tolerate his sacrileges.'

Johann shrugged, and the dwarf laughed again. The mirth was beginning to grate on him. He was unpleasantly reminded of Andreas's deathly laughter. Truly, he had fallen among madmen.

Darvi and another man were building corpse fires. They couldn't hope to burn all the dead, but they were managing to clear the area nearest the hall. Those too big to be carried whole to the blaze were cut up and thrown on like logs. Katinka came to Kleinzack and offered him a bracelet she had found.

'Pretty-pretty,' he cooed, holding the bracelet up so its jewels caught the light. He slipped it over his wrist and admired it. Katinka hovered, bowed down, waiting for an indulgence. Kleinzack reached up and stroked her ratty hair. She hummed to herself in idiot contentment, and he sharply tweaked her ear. She cried out and he pushed her away.

'Back to work, hag. The days are short, and the nights are long.' Then, to Johann, 'Our work is never done, you see, excellency. Each night there are more. It never ends.'

A hand fell on Johann's shoulder, and squeezed. He turned. Vukotich was up, a broken lance serving as a staff. His face had kept its greenish look, the scars standing out white and hard, and there was pain behind his eyes. But his grip was still strong. Even hobbling, he radiated strength. He was still the Iron Man who inspired terror even in Cicatrice's worst.

'This is a Battlefield of Chaos, Johann. This is what Cicatrice has been heading for all along. It's nearly over. He'll be close by here, sleeping, with his creatures about him.'

Kleinzack bowed to Vukotich, shifting his sword slightly. 'You know about the battle, then?'

'I've heard of it,' said Vukotich. 'I was near here once when I was younger. I saw the Knights coming here.'

'For over a thousand years, they've been fighting among themselves, proving themselves. All the Champions come here sooner or later to see if they've got what they say they have. And most of them haven't. Most of them end up like these poor dead fools.'

'And that's how you live, dwarf,' spat Johann. 'Robbing the dead, selling their leavings?'

Kleinzack didn't seem offended. 'Of course. Someone has to. Bodies rot, other things don't. If it weren't for us, and for our forebears, this plain would be a mountain of rusting armour by now.'

'They sleep in great underground halls nearby,' said Vukotich, 'sleep like the dead. This is an important stage in their development, in their alteration. They lie comatose by day on warpstone slabs, changing form, ridding themselves of the last traces of humanity. And by night, they fight. In small groups, in single combat, at random, they fight. For a full lunar month, they fight. And if they survive, they go back into the world to spread their evil again.'

'And Cicatrice?'

'He'll be here. Asleep now, as befits a general. We'll find him, and Wolf with him.'

Vukotich looked tired. From his eyes, Johann could tell it would be over soon, one way or another.

'You,' Vukotich addressed Kleinzack, 'carrion crow. Have you found anything bearing this symbol?' He produced a cloak-clasp with the emblem of Cicatrice's band, the stylised human face deformed by a red lightning bolt in imitation of their leader's daemon-claw scar.

The dwarf held up a hand, and rubbed his thumb against his fingers. Vukotich tossed him the clasp, and he made a great show of examining it as if appraising the workmanship.

'I can perhaps recall some similar item...'

Vukotich produced a coin and cast it at Kleinzack's feet. The dwarf looked exaggeratedly insulted, and shrugged helplessly.

Johann dropped a purse of coins to join the single crown and Kleinzack smiled.

'It all comes back to me. The scar.' He passed a finger diagonally across his face, kinking a little over his nose. 'Very distinctive. Very unusual.'

'It's an unusual man we're after.'

'The man whose followers bear this design?'

'Yes. Cicatrice, the bandit.'

Kleinzack laughed again. 'I can do better than show you a man who bears the image of this scar...'

The dwarf spun the clasp in the air and caught it.

'I can show you the man who bears the scar itself.'

A CLAW GRASPED Johann's heart, and squeezed.

'Cicatrice?'

The dwarf nodded, smiling, and held out his open hand. Johann gave him money. Kleinzack made a great pretence of examining his payment, biting into one gold crown, leaving shallow marks across the Emperor's face. He looked at Johann and Vukotich, savouring his momentary power over them.

'Come,' he said, at length, 'follow me.'

Vukotich was still slowed by his wounds, but managed to hobble along with the dwarf. Johann felt frustrated by their measured pace as they went their way through the heaps of the dead, out onto the bloody steppe. For ten years, he had been waiting to confront Cicatrice. That scarred face – which he had never seen, but which eternally recurred on his men's emblem – had haunted his nights. He had never exchanged a blow or a word with the bandit, but Johann knew his history as well as he knew his own, and felt that by following in Cicatrice's tracks, he had become as close to him as to a brother. A hated brother. Now, he remembered their separate battles. He measured his bested foes against Cicatrice's, wondering whether he was truly the Chaos Champion's equal in battle. He supposed he would find out soon enough.

Johann was impatient. Ten years was too long. It was well past time to get this over with.

No. He slowed himself, keeping in step with Vukotich and Kleinzack, helping his tutor over the rougher patches of ground, reining in his unruly imaginings. He would not hasten now. He had stayed alive for this day, kept himself going beyond all human endurance. He would not fumble at the last and chance Wolf's life. He found a calm in the centre of his heart, and let it seep through his being. The tightness in his chest eased. He began to see with a deadly clarity.

Almost unconsciously, he checked his weapons. His knives were in their greased sheaths, his sword hung easily from his belt. The blades could be in his hands faster than a human eye could register. After ten years on the trail, he could kill sometimes faster than he could think. It was a habit of which he looked forward to purging himself.

He remembered the initial arrow, brushing the deer's hide, proceeding with what had seemed like supernatural slowness towards his brother's shoulder. Johann hadn't used a longbow since, preferring to concentrate on hand-to-hand iron and steel.

'It's not much further,' wheezed Kleinzack. The dwarf was out of breath, and his sword shivered each time he filled his lungs. 'Just over this ridge.'

The ridge was not a geographical feature, it was an arrangement of dead horsemen and their steeds, cut down by a row of cannons. The third or fourth charge had broken through, but the casualties had been appalling. Johann tried not to think of the ranks upon ranks of flesh underfoot as he helped Vukotich up over the obstacle. Kleinzack swarmed with surprising agility over the cavalry corpses, pulling himself along using belts and saddles as hand-holds.

Darvi and a group of rangy, dead-faced men were hard at work, cutting valuables loose from the bodies with saws and shears. They were working on a pile of felled knights. One man was tugging at a plumed helmet whose owner was still feebly resisting, despite the depth and number of his mortal wounds. This one was in the latter stages of the changes, limbs barely recognisable as human, leathery batwings torn and crumpled beneath him, torso swollen up by a breastbone that was thrusting through papery skin like a knifeblade. The tatterdemalion's head twisted this way and that with the helmet, but finally his robber got a good enough grip and with one determined tug pulled his prize away.

The altered was old, his cheeks sunken and serrated, all his teeth gone save for two yellow tusks that had worn grooves in his lips. His hair was white and sparse, knotted in rat-tails on one side where he had once been partially scalped. And a red scar ran diagonally across his face, kinking a little over the nose.

Their search was over.

But this was not the Cicatrice Johann had pictured. This was a dying misfit, altered beyond practicality, lost even to himself.

'I want to talk to him,' Johann told Kleinzack.

'That's of no mind to me, your excellency...'

The dwarf wandered off, signalling Darvi and his men to follow. There were still pickings to be had. Something was screaming a few hundred yards away. Kleinzack's crew ambled towards it, their killing tools ready for use.

Johann and Vukotich stood over the man they had followed for so long. He hardly seemed aware of their presence, being absorbed in the business of dying. Cicatrice was still vaguely trying to stand up, but ankles broken and swollen to the thickness of a normal man's waist wouldn't support him. Uncomprehending eyes opened and blinked on his bare shoulders, purposeless tendrils waved languidly in the flow of blood from the rib-deep wound over his heart.

'Cicatrice,' said Johann, feeling the syllables of the name on his tongue, 'listen to me...'

The old altered looked up with fast-dimming eyes, and managed a smile. Red treacle oozed from his mouth.

'Cicatrice, I am the Baron von Mecklenberg.'

Cicatrice coughed, somewhere between a sob and a laugh, and turned his head to Johann. For the first time, the hunter and the hunted looked upon each other. Johann saw recognition in Cicatrice's eyes. The dying monster knew who he was. And he would know what he had come for.

'Wolf. Where's Wolf?'

Cicatrice raised a six-taloned hand, and pointed down at the earth, then made a general gesture, indicating the whole area.

'Here?' Cicatrice nodded.

'What have you done to him?'

'What... have... I... done to... *him!*' Cicatrice gathered his voice, and forced the words out. 'What have I done to him? Why, my dear baron, surely you should ask... what has he done to me?'

He held a claw to his opened breast, and dipped it in the blood.

'Wolf fought you? Wounded you?'

The laugh came again – the laugh Johann had been hearing from too many throats since this began – and Cicatrice's smile became cruel and indignant. Johann could see the shadow of the fearsome warrior chieftain's face over the shrunken and abused features of this poor creature.

'Wolf has killed me.'

With a certain pride, Johann turned to Vukotich. The Iron Man was an iron statue, his face unreadable. 'You see, Vukotich,' he said, 'Wolf resisted all these years. Here, in the heart of darkness, Wolf has turned on his captors and escaped.'

'No,' said Cicatrice, barely able to control his spasming now. These were his last minutes, last seconds... 'No, he has not escaped. Wolf now leads my army. For two years now, he has ridden at the head of our columns, planned our raids. I'm an old man. I've been tolerated. Until now. Now the Scar is dead, and the Young Wolf will have his time.'

Cicatrice reached into his wound, and pulled at his beating heart, holding it up.

'At least your brother chose to kill me face to face. His blade didn't come from the back.'

Blood ran through Cicatrice's talons. His heart puffed up like a toad and then collapsed. With his last strength, the bandit squeezed out his own life.

ON THE WAY back to the village, it was Vukotich who supported Johann, guiding him as an enchanter might one of the raised dead. Suddenly, the thousands of miles he had travelled in the past ten years weighed heavy upon him, as if each were a measure of time, not distance.

He had been concentrating so hard upon his search, his quest, that he had failed to perceive the shifting circumstances that now rendered the whole endeavour all but meaningless.

Wolf was in no need of rescue. A few days ago, Wolf had sent four creatures to kill his brother. In the last two years, how many traps and schemes had he created? How he must wish him dead!

'It's not Wolf,' Vukotich said. 'Whatever he has become, it's not Wolf. Your brother died a long time ago, in the woods, in Sudenland. He spilled his innocent blood. What we must find – find and *destroy* – is like the thing we burned in the forest, a monstrosity using what's left of his body.'

Johann had no argument.

By the time they were back in the village, the sky was already darkening. Days really were short this far north. Johann heard distant thunder, in the ground, and imagined the hordes stirring from their sleep, examining themselves for new alterations, new improvements.

Would he even recognise Wolf?

Kleinzack was standing before his hall, surrounded by his people. Mischa was chanting, and dancing epileptically, invoking long-dead deities, calling for protection from all manner of perils. The villagers had stowed their day's prizes, and were preparing for another night of cowering.

Johann would have to stay outside this night, and search through the carnage for his brother, seek to challenge him to mortal combat. He had no doubt that he could survive in the thick of a melee, but he wondered if he could come so close to the creatures of the warpstone, with their roiling auras of evil, without himself beginning the long, slow metamorphosis into monstrosity. If he were to start altering, he thought he could trust Vukotich to stick a spear through him.

A circle noosed around his left ankle, biting into the leather of his boot, and he was pulled off balance. He saw the wire rising out of the earth as it was reeled in. Kleinzack jumped aside as the whirring machine behind him pulled the steel thread in yard by yard. Darvi was working a handle. Johann fell badly, jarring his back, and was dragged too fast across the ground to sit up and free himself. His clothes were abraded, and his sword-hilt dug into the ground like a plough. A net was thrown over him, and he felt a metal-tipped boot impact with his ribs. His arms were tangled in the net, and he felt heavy weights on them. Anna and Katinka were kneeling, pressing him to the ground as they hammered pegs down, pinning the net, limiting his movement.

Twisting his head, he saw Vukotich spinning his broken lance, surrounded by six or seven of Darvi's brawny corpse-strippers. He gored one through, but his weapon was tugged out of his grip and the circle closed. He went down under it. Later, when they'd avenged their friend with a severe pummelling, they dragged him to the hall and pinned him out beside Johann.

Approaching carefully, Kleinzack and Darvi extracted the weapons from Johann's sheaths. He tried to resist, but only got another kick for his pains. The dwarf made a great play of examining the sword, appreciating the workmanship, and then taking it away.

All the while, Mischa danced, sprinkling foul-smelling liquid on Johann, daubing arcane symbols on the earth, and reciting from various scrolls of manuscript he kept about his person.

Johann gathered he and Vukotich were being laid out to appease the gods. At least, that was what Mischa was telling the villagers.

Eventually, the mad priest stopped, and went inside with the rest of the villagers.

Above the net, the sky was nearly black. The subterranean sounds were louder now and Johann could feel the earth under him shaking. He tensed all his muscles and exerted as much pull as he could. One of the pegs popped out of the ground, and his right hand was free. He strained again. The pegs were loosening, but it would take time to fight his way out of the net.

Then a shadow fell over him, and he heard the now familiar laugh. It was Kleinzack.

'Happy now, excellency? You'll soon see your brother. I'm only sorry I shan't be here to witness your touching reunion, to see your first embrace after so many years...'

The dwarf's hands were on him, patting pockets for coins.

'Of course, your brother has already paid me well for arranging this little get-together, but I don't see why I shouldn't also extract some tribute from you. It's only fair.'

Kleinzack took the pouches from Johann's belt, and the amulet with the family crest from his neck. Then he tried to work off the signet ring from his right hand.

Johann grabbed the dwarf's hand and held tight. Kleinzack thumped him, hard, but was still held. He spat in the dwarf's face and, summoning all his strength, sat up. Pegs burst free – those driven by Anna seemed a shade less well-rooted than those Katinka had seen to – and the net gathered in Johann's lap as he fought loose of it.

Kleinzack's gloating smarm had bubbled away, and his face was a mask of terror. He started blubbering, begging for mercy.

The ground was trembling constantly now, and he could hear hooves, the clanking of armour, shouts of defiance and other, barely human, sounds. A great many creatures were coming this way.

He held Kleinzack at arms' length. The stubby legs kicked, but the mayor couldn't reach Johann's torso. He had adjusted his grip now, and held the dwarf by a fistful of jerkin, just under the protruding hilt of the sword.

'You've left me here, unarmed, to die, dwarf.'

Kleinzack didn't say anything, just drooled. His bowels had let go, and he was dripping.

'You took away my sword. Up here, that's as much murder as taking away my life.'

There were creatures around them in the darkness, human and otherwise.

'You owe me a sword, Kleinzack. I'll take yours.'

He threw Kleinzack upwards. The dwarf seemed to hang in the air for a moment, eyes wide with disbelief. Johann reached out and grasped the hilt of the sword in the mayor. The dwarf's weight dragged it down. Kleinzack screamed as the sharp blade shifted in his chest. The point of the sword dug a few inches into the ground. He put a boot on Kleinzack's belly, and pushed the dwarf's body down the length of the sword. The straps and belts came free, and Kleinzack flailed, the long-ago killing stroke finally accomplishing its purpose.

Johann drew his new sword from its scabbard of flesh, and kicked the dead dwarf away.

The fighting had begun, and the dark was pierced by bright flashes. Fires were started, and creatures hurled themselves against each other. An altered head rolled past Johann's feet as he cut Vukotich loose from his net. A cannonade exploded close by and Vukotich took a peppering of shot in one leg. Johann felt blood pouring down his face, from a chip lodged in his forehead, and tried to smear it away.

Nobody was paying particular attention to them, although Johann killed anything that came within a few yards of them, just to make sure. Vukotich took a two-bladed, dagger-topped waraxe from a fallen troll, and split the face of a bear-faced Norse warrior who was hefting a sword at him. As the bearman fell, Johann saw the scarface design on his belt-buckle. He had been one of Cicatrice's.

No, one of Wolf's.

Johann and Vukotich fell back against the hall, leaning on the roof. It was a defensible position. Before them, the warriors hacked and slashed at each other, not caring who they wounded. Ribbons of blood flew through the air. The killing continued.

They didn't have to wait long.

Among the frighteningly random conflict there walked one group who seemed cooler, murderous but purposefully so. They fought their way through the throng towards the hall, towards Johann and Vukotich. There were less than they might have expected – Wolf must have taken bad losses during the last week of fighting by night – but they were death-hardened. Each wore, somewhere about him, the scar.

And one luxuriously-maned, red-eyed, fang-snouted giant wore it as a blood-coloured tattoo across his face.

Wolf.

WOLF GROWLED, LOW and feral in the back of his throat. Then the growl rose to a snarl, and spittle flew from his lupine snout. Then the snarl ended with a gulped intake of air, and Wolf's chest swelled. He howled like the animal he had become, baying at the skies. He clutched and unclutched his great, furred fists.

He carried no weapons but the three-inch, razor-edged claws that ended his fingers and toes, and the rows of teeth in his face. Johann guessed that with those natural assets he wouldn't need to.

Again, Vukotich had been right. There was nothing, that he could see, left of his little brother.

Then the wolf smiled at him, and passed a claw through the air, bidding him come forward.

Wolf's bandits held back, keeping the rest of the battle away from the area now marked out for the fight to the death.

'Forgive me,' Johann said, as he lashed out with Kleinzack's sword. Wolf threw up an arm, tendons shifting beneath his pelt, and the swordblow was deflected. The altered Wolf must have iron in his muscle and bone. Johann's strike had left a graze, which trickled blood, but no more. It should have sheared through, severing the arm.

Wolf moved fast and Johann had to stumble backwards, losing his footing, to avoid the snipping of the claws. Wolf kicked out with a barbed, bootless foot, and a claw-toe raked across Johann's stomach, cutting through his layered-leather armour. He pushed upwards as he stood, grabbing Wolf's ankle with both hands and turning it, off-balancing the creature that had been his brother. Almost immediately, he lost his grip and Wolf was righting himself. He stood like a man, ready to wrestle with the arts they had been taught as boys, but he fought like a beast, who had to use tooth and claw or go hungry tonight.

Vukotich was still leaning against the sloping roof of the hall, breathing heavily. He was watching his pupils, but also wary of Wolf's comrades, ready to pitch in with an axe if the strangely altered rules of fair combat were breached. Otherwise, he was leaving Johann and Wolf to their struggle.

Johann saw that Wolf had indeed grown with his alterations, finding a shape to fit his name, yet retaining every spark of his intelligence. His eyes were cruel but gleamed with sharpness of mind. The clawstroke across his face marked him as a leader. He would never have been baron, but he had proved that he could rise to power by his own designs.

Had Johann not missed his deer, what would Wolf have made of himself? How would his strength, now perverted into monstrosity, have been made manifest? Truly, the division between Hero and Hellspawn is fine, no thicker than a slender arrow...

The cut at his belly had gone deeper than he thought, and he felt his own blood soaking the inside of his clothes. Knots of pain were forming, too, and he tried not to think of the depth of his wounds. He had seen men vainly trying to coil their insides back in, and knew how permanent damage to the vitals was. Wolf showed no sign of hurt, although he had struck him again and again with the edge of Kleinzack's sword. His brother's hide was thicker than any armour.

They circled each other, like wrestlers looking for a good hold. He remembered that he had always bested his brother when they were boys. The three years between them gave him the advantage, and Wolf had been shamed only when Johann, hoping to give his brother a taste of victory, had held back and allowed himself to be beaten. Had that experience festered in the captive boy's mind while the powers of the warpstone were exerted on him? Was that the secret anger that had fuelled his alteration?

Johann bled from the shoulder now, almost the exact spot where he had wounded Wolf so many years ago, and wondered whether that claw-thrust had been a deliberate reminder.

Wolf wore a metal shoulderpiece with the mark of
Cicatrice picked out in jewels, covering the site of his long-
healed wound. It was one of several for-show scraps of
armour adorning his body.

Wolf jabbed again, with a blade-tipped forefinger, and
again gored his shoulder. Now, he was sure it was deliberate.
Wolf was drawing the fight out, reminding him of the long-
ago error that had brought them to this...

He heard a clash and a scream, and glimpsed a tableau
behind Wolf. One of the bandits had gone for Vukotich and
was on its knees in front of the Iron Man, axe embedded
between its eyes. The axe came free and Vukotich whirled to
take on another attacker. Things were coming to an end and
Wolf's men were clearing up the side issues.

Wolf dropped to all fours and charged like an animal, his
long, still-golden hair streaming behind him. His back
arched, and Johann saw the points of his vertebrae thrust
against his skin. With a two-handed grip, he sliced into
Wolf's humped back, aiming for the spinal column. Hide
peeled and the sword jarred in his hands. Wolf roared,
apparently feeling pain for the first time in the fight. He
twisted away, rolling in a ball, and then stood like a man
again, and closed with his brother.

Johann's swordpoint touched his breast, and he froze.
Wolf looked at Johann, the sword held between them.
Johann had a good grip and Wolf leaned forward into it. His
hairy skin dimpled around the sharp end of the blade, and
Johann felt the hilt pushed against his stomach. He could let
go of the sword and it would stay between them, held by
their bodies. For an instant, the brothers locked eyes, and he
knew he was lost. Wolf snarled, strings of saliva hanging
from his snout, and coals glowed deep in his blood-filled
eyes.

Wolf held his shoulders and pulled his brother towards
him in a killing embrace. The sword should have burst
through the skin, and pierced his heart neatly...

Instead, the sword bent. First, it simply strained and
Johann felt the pommel driving painfully into his wounded
gut. Then, with an agonising creak, a natural weakness in the

iron was worked on, and the weapon bent as easily as a green branch. Wolf's snarl continued and the sword was pulled out of Johann's hand. It fell away, useless.

Vukotich was still fighting. Three of Wolf's men were out, but the last two had him pinned to the roof, and were cutting him. The Iron Man was bleeding badly and his blood had an unhealthy, greenish tinge.

Wolf and Johann grappled with each other, wrestling again. He felt the claws going into his wounded shoulder, digging deep in the flesh. He brought his knee up, and slammed into Wolf's rock-hard belly. The blow had no effect. He took a handful of Wolf's hair, and tugged it sharply. A patch came away bloody, but Wolf didn't flinch. Wolf made a fist, and aimed for Johann's face. He took the blow on his chin, and reeled back, his head ringing, his vision shaking.

His shoulder was a fiery mass of pain now. And his left knee wasn't working properly. And he had no weapons save for his hands. And his mind.

Wolf howled, with a note of triumph, and came after him. He was tempted to turn and run. But he wouldn't get ten feet in the battle anyway. He might as well die by Wolf's hand as by that of an unknown minion of the night.

He made a hard-edge of his hand, as the monks of Nippon were known to do, and chopped at Wolf's neck. Wolf moved before the blow could land, and he skinned the leading edge of his hand on the jewelled armour plate.

Wolf screamed, and lashed out clumsily, claws closing in the air a foot to the left of Johann's face.

That was the reminder he needed. That was the message what was left of his brother had been giving him. He felt the pain in his own shoulder, but ignored it, and took hold of the scarface-marked armour piece.

He wrenched it off, and looked at the patch of untreated, rotted wound beneath. Worms writhed in it, a flash of bone could be seen in the mangled meat. The fur around was grey.

Wolf looked at Johann with the eyes of the boy he had been, and silently begged for it to be over.

Johann found a sword on the ground, bloodied but unbroken. Wolf was down on one knee, as if waiting to be knighted. Johann calculated that he could drive the blade through the old wound, past the shoulderbones, and into his brother's heart.

The flow of blood from his temple had halted, but there were tears on his face, salt stinging a cut on his cheek.

Johann hefted the sword aloft, and held it point-down above Wolf, ready to thrust deep, ready to finish his quest...

But things changed, and Vukotich was under him, between the brothers, mortally wounded but still moving. Johann had already begun to bring the blade down. It slipped into the Iron Man just below the v of his throat and slid through flesh and bone.

Incredibly, he stood up. Johann backed off. Wolf was curled up behind Vukotich, cheated of his death. Vukotich turned and pulled the sword from his neck. He held the weapon against him, point lodged beneath his chin, and then drew it across his body.

He opened himself and his blood fell upon Wolf. Innocent blood.

There was a coppery smell and Vukotich glowed with a violet light. He was mumbling at the last, reciting some charm or spell of his homeland, bleeding all over the thing he had once nurtured, taught and loved as a son.

Then he fell sideways, dead.

Johann went to Wolf, reaching for the sword in Vukotich's already-stiffening hands and found the source of the violet light. Wolf was glowing, surrounded by a man-shaped cloud of insubstantial mist. The glow pulsated, and the mist grew thicker. Johann couldn't see his brother through it.

Innocent blood. Never underestimate the power of innocent blood, Vukotich had said.

He tried to touch his brother, but his gloved hand couldn't penetrate the mist. It was yielding, but refused to break.

An enormous male altered with four-foot antlers charged them, and Johann brought his sword up, scraping the velvet from a tine. The stagman howled and his face was engorged purple with rushing blood. Johann cut him down expertly, and took on the two twin goblins who followed, tricking them into spearing each other. Then came an octopoid monstrosity with the eyes of a beautiful woman, and a tiny-headed giant with four mace-handed arms. And others, and others.

As if possessed, Johann fought them all. He stood over his cocooned brother, and held off the hordes until morning.

At first light, the battle stopped. It was like a combat sport. An unheard referee had ended the match and everyone could go home. Johann had been trading blows with an androgynous popinjay who wielded a thin, deadly rapier. When the sun first tainted the sky, the creature sheathed its sword and bowed elaborately to Johann, swishing a ruffled sleeve through the air. All around them, combatants had left off trying to kill each other and were breathing hard. The sudden quiet was unnerving.

Johann looked at his enemy of the moment. There was a disturbing touch of invitation, of frightful promise, in its womanish smile. Its beauty was almost elven, although its neutered but well-muscled form was human.

'Until tonight?' it said, gesturing in the air.

Johann was too exhausted to reply. He simply shook his head, conscious of the blood and sweat falling from his face.

'A pity,' it said. It kissed two fingers, and pressed them to Johann's lips, then turned and walked away, gorgeously embroidered cloak swinging from side to side, the buds of horns poking through its girlish hair. Johann wiped the scented blood taste from his mouth. It joined the others, and they trudged wearily away, leaving behind the losers of the night's conflict. They were tonight's losers, or the next night's, or a hundred nights from now and far from this place's. When you fight for Chaos, you fight with Chaos. And you can't fight with Chaos and win.

Johann fell to his knees beside Wolf. Vukotich's corpse was stiff as a statue now, and had suffered much abuse during the course of the night. But his normally hard face had softened. Johann realised just how little he really knew about the man he had lived with, fought alongside, travelled with and eaten with for ten years. At the end, though, Sigmar was with him. And magic had been in his blood. He traced a hammer in the earth.

Wolf's cocoon had stopped glowing, and was dry and papery now, with thick veins. Johann touched it, and it broke. Wolf was stirring. The unidentifiable matter fell away in dusty scales. Johann tore it away from his brother's head.

A thirteen-year-old face appeared.

There were people about now: Anna, Darvi, Dirt, Mischa. The mad priest gave thanks to another dawn. With a single glance, Johann convinced Darvi not to fight him. Dirt bent down by the brothers and grinned.

'You're the mayor now,' Johann told him. 'Get Katinka. My brother's been hurt and needs a poultice.'

There was an arrow wound in Wolf's shoulder, fresh and clean and bleeding.

THE WARHAWK

I

THE GROUND WAS his enemy, his prison. All his life, Warhawk had tried to escape its dreary pull. He was more comfortable up here on the rooftops than down below on the grimy cobbles, but his aim was higher still, in the freedom of the skies. On his wrist, Belle shifted slightly, hooded head bobbing. He envied her her wings, her flight. But soon, when the Device was complete, he would share her life, would truly be able to take her for his mistress and mate.

When, as the Device decreed, thirteen had died, he too would be able to soar above the dirt, plunge through the clouds, battle the cross-currents of the winds. Nine were dead already. And Number Ten was down below, an insectile speck crawling through cramped streets, never raising eyes from their boots, never dreaming of the wonders above. He did not know him or her yet, but they were already marked for death.

Warhawk had been capricious so far, choosing some of the sacrifices carefully, but picking others entirely at random. One of the most distinguished he had come upon by chance. It had never been explained satisfactorily why a cleric of Solkan, supposedly engaged in important archaeological work in the Grey Mountains, should be disguised as a ragged beggar in the streets of Altdorf, importuning the crowds outside the Vargr Breughel Memorial Playhouse. But that was precisely the activity in which Professor Bernabe Scheydt had been engaged when Belle took him. Warhawk knew all men led iceberg lives, four-fifths submerged in the dark. Death sometimes brought submerged things to the surface.

Balancing carefully, leaning to one side to counter Belle's weight, he walked along the knife-point roof-prow of the Temple of Shallya. He strode without fear across the gap between the temple and the Imperial Bank, scaled the gabled cone of the bank's upper cupola, and finally reached his chosen perch for the night – the service platform just below the great clock. Inside the cupola, machinery ground together, time relentlessly marching forward with the hands on the clockface. In a world slowly eaten away by Chaos, time was a certainty, and the bank clock was a byword for reliability. It was accurate to a quarter-hour, probably the most sophisticated timepiece in the Empire.

Down below, as the night people emerged, the Konigplatz became busy, crowded. It was chilly, but Warhawk, wrapped in his padded leather armour, felt nothing. His body bruised by too many falls, he had been careful in stitching together his black protective suit. A close-fitting hood covered his face, stylised hawk's beak picked out on the leather, feathery swirls around the eyeholes. The few who had seen him swore he was a ghost, or a bird-headed altered.

He looked across the Konigplatz, the Place of Kings, at the cluster of Imperial statues forming a crowd of their own, jostling around the great form of hammer-wielding Sigmar, the earliest emperors faceless lumps of stone, the most recent vulgar caricatures, each vying for a better position. It was the tradition for a new-elected emperor to commission his own statue to add to those of his predecessors. After two and a half thousand years, it proved politic to let the oldest statues crumble away to make room. Still, another period like the Year of the Seven Emperors, which followed the death of the Emperor Carolus twelve hundred years ago, would require the demolition of one of the buildings abutting the Konigplatz to make space for the figures.

Belle's talons were tight on his wrist, razored extensions snug in the grooves of his thick, reinforced glove. She was a good bird, the best he had ever trained – schooled almost from the egg to be a huntress, a weapon – and she would be the greatest of her age. His father would have been proud of Belle. She was easily the equal of the famous Sebastian or Boris the Ferocious, and, in time, she might be as fearsome as Minya, the huge she-hawk who had turned the Battle of Axe-Bite Pass, taking out the eye of Cervello the Traitor, and dying to save his father on the upper slopes of the Fastness of Jagrandhra Dane.

He looked down, scanning the crowds for a sign. From a full five storeys above, they were all tiny, insignificant creatures. His sacrifice was down there somewhere, waiting for a death that was the next movement of the Device. Some gesture, some colour, some sound drifting up. Something would call out. It always did. Meanwhile, Belle was patient. With Belle, the Warhawk had no need of jesses to restrain her ankles or hood to cover her eyes. She would not take to the air until he signalled.

The watchman, Kleindeinst, reminded Warhawk of his father. They had the same hard eyes, the same scarred determination. He had seen Harald Kleindeinst in public several times, even attended a citizens' meeting where angry questions had been directed ceaselessly at the captain. Kleindeinst swore he would clip Warhawk's wings, but had accomplished nothing. At first, the Warhawk thought Kleindeinst might prove a worthy adversary. The copper had brought down the Beast Yefimovich last year, ending the series of murders that had shaken the city during the fog riots. The palace itself had requested the watchman be given charge of the current investigation. Warhawk had sat with the broadsheet writers and concerned businessman, and watched Kleindeinst reel as he was angrily denounced by speaker after speaker. The people of Altdorf wanted decisive action, and couldn't see how powerless the watchman truly was. Kleindeinst would never understand the Device, much less impede its workings. Before the meeting's scheduled end, Captain Kleindeinst had left the room and stalked out alone, renewing his vow, striding from the watch station ahead of the crowd's jeers.

Down below, small knots of people were assembling around the empty bases of the oldest statues. In the evenings, speakers would take advantage of these ready-made platforms to address the crowds, preaching the worship of a lesser god, advocating the institution of an unheard-of political system, spreading gossip and sedition, or making public some commercial venture. In the past, Warhawk had himself spoken in that manner, declaring his intention to conquer the skies, ignoring the laughter of the unwashed mob and the sneers of the wizards. A Brustellinite revolutionist occupied his old pedestal. He was calling for a general uprising against the Emperor, and his audience, loyalists to a man, were getting restless. A strolling watchman, club already out, was moving in on the speaker, doubtless ready to make an arrest, and give the revolutionist a chance to get acquainted with the worthies he decreed should be free by spending a few nights in a straw-and-dung-floored cell with pick-pockets, beggars and cutpurses.

Harald Kleindeinst had been a disappointment. Warhawk was almost sorry for the copper. With each sacrifice, Kleindeinst's position became more dangerous. By the time the Device was complete, the captain would be lucky to escape the wrath of the people he served. His body would hang on the docks for the river-birds. While he was rotting, Warhawk would be learning the ways of the air, striving ever higher, released at last from the tyranny of mud and stone. Still, Kleindeinst was as much a part of the Device as he was himself. He remembered his father saying that you should choose your enemies as carefully as you pick your friends.

It was his father who first told him of the Device, who had explained its workings. It was not magic, but alchemy, a true science. Magic only worked for wizards, but alchemy was for all who followed the steps. Wizards were arrogant, conjuring

fire from the phlogiston in the air and sneering at ordinary
men with their sulphur-sticks. But eventually magic would
be swept away, and the Warhawk would fly, not through
clouds of mystery and superstition, but upon solid princi-
ples of logic and balance. In the mean time, blood sacrifice
must be made.

The watchman shouldered through the crowd and laid a
hand on the revolutionist's leg. Everyone was shouting. The
unkempt Brustellinite jumped upwards, making a grab for
the outstretched arm of the statue of the Empress Magritta,
and swung like an ape. The copper scrambled up after the
fire-breather, egged on by the crowd.

Warhawk knew.

He pointed leisurely, shrugging with his wrist. Belle's
wings spread elegantly and flapped. The bird rose from her
perch, and swayed into the air, almost floating, beating her
wings only when absolutely necessary. That was one of his
father's tricks: teaching the bird to glide silently towards the
victim.

The empress's arm broke at the shoulder and the revolutionist fell into the hostile crowd, who set about
pummelling and kicking him. The watchman, sweating
from his exertions, looked down. He removed his cap and
used it to wipe his forehead.

Belle brought her feet down like a diver executing a back-
flip and settled, claws-first, around the copper's head, her
beak digging into the back of his neck, her knife-ended
claws rending his cheeks and throat. The crowd were too
busy with the Brustellinite to notice the sacrifice. Warhawk
felt the thrill of his kill, knowing the Device was one death
closer to completion. He already heard the clouds calling to
him and could feel the magnetic pull of the stars.

Belle let the watchman fall and his body tumbled into the
crowd. Shrieks and screams rose into the night and his bird
spiralled up away from the sacrifice.

He heard his name, repeated over and over, and stretched
out his wrist for his faithful servant.

People were pointing up at him. He took care to be sil-
houetted against the clockface. He was not like the Beast,

skulking in shadows and fogs. He was a clean predator of
the skies and his daring was a message. A message to the
ground-crawlers he despised, to the watchman who could
never catch him, to the spirit of his departed father.

He was the Warhawk!

Belle landed on his wrist and he brought her close to his
leather-covered mouth. He kissed her bloodied beak, feeling
the warm wetness through his mask.

Climbers were already attempting to scale the bank. But by
the time they reached his perch, he would have long since
flown. With the song of the air in his heart, his devoted bird
on his wrist, he disappeared from the clock platform. A
touch of disappointment leapt inside him – disappointment
that this was not the thirteenth sacrifice, that feet and hands
not wings were the instruments of his escape… He began to
make his pre-planned way down to the hated ground.

II

EVERY TIME THIS happened, more people found an excuse to
loiter around the abused corpse and get in the way. All of
them had shit they wanted to dump on Harald, but none of
them were prepared to get in an orderly queue and take their
turn. Standing by the dead watchman – undisturbed since
the killing – was like being in the middle of a group of
squawking vultures. They all shouted at him at once,
protesting, abusing, questioning.

Captain Harald Kleindeinst – 'Filthy Harald' to some –
tried to block out the noise and concentrate on the job. This
time, his job was Klaus-Ulric Stahlman, forty-three, consta-
ble of the watch, Altdorf-born, wife and three children, dead
in the Konigplatz gutter. A twenty-year flatfoot, his life had
been spent walking the streets, clubbing trouble-makers,
warming his swelling guts in defiance of regulations with
peach schnapps, hauling in the more obvious drunks and
whores, chasing fleetfoot pick-pockets and hanging around
bored in the drizzle waiting for his shift to end. His record
showed no promotions, no commendations, no complaints, nothing. The station captain, Katz, could barely
remember him.

Stahlman had to be identified from his badge number. The bird had lifted the scalp and skin off his skull as if removing a hood. The collar of his uniform and the front of his tabard were stained with his blood, and there were vertical slashes where scrabbling claws – augmented by sharpened metal attachments – had torn. Harald was long past losing his lunch over such things, but these mutilations were becoming monotonously familiar. The Warhawk was a great leveller; grand duchess or scrubwoman, great general or fat old copper: all were equal with their faces off.

Ignoring the ghoulish sensation-seekers, the crowd consisted of six ordinary watchmen, four from the Konigplatz district and two from Harald's own Atrocities Commission: Captain Katz of the Konigplatz, greatcoat over his nightshirt; three pests from competing broadsheets, scratching nasty details on little tablets; a pale-looking physician from the Temple of Shallya, who had been passing and was drafted in to give the gory details; Ehrich Viereck, former commandant of the Commission, still gnawing away at the edges of the case; and Rasselas, supposedly an official of the Imperial Bank, actually a spy in the pay of Chancellor Mornan Tybalt. Within minutes of the murder, the news was all over the city, and the vultures were gathering in the place where the hawk had been.

Harald nodded and one of his watchmen draped a canvas sheet over Stahlman. That made the bloodthirsters lose interest and drift away. Katz and Viereck were muttering together, hatching a scheme to haul Harald off the case. After nine – no, ten – corpses, Harald would not ordinarily have minded. Only he couldn't live with the idea of the Warhawk walking, or flapping, away free. These killings were a personal affront now, each corpse another bleeding wound. Harald would end them or be ended himself.

Rasselas was concerned that the men Harald had sent up to the cupola be careful not to disturb the delicate machine. He was being explicit on the point. Harald wondered whether the Warhawk had selected his perch on purpose, to involve Tybalt and the Imperial counting house in the investigation. Few things were as guaranteed to hinder the path of a watchman as the helpful hand of that olive-eyed, sallow-skinned, one-thumbed schemer. Harald had met Tybalt briefly during the Great Fog Riots, while in pursuit of the Beast, the last pattern-killer to plague the city.

'Well,' Viereck snapped, chewing at the wounds, 'this is what your "softly, softly" methods achieved, Kleindeinst. A watchman dead and the whole city laughing at us.'

'Feel free to apprehend and execute the Warhawk again, Ehrich,' Harald said, calmly, shutting Viereck up.

When the Warhawk had first struck, no one had believed there was a human agency involved in the killings, and the militia had gone around with crossbows skewering every pigeon and duck in the skies. Someone took it into his head to slaughter the ravens that traditionally flocked around the west tower of the Emperor's palace. Street-dwellers and hovel-huddlers who hadn't tasted meat in their lives were suddenly able to eat fowl every night. Then, when the black-hooded Warhawk had been seen with his bird, Viereck had taken over. His investigative methods were simple, brutal and grossly ineffective.

After each killing, he found a vaguely likely suspect – a commercial falconer, an unliked ornithologist, a rat-catcher who used a hawk – and made an arrest, announcing that he would put them to the torture until the case was solved. After a few days in Mundsen Keep with Viereck and some expensive equipment, the suspect would confess and be hanged, whereupon there would be jubilation in the street, Viereck would be declared the hero of the day, and the Warhawk would strike again, leaving another clawed corpse in the street and an Atrocities Commission in search of a new suspect.

'At least the investigation was making progress when I was in charge, Kleindeinst,' Viereck blustered.

Harald looked at the man, fixing him with his eyes, and Viereck looked away, sweating.

After three hangings, Viereck had been removed from his position – it was rumoured at the insistence of the Emperor himself – and Harald Kleindeinst had been seconded from the Dock Watch to head the investigation of the killings.

Now, three months and four victims later, he knew no more than the day he had first heard of the murders.

'This cannot go on,' Rasselas insisted, stating the obvious, 'business is suffering. People are withdrawing funds from the bank and leaving the city. There'll be a crisis.'

The first to leave the city – as usual, Harald reflected – had been the Imperial family. Officially, they were spending the summer on the Ostland estates of the Grand Prince Hals von Tasseninck, another green velvet-set jewel among mankind, so the young Prince Luitpold could gain some experience of life in the provinces. Harald guessed the House of the Second Wilhelm was actually scared of the caress of claws that held no respect for lineage and breeding.

These were not like the Beast's killings, when only street drabs had suffered. Thus far, clerics, militiamen, titled ladies, greengrocers and street urchins had fallen alike under the talons. Everyone was in danger, and those who could afford it were removing themselves.

'The shipping lines are taking all their business to Marienburg,' Rasselas prattled on. 'It's beyond reason.'

Baron Joachim von Unheimlich, patron of the ultra-aristocratic League of Karl-Franz, was advocating Altdorf be placed under martial law, and that troops quell the uprising obviously being fomented by the Warhawk. It was the Beast scenario all over again, the killings were being used by every faction to their own ends. It was Harald's job to set all these distractions aside and to home in on the killer himself. Or herself. In all probability, these were not political crimes, crimes for gain, or even crimes for sport. These were pattern killings, the work of a clever madman who made his own rules and stuck to them. If he could understand the Warhawk's rules, then he had a chance of catching him.

'The Konigplatz Watch Widows and Orphans Society will place an additional reward,' Katz of the 'platz announced to the scribblers, 'of one hundred crowns. Our fallen brother, Schlieman, will be avenged.'

'Stahlman?' asked an ink-fingered writer, only to be ignored.

Another broadsheet character had bribed a copper to lift the canvas and was sketching the dead man's red-covered skull.

Harald realised he was in danger of losing control of the investigation. The Atrocities Commission was not what he was used to. It had too many men, too many ledgers, too many conventions.

The resources should have helped, but he was hobbled by them. He missed the days when he was a lone hunter, just him and the quarry, stalking the streets until the chase was over.

Viereck knelt by the corpse, and began praying loudly to Ulric and Sigmar, calling their wrath down upon the foul murderer, then turning his profile so the sketch artist could include him in his picture. Noticing this, Katz too bent over, thrusting his studiedly grim face into the area the man was sketching, trying to look resolute. The two watchmen seemed more than ever like ghouls, lunching on the dead man's entrails.

'Captain Kleindeinst,' asked another of the reporters, 'how do you react to suggestions that your lax approach to wrong-doers has proved an encouragement to the Warhawk murderer?'

Years ago, when he had killed an elector's nephew who was on the point of raping and murdering a servant, this reporter's sheet had branded him a monstrous thug whose excesses should be curbed with the lash.

'I react by feeding the suggester his own boots and kicking him off the docks.'

The reporter made a great show of writing that down.

A fly coach trundled into the 'platz, and Harald felt almost relieved. With her around, things might start moving again. One of his watchmen opened the carriage door and a slim young woman with red hair stepped out. She didn't look like much, but she was the best hope Harald had of snaring the Warhawk.

'Let me through,' Rosanna Ophuls told the crowds, 'I'm a scryer.'

* * *

III

SCRYING THE 'PLATZ for a trace of the bird was like trying to catch a butterfly one-handed. It was what Rosanna had expected, she had been through it before at the scenes of the other Warhawk murders. It was a futile task, but it had to be done.

Someone hissed 'witch', and was shut up. The stab of anonymous hate and fear from the crowd still hurt her. It was hard to make people understand what she was. All her life, she had been called a witch, a freak, a monster. Only when she was needed did she become an angel of mercy, a saviour. And she hadn't saved anyone recently.

Harald kept them all back, and – through a heroic effort she could sense as if it were a blazing bonfire – kept them quiet, while she tried her best.

'It's mixed up with the residue of the dead man,' she explained, eyes tight shut, as she brushed the bloodied pedestal with her fingertips, shivering as the left-behind emotions of Klaus-Ulric Stahlman shot into her.

He had died in panic, like the others, unable to understand what was happening. Spurs had gouged his eyes, so he had seen nothing. As he screamed, talons raking away his cheeks and lips, he had heard the beating of wings, hard edges of bone cracking his skull. There had been no final prayer, no thought for his wife and children, no sense even of surprise. It had been quick, but agonising.

'There was another man on the pedestal,' she said, seeing him through the dead watchman's memory, 'an agitator, a revolutionist.'

'Liebenstein,' interrupted Katz, distracting her, 'We have him, a Brustellinite sewer rat.'

Rosanna opened her eyes and blinked, her contact with the past lost completely. The morning sights and smells flooded in, blotting out her scrying. Harald told the other captain to be quiet.

There were still sticky patches of gore everywhere, bright in the sunlight.

She shut her eyes, and was back in the night. It was hard to make people understand that scrying wasn't like scanning a page in a book, going straight to the sentence you needed and absorbing it instantly. It was like a children's game, reaching into a barrel of sawdust, not knowing whether you'd come up with a ripe apple or a cat's skull.

She heard the revolutionist ranting with all the fervour of a fanatical preacher espousing the worship of his god, holding up the martyred Professor Brustellin – dead in the fog riots – as the idol of a new kind of society, one without privilege or injustice, without hunger or crime.

Then Stahlman had intervened, and the Brustellinite – Liebenstein – was gone, lost in the darkness, and her focus was on the watchman. The bird speared into her consciousness and Stahlman was dying again. Rosanna tried to ignore the watchman, to latch onto the tiny mind-presence of the bird.

'It is a hawk,' she said, 'female, I think. A name beginning with B. Beate. Bella? No, Belle.'

'The hawk's master?' Harald prompted.

She concentrated hard. Animals were difficult, and birds – apart from fish – the most difficult of all. Their minds were focused on food and procreation to the exclusion of all else. They ignored so much, there was little impression worth reading.

'A black hood,' she said, seeing a distorted image she realised was the bird's field of vision, 'a kind hand...'

A chunk of red meat came near the bird's face, juicy and oozing, pinched between two gloved fingers. Rosanna gulped and swallowed nothing, echoing the bird's movements.

'He feeds her,' she said. 'He loves her, nurtures her.'

There was nothing more.

Rosanna opened her eyes. 'That's it,' she said, 'I'm sorry.'

She didn't need her scrying to sense their disappointment. Hope seeped out of them like air from a pin-pricked pig's bladder. She was cold and shaking. Harald wrapped her cloak around her shoulders.

Viereck, Katz from the 'platz and Rasselas were unimpressed, but Harald was solicitous.

'Thank you,' he said.

'I was no help.'

'We have a name. Belle.'

'A bird's name. Not a man's.'

Like Harald, she had been on this case since last year, paid a small salary by the Atrocities Commission. Like Harald, she was frustrated. All they had learned was negative.

There was no connection between the victims. There was no political, financial or personal motive. Before these killings, there had been no previous crimes of a similar nature. There was nothing to suggest the Warhawk was a member of any Proscribed Cult, although the killings might conceivably be sacrifices of some kind. The murders had taken place all over the city, with no pattern as to the locations.

Killings had taken place at all hours of the day and night, although mostly under the cover of darkness. A masked falconer had been seen, but he – or she – was of average height and build, face completely covered. The murderer left no calling cards, no signature clues, no indication at all as to who he might be or what his motive was.

Harald turned to Rasselas. 'Is the way up to the clock cleared?'

The bank official was about to protest, but Harald's hand unconsciously drifted to the prominent hilt of his Magnin throwing knife, and his ice-chip blue eyes narrowed. Rosanna felt the force of his personality narrowed like sunbeams by a magnifying glass, and saw Rasselas twitch under the glare.

'It's been arranged,' he said.

Harald nodded. 'Rosanna,' he said, 'the Warhawk set his bird on the watchman from above, as usual. He was seen on the platform below the clock.'

Rosanna looked up at the Imperial Bank. She had seen the clock practically every day since she came to the city – it was one of Altdorf's landmarks – but had never before noticed the small platform, bounded by low rails, beneath it. There was a watchman up there now, waiting.

'Let's go,' she said, swallowing spit.

'You're not afraid of heights, are you?' Harald asked.

'No,' she said, the bottoms of her feet curling with antici-
pated fear, 'not at all.'

'Good,' he nodded.

Rasselas led the way.

IV

HE HAD NOTHING to fear from the witch woman. With Belle
asleep on her perch back in his attic and his leather suit
hung in the closet alongside his father's old clothes, he was
no longer Warhawk. He was just himself, one of the crawling crowd. He didn't even look up at the skies with longing.
Only with Belle on his wrist and leather on his face was he
the man the witch was seeking, the beneficiary of the
Device.

The witch woman was not much more than a girl, a pretty
reed of a creature in a pale red dress, walking as if on
eggshells, hands held out slightly to ward others away. She
wasn't comfortable with people, he realised. She must see
into their hearts, into their secret lives. He had been careful
not to get near her.

At first, he had stayed away from the scenes of the sacrifices. It had been enough to take Belle home and to read in
the broadsheets of Captain Viereck's foolish attempts to
scare him off course. But when he realised how safe he was,
how impossible it would be for anyone to connect him with
Warhawk, he had ventured out.

Kleindeinst led Rosanna away, towards the bank.
Watchmen told the crowd to disperse, and most did. But he
stayed where he was, sucking on his pipe, for all the world
like an ordinary idler, mildly interested but no more. His
tobacco tasted sweet, and his gaze rose with the smoke from
his pipe-bowl. The smoke was pulled apart by the winds and
dispersed into the sky.

When Kleindeinst had taken over, he had got into the
habit of returning to observe the watchmen. Outside the
Vargr Breughel, while the torn and broken Scheydt was
being carted off, he had seen Detlef Sierck, the great actor,
and Genevieve Dieudonné, his famous vampire paramour,
and he had been most impressed.

Some people were born important, were born to be stars. It was nothing to do with breeding or position, but with a capability to affect the world, to change things, to get things done, to fulfil ambitions. His father and Prince Vastarien, Detlef and Genevieve, Imperial ministers and electors, even Kleindeinst and Rosanna. These were important people, stars. Detlef and Genevieve had defeated the Great Enchanter, Kleindeinst and Rosanna had tracked down the Beast. These were achievements. He had never been important, as his father had been, but he was becoming so. When the Device was complete, he would be the most important of all, the most outstanding. Everyone would know who he was, but no one would be able to lay a hand on him. He would fly higher than the strongest archer could shoot an arrow. His father had soared, but his wings would take him above his father. His wings would take him among the stars. He would be a star.

One interesting thing was that he was not the only face who showed up at each of the Warhawk sites. There were a couple of reporters from the broadsheets who always arrived within minutes, and interrogated the crowds. He had described himself – the black-suited, leather-cloaked Warhawk – to them several times, but he was so ordinary they did not even realise he was the same person. Others were just sensation-seekers or bizarre obsessives. He realised they were his admirers, just as the women who waited outside the Vargr Breughel for a glimpse of Detlef Sierck were the great actor's admirers. Their tight-lipped, hungry faces made him feel like a star.

He had seen his symbol, a bright-eyed hawk, chalked up on walls, and slogans encouraging his purpose. On the pedestal of the old Emperor Luitpold statue was written 'Fear the Warhawk'. That made him smile inside, made him feel the itching lines on his back where his wings would sprout.

Kleindeinst and Rosanna were climbing the bank, ascending to his perch.

'You,' said a burly watchman, 'move on.'

He smiled at the officer and bowed, then sauntered off, hands in his pockets, jauntily whistling 'Come Ye Back to

Bilbali, Estalian Mariner'. It was time he went to his birds.
Belle would need feeding, petting and rewarding.

His step was so light he could barely feel the hated cobbles beneath the soles of his boots. He was almost flying
already.

V

THERE WAS NOT enough room on the platform for all interested parties, so Harald took a delight in banning everyone
but Rosanna and himself. The others stood and watched
from inside the cupola, the vast and incomprehensible
wheels and works of the clock hanging above, holding their
hands over their ears to shut out the ticking, ringing, rending, wrestling sounds of the mechanism. Rasselas proudly
began to explain the mechanism to anyone interested,
whereupon his audience jammed fingers further into ears.

Rosanna leant lightly on the rail, hair whipped by the
wind, eyes shut, searching inside herself for whatever it was
she had that made her what she was. Harald had used her
on other cases, ever since their brush with the Beast, but he
still didn't really understand how scrying worked. He knew
it wasn't simple, knew it did things to her he could never
appreciate.

He noticed the girl's knuckles were white. She was gripping the rail as if it were life itself.

There were bird droppings on the platform, some fresh.
And bootprints – no special makers' marks or distinctive
treads to serve as clues, like in one of Ferring the Balladeer's
mysteries – in the dust. Without Rosanna's abilities, Harald
could reconstruct the killer's movements. The Warhawk had
stood here a while, picking his target. He had stood still –
the prints were clear, not overlapped – and unmoving,
patiently waiting. Handprints showed the holds he had used
when escaping. Harald's stomach roiled, as it often did
when he caught a scent of crime.

Stahlman regularly patrolled the 'platz, so the Warhawk
could have picked him as a victim well in advance and
turned up in order to get him. But it was more likely that he
chose his perch first, and then selected the man who was to

die. Still, killing a watchman was an obvious taunt. He wondered whether the Warhawk was trying to speak directly to him, taking a copper as a demonstration that he could defy Filthy Harald and live.

The first watchman up here had found a feather. After ten killings, the Atrocities Commission had enough feathers to stuff an eiderdown for that luxury-loving slut, Countess Emmanuelle of Nuln. Like the others, this specimen was undistinctive. All the second-best ornithologist in the city could tell was that it came from an ordinary hawk, and that the bird was in good health and probably well-groomed. Of course, the man had hardly been disposed to cooperate with the watch after the way Viereck had treated the best ornithologist in the city.

'I feel him,' Rosanna said, in a matter-of-fact way. 'It is a he, a man. He's dark inside, not much there. Like an empty suit of armour. An empty suit of leather armour.'

Harald paid attention, taking care not to get too near the girl. She could be confused that way. The wind was changing, blowing her hair across her face. If she were not so haunted, Rosanna would have reminded him of his wife.

His dead wife.

She was shaking now, her body jarring the rail, her chin bobbing, her head making strange – birdlike? – little movements.

'I am him,' she said, 'I am the Warhawk.'

'What's he thinking of?'

She hesitated. 'He has no real mind. And yet, he remembers his father. A taller, bigger man. Of course, in his memory he's a child and his father towers over him. But there's something. He constantly matches himself against his father, trying to outdo him, trying to fill his shadow…'

That was common enough among pattern-killers. There was always something in their childhood, their family background. Then again, considering the number of wretched parents around, it was a miracle the world wasn't overrun by pattern killers.

'His father… is… was…'

'Yes?'

Rosanna was shaking violently now, as if in the early stages of a seizure. He was worried for her and stepped nearer.

'His father was the Warhawk.'

'The Warhawk.'

She nodded, her hair whipping. She was turned away from him, but he knew her eyes were still shut. Beyond her, he could see the statues of all the emperors since the time of Sigmar. Pigeons – a rarity in Altdorf these days – roosted in Sigmar's helmet and flocked on his dropping-encrusted hammer.

There was a wrenching sound, like a sword being pulled out of a stone wall and Rosanna lurched forwards, a scream starting from her mouth. Harald reached forward, grabbing her shoulders, holding hard. The clock's bells began chiming, impossibly, torturously loud.

The rail had come out of the masonry and Rosanna was toppling from the platform. Her weight pulled at him and one of her feet slipped over the edge.

'In his mind,' she shouted over the din of the chimes, 'he's flying, he's with the hawk!'

Her legs were over the lip of the platform now and she was gripping his arm. For an awful moment, he thought they would fall. He grabbed the end of the rail still embedded in the wall and pulled, hauling her away from the edge. She got both feet back on the platform. The others were crowding around the door, concerned. Katz reached out, feet well braced, and held his arm. Rosanna clung tight to him. She had very nearly gone off the front of the building.

They stood up and leaned away from the edge. Rosanna whistled out a breath and shook her head, smiling shakily. She gripped him hard. Then her hold relaxed and she pushed herself away, slipping into the cupola. The others got out of her way.

What had she read? What had she read from him?

He was shaking himself, as if fear had bled out of her mind into his. He stopped his trembling, stilling his own heart with an iron fist inside his chest.

Harald followed Rosanna inside. The chimes finished.

* * *

VI

IN THE ATTIC, his birds were mostly asleep. He had trained them to be night flyers.

He prowled between the coops and perches, checking on his favourites. Belle was resting, head tucked under one wing. The barbs attached to her feet weren't chafing her. A good attack bird should have weapons as grown-in as a never-removed wedding ring.

His back, where the wings would grow, was itching constantly, two invisible rashes on his shoulderblades. Candlewax dripped on his hand, stinging.

He remembered his father, a statue on the hillside, mind soaring up in the body of his Minya. The Warhawk, the first Warhawk, had left his son in early childhood. Each of the boy's memories of the man was a polished perfect cameo that would stay with him forever.

Some of the birds shifted. It was comfortably hot up here in the windowless dark, only occasional shafts of light beamed in through the slats around the hatchways. The natural smells were strong, comforting, constant.

In his memory, his father was always still, a shell, his true self absent. He remembered looking from his father's impassive mask of a face to the dancing shape in the sky, and feeling the beginnings of understanding.

He lined the birds' coops with broadsheets that contained stories about the latest sacrifice.

The next movement of the Device must be bold.

In a corner of the attic, he contemplated the detritus of his earlier paths. Here were the remains of his first machines, bent metal and torn canvas, broken-toothed clockwheels and tangles of snapped wire. He had wasted years. He had always known that the answer was in science, not magic. But it was only recently that he had remembered his father's talk of the Device.

A clever man might fly. A man with no magic, but with the love of the sky in his heart.

Once, he had consulted a wizard about the Device, and the man had laughed at him, concealing his terror and envy with scorn. Wizards were all afraid of being caught out, of

being shown up as frauds. They all pretended that Devices
were nonsense, jealously guarding their own exclusive powers.

When he could fly, he would take a delight in tormenting
wizards.

He must sacrifice again, soon. This time the sacrifice must
be deliberately chosen. As it neared its completion, the
Device had to be tended carefully, each move provoking its
successor.

He thought of Kleindeinst and his witch woman, wondering if they were ready for what they must do next.

It would be a gamble, but it was his only possible move.
Would his father have approved? He didn't know. It didn't
matter. When the Device was complete, there would only be
one Warhawk.

He went downstairs, and put on his hood.

VII

THE OFFICES OF the Atrocities Commission were in the watch
station on Luitpoldstrasse, the largest in the city. Harald had
a desk there, and notional control over a small army of
clerks and record-keepers, but Rosanna knew he spent as little time as possible surrounded by quill-pushers and
inkwells. A street copper, he had no patience with ledgers.

But now they were forced to fall back on dusty books.
Every surface in the room was piled high with yellowing
paper. Viereck was a poor organiser and the files from his
period of command were chaotic. Anything of an earlier vin-
tage – and there'd been a watch station on Luitpoldstrasse
for centuries – was as likely to have been used as a taper for
lighting cigars as to have been preserved. By the inexorable
law of bureaucracy, the chances of a document's survival
could be reckoned in inverse proportion to its usefulness,
which meant that anything with a possible bearing on the
case was liable to be ashes on the wind, while badly-spelled
grocery lists or Imperially-decreed alterations to the watch
uniform were preserved for posterity.

'I should have made the connection before,' Harald was
fretting. 'Warhawk isn't exactly a commonplace name.'

Rosanna was less sure of this. Now it had come up she knew she'd heard the name before these killings, but not in any context that could possibly apply to the current crimes.

'Surely, the first Warhawk wasn't a murderer? He was some kind of hero, wasn't he?'

She dimly recalled a ballad recounting great victories and a noble death.

'Good question. But you get to be a hero by doing the same thing murderers do.'

'Killing?'

'There's nothing wrong with killing,' he snarled, 'just so long as the right people get killed.'

As Harald flicked furiously through forty- and fifty-year old gazetteers, Rosanna's eyes watered from the raised dust. It was late afternoon and the lantern in the office was smoking badly. One bad sputter from lantern to papers and this place would burn like a Mondstille bonfire. She had already been hauled out of one burning watch station by Harald Kleindeinst, and had no intention of repeating the experience. She opened the lantern and trimmed the wick.

'After all,' Harald continued, 'who killed most often, the Beast or Sigmar? Killing for a cause may be all well and good, but there are some for whom the killing is more important than the cause.'

'When did our murderer start being called Warhawk?'

'Another good question, and one our friend Viereck should have troubled himself to answer.'

'I've seen it chalked up on walls.'

'Usually, the names of pattern-killers – the Beast, the Slasher, the Ripper – start in the broadsheets, but this time I think it just appeared out of the air, like our quarry's bird.'

Rosanna thought back to her scrying of the Warhawk. She could pick up names sometimes. It depended on how people, in the supposed secrecy of their skull, thought of themselves. One of the fundamentals of magic was the true naming of things and individuals. Once you knew a person's true name, you had a measure of power over him or her. In this business, that was literally the case. If they knew the Warhawk's true name, he could be tracked down and stopped.

Harald coughed as another cloud of dust rose from an unrolled scroll.

In his private self, the killer thought of himself as Warhawk, but behind him was a greater shadow, the Warhawk. Unmistakably, the Warhawk was the murderer's father. Rosanna had sampled his childhood, his memories of punishments and favours.

A clerk, cheek permanently stained by the ink-dribble from the feather-pen lodged above his ear, staggered in, and deposited another armful of documents on an already over-burdened table.

'Found it,' Harald said, quietly.

Rosanna crossed the room and looked over the captain's shoulder.

The scroll was an old indictment, dated nearly thirty years ago. It bore the seal of the Emperor Luitpold, and it was a list of charges laid against Prince Vastarien, beginning with disloyalty to the Empire and concluding with the raising of a private army to pursue the prince's own military ends.

'Vastarien's Vanquishers,' Harald said, through gritted teeth.

'Who were they?' she asked.

'I keep forgetting you're young,' he said. 'Prince Vastarien was before you were born.'

'I know the name.'

'Mention it to anyone my age and you'll get an interesting reaction one way or the other, an eternal curse or a prayer to Sigmar. Whatever the prince was, he was extreme about it.'

'Was he a hero?'

'A lot of people thought so. A lot of other people – obviously including the old Emperor and most of the court – disagreed violently. No one really knows what happened to him in the end, up in the Fastness of Jagrandhra Dane, but if he'd come back he would as likely have spent the remainder of his life in Mundsen Keep as have been weighed down with honours and glory.'

Rosanna read the charges against the prince. They were lengthy and detailed, alleging all manner of moral turpitude, unseemly conduct and dangerous behaviour. It appeared that a raid against river pirates on the Urskoy had almost caused a tiny war between the Empire and Kislev, rattling Tsar Radii Bokha's cage enough to prompt a strong diplomatic complaint. However, scrawled in a different hand from the rest of the document was an instruction that the indictment not be proceeded with, over the personal signature of Maximilian von Konigswald, one of the old Emperor's closest advisors. Evidently, Prince Vastarien had been let off, the tsar appeased some other way.

'Who are the heroes of the day, Rosanna?' Harald asked. 'That mysterious fellow who's said to be the scourge of goblins and beastmen? Detlef Sierck, genius and defier of Drachenfels? Hagedorn, the wrestler who could put anyone on the mat three out of three falls? Graf Rudiger von Unheimlich, the foremost huntsman of the Empire? Your intrepid swordsman friend, the Baron Johann von Mecklenberg?'

Rosanna blushed at the mention of Johann. He was with his brother, back on their estates in the Sudenland.

'Well, when I was a lad, Prince Vastarien was one of those names. The traitor Oswald von Konigswald was another, so that goes to show how seriously you should place your trust in heroes. If Vastarien did a tenth of the things the ballads and chap-books claim he did, he was the greatest citizen of the Empire since Sigmar. He was also probably the most completely insane fool that ever lived. He raised his own cadre of fellow heroes, and fought his campaigns, ignoring Imperial edicts, smiting whoever he decided was the enemy of his cause.'

'Vastarien's Vanquishers?'

'That's what they called themselves. Next time you see the Baron Johann, ask him about a man called Vukotich. Iron Man Vukotich.'

'I am not likely to be seeing…'

'I'm sorry,' he said, in a rare moment of solicitousness, 'I shouldn't tease like that. We all have our scars. Anyway, our

Warhawk – the first Warhawk – was one of the prince's heroes.'

He turned the scroll over, and tapped a list of names, written in a watery ink that had faded to pale blue.

'Here,' he said, 'see...'

Rosanna's eyes ran down the list. The Vukotich Harald had mentioned was there. And, near the bottom, the single word, 'Warhawk'.

VIII

HARALD DIDN'T GET out to Mundsen Keep very often. Too many old acquaintances were permanent guests here. This black, slit-windowed pile beyond the city walls was where Altdorf dumped its human refuse. Debtors and murderers, revolutionists and thieves, out-of-favour courtiers and long-forgotten scapegoats. All ended up in the depths of the Keep. Even here, in the governor's airy and well-lit apartments, the aura of misery was strong.

Rosanna had never visited the prison, and he could tell she was appalled by the place. The Keep was outside the city walls because no one could stand to live too close to the human stench that hung around it. No amount of lye and water could dispel the stink.

She didn't say anything, but Harald knew she was thinking of the criminals she'd helped send here. Since Baron Johann left for the Sudenland, Rosanna had been very helpful to the watch. Without her, there would be a few more felons loose in the streets and sewers. And without the watch – now she was no longer welcome at the Temple of Sigmar – Rosanna would have no means of income.

Governor Gerd van Zandt received them in his office, and listened patiently to Harald's request.

'Out of the question,' Van Zandt said, fluttering a heavily-scented handkerchief under his large nose.

'The prisoner Stieglitz is in solitary confinement and is to have no contact with the outside world. There are revolutionists everywhere, they constantly try to smuggle messages in or out...'

'Are you suggesting that I'm a Brustellinite?'

Harald glared at the governor, who quivered and looked away.

'No, er, not at all, Captain Kleindeinst. It's just that… rules and regulations, you know… we must have discipline.'

'Rickard Stieglitz is still alive?'

'Um, yes,' Van Zandt sputtered.

'Fine, then it is imperative we speak with him.'

'As I said, that is, um, not possible.'

Harald leaned over, and took hold of Van Zandt's ruffled shirt-front, getting a good grip, hoping some of his flabby flesh was caught in the folds. He hauled the man out of his padded chair and lifted him into the air, letting his skinny legs dangle.

'Nothing is impossible in Mundsen Keep, governor. Prisoners can get extra food, ale enough to drown a halfling, a supply of weirdroot, jars of olla milk, even the occasional woman or pretty-boy. All it takes is influence, money, a favour. We both know that. And we both know no money changes hands in the Keep without a tithe slipping your way.'

'This is outrageous… these charges… ridiculous…'

'I don't care, Van Zandt. I send them here and that's an end of it. What you do then is up to you. And the Imperial Prison Reform Committee. I have friends on that committee. Maybe I should see my old friends more often. Talk things through. I'm well-known for my strict views on penal conditions. I could be called in to give testimony. And that testimony could go either way.'

'Ah… ah… ah…'

'I hate criminals. They make my stomach churn. And do you know how my stomach feels now? Like a storm at sea, Van Zandt. As if there were a criminal very close by. Almost as close as the end of my arm.'

Van Zandt's shirt was tearing and blood had drained out of his face.

'You understand me?' Harald said, dropping the governor back into his chair.

Van Zandt nodded. 'Yes, I understand.'

'Good, now arrange for my associate and I to see the prisoner, Stieglitz.'

'Yes, of course, right away, captain…'

Van Zandt hurried out of his office. Harald turned to Rosanna, and shrugged.

'What else could I do?'

The scryer must disapprove of him, of his methods. But they worked well together. She would accept anything that bore fruit. Before, he had not been the kind of watchman who did well with a partner – he'd buried too many good men – but Rosanna Ophuls was different. Her expertise was in a different area, and complemented his. His stomach and her conscience had given many criminals cause to regret their sins.

'I still don't understand,' she said. 'This revolutionist, what does he have to do with the Warhawk?'

Harald patted the scroll, rolled up in his belt.

'One of the habits of heroes is that they die young. Plain men like me live to an old age, but heroes tend to go down fighting. Do you think that Konrad fellow intends to die in bed of the gout? So, it follows that a thirty-year-old list of Vastarien's Vanquishers isn't likely to have many still-warm bodies on it.'

'Stieglitz is one of them?'

'That's right. Lucky for us. In his youth, before he fell in with Brustellin and Kloszowski and the rest of the fire-brands, Rickard Stieglitz was one of Vastarien's muscle-flexers. An axe-hefting mountain of meat and bone.'

'How did someone like that wind up dedicated to the overthrow of the aristocracy?'

'Someone with a title took his wife, killed his children and cut off his arm.'

'That would do it.'

'When he was captured after the fog riots, he had his ears clipped. I understand there's not much of him left.'

Harald had never been with the special corps who rousted the ten brands of revolutionist who preached sedition against the Emperor. That was a militia job. Sometimes the palace guard or the Knights Templars of Sigmar helped out. A simple copper had no politics.

'You hope he'll be sane enough to remember the Warhawk's real name, if he ever knew it, and well-disposed enough towards the watch, who penned him up here, to share the knowledge with us?'

Harald's stomach was eating away at him again.

'He has no reason not to, Rosanna. Our murderer is no champion of the oppressed. The Warhawk is just a scummy killer. If Stieglitz is still enough of an idealist to want justice for all, he'll help.'

'Sometimes you sound like a Brustellinite yourself.'

Harald spat. 'Revolutionists? I hate 'em. Dreamers and bullies and trouble-makers.'

The door opened, and a prisoner was dragged in by two trusties. The man was weighed down with chains, his head hung. His ears were scabbed over, his face a ruin of scars and his left arm missing. Those were the injuries Harald had been expecting. Also, one of his eyes was gone, one bare foot was inflated with pus to the size of a football, only the little finger and thumb remained on his right hand, and through his rags there were obvious burn-marks on his back and chest. The mountain of meat and bone had been worn down to a pathetic hump.

Rosanna shuddered and stifled a cry. The trusties dropped the prisoner on the floor and the scryer went to him, helping him huddle into a sitting position.

Harald looked at the governor, accusing him.

'Revolutionists are not popular with the other prisoners,' Van Zandt explained. 'Murderers and rapists resent being walled in with filth who advocate disloyalty to Karl-Franz. He was in the hole for his own protection.'

'I'm sure.'

'Harald,' Rosanna said, 'how can we question this man?'

'What do you mean?'

'He has no ears to hear what we ask, and no tongue to give answer.'

'No tongue?'

Stieglitz's mouth gaped open and Harald saw the scryer was right. Beyond his few remaining teeth was a black hole. Harald looked again at the governor.

'He kept shouting Brustellinite slogans from his hole, slanders against the Imperial family and the electors. "Throw off your chains, kill your betters, seize the land," things like that. I thought it best he be silenced.'

'If you acted this way within the city walls, Van Zandt, you'd answer to me. It'd be interesting to see the kind of treatment you would get from your fellow convicts if, through some malfeasance, you were yourself sentenced to serve time in Mundsen Keep.'

Van Zandt turned a sickly colour. It must be his greatest nightmare, to wake up one morning chained on filthy straw, as an inmate rather than the master of this place.

'Can he read?' he asked.

'I don't know. I doubt it.'

Rosanna held up a paper from Van Zandt's desk, and ran her finger along a line of writing, a question in her eyes. Stieglitz nodded. He could read.

Harald gave the scryer the scroll. She showed the prisoner the list, pointing out his own name, then indicating the Warhawk's.

Stieglitz's single eye narrowed. He was trying to understand. In his cage of abused flesh, he was still a thinking man.

Harald gave Rosanna a pencil, and she wrote on the scroll.

What was the Warhawk's true name?

A ghastly keening came from the back of the prisoner's throat as he tried to give an answer. For some reason, he did want to help. Maybe he had no cause to love his old comrade in the Vanquishers? Maybe he was completely broken and pliable?

'The stink in here,' complained Van Zandt, waving his handkerchief. 'These people have no concept of personal cleanliness. Myself, I bathe once or twice a month.'

Van Zandt signalled to a trusty, who opened one of the casements, letting in a waft of forest-scented air. From the window, it was a hundred-foot sheer drop. The trusty, as much a prisoner as the ruin on the floor, looked out at the city walls, the trees and the road below, with a yearning that was like a knife in Harald's gut.

Stieglitz stopped gurgling and Rosanna handed him a pencil and the scroll. His remaining fingers couldn't hold the pencil properly and he dropped it. Rosanna picked it up and slipped it back into his hand, keeping it there with her own fingers.

'He was left-handed,' Van Zandt explained, 'that was why the duke, um, er… you know…'

Harald knew.

Between them, Stieglitz and Rosanna made a mark on the parchment. It was useless. The first letter might have been an M, or an A, or an E, or a dwarfish rune, or a meaningless squiggle – or anything.

They gave up. Stieglitz sagged, dejected.

Harald wanted to break Van Zandt's neck. In taking away Stieglitz's tongue, he was as responsible for the next death – and the one after that, and the one after that, and all the others – as the Warhawk himself.

Rosanna sighed.

'I'll have to scry him,' she said, reluctantly. 'The name must be uppermost in his mind. He's been trying to write it.'

Harald knew why she was unhappy. Sharing what was in Stieglitz's skull – the pain, the suffering, the hatred – would be a filthy business, like fishing for a jewel in a cesspit.

Rosanna took the prisoner's hand, and shut her eyes.

From the window, the trusty screamed, and fell out of the way. Harald turned, his Magnin suddenly in his hand.

The bird came into the office, its huge wings beating, and moved as fast as water on an incline. Van Zandt covered his head and dived behind a desk.

A beak sliced down, across the trusty's chest, loosing a bright red trail of blood. Then, the creature went for Rosanna.

Harald slashed, but missed. A heavy wing struck his wrist, stunning him, and his knife thumped against carpeted stone.

Rosanna's hands were over her face, her contact with Stieglitz broken. With the hand that still had feeling, Harald grabbed at the bird. He felt feathers come free, but it dodged him.

Then it struck at Stieglitz's neck, the force of the beak-blow breaching his artery. A fountain of blood splashed over the hawk, spattering its wings, masking its face. It attacked silently, not a squawking terror but a resolute instrument of murder as conscienceless and perfect as an arrow.

Harald had his knife again, and threw. It sliced cleanly through the distance.

The bird was out of the way, and the knife jammed to the hilt into a wooden panel by Stieglitz's hanging head, vibrating fiercely.

The mercenary revolutionist was dead, what was left of his life ripped from him, his blood soaking the rags on his chest and pooling around him. The flow of his own blood washed part of him clean, revealing white skin beneath the grime of the Keep.

Harald tried to catch the bird, but it was gone through the window in an instant, flapping back towards the city. It circled a tall tree a quarter of a mile off, and landed in the branches as if finding a nest. He could see a tiny figure, all in black, receiving his murderous pet.

He made huge fists and slammed them against the windowsill, imagining laughter on the wind.

IX

HE SLITHERED DOWN the tree like a monkey, gripping with his knees, Belle on his shoulder. Number Eleven had been the trickiest yet, but it was a clean kill, a clever kill. The Device was functioning perfectly.

Kleindeinst had been there, as he had expected – known – he would be. He had almost guided the watchman himself, directing him as he would one of his birds.

He let Belle go, and leaped from tree to tree, relishing the moments he was in open air with nothing beneath him. When he began to plummet, he would put out a hand and catch a branch. Over the years, his body had become creaky through disuse. But, with the Device in motion, he had been training himself as rigorously as he trained his birds. When he had wings, he would need to be agile, to bend himself to the ways of the sky.

With an inevitable disappointment, he finally came to ground, thumping against the softly-grassed forest floor. The jolt shot through his entire skeleton, making him bite his tongue, and he stumbled against the bole of a tree, gripping until his balance returned.

On the ground, he was clumsy.

He held out his wrist and Belle settled.

'Two to go,' he said. 'And we'll be together always.'

X

CAPTAIN VIERECK WAS back in the office at the Atrocities Commission by the time they returned from Mundsen Keep. He must have spies everywhere. Rosanna was not surprised.

She had been too close to Stieglitz at his death, and the tongueless scream that poured from his broken mind still echoed inside her. In the carriage, Harald had been slumped and brooding. He felt his defeat keenly. Sometimes Rosanna was surprised at the depths of fellow-feeling 'Filthy Harald' was capable of. She wondered about his wife. The dead one he didn't talk about. Ever.

By the end of the day, it was official. Harald Kleindeinst was back on the Dock Watch, and the Warhawk investigation was Viereck's responsibility. By the end of the evening, the case was back on its original course, with an acrobat – who had been accused in an anonymous letter – under arrest and on his way to Van Zandt's pet torturers. Harald disappeared while Rosanna was being seen to by the Luitpoldstrasse station physician, getting salve pasted on her superficial cuts.

Of course, she was off the case too.

She had tried. She went to Viereck, and found him with Rasselas, toasting their capture of the Warhawk. She explained their line of inquiry to them, laying out all she knew about Vastarien's Vanquishers, the first Warhawk, and Stieglitz.

They thanked her for her concern and had her escorted out into the streets.

It was a cold evening, with the first traces of an Altdorf fog. She looked up at the night skies and imagined a bird passing across the face of the visible moon. A bird of prey, alone and hungry, impersonally cruel and casually deadly.

As so often happened since she left the Order of Sigmar, where she had been cloistered since girlhood, Rosanna felt alone and uncertain. She could see so many things – random and useless information poured from the heads of passersby, from the cobblestones under her shoes – but if she turned her scrying in upon herself, there was just a blank space, a vacuum in the centre of a whirlpool.

She supposed she should go back to her lodgings. And sleep.

XI

UNTIL HIS CAPTAINCY could be reviewed by a board which – including, as it did, Rasselas of the Imperial Bank and a colonel of the watch he knew to be in the pay of Hals von Tasseninck – would recommend either his demotion to beat-pounding serf or dismissal (again) from the watch, Harald still had his copper badge. And he would always have his Magnin.

The heaviest throwing knife in the world, the Magnin had been his friend through innumerable bloody nights. He noticed Rosanna shrank away from it as if it were a red-hot poker, and assumed she must be able to flash visions of the knife's past experiences.

With his Magnin in its sheath on his hip, and his badge pinned on the breast of his tunic, he strolled into the Sullen Knight, a hostelry that fully deserved its reputation as the rowdiest, most dangerous, most violent on the Street of a Hundred Taverns. Normally, watchmen only ventured into the Sullen Knight in groups of four or more, with swords drawn and pistols primed. But tonight, he was alone.

He elbowed his way between two young men who were attempting to strangle each other and glanced around. Several brawlers looked up from their fights, alerted by the flash of copper.

A broad-shouldered Kislevite, beaded braids hanging from the unshaved half of his scalp, roared and charged Harald, seeing only the badge. It was Bolakov, a perennial visitor to the cells in Luitpoldstrasse when there were enough watchmen available to subdue him. By the time the foreigner got to him, Harald had a fist out ready for the thug's face.

Bolakov crumpled and fell. He must be too drunk to recognise Filthy Harald. No one else made his mistake. Still feeling acid in his guts from his bad day, Harald sunk his boot into Bolakov's side, denting his ribs. A few grinding broken bones would take the Kislevite bully boy out of the brawling business for a few days.

Harald ordered a bottle of schnapps from Sam the barman and looked around, wondering if there were any other heads he should bother to thump. He saw a thin man in a black leather jacket trying to slip out the back way and knew he was in luck.

'Stop, Ruger,' he shouted, 'or find out if I can throw this knife faster than you can get through that door!'

Mack Ruger froze, hands well away from the docker's hook on his belt, and turned.

'Good choice,' Harald told the weirdroot vendor.

Ruger looked guilty, wondering which of his crimes was coming back to haunt him. Harald knew there was quite a list.

'Drink with me,' Harald ordered.

'I… uh… no thank you, sir, I was just leaving…'

'That was not an invitation, Ruger.'

'No, of course.'

Ruger, a Hook – a member of one of the waterfront gangs – sat down, and Harald pulled a chair up to his table, setting the schnapps down between them. Someone thought that Harald turning his back gave them an opening – evidently not noticing the useful full-length mirror behind the bar – and reached for a leadweight at his belt. Harald tossed a heavy pint-pot over his shoulder, and smashed the coshman's wrist without even turning to look.

'Still in business?' he asked Ruger.

'This and that, you know,' the Hook replied.

'You usually set up shop at the Breasts of Myrmidia so you can sell your foul stuff to the students from the University, don't you?'

Ruger didn't bother to deny it. He could probably lay his hands on more arcane herbs and potions than one of the university's tame wizards or a palace physician.

'Of course, what with the Fish taking over the Breasts, you must have had to find a new territory.'

Ruger tried a shrug. The Fish were the Hooks' deadliest rivals, and the two factions had been feuding for generations. Harald had personally ended the last Waterfront War, and his reputation was etched into the gangs' consciousnesses as if by acid.

'Nothing is certain in this life, Ruger. Are you carrying?'

Ruger began to say no, but gave up.

'I need something,' Harald said. 'Something in your line.'

A crack of a knowing smile started, but Harald slapped it off the degenerate's face. 'Don't think you know anything about me, Ruger. Don't ever make that mistake.'

'No, captain.'

The angry mark on the vendor's cheek was like a birthmark.

'The berserkers of Norsca snort a herbal powder before they go into battle,' Harald said. 'It takes away their pain, makes them feel stronger, almost invincible.'

'Daemon dust.'

'That's the stuff. Give me some.'

Ruger was about to protest, but Harald took the Magnin out and laid it on the table.

'Look at the beautiful line of the blade,' Harald commented, 'a work of art.'

The vendor sorted through his pouch, and came up with three bundles, dried leaves twisted into balls.

'This is expensive,' Ruger said.

'I get a watchman's discount.'

That meant he was stealing the daemon dust. Ruger knew there was nothing he could do about it.

Harald took the first leaf and crumbled it. A blue powder spilled into his palm. He pinched it like snuff, and shoved it up one nostril, inhaling sharply.

Turning to the barman, he said, 'Sam, find the four biggest, meanest, hardest, toughest bruisers in the place and tell them from me that their mothers enjoyed sexual congress with farm animals.'

The daemon dust exploded in his brain as he swallowed half the schnapps. This was dangerous, but he needed something to make him not care how hurt he got in the next few hours. Liquid fire ran through his veins, and he held his breath to keep himself from exploding.

Being a detective hadn't helped him catch the Warhawk. Now, he would try being a berserker.

By the time he was ready, Sam had more than four roughs for him. It took him nearly a minute to disable them all. He broke a stool over Ruger's head as a thank you for the dust and hurled his empty bottle at Sam's head, then tossed a table at the long mirror, enjoying the tinkling of the broken fragments as they showered onto the floorboards. This shut everyone up, and got the attention of even those so absorbed in their own fights that they had ignored his devastation of the bruisers. Then, he made an announcement he intended to repeat in every tavern on the street.

'My name is Harald Kleindeinst, captain of the Dock Watch, late of the Atrocities Commission. Filthy Harald. I'm declaring my own war on the crime on this street. Every whore, every weedroot vendor, every cutpurse, every Hook, every Fish, every non-aligned thug, every pimp, every fortune teller, every assassin, every cudgel artist, every knifeman, every burglar, every mountebank, every swindler, every dwarf-molesting mother's ruin of you, take notice. My war will continue until someone gives me the name I want, or the name of someone who knows the name I want. Then things will be back to business as usual. All of you, listen, and remember. My war will go on, until I have the true name of the man they call the Warhawk.'

Harald stepped over Bolakov on his way out of the Sullen Knight. The dust put off any pain he should have been feeling. His face must be bruised badly, and he felt himself bleeding into his shirt. He didn't want to think about what would happen when the daemon dust wore off...

* * *

XII

HE WAS ON the Street of a Hundred Taverns, buying a paper of roast chestnuts from a stall by the Drunken Bastard, when Kleindeinst exploded out of the Sullen Knight, spilling bodies all around him.

Even though the watchman was off the case, he knew Kleindeinst would not stop searching for him. Kleindeinst stumped across the road as if wearing a heavy suit of armour and pushed into the Drunken Bastard, an establishment that catered exclusively to miserable, solitary drinkers and the nimble-fingered pickpockets who preyed on their depleted coin-pouches.

Chewing on a nut, he wandered near the door, and listened to the speech Kleindeinst made to the surprised sots. It gave him a thrill, and he was pleased.

The Device was moving smoothly.

Kleindeinst strode out of the Drunken Bastard and pushed through the queue by the chestnut stall.

'You have your Imperial permit?' he asked the trader.

The man fumbled in a satchel, not for the permit but for a bribe. Kleindeinst grinned down at the pathetic coins in his hand and flung them to the ground, whereupon a pack of urchins appeared from the alleyways and descended on the pickings like hungry wolves, fighting and tearing.

Kleindeinst took the chestnut trader's brazier and poured it over his stall, spreading hot coals.

'You're closed, criminal,' he spat.

The watchman stalked away from the mess he left – other stall-holders in his path shutting up their belongings and retreating – and shoved his way into the next tavern, the Beard of Ulric.

Warhawk chewed his chestnuts, and waited.

A body came flying out of the Beard of Ulric and skidded into the gutter.

Warhawk tittered.

XIII

BY THE TIME the sun came up, Harald had covered the entire Street of a Hundred Taverns, and spread his message throughout Altdorf. He broke the neck of a Fish who tried to knife him outside Bruno's Brewhouse and he stopped the heart of a poison-clawed Hook with the heavy wedge of his Magnin in the tap room of the Wayfarer's Rest. In the Holy Hammer of Sigmar, the gathering place of professional murderers, he beat Ettore Fulci, the noted Tilean strangler, to a bloody pulp. Then he had impressed the cultivated Quex – acknowledged fashion leader of the city's assassins – with the need to find some way of ending the career of the amateur Warhawk if he wanted to be able to ply his trade without extraordinary difficulty. Quex was reluctant, so Harald broke three of his fingers and shredded his best cloak. Venturing into the Crescent Moon, haunt of the unquiet dead, Harald slipped his Magnin into the dry throat of a thousand-year-old hag, letting air whistle into her skull as he told the assembly of the thirsty dead what his conditions were for letting them remain in this world. In the rooms above the Crown and Two Chairmen, he used open hands on the girls, not hurting them overmuch but bruising their faces enough to dent their trade for a few nights.

Having recently learned that the nervous landlord of the Staff of Verena was paying the highest rate of protection money on the street to both the Hooks and Fish, as well as a retainer to the regulars of the Holy Hammer of Sigmar, all to ensure the safety of his business and patrons, Harald paid the Staff a visit and did as much damage as possible. He left the place a ruin, and the landlord howling at how little protection his illicit outlay had actually purchased. Finding a couple of officers from the Dock Watch standing guard outside an illegal dice tourney in the basement of the Von Neuwald Arms, he slammed their skulls together and tossed their badges into the sewers. Then he stormed into the tourney, breaking heads, hands and legs with a stout oak chair. He took the gamblers' coins from the grid and threw them into the gutter for the beggars.

It was a watchman's maxim that the solution to every crime in the Empire could be discovered on the Street of a Hundred Taverns. Still, there were other places, and so in the small hours, Harald ventured off the thoroughfare. The Fish

had a place on the docks, a warehouse where they stored all
the goods that 'slipped overboard during unloading', and
Harald broke in while the guards were snoring drunkenly.
He emptied a cask of Estalian brandy over a dozen bolts of
Bretonnian silk, and then carelessly dropped a flaming torch
onto the soaked material, leaping through a trapdoor to
escape the resulting explosion.

The daemon dust in his mind prevented the cold of the
river from biting through his flesh and he didn't come out
of the Reik until he was past the Three Toll Bridge. He found
'Count' Bernhard Brillhauser scraping the pavement with his
feathered cap on Temple Street, offering to take any provin-
cials who were new in town on a tour of the 'exciting'
underworld of the city. It was said that you hadn't really visited the capital city of the Empire unless you'd been fleeced
by the 'Count'. Along with the changing of the Imperial
Guard, a visit to the Konigplatz and the latest presentation
at the Vargr Breughel Memorial Playhouse, it was one of the
experiences of Altdorf.

Leaving the 'Count' with his hat in the back of his throat,
Harald barged into the Temple Street Gymnasium, where a
trial of strength was on between Hagedorn, the famous
wrestler, and Arne the Body, the gym's proprietor. Arne was
known for his perfectly-developed limbs, and, from time to
time, for his availability to any of his wealthy clientele who
might require some discreet pain-infliction.

Harald pulled Arne out of the ring, just as the contes-
tants were bending iron bars with much bicep-flexing and
neck-straining, and tossed him against a climbing frame,
the dust-strength in his body giving him an edge over the
perfect physical specimen. As far as he knew, Hagedorn
had never broken the law, so he left the bewildered hay-
seed – a blinking column of muscle surrounded by
fawning women – alone. With the second pinch of daemon dust up his nose, he felt he could probably have
tangled with the master of the mats and won. He took
Arne's half-bent iron and wrapped it around his neck, fixing him to the frame. Then he punched the trainer's
rock-hard gut muscles a few times. The Body swore he

knew nothing about the Warhawk, and Harald told him he'd be coming back if Arne were lying.

He didn't need sleep. In fact, he felt stronger by the moment and jogged through the early morning streets, bursting with energy he needed to burn off. A dozen or so people had come to him with spurious help, trying to frame their enemies for the Warhawk crimes, others sincerely dumping information on him, or just flapping their lips. Nothing usable had come to light.

He made his way across the city to the University, where he wanted to throw a scare into the cut-ups of the League of Karl-Franz, and shake the cobwebs of the revolutionist movement. The Imperial loyalists – all of whom, he suspected, were supported by that shadowy kingmaker, Graf Rudiger von Unheimlich – and the revolutionists – split into Brustellinite, Kloszowskist and Yefimovite factions, but still tied together by hatred for the aristocracy – were closely linked with the rest of the city's human vermin, and he didn't see why, if he was coming down so hard on pimps and killers, he should let them off lightly.

In one of the coffee houses near the university, he found Detlef Sierck, the actor, drinking off a hangover and moaning to anyone who would listen about the fickleness of women, all the while handing out flyers for his latest production, *She Served Him Ill*.

One of the early murders had taken place outside Sierck's theatre on Temple Street, and Harald had questioned the man – and his now-vanished vampire mistress – closely. Sierck was still too drunk to remember him and, since he was completely ruled out of the investigation, Harald left him to his headache.

In the university square, he encountered Brand, a soberly-dressed cleric of Ranald he remembered from a series of assaults on priestesses of Shallya. None of the victims had been willing to identify the cleric as the degenerate, but Harald had known the man was guilty. Judging that this was as good a time as any to make up for the deficiencies of the justice system, Harald dragged Brand to the gates of the Ueli von Tasseninck School of Religious Studies, and beat a

confession out of him, continuing the beating long after the
culprit had yielded up all his sins, then draping his battered
but breathing body over the statue of that invert Ueli von
Tasseninck that his uncle, Grand Duke Hals, had spon-
sored. The statue reminded Harald of the time he had first
been expelled from the watch, for foolishly assuming the
laws against rape and murder applied even to people whose
uncles were electors of the Empire, so he prised an iron bar
out of a fence and returned to chip away Ueli's sainted face.
Quite a crowd gathered – students, harlots, lecturers, guilty
bystanders – and he made his speech to them.

It got better every time.

'My name is Harald Kleindeinst, captain of the Dock
Watch,' he began. 'Filthy Harald. I'm declaring my own
war...'

Suddenly, like a towel falling from his eyes, the daemon
dust wore off. All the pain of the world flooded into his
body.

He didn't even scream, he just collapsed.

XIV

EVEN TWO DAYS after Harald's rampage, the Street of a
Hundred Taverns looked as if a raiding party of Chaos
Knights had laid waste to the thoroughfare. And then a wave
of goblin scavengers had gone through, mistreating the
wounded and breaking whatever had been left whole by the
first assault. It was hard to believe one man – even Harald
Kleindeinst – had done this much damage.

As usual, beggar children tugged at Rosanna's shawl. As
usual, she gave them more than she should. Every loiterer
on the street seemed injured in some way, superficially or
seriously. Workmen were everywhere, repairing windows,
carting away broken furniture, re-hanging smashed signs,
painting over bloodstained walls. The gutters glittered with
shards of broken mirror glass.

A couple of patrolling watchmen were exchanging jokes,
where usually they would be venturing carefully, hands on
clubs. The ordinary run of street crime had dropped almost
to nothing in the last two days. Pickpockets had broken

fingers, whores bore unsightly facial bruises, and cudgel-artists wouldn't be hefting a weapon until broken elbows set. But none of this had stopped the Warhawk.

Twelve dead – one since Harald's rampage. Rosanna felt a Harald-like need to put an end to the killing spree. With every death, the whole case changed, turned about-face. She wondered how Harald would feel when he heard about the latest atrocity.

'Miss Ophuls,' a voice called.

She turned. A nondescript man, in early middle age, leaned against a lamp-post, painfully eating an apple. His lip was split and bruised. She had a presentiment that the Warhawk case was about to crack open down the middle.

'Rosanna Ophuls?'

She couldn't scry much from him. He was a typical non-entity, nothing strong enough inside him to count as an identity.

'You work with Kleindeinst?'

Rosanna nodded.

'Mack Ruger,' he said, introducing himself with a thumb to his chest. 'Your friend paid me a visit two nights back.'

'So I see.'

He rubbed his face. 'I got off easy compared to some.'

'Pimp, right?'

'Your reputation is exaggerated. Weirdroot.'

'A thriving trade, I suppose.'

'I do bearably. Everyone has a right to dream.'

'If they've money.'

'I'm a businessman.'

Rosanna would have laughed, but there was an image in Ruger's mind he could not keep shielded. A swooping bird.

'You know the name?' she said, suddenly intuiting.

He shook his head. 'No, but Stieglitz wasn't the last of Vastarien's Vanquishers. There are other survivors. One can be found on this street.'

'How much?'

He shook his head. 'This is a gift. Just be sure you tell Kleindeinst this came from me. He already owes me for the face. I'll want concessions.'

Rosanna almost felt as if she were Harald, the rage boiling inside until it had to volcano through the top of her skull.

'Give me the name,' she said, 'or I'll be sure to tell Captain Kleindeinst you withheld it.'

Ruger paled behind his bruise.

'Gurnisson,' he said. 'Gotrek Gurnisson.'

'A dwarf?'

Ruger nodded. 'He's at the Crooked Spear, with a human tagalong, Felix Jaeger.'

Rosanna thought she might have heard of Gurnisson. Dwarfs were long-lived and had good memories. If he had served with the first Warhawk, Gurnisson would know his true name.

'Tell Kleindeinst to be careful with the dwarf. Gurnisson won't appreciate his usual rough treatment. He's a troll-slayer.'

'That won't matter,' Rosanna said.

'I warned you,' Ruger said. 'That's all I could do.'

Without thanking the man, Rosanna left, looking for a vacant carriage.

XV

IN HIS DREAMS, Eleni had been alive again. There was no crime in the city. Pattern killers were mythical creatures. His stomach didn't play up. And the Emperor was concerned with the welfare of his subjects.

When he woke up, the world was a festering wound and he was a squashed maggot writhing inside it.

The daemon dust was flushed from his body, and his first urge was to reach to his belt for the third leaf-twist. Everything ached, hurt, screamed or burned.

He was out of his clothes, in a bed, under blankets. The dust was gone.

'Easy,' a voice said. A cool, feminine voice. An angel's.

Sitting up, he felt hammerblows to his head. He was strong. He told the pain to go away. It was stronger.

Gripping the edge of the bed, he stayed upright.

'You're in the Luitpoldstrasse Station,' the voice said. 'You've been asleep for two days.'

'Eleni?'

His eyes focused, and he saw Rosanna. She looked surprised.

'Eleni?' she asked.

'Never mind.'

Rosanna was by his bedside. There were others in the room. Rasselas was there, bowed low beside his master, Mornan Tybalt. And Graf Rudiger von Unheimlich, sneering with distaste at the commoners.

'What happened?'

'You're back on the case,' Rosanna told him.

Harald looked at Tybalt and von Unheimlich. They both nodded, brief acknowledgements that this was true.

'Viereck?'

'The twelfth victim.'

Harald clutched the blankets and started forwards, a wave of agony convulsing him.

'What?'

'He was on execution dock,' Rasselas explained, 'supervising the hanging of the acrobat. The bird came from nowhere and took his head almost off.'

'The hawk left a message, like a carrier pigeon. It was for you.'

Rosanna gave him a slip of paper. He managed to hold it with his banana-clumsy fingers, and focused on the few words.

'COME AND GET ME, KLEINDEINST.'

It bore a seal with the imprint of a hawk's clawfoot.

Rosanna, while close to him, whispered, 'I have a name. Another of Vastarien's Vanquishers.'

She didn't want the others to hear. He understood immediately. In this case, no one could be trusted.

'Get me some clothes,' Harald shouted at the dignitaries, 'and a pot of strong coffee.'

He thought Rasselas might be smiling, but the Imperial Chancellor and the Patron of the League of Karl-Franz remained grim and set in their expressions.

'By the way,' said the chancellor, 'that business of you brutalising every criminal in the city?'

'Yes.'

'Disgraceful. Consider yourself reprimanded.'

'Got to keep the customers satisfied, eh?'

Tybalt looked as if he had mistaken an onion for an apple and taken a big bite.

Praying for the pain to go away, Harald got out of bed.

XVI

HIS BACK WAS on fire now, only the leathered weight of the cloak, so like wings, could cool him. Venturing out without his Warhawk suit had been torture today. From now on, until the Device was complete, he would wear the leather constantly. He adjusted the hood, until it settled like a new skin.

One more sacrifice, and the air would be his realm.

The watch captain had died pitifully, screaming and fouling himself. Viereck was a poor specimen next to Kleindeinst.

He thought back to the night of Kleindeinst's rampage. The watchman had mistaken him for a panderer, and roughed him up a little. Warhawk had been almost amused and unable to stifle his laughter. The watchman must have thought him mad, or one of those inverts who gain pleasure from pain. Kleindeinst had pushed him into the gutter outside the Beard of Ulric, and left him giggling.

'We have chosen our instrument well, Belle,' he told his bird. 'He shall be the last component of the Device.'

The hatch in the roof was open, and beyond was the sky.

XVII

IN THE SALOON of the Crooked Spear, it was impossible to miss the dwarf. He had climbed a stool and was hunched over the long bar, an axe half his size set down amid a small forest of foam-smeared empties. To Harald, the trollslayer looked like what you'd get if you sawed off Arne the Body's legs at the knees. He was still drinking, despite the occasional complaints of a reedy-looking young man at his elbow. Harald knew Gurnisson had a reputation as a brawler, and it was said the last time he'd been drunk enough to be penned in a cell he'd got out by chewing through the bars.

There was a piper in the corner, half-way through an assault on a popular sea-shanty. Rosanna was the only woman in the place. The other drinkers were heavily muscled warrior-types, proud of their fighting scars, prouder of their barrel-shaped limbs. Doubtless, they all exercised daily at Arne's gymnasium, and nightly in the back-alleys of the Street of a Hundred Taverns, exchanging blows with each other. The Sullen Knight was the inn for amateur bruisers and brawlers. The Crooked Spear was where the seriously violent misfits came.

And Gurnisson was the most seriously violent misfit in the place.

Well, maybe the second...

'Gurnisson,' he announced, loud enough to shut up the piper.

The dwarf didn't turn from his drink, but his shoulders heaved enormously, straining the stitching of the back of his jerkin.

'Couldn't you try just asking him politely?' Rosanna suggested. 'Maybe he'll want to help.'

'Gotrek Gurnisson,' he said, louder.

The trollslayer looked over his shoulder, a bleary eye casting around for the man who'd spoken his name.

'Who wants to know?' he asked, hand tightening on the shaft of his axe.

'Captain Harald Kleindeinst of the Dock Watch.'

Gurnisson's companion, who'd obviously heard about Filthy Harald, rolled his eyes upwards and prayed silently for deliverance. The inn was thick with the scent of impending combat.

'Bastard,' someone shouted behind him, 'you broke my brother's arm!'

An enormous young man who didn't look familiar lunged at Harald. He stepped out of the way, and made a simple move with his elbow, listening for the crack of bones giving way in the hulk's forearm.

'There,' he said, 'now you're twins.'

Screaming in a high-pitched yelp, the would-be avenger retreated. Gurnisson grinned.

'Nicely done, copper.'

'It was nothing,' Harald said, pulling up a stool next to the trollslayer.

'We don't serve her kind here,' the ear-, nose- and lip-ringed barman said, nodding with distaste at Rosanna, who was being given a chair by Gurnisson's companion.

'Witches,' the barman said, and spat.

'You just changed your policy,' Harald told him.

The barman considered it a moment, and went along with Harald's suggestion.

'Schnapps for me, sherry for the lady, and whatever these gentlemen are drinking.'

The drinks came.

'You made a noise on the street a few nights gone, copper,' Gurnisson said.

Harald agreed.

'A good thing you didn't run into me.'

'Good for you, or good for me?'

The dwarf showed his sharp yellow teeth, and his face flared in an angry-looking grin.

'Let's say it was good for the city,' Gurnisson's companion suggested as a compromise.

'Felix Jaeger,' he said, shaking Harald's hand and kissing Rosanna's.

'Why do you seek me out, copper? Have there been complaints?'

'No more than usual. I just want a name from you. The name of a criminal.'

'I be no snitch.'

'This be no ordinary criminal. I'm talking about the Warhawk.'

Gurnisson looked puzzled. 'The murderer? Why should I know his name?'

'You knew his father.'

'Knew a lot of people's fathers, and grandfathers, and great-grandfathers.'

'You were with Prince Vastarien?'

Gurnisson's thick features twisted into an expression approximating the wistful. 'A long time ago. We were fools then. All of us.'

'There was another Warhawk.'

Gurnisson looked as if he'd just bitten into a rancid rat. He tried to wash the taste out of his mouth with a swig of ale.

'A bad one, he was. Some like soldiering too much. It lets them do things they couldn't do as civilians without being chased by people like you.'

Harald wondered what it must have been like in the Vanquishers. Had they been heroes or monsters? Or a mixture of both?

'Kept to himself, did Warhawk. Always with his precious birdies. Minya, Sebastian. Cheep cheep cheep. They were his childlings. The only things he cared for, the only things real to him.'

'He had a name?'

Gurnisson paused, took another swig.

'Robida,' he said. 'Andrzej Robida, curse his dead and rotten-to-Khorne guts.'

Now it had come, it was a disappointment. Sometimes, the answer to a mystery was like a daemon dust rush, a sudden influx of understanding and vision.

The name Andrzej Robida meant nothing to him.

XVIII

HE TOOK OUT his father's falconer's clothes, and laid them on the floor. With the lamp behind him, his shadow filled the suit. Old Andrzej had been a bigger man than his son. But Warhawk would outgrow the dead man's stature.

Belle flexed her wings on the stand, as Warhawk took a knife to the old clothes, ripping the rotten material apart, scratching the floor.

The birds reacted to the noise, and began calling to each other, screeching, squawking, scratching.

Warhawk stabbed the shadow, gouging the wood of the floorboards.

Soon...

* * *

XIX

ROSANNA WAITED UNTIL they were out on the street to tell him. Since meeting Ruger, she had become cautious. She had scried something from the weirdroot dealer that made her trust only Harald. Treachery was a part of this thing.

'I know of an Andrzej Robida,' she said.

Harald stopped in his tracks, and turned to her. In the lamplight, his face seemed set as a statue's.

'He was well known a few years ago, especially at the Temple of Sigmar. He was a patron of the sciences. He knew the old lector, Mikael Hasselstein. They used to debate the possibilities of human invention.'

'Tell me, quickly,' Harald said.

'Robida was the sponsor of the inventors' contest. You remember, he offered one hundred thousand crowns to anyone who devised a machine which could fly under its own power. A machine, not a magic trick. All those rickety winged creations plunging from the walls of the city, into the Reik, into the trees. The crowds assembled to laugh at each new failure. Wax wings, inflated silk bladders, man-lifting kites.'

'Wings,' Harald said. 'All through this, I've been hearing the cursed flutter of wings.'

There was a watchman coming down the street, on his rounds. And an unoccupied carriage trundling, idling, looking for trade.

'Robida is a rich man. He has a big house near the palace.'

'He must be the Warhawk.'

'Yes,' she said, thinking, 'he must.'

Shockingly, suddenly, Harald embraced her, kissed her. Then, he was hailing the carriage.

'Get to the Luitpoldstrasse and send the watchmen after me,' he said, climbing in. 'Klove,' he shouted to the watchman, flashing his copper, 'look after this woman.'

Her mind was racing. During their brief contact, Harald had poured images from his mind into hers. She knew he was going after Robida alone, leaving her behind to protect her.

There was something else nagging her.

She watched the carriage rattle off down the street.

'Miss?' the watchman, Klove, asked.

Rosanna was about to say something, but a drunk was expelled from Bruno's Brewhouse, and staggered against them.

Klove clouted the man, and sent him reeling into the gutter.

'Be off with you, Ruger,' he shouted at the drunk. 'And keep quiet, or I'll confiscate your pouch.'

Wheels were whirring inside her head.

'Is that Mack Ruger?' she asked the copper.

'Yes,' he spat, 'the pest. Not worth the trouble of hauling him in.'

Ruger twisted in the gutter and looked up, grinning. He was not just drunk. Weirdjuice dribbled down his chin, and his eyeballs were swimming.

Rosanna had never seen him before.

XX

A BIG HOUSE near the palace.

That wasn't much of an address, but it would have to do. Harald had ordered the carriage-man to take him to the palace district. Former Lector Hasselstein – whom Harald had no cause to remember fondly – had retired from public life and entered a secluded order, but Harald hoped he could scare up someone at the Temple of Sigmar who could tell him where Andrzej Robida lived.

It felt right in his guts. Robida was the Warhawk.

This all had something to do with wings.

'Faster,' he ordered the intimidated carriage-man. 'This is life or death.'

He would find Robida's address within the hour, even if he failed at the temple. If necessary, he would break into the palace itself and find some toady who knew the patron of the sciences.

It would be over soon.

XXI

BELLE WAS TOO good a bird to be impatient.

Warhawk stroked her wings.

The blood of twelve was on her beak. Soon, it would be the blood of thirteen.

The Device was almost complete.

The blood of just one more sacrifice was needed.

He regretted the time he had wasted on the mechanical sciences. All those strange flapping, churning, straining machines plummeting from the walls. He should have thought of magic first.

It was all so simple.

Thirteen sacrifices, and the freedom of the skies would be his.

Kleindeinst must be out there already, on his way. Warhawk had been spacing out the sacrifices, waiting until he knew Gotrek Gurnisson was in the city.

Gurnisson was a part of the Device too. Just as they all were, all the dead, all the flies buzzing around the sacrifices. The witch-woman, Kleindeinst, the criminal he had impersonated, the poor dupes Viereck had hanged...

It was as his father had told him, so many years ago. Thirteen must die by one bird, and that bird's master would be free of the ground.

But there were other rules.

The first sacrifice must be a child.

The fifth a woman of the aristocracy.

The tenth a man of authority.

The twelfth a slayer of innocent men.

And the thirteenth...

Belle's head rubbed against his black leather glove. Kleindeinst was out there, coming closer...

The thirteenth must come to the sacrifice of their own accord.

XXII

MAGISTER SPIELBRUNNER DID not relish being hauled out of his bed by a scryer and quizzed intently about alchemical spells. But he was coming around to accepting it.

'Flight,' the wizard said, 'that's an old one.'

Spielbrunner was young for a wizard, almost boyish. Rosanna had met him briefly when she was with the temple, and remembered his obvious interest in her. He was still interested, and that meant he was putting up with this intrusion into his home.

'After lead-into-gold, rejuvenation, invincibility, sexual potency and foretelling the future, flight is the most popular lunatic fancy. People always come to wizards begging for wings. As if we could work miracles...'

They were in Spielbrunner's study, a modern and uncluttered room, with a no nonsense air about it. His books were dusted regularly and well-kept, and his equipment was stored precisely and in order.

'There are many methods for attempting the power of flight,' he continued, flattening his hair with one hand, and pulling his night-robe tight about his thin body. 'None of them work, of course,' he added. 'Not really. Not for long. Although temporary power of flight – to get you out of a tight situation, say – is comparatively easy for the trained magician. Ten years of study and contemplation, a strict spiritual discipline and a few of the right incantations, and... whoosh!'

'Our man isn't interested in a temporary power of flight. He wants actual wings.'

'Some altereds of Chaos sprout wings. And other things.'

Spielbrunner was picking through books, looking for something.

'This would have to involve murders,' she prompted. 'A number of them.'

'Oh, you mean a Device,' he said, with disgust. 'Superstitious rubbish, like all short-cuts. Popular for a while with unlettered idiots trying to poach some of the benefits of wizardry – meagre though they are, I assure you – without going through the irksome business of actually acquiring magical skills. Everybody wants to be a magician...'

Not everybody, she thought.

'But nobody wants to give up their entire life to becoming one. And that, I am sorry to say, is the only way to get there. As for Devices – nasty, barbarous things – nobody bothers with them any more.'

'Someone still bothers,' she said, unpleasant pictures in her mind.

'Oh dear.'

XXIII

IT WAS NEARLY dawn, and he had wasted time at the temple, going through the former lector's neglected papers while a dim-witted novice held the candle and shivered. Finally, a couple of Templars turned up and he had to dissuade them from throwing him out. But, as it happened, he had found nothing. In the end, Harald got the address the way he should have done in the first place, by asking a watchman.

On this side of the river, the watchmen weren't what he was used to on the docks. Patrolling the palace, the embassies and the temple districts – all well equipped with their own armed guards – these coppers spent more time making sure their uniforms were smart than chasing cutpurses or roughing up Hooks and Fish.

Still, a flash of the badge got him cooperation from an officer in the Templeplatz Station, and precise directions to the Robida Estate. Harald had looked around at the languid night staff of the station and decided he would do best to go alone.

Knife in hand, he stood before the nondescript but elegant house. Above the door, the name 'Robida' was picked out in elaborate scrollwork, a soaring hawk bas-relief above it.

It was as if Warhawk were announcing himself.

The door was open. Inside, he fancied he heard the flutter of wings.

The first light was in the sky as Harald walked up to the house, and pushed the door open with his boot.

'Don't,' a familiar voice shouted from across the street, 'you're expected!'

XXIV

ROSANNA HAD TRACKED Harald from the temple to the watch station, pushing Spielbrunner's carriage-man to speed at each turn. The wizard had explained the Device to her and let her have the use of his coach. She now owed him favours, and that was sunk into her like a fish-hook. It was not generally a good thing to be in a wizard's debt.

'He's been pulling you here all along,' she explained.

Harald stepped over the threshold, into the gloomy hallway. Dawnlight streamed in through a dull window at the far end.

'It's part of the Device.'

She kept up with Harald, but he ignored her explanations.

The house was filthy, its floor matted with dry birdlime and trodden-in feathers. The wall-hangings had been rent apart by beaks and claws. There were chewed bones everywhere.

They went upstairs, following the point of Harald's knife.

'If he kills one more, he believes he'll be able to fly.'

Harald snorted a laugh. 'That's madness.'

'Yes, madness.'

They looked around the landing. There were paths on the floor, but wherever the master of this house chose not to venture was abandoned, cobweb-ridden rubbish.

The smell was worse than Mundsen Keep.

They followed the largest path, where a track had been worn through the bird droppings almost to the faded carpet.

At the end of the corridor was a ladder, which led up through an open trapdoor in the ceiling. Above, she heard the small sounds of birds.

She scried danger.

Carefully, Magnin out, Harald pulled himself up one-handed. Birds squawked, but no attack came.

She followed him. There was a hatch in the attic, a gable leading to the roof. A slight wind blew in. Rosanna saw the sun rising over the roofs of the city.

'He's out there,' she said. 'Waiting.'

XXV

IT WAS PERFECT.

They came through the hatch and stood on his roof.

'He's brought you here,' the witch-woman was saying, unsteady on her feet, 'for the Device. You're to be the last sacrifice.'

Warhawk laughed silently inside his hood, and stood up. Belle's wings spread. 'No, my dove,' he said, 'not him, you.'

Belle glided in silence, beak aimed at the scryer's heart.

Warhawk saw the mask of fear on her face. He had known earlier, when they met in the Street of a Hundred Taverns, that Kleindeinst was the string which would pull her to this site.

'You came of your own accord, remember.'

Belle's arched wings flattened out, and she began to dive. The witch-woman's feet slipped, and she fell away from Kleindeinst. Warhawk realised she was terrified up here, afraid of heights.

He was almost there. In an instant, the Device would be complete and he could fly from this rooftop.

Kleindeinst's hand moved, and something shiny flew from it, turning over and over, scything the air.

Belle tumbled from the sky, and Warhawk felt a beak in his own heart. His bird, his twelve-times-blooded bird, thumped against the slates.

Screeching himself, he attacked, leaping across the gap between the roofs, his boots steady on the shifting tile, and scooped up Belle in his arms.

She was still living.

It could still be done.

XXVI

THE HOODED FIGURE charged them, waving his bird like a shield, and leaped from a ledge a man's height from their level, landing hard on Rosanna. He set about lashing her with the bird.

She couldn't see anything, but she could feel what he was doing. The bird's beak bit into her.

'Die, die, die,' he grunted through his mask.

She imagined the face of the man who had represented himself to her as Mack Ruger, contorted behind the black leather.

The beak tore at her clothes. The bird was still alive, spitted with the knife, but clinging on until the Device was complete.

'Die, die, die…'

The Warhawk – Andrzej Robida – sounded like a bird himself, a pecking, gouging bird.

'Die, die, die…'

Gods, she thought, what if Speilbrunner was wrong? What if the last thing she were to see in this life was the Warhawk taking to the skies, proud wings spread, blood dripping from his talons?

Fear had enveloped her as soon as she had emerged from the attic hatch and realised how far above the cobbles of the city street she was. Now, the fear was threaded through with pain and panic.

The force of Warhawk's rage, of his need, pummelled her as much as his blows. She scrabbled with her hands, biting back her screams, praying…

'Die, die, die…'

XXVII

HARALD'S STOMACH CHURNED and tore itself apart.

The Warhawk was on Rosanna, battering her with his dying bird. He made bird sounds as he assaulted the scryer. Again, Harald had sought a monster and found only a mad-man.

He strode across the roof, his hands out. The Magnin had taken care of the damned bird, and now it was down to him to deal with the bird's master.

He took Warhawk by the back of the neck, gripping the collar of his leather cloak, and pulled him away.

The murderer was no stronger than the average man, but he was frenzied and determined. He scratched at Harald's arms, twisting in the copper's grip.

Rosanna, sobbing and bleeding, crawled away and clung to a chimney. She was scratched, but she would live.

The Warhawk kicked backwards at Harald's shins. He couldn't hurt him any more than he was already hurting. The murderer could not stop him. It was all over.

Harald turned the Warhawk around, and looked into the mad eyes that stared out through his mask.

He lifted the man off his feet.

'So you want to fly, do you?'

Warhawk squawked.

He heaved the murderer above his head, and tossed him as far as possible out over the street. For the briefest of moments, the black leather silhouette hung in the air, cloak spread behind him.

'Try flapping your arms,' Harald suggested.

THE IBBY THE FISH FACTOR

I

IT WAS THE worst kind of sunset. The sky, red to the west, churned with cloud the angry colour of fresh-spilled blood. Even squat statues cast shadows as long as temple steeples. Passersby were fringed incarnadine in the dying sun. At the eastern end of Konigplatz was the colossal building that housed Altdorf's law courts and the headsman's offices: its thousand leaded windows caught the last light and flashed vivid, painful orange into her sensitive eyes.

As the dark crept across the 'platz, her vampire senses quickened. Mites and motes dancing in the summer evening caught her attention. Genevieve could distinguish each and every speck – dust or insect – and chart its random course. The background chatter of city noise rose like an orchestra tuning up, and she could make out words spoken in anger or affection across the square. The calls of birds pecking each other over scraps of food and the cries of competing pro-claimers became an assault on her ears. Despite her need to pass as ordinary, nightfall brought her to full life, pricking the red thirst she must not slake. Sharpening nails cramped

191

inside her too-tight velvet gloves, curling in on themselves
like hooks. She ground her teeth, trying to keep her lips
demurely clamped over swelling, razor-edged fangs.

Her eyes hurt most. She saw too many ghosts in the last
light of day.

This season, with Clause 17 proclaimed all over the capital of the Empire, it wasn't a good idea to wear smoked
glasses on the streets. Let alone affect a red-lined black cloak,
sleep in a coffin, neglect to cast a reflection, shapeshift into
a bat or wolf, flinch from an icon, or ask for six hundred and
seventy-six candles on her birthday cake.

Or smile too sharply.

Genevieve had never been a cloaks-and-coffins sort of
vampire. She couldn't transform into anything except an
angrier, sharper-toothed and clawed version of her regular
self. She could bear garlic, a useful trait in a person forced
occasionally to subsist on the blood of Tileans who bathe
their food in the stuff. Her conscience was clear enough that
holy emblems held no horror for her.

But sunlight made her eyes ache. Enough of it would start
her skin peeling.

And she needed to drink warm human blood quite often.
That was never going to make her popular. This summer,
with Antiochus Bland's Sanitation Bill posted all over this
part of the Empire, it was also an invitation to be guest of
honour at a corpse-burning party.

At the city gates this afternoon, Genevieve had pointedly
been asked to kiss a blessed amulet by a bored watchman
who didn't take the trouble to clean the baubles between
uses. Symbols of Shallya, Verena, Ulric and Sigmar were
available. Just ahead of her in the queue, a fastidious merchant cringed at being handed a Sigmarite hammer still
glistening with the slobber of a sickly farmer's boy. The silk-
seller, unfortunate enough to have eyebrows that met
suspiciously over his nose, was hauled out of the line by a
couple of black-robed clerics of Morr and put to the
Question. She gave thanks that Bland's Boyos were too intent
on the merchant to pay attention to her insignificant person,
and chastely pressed closed lips to a pewter Dove of Verena.

She slipped through the gate, trying to ignore the yelps of indignation and worse emanating from the hut-like shrine of Morr set up beside the watch-point. Now she knew how stringently Clause 17 was being enforced. She had chosen one of the market gates, because word was that the daily stream of dodgy characters that flowed in and out of the Imperial city dissuaded the Cult of Morr from using silver icons – several sets had gone missing – in the kiss-the-god test. A clean conscience wouldn't have helped her with silver.

Since then, she had dawdled in the Konigplatz like a first-time visitor from the sticks, pretending to count the jostling statues of past emperors, not talking to strangers like her mama had told her, hoping to see someone famous in the flesh. She pointedly bought half a dozen apples, eating them pips and all. Anyone who cared to pay attention would know she was the sort of girl whose diet didn't extend far beyond fruit, bread, cheese and the occasional turnip pasty.

She had made sure to get green apples, not red.

Yum yum. Human food. Wouldn't eat anything else, no sirrah.

Never eat anything red. Or drink it either.

The red thirst was starting to bite. Her fang-teeth ached and tore the inside of her mouth. The taste of her own blood made it worse.

She had not fed in weeks. That made her crotchety.

Apart from other inconveniences, she felt stuffed inside. Well-chewed apples filled her like mud. Her stomach and bowels weren't used to stubborn solids. It was an effort to keep the food down. How horribly ironic it would be: to pass all the other tests and be given away by undigested fruit-pulp.

Under the great statue of Sigmar, cloaked in the cool dark of its swelling shadow, she held her body still. Sudden movements would betray her as not human. She deliberately lifted the last apple to her mouth, arm slower than the human eye, imagining the air as thick as water. She overdid it to the point where she might be mistaken for one of those strange street performers who do things as if living only half as fast as everyone else.

The moons came out, shiny as new pfennigs.

She was reminded of feeding and her fangs became needle-keen.

She bit into the big apple, jaw-hinges dislocating momentarily, and took the whole core out. Her mouth was full, cheeks bulging like a hamster's, and she had to push with her fingers to get it all in. The trick of distension didn't work for her gullet, and she had to thump her throat to keep from choking.

'Gone down the wrong hole, eh?' said a loiterer.

She couldn't speak, but tried to swallow. A cannonball was lodged somewhere between her voice box and her stomach.

The loiterer got close enough for a lot of little details to come in focus. His doublet had been tailored for someone else but invisibly mended to fit him, and was embroidered with mock cloth-of-gold. His boots were cheap too, tricked up with shiny buckles to look expensive. She scented a wrong 'un, but mostly saw the tiny throb of the pulse in his throat, between the ruff of his shirt and the sharply defined line of his beard. Under pink skin, she saw red and blue.

She heard his heartbeat and perceived the flow of blood under his skin.

He patted her on the back with one hand, dislodging the last of the cannonball and reached for her purse with the other.

She swallowed gratefully and pinched his wrist instinctively, halting his grab.

'You misunderstand,' he tried to wheedle. 'I am merely pointing out the vulnerability of your poke. The 'platz is full of thieves at this hour. And you must protect yourself.'

'Quite so,' she said.

She exerted pressure with her thumb and forefinger, digging into the loiterer's wrist. A shiny sliver dropped from his fingers to the cobbles – an edge rather than a blade, but keen enough to do the job.

'You're a cutpurse,' she said.

His face was screwed up with pain. Nails had forced through the finger-seams of her glove and were stuck into his wrist. Bright blood welled up like a soap bubble and fell, tumbling over itself, to splash on cobbles.

The blood shone with colours only she could see.

She had to force herself not to throw herself on the ground and lick up the spillage.

She looked into the cutpurse's eyes. And saw no reflection of her face.

He was terrified. Then cunning, growing too confident.

'And you're a leech,' he sneered. 'Unhand me, monster!'

A small crowd was gathering. Fellow pickpockets, she guessed, come to admire or critique the sham swell's technique. The professionals must have noticed her quickness at fending off his expert poke-grab. No one now thought she was an innocent girl on her first visit to the big city.

A watchman was coming this way. By his helmet, with its feather and shiny badge, she knew him for one of the ceremonial toy soldiers who policed the more public and official districts.

She let go of the thief's wrist, but he took hold of hers.

'We've got one of them!' he shouted. 'Officer, send for Bland's Boyos. This foul inhuman creature must be turned over to the Cult of Morr. We've a leech for the burning!'

A cobblestone bounced off her forehead. Insults and excoriations were called out. Several of the crowd held up flaming torches on long sticks. The lamplighters, of course. As the hisses and mutters spread, the effect was uncomfortably close to mobs she remembered of old. Yokels with firebrands and farm implements, swarming over the countryside. Ranting clerics and pompous rural burgermeisters, leading from behind. Execution without trial, and the shrill cry of 'Death to the dead!'

Five hundred years ago, well before Antiochus Bland ascended to the Temple Fathership of the Cult of Morr, the Undead Wars – fomented by the von Carstein clan, those Sylvanian lunatics who claimed to speak for all vampirekind – had set off the worst of the persecutions. The average Count von Carstein proved enormously keen on leading armies of rotting mindless strigoi against the higher races and dreaming of an eternal feast of blood. However, those master tacticians tended not to be about when vampires you could actually hold a conversation with were picked off in ones and twos by those doughty bands of scythe-waving, fire-building, stake-brandishing clods every village had sitting around the inn waiting to impale, incinerate or quarter anyone to whom they took a dislike.

'Off with her head,' shouted some silly woman.

'Beheading's too good for the likes of her!'

The rake Chandagnac, her own father-in-darkness, had been among many comparatively blameless purge victims, hunted down and destroyed by clerics of Ulric. Since Chandagnac had also gifted the ill-remembered Tsarina Kattarin with the Dark Kiss, Genevieve supposed he was indirectly responsible for as much bother as the von Carsteins. Just as the Undead Wars were dying down, Kattarin overwhelmed her addle-headed mortal husband to become absolute ruler of Kislev, exerting a bloody grip that lasted centuries. She'd be on the throne still if her great-great-great grandchildren hadn't got fed up with an immortal ice queen blocking succession and conspired to transfix her like a butterfly. The body, preserved by the cold of Kislev's Frost Palace, was still on display as an Awful Warning.

'Put silver needles in her eyes,' shouted a thin girl with more imagination than most. Genevieve had not heard that one before.

'That's a good idea, Hanna,' said a friend of the clever-clogs. 'Silver needles!'

She found herself backed up against the base of the statue of Sigmar.

The torch-flames got closer. The watchman forced his way to the front of the crowd.

'What's all this, then?' said the copper. 'Move along smartly, you lot.'

The watchman, tabard let out over his comfortable stomach, caught sight of the cutpurse and reached for his cudgel.

'Oh, it's you, Donowitz. Still dunking for pokes? And picking on the young ones again. It'll be Mundsen Keep this time. No more warnings.'

Genevieve noticed that Donowitz wore his cap aslant to conceal a wax ear. He'd been clipped at least once.

'I am entirely innocent, your worship,' said the cutpurse. 'I found this daughter of darkness preying on decent living folks. She's a ghastly monster of the night. An undead hag in a girlish shape. Look at the red in her eyes. See how she shows her fangs and claws.'

Genevieve became acutely aware that her mouth was open and her gloves shredded. Her red thirst was up, she was coiled to spring. If it was to end tonight, she'd take some human bastards to true death with her. They might have her head off, but she'd go out with the taste of Altdorf blood in her throat.

'We're going to do what Temple Father Bland says, and treat her properly,' said Donowitz, instantly self-elected mob-leader. 'Strip her for the Question, lay silver lashes on her skin, then despatch her with stake, fire and sickle.'

'Oh aye,' said rather too many enthusiasts.

'Hold on,' said one fellow. 'I must rush home and fetch me old dad. He wouldn't want to miss this.'

'Sell tickets, why don't you?' Genevieve shouted at the dutiful son as he scurried off.

'None of your lip, monster,' said the watchman.

'Officer,' she said to him. 'It's a fair cop. My name is Genevieve Dieudonné. I am indeed a vampire... ghastly monster, undead hag and so forth. I freely surrender myself to the Konigplatz Watch. Kindly escort me to a cell to await the laying of actual criminal or spiritual charges against me. I should like to stand on my right as a citizen of the Empire in good standing to send one written message, to my friend the Emperor Karl-Franz, whose life I happened to save from the infernal designs of the traitor Oswald von Konigswald and the Great Enchanter Constant Drachenfels.'

She hated bringing it up all the time, but the situation seemed to demand it.

The copper scratched his chin. Someone poked her leg with a stick and she involuntarily snarled.

'Well, um, miss, I, er...'

'Don't be blinded by her vampire powers of fascination,' said Donowitz. 'And don't hark to all this legal nonsense. She's a dreaded leech and we've caught her in bloodsuckery. She's no more rights than any other abomination.'

'Didn't you people hear what I said?' Genevieve shouted, annoyed. 'Thirteen years ago, I saved the whole Empire!'

'That's as may be,' said Silver Needles Hanna, 'but what have you done for us lately?'

She was prodded again. A mean-eyed dwarf in short lederhosen had got between everyone's legs and was close to her. He had a special prodding-stick.

'Death to the dead!'

The cry was taken up.

She was prodded again, through her skirt. The gnarled stick was a bit sharp.

'Shove it in her heart, Shorty,' said Hanna. Genevieve had expected more from Silver Needles, but people always turned out to be disappointments.

With that in mind, she still tried to look imploring to the watchman.

Someone tipped his helmet from behind and the peak slid over his eyes.

'I have your watch-number officer,' she said. 'I'll remember it if you let this unruly mob run riot.'

She had misjudged the copper. He looked stricken at being singled out.

'See, she's divined this poor fellow's watch-number with her magic powers,' said the vendor who'd been happy to sell her unripe apples all afternoon. 'She's a witch as well as a vampire.'

'It's written on his helmet, goathead,' said Hanna helpfully.

'I can't be doing with all this,' said the watchman. 'My shift ended at nightfall. Just be sure you do a decent job of it.'

He turned and walked away.

The prodding dwarf was closer, gurning up at her with yellowed teeth and eyes.

'You think that once they've done for all the vampires they won't turn on dwarfs next?'

Another mistake. Shorty lifted her skirt with his stick and leered at her knees. Half the crowd laughed. The other half complained this wasn't in the dignified spirit of a proper vampire-slaying.

'Oh, let Shorty have his fun. It's not as if she were human.'

The dwarf put his face to her skirts and drew in a huge breath, sucking at her scent.

This was just disgusting!

'Hang this lark for a game of tin soldiers,' said Genevieve.

She braced herself against Sigmar's plinth and stamped on Shorty's face, jabbing her heel against his squash nose. Her kick propelled Shorty off the cobbles. He cannoned through the crowd and splashed down satisfyingly in a puddle.

'What a bully,' said Silver Needles Hanna. 'Vampires are all the same.'

Genevieve had inherited the dwarf's prodding stick, which seemed a lot shorter in her grip than it had in Shorty's stubby fingers. She held it up like a duelling blade. People pulled out the knives and swords kept out of sight when the watch was around. Someone even started powdering a pistol.

'Before we proceed further,' she said, 'there's one thing I'd like to get perfectly clear. You're all criminals. Cutpurses, ponces, jack-up artists, hugger-muggers, layabouts, bawds and the like. And you're about to *murder* me. But you feel pretty good about it. You've had a hard day stealing, fleecing, whoring and cheating, but you think killing me is, as it were, your *good deed for the week*. Doesn't that strike any of you as *insane*? Have I ever hurt any of you? Except "Dunkin" Donowitz and the prod-happy pervert, both of whom started any trouble they got. So far as you know, have I ever hurt anyone you've ever met?'

'It's not what you've *done*,' said Hanna, 'it's what you *are*!'

'I thought as much.'

Genevieve flung the stick away. She invoked whichever Gods of Law were left over to care about justice for the undead. Tensing her thighs and calves in a semi-crouch, she fixed her mind on a point thirty feet above her head and sprang up into the air. With a run-up, she might have made

it to the raised warhammer. As it was, she slammed against
the statue's broad belt, face scraping weathered stone belly-
muscles. Her clumsy hands found no hold, and she slid
down between Sigmar's mighty thews. She scrabbled for
something – anything! – to grab.

'Sacrilege!' shouted too many people.

Genevieve had cause to thank the sculptor who defied
conventional morality by insisting that the greatest
memorial to the founding hero of Empire be anatomically
correct and heroically proportioned enough to get a grip
on. When Altdorfers swore by Sigmar's holy hammer, they
didn't just mean the one he held up ready to smash goblin skulls.

She found rests in the muscles of Sigmar's knees for her
boot-toes, drew in a breath, and climbed the statue monkey-
fashion, swarming up over the hero's waist and chest.
Perching on his shoulder like a gargoyle, she leant against
the flaring wings of his helm. Up close, she realised that the
white texture of his beard came from centuries of inconti-
nent pigeons.

'That's what we have in common, my lord,' she breathed.
'One minute, you're a hero of the Empire. The next, they're
crapping all over you.'

Just about now, being able to shapeshift into bat-form
would have been a useful attribute.

Something burning spanged against Sigmar's helm. A
lamplighter's torch, thrown as a makeshift spear. Someone
down there in the swelling crowd would probably have a
crossbow.

It was time to make a dignified exit.

'Death to the dead!'

There was a flash, a sizzle and some screaming. The pis-
tolier had fumbled his loading and set fire to himself. They
couldn't blame her for... who was she fooling? In their current mood, the crowd was likely to blame her for sour milk
and clogged drains.

A couple of bold would-be vampire-slayers were trying to
scale Sigmar's plinth. One fell off and was caught by the
crowd, then tossed up to try again.

Genevieve took a run along Sigmar's heroic arm, got her hands around the shaft of his more conventional hammer and swung a couple of times, trying to remember the tumbling moves she had learned in Cathay from Master Po. She launched herself into space and reached forward like an acrobat, aiming herself at the huge flat green scowl of the Empress Magritta.

The tradition was that every new emperor and empress was supposed to commemorate their investiture by commissioning their own statue and adding it to the crowd in Konigplatz. After two and a half millennia, space was at a premium. Most of early post-Sigmar emperors were worn down to little more than stubs. City planners still dreaded another upheaval like the Year of Seven Emperors, which had forced them to demolish the beautiful little shrine of Repanse de Lyonesse to make way for a spectacularly ugly and undignified jostle of poisoned, stabbed, hot-collared and defenestrated one-week wonders.

Even that was less of a disaster than the statue of the Empress Magritta. After the Bronze Lady browbeat the electors into giving her the throne, she decreed her statue should reflect her stature and be twice the height of Sigmar's. When she was eventually succeeded, after a deft bit of backstabbery, the often-forgotten Emperor Johann the Grey was acutely embarrassed by the colossa frowning down disapproval on the whole city, and wondered how to go about breaking tradition by getting rid of the thing.

The problem was half-solved when the statue proved so heavy that it plunged through its shoddy sandstone plinth and lost three-quarters of its height by sinking long legs and most of its body into the sewers and tarns under Altdorf. A story went that on the night of the Big Plunge, the stern stone face of the Sigmar statue was seen to smile broadly. Die-hards who spent centuries whining that things were never right again after the Bronze Lady was booted out perpetually sought to raise public subscriptions for the re-elevation of the statue to its former glory.

As it was, Magritta's spiked crown was in just the right place.

Genevieve caught the spikes and vaulted over them, concealing herself neatly inside the sculpted crown.

Most of the Konigplatz emperors were solid stone, but Magritta was hollow metal. Before the big plunge, it had been possible to climb up inside the statue and peer out over the city from the crown. There must be a hatch somewhere. Rooting through the clogged detritus inside the crown – the contents of which she didn't want to think about – she found a ring. At the first pull, it came off in her hand.

Trying to ignore the shouting from below and the flaming arrows striking Magritta's solid hair, she felt out the edges of the hatch.

An arrow arced down into the crown, narrowly missing her leg. The fire blotted her vision with dazzling squiggles, but after the flare the light was useful. She was in a large bird's nest, surrounded by fragments of eggshell and hundreds of animal bones. Since there were few twigs in the city, the nest was woven of whatever came to beak: stolen items of clothing, at least six parasols and umbrellas, entire potted shrubs and a lot of simple garbage. A still-living weirdroot sported healthy bulbs, presumably enabling the dweller in this nest to fly higher than any other bird in the city.

She pulled the stoutest umbrella skeleton out of the nest and slid it into the hatch-crack, lifting the heavy metal flap enough to get her hand under its lip.

As well as shouting from below, she heard angry squawking from above.

A city legend had it that after 'Filthy' Harald Kleindeinst ended the career of the pattern killer Warhawk, the murderous trainer's birds escaped and took to the high perches of Altdorf. The hardy, vicious, overlarge sky pirates stole babies and dogs to feed their young.

She didn't need to find out if that was true or not.

Hauling up the hatch, she slid into the comforting if odorous gloom and let herself fall a dozen feet. The hatch clanged shut above her. Light filtered through the green lenses in Magritta's eyes. The crowd sound was muffled.

Now she just had to work her way down to the base of the statue and leave through the door in the empress's heel. Which was a thousand feet below her, and underwater.

It was a good thing she didn't need to breathe.

II

'DETLEF, I'M DEEPLY disappointed that you of all people should take this unproductive attitude. I can't understand why you'd wish to display such an unbalanced – indeed, unnatural – view of the undead in such an influential space as the theatre. Young people – indeed, children – patronise this place, they have unformed and easily-influenced minds. Surely, you concede that you have a duty by everything holy to present all arguments before coming down firmly on the side of the living?'

Detlef Sierck, actor/manager/playwright-in-residence of the Vargr Breughel Memorial Theatre, considered his visitor. The wheedling, smiling, Antiochus Bland was not physically impressive. Detlef had inches on the man and outweighed him by half, but the Temple Father of the Cult of Morr acted as if this snug room was his office, not Detlef's. Usually, the broad desk gave Detlef a sense of power over supplicants and auditionees, but now he felt trapped, wedged in by furniture that pressed on his substantial belly, pinned back by Bland's fixed eyes.

Elsie, the angelic foundling Poppa Fritz had taken on to sell programs and interval sweetmeats, brought in a tray with a pot of fresh beef tea and a couple of goblets. Bland looked at the reddish liquid suspiciously, but the twelve-year-old's open face won him over. There had been some backstage talk of dosing Bland's tea with weirdroot, but Detlef hoped nothing had come of it. The Temple Father could hardly become *more* dream-haunted, deranged and obsessive.

'Thank you most kindly, missy,' said Bland, turning his smile on the girl. He fished a pfennig from his tummy-pouch and gave it to her. 'It must be very sad – indeed, tragic – to be an orphan. I often worry about what might happen to my own three lovely children if their dear mama should be snatched away by fiendish creatures of darkness. There's nothing more important – indeed, prudent – than a good solid savings account with a respectable house of bankers. If you invest this tiny chap wisely, it might grow up to be a great big schilling.'

Little Orphan Elsie, an expert judge of character and coinage, raised the pfennig to the corner of her mouth, eye-teeth bared for a healthy bite. Detlef caught her eye with a quick head-shake, dissuading her from treating the Temple Father like a palmer-off of snide coins.

Elsie thanked Bland for the pfennig and left. Detlef hoped the child was sensible – indeed, human – enough to squander the coin on a hair-ribbon or an almond biscuit. To the gallows with good solid savings accounts and respectable houses of bankers. Ulric knows he hadn't saved anything as dull as money at her age; or at any age since then, come to that. It all went back into the theatre. He was only one flop away from his old debtor's cell at Mundsen Keep.

He drank his own beef tea, the closest he'd get to meat this week, and didn't cringe when Bland's shark-smile was turned back on him.

It was too easy to think that, with a new production in rehearsal, he had better things to do than debate Clause 17. Actually, this little chat with the Temple Father was the most important meeting he had had all year. If he didn't play this scene as masterfully as any he'd ever enacted, there wouldn't be a new production and, in all probability, wouldn't even be a theatre.

He was holding back mention of the fact that he had once saved the Empire.

That and half-a-pfennig was enough to get buy a bun from Elsie's tray these days.

Understandably, Karl-Franz chose not to patronise the theatre. The last time the Emperor showed up for a Detlef Sierck premiere, the traitor Oswald had tried to kill him and the Great Enchanter Drachenfels nearly came back from the dead to take over the Known World – which at least pre-vented him from falling asleep in his chair and having to rely on an advisor to tell him how much he liked the show. But his son Prince Luitpold, the eager teenager of the old days grown into a straight young blade, had never missed a Vargr Breughel opening (or closing). According to the scurrilous newsheet *Boulevardpresse*, the heir presumptive had the largest private collection of immodest paintings of the company's leading lady, Eva Savinien, in the city. There were flower-growing smallholders in far-off Upper Gris Mere whose entire business depended on the prince's habit of sending Eva a dozen bouquets of rare blooms every night she appeared on the stage. However, this morning the palace had returned the complimentary tickets to the Imperial box with a curt note from a steward stating that Prince Luitpold would be unavoidably detained on the night the theatre was holding the gala debut of Detlef's new play, *Genevieve and Vukotich; or: A Celestial Plot in Zhufbar*. This afternoon, messengers from all over the city – all over the Empire, it seems – returned half a house's worth of invitations. Most of them couldn't even be bothered to think up a half-decent prior engagement.

The current situation didn't make it advisable to support *Genevieve and Vukotich*.

'The cultural industry has a vital – indeed, crucial – part to play in maintaining the moral health of the Empire, Detlef,' purred Bland. 'Look to the Imperial Tarradasch Players and *Death to the Dead!* Educational and instructive stuff. And a sound investment. Folk too often forget the Undead Wars, you know. I'm insisting that they be in the core curriculum of all schools of history. And what of those mummers who put on Wilhelm Konig's verse drama *Vampireslayer* for the children? Could that fine work not be adapted for the legitimate stage? You would be perfectly – indeed, superbly – cast as stouthearted Gotrek, scourge of the undead.'

Gotrek was a dwarf! Detlef didn't play parts which required him to wear boots on his knees.

'There are so many fine subjects. The evil of the Vlad von Carstein and his whole rotten dynasty. The depredations of Bloody Kattarin. The murders of the vampire Wietzak. With so much wonderful – indeed, inspirational – material to choose from, I can't quite see your problem. Why do you have to bring up this Zhufbar business?'

'It happened, Temple Father.'

'Many things happened. That doesn't mean they should be raked up on stage at every opportunity. With so much wholesome – indeed, life-enhancing – matter to write about, why must you dwell on the undead? On the filthy, stinking, bloodlusting, crawled-up-from-the-unhallowed-grave monsters who so threaten the fabric of our unparalleled Imperial society? Of course that's only my opinion. You are free to hold another. This city isn't ruled by a tyrannical absolutist like Kattarin the Great. She used to kill poets, you know. Slowly. If you wrote something she didn't like, you wouldn't be reasoned with. Indeed, you'd be exsanguinated and tossed to the wolves.'

'Genevieve isn't Kattarin.'

'They are sisters, though. Sisters-in-darkness. Who's to know when the smile will turn pointy?'

Temple Father Bland was potty about vampires.

Detlef had assumed his entire family was killed in an undead clan raid, but it wasn't so simple. Though no vampire had ever actually done anything to hurt Bland, the very idea of them crawled under his skin and festered. Most people didn't feel anything either way about leeches. If something was tearing open their necks, they were agin; if something was saving the Emperor from Drachenfels, they were for. Otherwise, live and let live – or unlive, or whatever. There were orc hordes and daemons to worry about, so what was a little nip here and there? And, really, weren't most vampires just human beings with longer lives and differing dietary habits? To Detlef's mind, actresses were a lot creepier – you never knew what they were thinking or whose throat they'd go for next. And all the worst villains Detlef had met were full humans, even counting drama critics.

But Bland was a fanatic on the subject and there was no talking to him about it.

If he were just a ranter, no one would have noticed, but the cleric was far cannier than that. He had bided his time, smiling and working energetically, climbing his way up within the Cult of Morr, god of the dead. Now, he was the youngest Temple Father anyone could remember. Detlef, at forty-five, had a good half decade on Tio Bland. The only lines on the cleric's face were the stretches around his perpetual smile.

Traditionally, the Cult of Morr wasn't even one of the major faiths; it was chiefly concerned with burial rites and grounds and respect for those who had the decency to lie down when they died. But in the last ten years, a succession of scandals had rocked the traditional allies of Imperial power. The rot had started with Oswald von Konigswald – if you couldn't trust an elector not to conspire with ancient evil, anyone was liable to turn out to be crooked as a corkscrew.

As demonstrated by the satirical revues Detlef mounted late at night after the main show to bring in the inky student and grumbling would-be revolutionist audience, holders of high office could no longer automatically expect undiluted respect. With the likes of Temple Father Mikael Hasselstein of the Cult of Sigmar, Graf Rudiger von Unheimlich of the League of Karl-Franz or one-thumbed chancellor Mornan Tybalt – rogues and schemers, all – retired, dead or out of favour, even minor court players saw their chances to make moves.

Bland's opportunity came with a minor septicaemic plague scare. With bodies lying where they fell and watchmen and the militia terrified to touch them, the Cult of Morr stepped forward and offered to take over the collection and disposal of the dead. It was no more than a traditional sacred duty. Bland, then in his first months of office, worked so tirelessly, personally supervising the corpse-harvest, and the outbreak was quelled before it could fully blossom. A few tiresome relatives complained of undue haste in hefting departed uncles into the cremation pits, but that was a small price to pay.

Then, somehow, the cult's remit in dealing with bodies had expanded. In the satirical revue *Altdorf After Dark*, Detlef had pinned his face into an approximation of the Bland smile and played the part of 'Antoninius Blamed' and

explained reasonably – indeed, sincerely – that the clerics of
Morr correctly judged that everyone walking round was a
potential body. Thus, the cult felt they more or less had the
right – indeed, responsibility – to bury or burn people on
the assumption that they'd become corpses eventually. It
was as well to get the funerary arrangements over with while
the pre-deceased could still appreciate them.

Bland made a point of seeing the show and laughing very
loudly.

He wasn't laughing now. Up close, Detlef realised Bland
didn't even smile properly. It was only his lips and teeth. His
eyes were frozen and scary, never blinking, all pupil.

'Maybe you're too close to the subject matter, Detlef…'

Detlef bristled. He knew where this was leading.

'You draw too much from one person's account of the
kerfuffle in Zhufbar all those years ago. Current – indeed,
dominant – thought holds that the situation was by no
means as clear-cut as interested parties have made out.
History may look more kindly on Claes Glinka's well-
intentioned moral crusade than you do in your work…'

Detlef did not know how Bland had got hold of a manuscript copy of his as-yet unperformed play. When he found
out, someone was going to be fired, without references but
with bruises.

'Who knows, maybe Wladislaw Blasko may emerge in the
corrected historical accounts as a much-maligned figure? As
an artist – indeed, as an honest recorder – can you afford to
stake your reputation on the word of… of a dead-alive thing
in woman-shape, a bloodlusting nosferatu who'd drink the
world if we let her. Indeed, a bitch vampire!'

'Hold it there, Bland,' said Detlef, making fists under his
desk. 'You're talking about the woman I love.'

Bland sniffed. 'There are laws against interfering with
corpses,' he said, darkly.

'There are many laws.'

Bland had bored everyone he spoke to on the subject of
vampires for years, but learned his lesson. His Sanitation
Bill had not, on the face of it, seemed to have anything to
do with his hobby-horse. The Cult of Morr, after the plague

crisis, formed a commission with city-planners, watch commanders and officials of the court, then drafted a program of suggestions to prevent further outbreaks. It seemed like a good idea. Detlef himself signed a petition asking that the findings of the report be ratified as the law of the city. The Emperor graciously acceded, extending the shield of the Sanitation Bill to all the Empire. Into the bill, Bland had smuggled the legal grounds for his personal crusade, Clause 17: 'Any body unclaimed by a family member within three days of death is to be turned over to the Cult of Morr for burial or burning.' The dead should be ashes or under the ground and that was the end of it.

Of course, the sting came in the definition of 'dead'.

'Temple Father, how's this for a compromise? I shall retitle the work *Vukotich and Genevieve.*'

Bland's smile stretched still further as, behind his eyes, he thought it through. It took long seconds for the pfennig to drop. He rumbled that he was being spoofed again. His eyebrows pointed up in the middle and honest-to-Verena moist droplets started from his knotty pink tear-ducts.

'I'm going out of my way to accommodate you, Detlef, with regards to your status as a pre-eminent – indeed, paramount – artist of the Empire. I know how many crowns the theatre contributes to the city treasury. It wounds me that you should treat this business with such undue levity. If you only knew the work – indeed, thought – that has gone into all this. I've carted plague-ridden corpses to the burning-pits when everyone else has fled, Detlef. My dear wife and three lovely children begged me – indeed, pleaded heart-rendingly – to stay home safe from infection, but I saw my duty and shrank not from it. I was willing to get my hands dirty to do the right thing. Can you say the same?'

Now might be the time to mention saving the Empire.

Bland stood up. The silver sword he wore over his robes got caught up in the trailing hem. He affected a bandolier of wooden knives and squeeze-bulbs of garlic (one of which was leaking). As far as Detlef knew, Bland had never slain so much as a tick. It was possible that he had never actually been in a room with a vampire – the undead weren't that common in Altdorf.

Not for the first time, Detlef wondered what was eating the Temple Father.

Poppa Fritz, eternally-aged stage-manager and general factotum of the Vargr Breughel, popped into the office just in time to show Bland the way to the street, where a couple of pike-toting clerics awaited their master. From the window, Detlef saw the Temple Father shake hands with various members of the crowd of permanent protest, hugging old ladies and kissing held-up babies, before heading for his black hearse-like carriage. As Bland passed, the scowling crowd cheered up momentarily. When he was gone, they went back to their dignified 'Death to the Dead' chants and harassment of anyone coming and going.

Detlef's back hurt from sitting and listening to rot for so long. He could have demolished a seven-course meal, but was on one of his periodic beef-tea diets, to get his weight down so he could offer a reasonable simulation of the lean, hard 'Iron Man' Vukotich opposite Eva Savinien's lithe impersonation of She-Who-Must-Not-Be-Mentioned-Except-on-Stage.

It was a long time since maidens collected portraits of Detlef Sierck. The drama critic of the Altdorf *Spieler* had pointed out that in his last two productions, Detlef had taken the roles of kings, Magnus the Pious and Boris the Incompetent, and had managed to get through the runs of both plays without getting off his throne except to make a curtain speech or fall down dead. Detlef considered challenging the upstart scribbler to a duel, but realised it was true – which was why *Genevieve and Vukotich* was full of fight scenes, active lovemaking, general dashing about and hanging from the rafters. He was spending his mornings at the Temple Street gymnasium where Arne the Body was either trying to get him in shape or murder him in the most humiliating manner imaginable. Strangely, all the theatre cats seemed to have gone on a diet too – Poppa Fritz reported that they were losing weight mysteriously, one more thing to worry about.

Maybe Bland had something. It was nearly ten years since Genevieve had left the city. Time to let the memory go.

His neck-bites, long-healed and invisible to everyone else, itched.

Would it be easier if he knew she was dead? Bland's Clause 17 could scoop her up as easily as any other poor leech. No, she'd survived this long. She'd outlive the persecutions, outlive Detlef.

There was a smell in the office. Not garlic.

A tapping came.

The Vargr Breughel was shot through with secret passageways, sliding panels and hidden hollows. The theatre had once been haunted by the creature they had called the Trapdoor Daemon, who moved behind the walls and spied through one-way dressing room mirrors. That was also a painful memory, yet another Genevieve anecdote saved for a later play – one with a last act he still didn't feel ready to write. Besides, audiences didn't like it when the girl left the boy at the end. *Downbeat* closed on the second week of previews. Bruno Malvoisin, the Trapdoor Daemon, had been a shapeless squid-human mutant hidden under a huge cloak and hat – a role Detlef could play without fasting or exercise.

Detlef went to the case where bound folios of his scripts were kept. The tapping came from behind it. And the smell.

Water was seeping under the panel. Had the Trapdoor Daemon returned? Surely, poor Malvoisin was dead.

Trembling, Detlef tripped the hidden catch. A small creature, hair in wet rat-tails, filth all over her, tumbled out.

Instantly recognisable green eyes opened in her mask of dirt.

'You came back,' he said.

Not one of his better speeches.

'I had to,' Genevieve replied.

Detlef had a moment of might-have-been panic. If she'd tapped only a few minutes earlier, she would have come out of the wall while the Empire's premier vampire-hater was in the room, with expert pikemen within his call and a beltful of sharpened stakes. He swore he'd have fought for her, but the outcome would not have been in doubt.

Under the ground or in ashes.

Genevieve wiped off her face with a muddy sleeve. She still looked like a lass of sixteen summers.

She touched him. His knees wouldn't support him.

They held each other.

III

THE OFFICE WAS the same, but Detlef looked older. Not just bigger, but softer, greyer. However, the fire in him was the same. Genius still flickered like a half-crazy light behind his eyes. She had not expected her thirst for him to rush back in such a flood, as if she'd tasted his blood last night, not ten years ago.

The room smelled of blood. And of her.

She'd been in the tunnels under the Vargr Breughel Memorial Playhouse before, but never had to swim out of a filth-clogged bronze empress and wade through the vile main sewers of Altdorf to make her entrance. She was a stinking ruin.

Detlef took a speaking-tube from a hook and whistled into it.

'Poppa Fritz…'

'Is Poppa Fritz still here? Still alive? He must be older than I am. It's wonderful that someone else doesn't change.'

Detlef waved her quiet.

'Poppa, I've, um, spilled something all over myself… Yes, yes, I should try to keep my temper, but you know Tio Bland… Could you send up Renastic with a tub of warm water and some soap? And towels.'

Genevieve stood in the middle of the room, trying not to drip on anything precious. The hideous embroidered elf carpet, which Detlef had said would be the first thing to go when he took over the theatre, was still here.

'You get used to it,' Detlef said to her, hand briefly over the tube. 'It's not so bad.'

He still had the trick of reading her oddest thoughts.

'Just coughing, Poppa… Oh, and could you get Elsie to look in Kerreth's workshop and fetch the Genevieve costumes, if they're finished.'

'Genevieve costumes?'

He waved her quiet again.

'Splendid... No, there's no rush. Thanks, Poppa.'

Detlef hung up the hook.

'The one thing you could say that would make him suspicious, darling, was "there's no rush". With you, with this place, there's always a rush.'

'I suppose you're right. I wasn't thinking.'

Detlef was overwhelmed and not just by the sewer smell. She should have expected that. He had smears on his face and chest from hugging her. He wore a big, unbelted smock and even that was over-filled.

'You haven't changed,' he said. 'You could be my granddaughter.'

'You haven't changed either. Not where it counts.'

He shrugged sadly, not believing her. She took his hands and gripped.

'Your eyes are the same.'

'I need lenses to con my own scripts.'

'That's not what I mean.'

The taste of blood was in the air. Her tongue slithered over the razor-points of her teeth.

On the desk stood a big pot of beef tea. Her eyes darted to it.

'You haven't... eaten?' he ventured.

She shook her head. He let her hands go and picked up the pot.

'Do you mind using my goblet? I can get a fresh one if you'd rather?'

She took the pot from him and tipped the spout to her mouth. She opened wide and poured. It took half a minute to drain the tea. She set it down and wiped her lips on the back of her hand.

'Better?'

'Takes the edge off,' she said. 'It's not blood, but what is?'

His hands crept up, involuntarily, to his collar, as if the room were too hot and he was buttoned up too tight.

She'd drunk a lot of blood, in passion and anger, since she was last here, but she'd never let herself be touched by the living men and women whose veins she tapped. She had known friends, victims, hosts, servants, pick-ups, enemies, meals, sacrifices. While he lived, Detlef was her only lover.

But she could not ask him to let her batten on him.

It would not be fair to bleed him and leave.

'I've missed you,' she admitted.

He sighed, in agony. 'I've not missed you, Gené. Because in my mind you were never gone.'

She noticed a playscript on the desk and picked it up.

'*Genevieve and Vukotich*. What can this be about?'

She flipped over the pages. She remembered telling Detlef about the bad business in Zhufbar, when she had been shackled to the mercenary Vukotich and nagged him into thwarting a scheme of the Chaos champions Dien Ch'ing and Yevgeny Yefimovich. When sharing with him the whole story, tactfully omitting full details of a bedroom scene she realised was represented with uncanny accuracy in this playscript, she had realised that in the middle of it came their first meeting, when he was just a little boy and she a runaway from Claes Glinka's moral crusade.

'It's a good story,' he said, a little sheepish. 'It'll be very popular. I wonder how that warm water's coming.'

She looked at more scenes. She wondered how Detlef intended to pull off the confrontation with the five Celestial elementals. He usually resisted big special effects, claiming the most important magic in the theatre was in the verse and the acting and that giant gasp-inducing daemon apparitions transformations were just a sideshow. If audiences left the play talking about the monsters, then they had been distracted from the true import of the drama.

It occurred to her that a play with a vampire heroine might not be kindly met in this season of Clause 17.

'Detlef,' she said, 'you're too brave. This could be the ruin of you, but it's so sweet. Though I feel your "Genevieve" is a little nicer than the original. Back then, I was basically earning a living as a dancing slut, remember? You shouldn't make me out to be some priestess of Shallya.'

'It's just an entertainment.'

'You don't write anything that's "just an entertainment"'.'

'How would you know? You've missed ten years. I've downslid. I do jokes and murdered kings and write myself parts which involve a great deal of sitting down. It's a while since I did anything really fine. You can't be a child prodigy at my age. A lot of things I've not even been able to finish.'

He was acting, out of habit.

'Rot and rubbish, Detlef. I've not been here to see you act, but I can still read. Your folios are available even in the savage outlands where I've spent most of my time.'

'Pirated editions from which I've not seen a pfennig.'

'And there are the sonnets.'

He blushed red. All his poems were about her.

'You've read them?'

'Not all the run of *To My Unchanging Lady* were destroyed. Students pass copies around, some hand-written and bound inside misleading boards to throw off the book-burners. Do you know how much you have to pay to get hold of a suppressed work?'

'Yes. I bribe the provincial censors to ban my best material so I can charge outrageously. Makes up for what I lose on those damned unauthorised folios. Being illegal is always good for cash businesses. Weirdroot tubers cost a lot more than potatoes.'

She giggled and he laughed.

'This is somewhere between uncomfortable and wonderful,' he said.

'Wasn't it always?'

Poppa Fritz came upstairs with Renastic, a new scene-shifter Detlef claimed was surprisingly strong for one so thin and sallow-looking, carrying a hip-bath full of warm water between them. Detlef had her hide behind the door. She was sorry for the deception: she liked Poppa Fritz and looked forward to cuddling with the old man. But Detlef was right: it wouldn't do just yet to let too many people know the vampire Genevieve was back in town. Renastic, a Sylvanian with a widow's peak, had potent breath and she was surprised to recognise him. She knew she would have to pass on the odd little scene she had witnessed from the secret passageway.

Stripped of her vile clothes, she slid luxuriously into the water, sighing with pleasure. In an ever-changing world, some delights were eternal – like a warm bath after a long dirty spell.

'One thing about that Renastic fellow,' she said. 'He has an odd little friend.'

'What do you mean?'

'As I was making my way through the old Trapdoor Daemon tunnels, I saw through one of the mirrors into a dressing room. There was only one candle lit, so it was dark, and the mirror is almost entirely crusted over with muck so I couldn't make much out. But your friend Renastic was there, in full evening dress with black cloak and all, dandling something on his lap that I couldn't quite see. Someone, rather. Someone child- or goblin-sized. Not a child, though. And not a goblin either, I think. He was playing with it, like a pet or a familiar. But the talk was heated. They were having quite a lively discussion, an argument.'

'I've no idea who this small person might be.'

'I had one of my weird feelings about him. Like there was no one there, at least no one with a soul. There was a certain amount of "yes, master"-ing. They were talking about someone or something called "Gottle".'

'Sounds dwarfish.'

'That's what I thought. "Gottle of Glood". I heard another name, one which doesn't have very pleasant associations: "Vlad".'

'So Alvdnov's little friend is named after Vlad von Carstein? No wonder he doesn't show his face much. He isn't liable to be very popular in the current climate.'

'"Alvdnov Renastic"? There's something strange going on there.'

'There's something strange going on everywhere. Tell me something I don't know, Gené.'

'That'll have to wait until after I'm clean.'

She sank under the water, letting it close over her face. Her knees rose from the seas like mythical islands, her hair floated like catchweed and trapped the toy ships Poppa Fritz had put into the bath.

IV

THE CORPSE WITH the gaping hole under his chin lay face-up in the gutter of the Street of a Hundred Taverns, ringed by clerics and coppers.

'His worries are over,' said Johannes Munch. 'This could have waited.'

Bland turned furiously on the watchman, struck speechless by such rank stupidity. Surely the Sergeant with Special Responsibility for Unlawful Killing must heed the undead menace. With each passing minute, the dead man became more dangerous.

'I think, sergeant,' interpreted Liesel von Sutin, Bland's scribe-proclaimer, 'that the Temple Father feels it is exactly that unhelpful attitude which has brought us to this dreadful pass.'

Munch looked wearily at Bland and Liesel.

'I lament for the old days, when the clerics of Morr stood decently back and let a copper do his job, then quietly came in and dragged the stiff off to the Temple for disposal.'

Bland wondered if there was anything suspect about the reddish glint in the sergeant's eyes. It mightn't just be a devotion to cheap Estalian wine. A question would have to be asked about Sergeant Johannes Munch.

A Clause 17 sympathiser in the Old Town Watch had sent a runner to the Temple of Morr with word of the suspect slaying. Bland had known straight away that this marked the start in earnest of the campaign. Everything else had just been preliminary. With a quivering sense of purpose, Bland had rallied his core team – Liesel, undeadslayers Preiss and Bruin – and held a brief prayer circle, then hastened over to the site of the homicide. The Temple Father had taken resolute charge of the situation, ordering Dibble, the cloddish watchman who had first tripped over the dead man, to fetch the Sergeant with Special Responsibility. The pockmarked Munch was initially hard to locate because he was 'at choir practice' – an accepted euphemism for getting blind drunk while telling lies about old cases down at The Blue Lantern, the coppers' tavern.

Munch didn't seem to feel this particular man-slaying worth interrupting a good Filthy Harald anecdote over. Bland, expecting as much, had gone over the watchman's head and summoned a specialist from private practice. Her carriage had just arrived and she was crossing the street.

'Now we shall see some progress,' Bland announced.

Rosanna Ophuls, scryer-for-hire, slid between Munch and Liesel, then took a casual glance at the dead man.

'Throat torn out with a docker's hook,' she said. 'Gang killing. Fifteen crowns please, Temple Father.'

Bland knew Ophuls was wrong.

This was the Street of a Hundred Taverns. And among those hundred was the Crescent Moon, notorious haunt of the vermin undead. It was a problem to determine exactly where the establishment was, though Bland didn't believe the rumours that the Crescent Moon shifted its physical building nightly. Just as soon as the place hung up a sign visible to proper human eyes, he would have the damned haunt of noxious evil closed down and put to the torch.

If you let the leeches run loose, this was what happened.

The dead man's wound was ragged and dry, black rather than red. His eyes were open, frozen in terror.

The scryer stood with her arms folded, tapping her foot. Bland judged her for an irritating person, a woman who would never show the commitment necessary for the campaign. It was time for another proclamation from the Cult of Morr, against the 'nay-saying ninnies' who heeded not 'the dangers of the dark'. He made a mental note to have Liesel work something up. With the campaign in full boom, the cult's scribe-proclaimer was busier and busier.

'With respect to your professional abilities, Miss Ophuls, might not a second glance – indeed, a proper scrying – reveal that this is merely *supposed* to look like a gang killing?'

The woman looked down at the dead person.

'Surely, the bloodlusting fiend, consumed by the madness of his or her red thirst, fell on this poor – indeed, innocent

– soul and drained him dry, then used a hook or some other such implement to cover up the crime, to cast suspicion elsewhere.'

Ophuls wasn't convinced. She was not doing the job she expected to be paid for.

'You haven't even touched him,' Bland said.

'She doesn't really need to, Temple Father,' said Munch. 'That "poor – indeed, innocent – soul" is Ibrahim Fleuchtweig, war chief of the Fish. Last week, three Hooks were trussed up and thrown in the Reik. On his orders. This is an escalation of the feud. If a Fish is hooked, or a Hook drowned, it doesn't take a divining witch – no offence, Rosie – to tell you who's responsible.'

'The sergeant is right, sir,' said Dibble. 'We all know Ibby the Fish in the Tavern Watch. A warrant was out for him in connection with the murders of Nosy the Cripple, Josten the Grabber and Dirk the Dirk.'

'Don't think I'm convinced by all these ridiculous names,' said Bland. 'You make them up to suggest your squalid calling is glamorous.'

Ophuls shrugged and made a *pfui* sound.

'You're being paid – indeed, well-paid – to do a job,' Bland insisted. 'Now get down in the gutter and scry.'

She looked at Bland as if she were exceeding her brief and trying to divine something about *him*. Then, she made a decision.

'Very well. Stand back, lads. I don't want your sins crowding in.'

Everyone except Bland moved away sharply, giving Ophuls a clear circle around the dead man to work in.

'You too, Temple Father.'

He naturally hadn't assumed she included him.

Arranging a muffler on the cobbles so she could kneel, Ophuls took off her mittens and rubbed her hands together.

'Cold night,' she said. 'Have to get some feeling in.'

She flexed her fingers and waved her hands hocus-pocus fashion over the corpse. She touched him, patting his jacket first and working towards the mess around his neck. Closing her eyes, she put her hands on the wound.

Bland's skin crawled. There was something not human about scryers.

The undead had a knack for *knowing*, too. This woman might not drink blood, but she'd bear watching. Better to be safe than sorry, and one could always apologise afterwards.

'I sense a lot of drinking.'

Munch snickered. Bland gave him a nasty look that shut him up. There was no room for levity when a vampire attack was being detected.

'A *lot* of drinking. Bugman's Six-X. Enough to float a riverbarge and addle a thaumaturgy professor. An enormously full bladder. A stagger into the alleyway behind Bruno's Brewhouse. A flash in the dark. Something sharp?'

'Fangs?'

She shook her head and let the corpse alone. 'A docker's hook, as used by the Hooks, the dockyard gang notoriously at war with the Fish, the dockyard gang to which the deceased was affiliated.'

He didn't like her tone of voice. She was pulling her mittens back on.

'You can't be certain.'

'No one can be *certain*, Temple Father, but you hired a scryer so you could get closer to certain than you were. You have had my professional opinion. If you want some free advice on top of that, you should take my word as being as near certain as you're likely to get.'

'Why is the corpse so pale? Indeed, bloodless?'

She looked up at the moons and down at the dead face. For a moment she was quiet, seeing something.

'This is the way the dead look,' she said, closing the corpse's eyes with her fingertips. 'Empty and abandoned.'

'At the Temple of Morr, we are quite familiar with the dead,' said Liesel. 'It is our duty to reverence the broken vessel to ease the path of the departing spirit. And to dispose of the vessel lest it be refilled by something unholy and unclean.'

Ophuls stood up and wrapped her muffler around her neck.

'If that's settled, Temple Father,' said Munch, 'you can do the job you're supposed to and cart Ibby away now. His gang-buddies have already forgotten him and won't claim the body, so it's up to you to get it off the cobbles.'

Thanks to the Sanitation Bill, the temple had to be alerted about any sudden death. Bland had been keeping an eye out for suspect reports like this one. He knew how the body should be served.

Bland wasn't ready to let go yet.

'What did you see?' he asked Ophuls.

'I beg your pardon, Temple Father?'

'Just then. You scried something.'

'Nothing important. Just the scrap of a life. It's odd what people think about when they're dying.'

'Their families?'

Bland thought of his dear wife and three lovely children.

'Sometimes. Mostly it's stuff you can't understand. Personal things they couldn't explain even if you could ask them. And sometimes it's random, as if they wanted to be distracted from the business of dying. Ibby thought it had turned cold all of a sudden. How's that for a way to spend your final seconds? Grumbling about the weather?'

Bland shook his head and raised a finger. 'You scry but you don't *see*. Think on what she said the dead man thought. "It had turned cold *all of a sudden*." Unnatural cold. They travel about inside their own evil clouds sometimes. They can become black fog or white mist and creep up on their victims. The undead. This proves – indeed, conclusively proves – what I've been saying all along. This was a vampire killing.'

Ophuls began to say something, but he continued, silencing her.

'They've been biding their time, waiting for a chance to strike at me. Ever since I showed my colours. They know I'm their enemy – indeed, their destroyer. This is the beginning of a war, a war between the living and the dead. It's the von Carstein days all over again. You'll all have to decide which side you're on and Morr help you if you go against the live and holy.'

Dibble scratched his head under his helmet.

Ophuls was frightened now, shrinking away from him. Good. What did she see? That he was right, of course.

'The dead are dangerous. The Cult of Morr will take over now. Preiss, you know the procedure.'

The tall cleric muscled through and stood over the dead man.

'Don't think you'll be rising again to bedevil the living,' vowed Preiss.

The cleric raised his staff and sank the sharpened end into the ribcage. Bland heard the point scrape cobbles. It was important to transfix the dead thing to the ground. Most people got it wrong and thought it was enough to sink a stake into the heart or spear the undead standing up. Impalement was merely a preliminary binding, fixing the monster – potential monster, in this case – to the holy earth. Preiss leant on his staff with all his weight, digging between the cobbles. It wasn't easy, which is why the cult had acolytes like Preiss, a former pupil of Hagedorn the wrestler, on hand.

'That's disgusting,' whined Munch.

'Disgusting,' snapped Bland. 'I'll tell you what's disgusting. A grave-rotted thirsty monster glutting itself fat on the blood of your lovely children or dear old grandma. That's what's disgusting.'

'Leave it alone,' said Ophuls, quietly.

'Not until the job's done.'

'But it's an old wives' tale that all those killed by vampires rise as vampires themselves. Sire vampires turn their get by the Dark Kiss. That means they give their own altered blood to favoured victims as they drink from them.'

'So you admit that this was a vampire killing?'

Ophuls threw her hands up.

'You can go now,' said Bland. 'Your part in this is over.'

Liesel took Ophuls by the elbow and steered her away. 'Present your chit at the Temple of Morr after one o'clock tomorrow,' said the scribe-proclaimer, 'and your price will be met in full, less Imperial tax.'

Preiss had Ibrahim Fleuchtweig fully skewered. He gave the nod to Braun, who came in with his silver-bladed axe and hacked off the corpse's head. It took a few blows and some sawing.

'You might have ruined a good evening's wine-bibbing,' said Munch, 'but I can't complain that the clerics of Morr don't lay on any entertainment. Ibby has been more thoroughly killed than any other corpse I've seen this month.'

'It's not done yet,' Liesel told him. 'The Temple Father must perform a final rite.'

Bland pulled on thick leather gauntlets. He picked up the startled-looking head, then stuffed its mouth with garlic taken from a pouch on his belt.

'Unclean undead spirit, I cast thee out.'

Liesel made a lightning sketch, preserving the moment of triumph.

'Could you hold the head up higher, Temple Father? Get the light from the streetlamp. And could Brother Preiss step out of the way? There, that's perfect.'

By tomorrow, Liesel's sketch would be copied and posted all over the city. Woodcuts would be sent to all the broadsheets, and this time they would have to run the pictures. Until now, the campaign had consisted only of speeches and dull legal matters. This was news, and news was what the vulgar masses craved above all else.

Everyone in the Empire would soon know that Antiochus Bland had personally prevented Ibrahim Fleuchtweig's rising from the dead as an unhallowed thing intent upon stalking the innocent. The Temple Father didn't care a jot for the glory of the deed, but he knew every holy campaign needed its leaders, its heroes. The people needed his example.

When Liesel was done, he dropped the head and left final disposal – hauling the thing away in the cart and its immolation in the eternally-burning corpse fires of the temple – to Preiss and Braun.

'That's another leech up the chimney, Temple Father,' said Liesel.

Bland was proud of himself, proud of his cult, proud of his purpose.

* * *

V

NOW SHE WAS cleaned up and dressed, Detlef thought the
vampire looked even younger. Eva Savinien was tall: her
'Genevieve' costume made the real woman seem like Little
Orphan Elsie dressed in a grown-up's gown. Genevieve
fussed with the belt and raised the hemline above her
ankles.

'That's better,' she said. 'Now I don't have to wade.'

Detlef knew he was scratching his bites.

The fact that Genevieve was back was enormous. It could
change anything, or mean nothing. He was tantalised,
which was doubtless the point. In vampire terms, a ten-
year absence might be the equivalent of him nipping out
for a pouch of ready-rubbed from the tobacco merchant on
Luitpoldstrasse and dawdling a bit in a café on the way
back. Genevieve might move back in here for good and
give in and marry him, but she might also disappear before
the 'platz clock struck midnight and never think of him
again.

That wasn't fair. She thought of him, obviously.

She was here.

She moved swiftly about the room, doing that vampire act
of shifting at speed between languid poses so that she
seemed to vanish and appear all over the place. It was a
habit of hers when she was excited. Or just-fed. She kept asking questions about mutual friends and acquaintances.

'And young Prince Luitpold, how is he?'

'Otherwise engaged for our first night, it seems. Tio Bland
is listened to at the palace.'

'That's their loss. I'd thought better of the boy.'

'Not a boy any more. He looks like a juvenile lead.'

'I hope they let him have some fun before marrying him
off to Clothilde of Averheim.'

'He's rather taken with Eva.'

Genevieve laughed, like music. Detlef recalled she had
never warmed to Eva Savinien. It was understandable: while
possessed by something left behind by the Great Enchanter,
Eva had tried to kill them both.

'Eva plays me, I gather.'

'She's very good. Got over that whole brouhaha with the animus and the Trapdoor Daemon. She's undoubtedly the best you since, well, since you.'

'I am retired from the stage. I had a very limited range. I could only play myself.'

'That's the story with half the great stars of the theatre.'

She settled in the chair that had been warmed by Temple Father Bland.

Reality crept back. He had been dazzled a while by the delight of having her here. Now he remembered the danger.

'Gené, you know it's not safe in the city for, ah, people like you.'

'Bretonnian girls? That's not news. Our governesses tell us from infancy about the perils awaiting in Altdorf for innocent mademoiselles fresh off the barge.'

'Vampires, Gené. This Clause 17 business...'

'Whose bloody silly idea was that? I tell you, if I'd signed a petition in favour of it I'd be utterly ashamed and prostrate with apology.'

She peeped out at him from under a curtain of drying hair.

'You're teasing.'

'You're scowling. Wind'll change and your face'll set.'

'Not my face. I'm a master of disguise. You're the one who can't change her looks.'

She made a vampire mask, flared eyebrows and fangs.

'See, I'm a monster. Fit only to be ashes or under the ground.'

Then she poked her tongue out.

'You could have stayed in the forests, or gone back to that convent at the other end of the world. All this would have passed and you'd be safe again.'

Suddenly, she was serious.

'Detlef, I've had enough of hiding, of being safe. What if Glinka's moral crusade came back and all theatrical performances were prohibited? Do you think you'd be happy in a monastery waiting for it to pass? You know you'd organise plays in the back-rooms of inns and woodland clearings and anywhere you could gather an audience. If they sent you to

the headsman for being an actor, you'd deliver a soliloquy
from the block and wouldn't shut up for a full fifteen minutes after the axe had fallen. It's like that with me. I can't
pretend I'm what I'm not.'

'You weren't always a vampire.'

'Like you weren't always an actor. I was a child once. Most
of us were. Now I'm… well… I'm…'

'Genevieve Sandrine de Pointe du Lac Dieudonné.'

'You remember all of it. Darling, you're the only one who
does.'

She was over the desk and in his lap. His mouth was on
hers, carefully. He remembered how to kiss her without getting cut open.

'You're still thirsty,' he whispered, 'not for beef tea.'

'I can't ask you for that,' she said, suddenly sounding old.

'You can't ask me to let you starve.'

Her forehead wrinkled as he pulled his collar away from
his neck.

'Gené, bite me. You won't really have come back until you
do.'

She pulled away from him, wiped her hair out of her face
and looked close into his eyes, running her fingernails across
the furrows around his temples and into his hair. Her face
was in shadow, but her eyes shone green as the southern sea.

'You haven't changed,' she said.

She pounced like a cat and her teeth slipped into his neck.

He held her tight as his blood pulsed into her mouth, feeling her ribs with his elbows, his hands knotted in her hair.

He told her he loved her. She murmured and he knew
what she meant.

VI

DETLEF'S OFFICE WASN'T a boudoir. Genevieve knew he
wouldn't have a divan in there, he was fed up with jokes
about eager young actresses and the casting couch. They
would have to make do with his padded chair and the
broad top of the desk.

Without detaching her mouth from his rich throat, she
slid out of her loose dress and helped him with his clothes.

There was more of him than she remembered, and he complained about his back when she dragged him out of the chair, but nothing had changed between them.

She couldn't keep her hands off him, though she had to be careful about her talons. It was too easy to get carried away.

'This is the second most impressive organ of maleness I've got a hold on this evening,' she said.

He looked at her oddly.

'Wrong time for that story,' she admitted.

'You can't expect me to let it lie at a time like this,' he said. 'Look at it from my position.'

'I'm not naked flat on my back on a desk with a vampire nuzzling my throat.'

Surprisingly, with the agility of his old stage heroes, Detlef heaved her off him and reversed their positions, pinning her like a wrestler. He carefully lowered himself onto her and started tickling the hollow of her own throat with his beard.

'This torture continues until you talk, vampire wench.'

She laughed and gave in. 'I had to climb the statue of Sigmar in the 'platz.'

'Oh no, not the one with the enormous–'

'Oh yes. That one.'

'Holy hammer of Sigmar!'

'Absolutely.'

Then, with an ease that comes from practice, his own hammer struck her anvil.

With his blood in her, she was stronger, faster, better. But it was his life that infused her, the peppery tang of everything that he was. When younger, he used to introduce himself as 'Detlef Sierck, genius'. Then, it had been a defence against criticism. Now, when he mostly passed himself off as a hack, it was true. She tasted the poetry he hadn't yet written.

Most of the night passed. Detlef dozed between exertions, but she became more awake as moonlight shone in through the office window.

'You've not said why you're here,' he murmured.

'In Altdorf? In the Vargr Breughel?'

'Both. Either.'

'Don't be upset, but I came to see someone who isn't you.'

He was fully awake again. She'd known that would sting. 'There's someone *else?*'

'Not like that. Believe me, there's no one else like you. Strange as it seems, you come along only once in even a life-time like mine. I've come to see another vampire. A very important one.'

'Here?'

He looked around, shivering.

'Uh-huh,' she said. 'Under your own roof, passing for alive.'

'Impossible!'

He got off the desk and began pulling on his trews. She whipped into the dress. Vampire swiftness took the drudgery out of all those dozens of little hooks and buttons. She was dressed before he could get to his smock, and helped him into it like a mother with a baby.

'It's that Sylvanian scene-shifter, isn't it?' blurted Detlef.

'No, no, Renastic isn't the vampire who sent for me.'

They weren't alone in the room. Genevieve wasn't sure when the other had crept in. For modesty's sake, she hoped it had only been within the last few minutes.

'It's about time, granddaughter-in-darkness,' said the high, familiar voice.

Genevieve looked at a shadowed corner and there she was. Her little face was silvered in the moonlight.

'Elsie?' blurted Detlef, aghast. 'Little Orphan Elsie?'

'I'd best make an introduction,' said Genevieve. 'This is the sire of my sire, the Lady Melissa d'Acques. She's an elder, one of the senior vampires of the Known World.'

'You're t-t-twelve,' sputtered Detlef. 'That's what you said. And you lost your parents in a coach accident.'

'I'm well over eleven hundred, actually. And I did lose my parents in a coach accident, only it happened a very long time ago. I've quite got over it. Most important things happened long enough ago for me to get over them. But I'm fed up with all the fetching and carrying you and that goat Fritz have had me do these last weeks, while I was waiting for my dear grand-get to arrive. It's sheer exploitation of child labour, that's what it is.'

Detlef lay back down on the desk and covered his eyes.

'I don't know why he's so upset,' said Lady Melissa. 'I let you love-bats have enough canoodling-time together before pushing in so we can get on with the matter for which I summoned you.'

'I'm dreaming,' he said. 'This isn't happening.'

'Don't mind him,' Genevieve told Lady Melissa. 'He's a genius. You have to make allowances.'

'We didn't have geniuses in my day.'

Detlef groaned.

Genevieve swept the very old lady up in her arms and danced her around the room like a real little girl. Lady Melissa was all right if you could get her to smile and be playful for a while. When she was serious, people tended to die.

'I've missed you too, grand-mama,' she said, kissing Lady Melissa's cold cheek.

VII

'WE MISSED YOU at the last gathering,' the Lady Melissa told her grand-get. 'Elder vampires from all over the Known World were represented at the Convent of Eternal Night and Solace.'

The girl had the decency to look a touch guilty. Her fat human pet was merely puzzled. Melissa knew it was rarely much use explaining anything to shortlivers. In this case, she would probably have to spell it out letter by letter: a day-walking serf was sadly going to be a necessity.

'I was travelling, grand-mama. I didn't receive my invitation until it was too late.'

She knew better than to credit that, but didn't mind.

'I can't blame you, child. There's nothing more *boring* than a gathering of elder vampires. Believe me, I've suffered enough of them in my centuries. All those long grey faces and ragged black cloaks. The stag-at-rut jousts as two old fools get in a squabble about some mortal morsel. You hear the same stories over and over. Mostly, yarns about how we didn't really lose the Undead Wars blah blah blah and are just biding our time before we emerge from our mountain fastnesses and take up rightful positions as rulers of humanity blah blah blah fountains of virgin blood as our right delivered up by the unworthy blah blah blah enough to make you stuff your ears with wax and spend a century sulking in a tomb hoping the prattle will end.'

Sierck was still looking strangely at her. She bugged her eyes out back at him and he flinched.

'Pity the poor little orphan, sirrah,' she said in her squeaky, whiny Elsie voice. All these supposed theatre folk around and no one had seen through her. 'I've had to chase rats, you know. This hasn't been easy for me.'

'I'm terribly sorry, ah, my lady.'

'And well you might be, shortlife. But you're just a blood-cow. You'll be gone in a few years.'

'Grand-mama!' Genevieve was shocked.

'Don't chide your elders, child. It's very unbecoming. I'm sorry to have to hurt your feelings, Herr Genius, but there's no point pretending, is there? Then again, I suppose pretending is what you mostly do. Oh, I can't be bothered with this being-polite-to-the-food business. Genevieve, we'll have to deal with this Tio Bland fellow ourselves. The cattle won't be any help at all. And you never know when they'll turn on you. They're your devoted slaves one moment and chasing you with sharp sticks the next. Did I ever tell you about that witch-hunter in Quenelles in the time of the Red Pox? Of course I did. No need to be kind about it. I tell the same stories too many times, just like all the other cobwebbed elder vampire bores.'

'Is she always like this?' Sierck asked.

Genevieve nodded. 'Isn't she adorable?'

'Less of that cheek, child,' Melissa snapped. 'Where was I? Ah, yes. The gathering. This Clause 17 nonsense was much debated. Elder Honorio is concerned, and you know how unflappable he is. Baron Wietzak of Karak Varn chewed through a stone table. He actually did it. I saw the bite he took out of the thing. Ugly table, actually. dwarf manufacture. Have you noticed how they deliberately make the legs

too short for humans? Just right for me, though. So hard
cheese to their nasty little schemes. I'm babbling, am I not?
That's what comes of being Little Orphan Elsie for weeks
and weeks.'

Sierck's mouth was an O of astonishment.

'I take it back,' said Genevieve. 'She's not usually this bad.'

'I'm not usually trying to save vampirekind from extinc-
tion.'

Melissa sensed a rat behind the books on one of the
shelves, little heart beating at ramming speed, warm blood
pulsing through its thready veins.

'Excuse me,' she said. 'Some of us have to make do.'

She was across the room and back in a beat, having fer-
reted the furry creature out and even rearranged the books
in order. She sensed the animal's panic and looked into its
glittering eyes, ordering its tiny brain to go to sleep and not
mind what was going to happen next.

She popped the rat into her mouth and ate it whole.

Then she dabbed her lips with a kerchief, looking to
Genevieve for approval. Without mirrors, vampires had to
rely on each other when it came to presenting a face to the
human world.

'A scrap on the upper lip.'

Melissa dabbed.

'There,' said Genevieve. 'Got it. You look pretty as a picture
again.'

Genevieve chucked Sierck's chin and finally shut his
mouth.

'The starving cats,' he said. 'You're the reason why they
haven't been eating well.'

'Kitty-kitties are overrated,' she said. 'Your ratters were fat
and lazy. I'll have to start on them once the rats run out. So
be warned. Unless, Herr Kind Genius, you'd care to open a
vein for a poor little orphan without a friend in the world.'

'Now now, grand-mama, none of that.'

Melissa stuck out her lower lip.

'You were talking about saving vampirekind from extinc-
tion.'

'So I was, child. Very conscientious of you to remind me.'

'Who are all these people she's talking about?' asked Sierck. 'It's as if I've come in on the fifth act.'

'I've told you about the Convent of Eternal Night and Solace,' Genevieve told the human. 'The retreat for vampires in the World's Edge Mountains. Elder Honorio is the master there.'

'A very old-womanish sort of master,' sniped Melissa.

'You are hardly one to throw that accusation at anyone.'

'What's a gathering?'

'Just what it sounds like,' Genevieve explained. 'Elder vampires *gathering* together for a set period. It's not that different from the drinking, hunting and yarning festivals the League of Karl-Franz or any other fraternal organisation throws at any opportunity.'

'Drinking and hunting?' Sierck looked stricken.

'You've upset him, child.'

'Shush, grand-mama. Detlef knows what vampires are like. Just because Tio Bland is an idiot doesn't mean that some, and I mean *some*, of us aren't bloodthirsty barbarians. Sadly, Kattarin wasn't that atypical of vampirekind.'

Melissa remembered the tsarina well. She had been fond of bathing in the blood of her courtiers' children. Anyone could see that was excessive and would lead to trouble.

'I told your sire not to make get of that Kislevite princess, child. Kattarin had a daemon in her before she was turned. But would Chandagnac listen? None of you fledgling vampires heeds your sire. That's something I agree with Honorio about. If you had respect for tradition none of this would have happened. Now, about this assassination plot against Tio Bland...'

Sierck gasped again, tiresomely.

'The pair of you are here to assassinate Tio Bland?'

Trust a human to get the wrong end of the stake.

'Merciful Shallya no,' said Melissa. 'We're here to *stop* him being assassinated.'

The rat-tail twisted in her stomach and she burped.

'I do beg your pardon,' she said. The back of her throat clogged and she began to cough. 'It all comes from the wrong diet.'

She hacked and spat a hairball out on the back of her hand. She was ready to scrape it off on the wall, but Genevieve hemmed and pointed at the waste-paper basket. Exaggeratedly, Melissa tidied the ball up and disposed of it properly.

'Happy now?'

'That's better, grand-mama. No need to make a mess.'

Unlike Genevieve, Melissa d'Acques had sired prodigiously. Over the centuries, she'd made over a hundred sons-in-darkness. They had given her grand-get without count. But they'd mostly drifted, finding their own paths through life and death, barely remembering that she still lived. Too many of her bloodline had listened to the Counts von Carstein and wound up destroyed in the Undead Wars or the persecutions.

Genevieve wasn't the sole survivor of Melissa's line, that of the great Lahmia, but she was the nearest thing the old woman had to family in the human sense. She thought that without Genevieve she would no longer take an interest in the affairs of the world, and for that connection she was grateful.

It was all very well to retreat into contemplation like Elder Honorio or lose oneself in the red thirst like Kattarin, but it wasn't living. And being undead meant you still lived, no matter what the vampire-haters might say.

She looked at Genevieve and Sierck.

'It was Wietzak's fool idea,' Melissa said. 'He actually wants another Undead War. He is claiming kinship to that Sylvanian rabble. He went to his keep at Karak Varn, to terrorise the peasants and raise up bands of strigoi warriors. You know what strigoi vampires are like, my dear. No finesse at all. Just mindless mouths on legs, purpose-made footsoldiers. The von Carsteins relied too much on them, and we all know where that led. Baron Wietzak has decreed that all enemies of vampirekind should be smitten down blah blah blah terrible vengeance against the human upstart who dares bibbledy-babbledy-boo sure and certain swift angel of painful death and so forth.'

'Wietzak is here?' asked Genevieve. 'Stalking Tio Bland?'

'He's not that mad. No, he's sent assassins. Or hired some local leech to do the job for him. He's not short of a golden hoard or two.'

'You won't find me grieving for Bland,' said Sierck. 'Death will shut the little stoat up, if nothing else will.'

That had occurred to Melissa. Only a few hours ago, when the Temple Father gave her a pfennig and some blather about investment it had been all she could do not to sink her fangs into the soft pouch of flab beneath his chin and tear into a major artery. Still, she had to be reasonable about these things.

'You know that's not true, Detlef,' said Genevieve. 'If a vampire kills Bland, it will prove everything he's been saying about us. He might be dead, but his cause will be taken seriously. Others will fill his place, and they'll be a lot less clownlike. Have you ever heard of the Tsarevich Pavel Society?'

'Pavel was the one who did for Kattarin?' he asked.

'Eventually, yes. There's been a Kislevite society in his name ever since. Die-hard vampire haters in high positions. They'll be watching Bland, seeing how popular his message becomes. I was nearly impaled by a mob this evening. Imagine those same mobs with watchmen and men-at-arms and witchfinders in their midst, backed by the force of Imperial decree. It won't matter if a vampire is guilty, innocent or a monster, we'll all be ashes or under the ground. And I personally will probably be killed, against which I happen strongly to be.'

'Ah, me too,' agreed the overwhelmed human.

'Now that's settled,' said Melissa, 'how are you two going to go about saving this Bland person's miserable neck?'

VIII

A HUGE POSTER outside the Temple of Morr showed fearless vampire-slayer Tio Bland holding up an annoyed-looking, enormously-fanged and red-eyed severed head in triumph. A banner-line read 'Death to the dead!' and an engraving which was supposed to look like spontaneous graffiti declared 'Ashes or under the ground!'

A stuffed black bat child's plaything with big red eyes and comical teeth, was impaled against a board with a wooden spike, red paint splashed around the heart-wound, with dribbles artfully swirled to spell out 'Rule one: no leeches!' In the bright light of early afternoon, Genevieve thought yet again that she was never going to get away with this.

A pair of black-robed acolytes, just like the thugs who had roughed up the silk-merchant yesterday, guarded the temple door. They seemed to be comparing the length of their weapons.

'I tell you, Willy, if a vampire attacked here and now, I would bring my silver-headed pike to bear and have its heart out in a trice.'

'Very impressive, Walther, but I'd have shoved my silver-bladed knife through the selfsame heart in half-a-trice.'

'That's as might be, but within the merest quarter-trice, I'd have…'

She could foresee where this conversation was going.

'Begging your leave, worshipful sirs,' she began, putting on an accent, 'be this the Temple of Morr?'

The temple-shaped building was jet-black, had a statue of the God of Death on the roof, was covered in symbols of Morr and had 'TEMPLE OF MORR' engraved in gold over the doorway.

'It might be,' said Willy the Knife. 'It depends on who's asking?'

'I be Jenny Godgift, come from far Wissenland.'

She did a little giggle thing in the back of her throat and rolled her eyes.

'That's a long journey for such a pretty little thing,' said Walther the Pike. 'You must have a good pair of legs under you.'

Genevieve brayed like an Estalian donkey, laughing through her nose.

'You be makin' me blush, illustrious personages. That be not kindly nor clever neither.'

Her cheeks were rouged to simulate blushing. Vampires couldn't redden with embarrassment, which was why dabs of rosiness here and there made such a useful disguise. Anyone might take her for a living human if they didn't look too closely. Detlef, master of all the theatrical arts, had been meticulous in applying a thin, subtle coat of face-paint. Her vampire pallor was covered, and she looked like a girl who had spent a lot of time outdoors in the sun. The strangest part of it had been sitting still in front of a dressing room mirror, seeing her long-lost face re-appear in ghost-form as Detlef layered make-up over her unreflecting skin. Did she really look like that? With a wig and lipstick, her reflection seemed complete – except for the socket-like eyeholes. She wouldn't pass a real looking-glass inspection, but if she happened to walk past a mirror – there were bound to be many in the temple – she'd at least not appear as a walking empty dress.

'Be this where the brave vampire-slayers work?' she asked.

She was sure she was overdoing it, but Detlef said an actor should never be afraid of the obvious. Most real people weren't. Witness: Willy and Walther, the comedy relief guards.

The clerics smiled indulgently at her. Genevieve let her lashes flutter. Thanks to facepaint on the eyelid, one of her eyes stuck shut. She got it open again before anyone noticed.

'Mistress Godgift,' said Willy, 'you need not fear the undead in this district.'

She made the signs of as many gods as she could remember, which came perilously close to an arm-dance.

'Gods be thanked,' she said. 'I've a powerful loathing for the undead in all their evil forms. I've come to join up.'

'Acolytes of Morr have to be apprenticed in childhood,' said Walther. 'Then work in a mortuary for two full years, pass exams in funerary rites, then…'

'But I wish only to slay the vampire creatures. Temple Father Bland must be endangered all the hours of the day and night, from bloodsucking fiends out to silence his holy pure words of justice. I am minded that one such as he needs a personal bodyguard.'

'I'm sure you mean well, mistress. But it takes more than a good heart.'

'I be practiced. I be very adept in all the latest techniques of vampire-slaying.'

Willy and Walther, a bit bored with her eager country girl act, shrugged at each other.

'I know how to put silver needles in their eyes.'

Willy looked a bit queasy at the thought.

'Leave your name with the mother superior's assistant,' said Walther, 'and a place where you can be reached by messenger. I'm sure we'll be in touch.'

'Be you brushing me off?'

Willy laughed uncomfortably. 'Not at all, Mistress Godgift.'

'Be you giving me the once-around-the-hayricks-and-left-in-the-spinney treatment?'

Walther was more to the point. 'We're on duty. We're much too important to deal with the likes of you.'

'Do you really think you be bravos enough to protect Antiochus Bland?'

She was worried that her country girl accent had turned abruptly piratical.

The guards were too annoyed to care. Willy tapped his knife-hilt, only it wasn't there. Genevieve held it up, careful not to touch the silver blade. She had lifted it from him with a swift grasp.

'Looking for this?'

Willy's face was dark. Walther's pike arced down. When its point scraped cobbles, Genevieve was out of its way. She had stood to one side, and had her foot poised to stamp down. She neatly snapped the pikeshaft.

'What if a vampire did that, sirs? What then?'

A few passersby stopped to pay attention. Willy and Walther liked that even less than having their toys taken away.

This was where she could use all those Celestial fighting arts she had studied under Master Po. A few passes of mantis style *gungfu*, and she'd be inside the temple and secure in her new job of bodyguard-in-chief to the Empire's most notorious vampire-hater. She reminded herself not to use teeth or claws. That would be a dead giveaway.

'Two schillings on the foreign wench,' said a gambler.

Genevieve would have bet on herself. Then someone barged out of the temple. He had to bend down to get under the lintel of the main door.

'Your two and raise you two,' said another gambler. 'That's Lupo Preiss, the wrestler.'

Oh wonderful. Genevieve gave up a silent lament for the days when clerics were reedy fellows with candlewax on their cuffs and weak eyes from too much reading. Back then, she could have trounced a whole temple-load of them without resorting to mantis-style. Sloth-style would have done.

'A crown on Brother Preiss,' went up the cry.

Genevieve's original champion muttered, 'Too rich for me.'

'What is this racket?' declared Brother Preiss.

'Mistress Nuisance is trying to force her way in,' said Willy No Knife.

'She says her name is Jenny Godgift,' said Walther the Half-Pike.

'I just feel Temple Father Bland should be properly protected,' she insisted.

Brother Preiss hefted up his sleeves and cracked his knuckles. He had the sort of hands that suggested he crushed rocks to powder to keep in trim.

'She damaged temple property,' whined Walther, holding up his broken pike.

'And stole some too,' moaned Willy.

Genevieve gave Willy his knife back. He made a play of cleaning its blade on his sleeve.

'Do you still want to fight, girl?' asked Preiss.

'I be a humble supplicant from far-off Wissen–'

Preiss took her by the shoulders and lifted her off the ground. Some of the crowd gasped. Genevieve wished she were back in Konigplatz with the vampire-killing mob. At least they were amateurs.

She turned in Preiss's grip, shrugging out of his fingers, and dropped to the ground. Taking her best shot first, she pivoted in her sprawl like a gypsy dancer, getting her shoulder and elbows against the cobbles so she could concentrate all the strength of her body into the tensed muscles of her right leg. She propelled a kick into Preiss's stomach.

Her boot-toe took him low, doubling him over.

She had to be fast to get out of the way as the ex-wrestler fell to his knees. Some bets started changing again. She made axe-blades of her fingers, a Nipponese trick Master Po had been fond of, and chopped down on Preiss's neck. His cowl protected him, but he must have felt the blow. She had to hop to avoid his grasping hand. If he got his fingers around any part of her, he wouldn't lose his grip a second time.

Honourably, she stood back and let Brother Preiss stand up.

An evil vampire would have kicked him in the head while he was down. She gave herself a gold star for being good, and hoped someone remembered her Shallya-like mercy at her funeral.

Preiss didn't show any sign of being hurt, though she must have given him at least a tummy-bruise with her first kick. She still felt the jarring of her foot against his packed-in meat, as if her leg-bones were jellied by the impact. The cleric was a trained fighter, which meant he didn't make the mistake of getting angry.

'Why are we wasting energy scrapping?' she asked. 'Surely, we all hate vampires. Nasty dead-alive things spewn from the grave to bedevil good folk such as we.'

Preiss made fists and came at her with a left-right-left hook-jab-jab combination. She leaned out of the first blows, but the third caught her on the forehead – she was sure he was aiming at her chin – and she staggered back.

Her first panicked thought was that her face-paint would have come off on his knuckles, but luckily her well-fixed wig had a fringe appropriate for her country girl disguise.

There were at least thirty-eight points on the male human body where a simple pass with her vampire talons or fangs would tap into wells of blood, leading within seconds to the loss of any capability of fighting back or even of life itself. Preiss left nine, or possibly ten, points totally unguarded. A vampire could easily take down the wrestling cleric and win herself supper into the bargain.

But she couldn't afford to fight like a vampire.

Remembering Master Po, she hooked her arms up and advanced, mantis style.

'She's a loony,' sneered Willy.

Preiss shook his head, knowing better. He assumed the correct defensive stance, right forearm out horizontally in front like a bar, left hand fisted and close to the stomach.

At the last moment, she switched to dragonclaw-style.

That got past his guard. She thumped him just above the ear, then again in the larynx. And her knee got to his side. She felt the impact again, but heard Preiss grunt as he took a blow to the kidney.

Judging at high-speed, she knew where to put her feet as she got her shoulder into Preiss's side where she had just kneed him. Then, with a strain on her own neck and spine, she lifted him off the ground. This was his own trick – wrestling, Hagedorn-style. She tossed him up and slammed him down.

Then she got a knee on his throat and her elbow poised over the bridge of his nose.

He said nothing but patted the ground three times.

She sprang away from him and bowed. There was some applause, but she kept her eyes on the ground. Preiss took his time about getting up, careful of his bruises. Willy and Walther busied themselves dispersing the crowd. Genevieve heard the clinking of coins passed from losers to winners. She regretted not having a slice of her own action.

'Brother Preiss,' she said. 'My humble apologies. I came here not to do any soul harm, but rather to prevent a great man – Temple Father Bland – from coming to harm.'

'She said she wanted to be Temple Father's bodyguard,' said Willy.

Preiss looked her up and down. Genevieve assumed the wrestler would not be disposed to like her. Then he smiled and she was horrified to realise that, contrary to expectation, Preiss liked her *quite a lot*. She gathered no woman had ever served him as she had. He found the novelty stimulating in all sorts of ways she didn't want to think about.

'Get Mistress Godgift a proper habit for a Temple Sister,' said Preiss. 'And tell mother superior to find her a place to lay her head. Not too far from the centre cloister. I want her always close by, and Temple Father Bland will agree with me. Since last night, we are at war with the undead. This woman will be first among our warriors.'

Genevieve saluted.

IX

WITH *GENEVIEVE AND Vukotich* in rehearsal, the Vargr Breughel Theatre would have been dark but for Detlef's 'open-stage nights' policy. The programme of an evening was set aside for all those who fancied themselves entertainers – jesters and jugglers mostly – to come up, be introduced to the paying throng – other jesters and jugglers, mostly – and try out their acts. Most hopefuls only lasted a minute or so before a volley of last week's vegetables silenced their venerable jokes or croaked songs. They would slink off into the wings, covered in rotten cabbage, vowing to go back to the counting-house or the tannery and forget any notions they had nurtured about a life of wealth, fame and unlimited beautiful lovers on the stage. The theatre only charged a modest admission fee and let in those who chanced performing free of charge, but the canny business manager Guglielmo Pentangeli had struck an agreement with the farmers' market to take away all the unsaleable fruit and veg at the end of the day. This was then sold to amateur critics who got far more enjoyment from pelting the acts than watching them. After each open-stage night, produce was gathered from the backdrop and sold again, as fodder for the carriage-company stables in Hasselhoff Street.

This evening, Detlef was preoccupied. He performed his usual duties as Master of Ceremonies, setting up each poor and trembling act with a few brief and witty introductory remarks, but his thoughts were with Genevieve in the Temple of Morr. He tried to comfort himself by believing that Bland would assume no vampire would be insane

enough voluntarily to walk into the one building in the city
where they were most likely to be impaled, beheaded and
consigned to the furnace. It wasn't much help.

Tonight's losers were even more pathetic than usual.

First up was a longshanks scholar from the University
who did impressions of notable Imperial personages. He
barely got into his satirical depiction of Konrad the Hero
when an entire vegetable marrow burst against his face,
hammering him against the backdrop. As the glowering
Renastic dragged the insensible scholar offstage, Detlef
supposed he should have mentioned that Konrad's Oath of
Devotion Society was in the house tonight. Then came an
Estalian guitarist with an enormous wave of oiled hair
cockatoo-combed up over his forehead. He actually managed to finish his number without so much as a tomato,
perhaps because the sweetness of his plucking was
matched by the extreme obscenity of his lyrics. A magic act
wasn't so lucky, and Renastic – whom Detlef still thought
bore close-watching – had to rush out with a bucket of
sand to smother the flames that had leaped from the wizard's brazier to his robes at the climax of his first and only
trick.

The Three Little Clots, dwarfs in loud check jerkins and
baggy trousers, came on and abused each other with eye-
pokes, beard-tugs and mallet-blows to the skull for five
minutes. They did each other more harm than any flung
fruit and had the wit to work the audience attack into their
routine – the bald-pated one with the knock-knees kept
snatching thrown edibles out of the air and stuffing them
into his mouth while the bespectacled one with an explosion of lightning-struck hair quipped that this was the best
meal they could expect all month.

After that, Detlef sacrificed a string of stuttering joke-
sters, an old woman who tied inflated pig-bladders into
strange shapes she claimed were animals, a temperance lec-
turer who mistakenly thought this was a fine opportunity
to take his message to the masses, an elf who dressed as a
human woman and propositioned sailors, another con-
jurer who made himself disappear and never came back

and a dock-labourer who took off his shirt and did peculiar things with his stomach tattoos.

It was always a good idea to wind up with a sure winner, so he brought on Antonia Marsillach, who danced athletically, and sans much in the way of costuming, behind strategically-placed roc-feather fans. The Three Little Clots came back, to popular acclaim, and snatched away Antonia's fans, which they used to batter each other as the unblushing dancer outdid the stomach-writher in assuming unlikely positions and the audience expressed their appreciation with a hail of flowers.

'Good show tonight,' said Guglielmo as Detlef rushed past him backstage.

'Sign the Clots to a long-term contract, extend Antonia for another two weeks and ask the greasy guitarist to come in next week for a proper audition. I never want to see any of the others in here again.'

'It shall be done, *maestro*.'

Genius was all very well, but Detlef knew he'd be back in debtors' prison if it weren't for Guglielmo's knack of arranging matters to keep a flow of money coming in and a trickle of money going out.

He found Lady Melissa in his dressing room, sat in his favourite chair, feet dangling over the edge, sharpening her teeth against a bit of old bone.

'I hope you're proud of that, Herr Genius. Very edifying and educational, I'm sure.'

'We don't admit children on open-stage nights, Missy.'

'I don't see why not. There's precious little to engage the grown-up intellect or the finer sensitivities. Captain Tattoo was tasty, though.'

Detlef noticed a red smear on the old girl's lips. He was momentarily horror-struck.

'Don't worry,' she said. 'He was knocked unconscious by a turnip. I just tapped him a little. He'll wake up with such a throbbing head that he won't notice the healed-over wound. And don't call me "Missy".'

'What if the Illustrated Churl runs into one of Bland's Boyos? They check up on suspect neck-bites, *Missy*.'

'I doubt they bother with big toes, though.'

'There's a vein in the big toe?'

She held her thumb and forefinger almost together. 'Just a titchy one. Useful for supping on the sleeping. You just have to lift the far edge of the quilt and take a nuzzle.'

'I could cheerfully have lived the rest of my life without knowing that.'

'What about your own neck, Herr Genius? It bears the unmistakable seal of Mademoiselle Dieudonné.'

Detlef was changing into street-clothes. He picked a shirt with a dandyish ruff, and arranged it over his bites. Then, he buttoned a waistcoat up over his stomach and looked to the vampire for approval.

'It'll pass for humans. But another vampire will spot you for cattle from across the room.'

Detlef was alarmed.

'Don't worry,' she said. 'It's an advantage where we're going. You're marked as the property of a vampire lady. Young bloods will steer well clear of your veins.'

'*Property?*'

'Don't get huffy. It's no worse than the way you shortlivers talk about your mistresses or pets. And I'm sure Gené is as fond of you as you are of any stray dog or passing trollop.'

Detlef couldn't decide whether Melissa was a nasty old lady or a horrid little girl. She was either too old or too young to care for anyone's feelings but her own. She was very unlike her granddaughter-in-darkness. He realised that he had only ever known one vampire, and he had made the mistake of thinking the nightbreed were all like Genevieve. It was much the same as Tio Bland thinking vampires were all like the Counts von Carstein.

'And don't look so hurt,' Melissa sniped. 'You had me skivvying and scurrying without a thought for putting me in school or seeking out my family. It's all about masters and servants, bleeders and bled.'

'How long is it since you received a good spanking?'

Melissa swallowed shock and put on her orphan face.

'You wouldn't...'

'If we can't be civil to each other, then we won't find out, will we, my lady? Now, have we had word from Genevieve?'

Melissa took a tied scroll from her sleeve.

'A messenger came while you were on stage. She has risen rapidly within the Cult of Morr and gained employment as a bodyguard to that Bland fellow. Very enterprising.'

This was better than they had hoped. But Detlef still had an image of Genevieve surrounded by flaming torches, stakes, mirror and silver scythes.

'So, one of us is close to the target,' said Detlef. 'It's up to us to go out and scare up the assassin.'

Melissa slid off the chair. She was dressed up in another stage costume, from Tarradasch's tear-jerker *The Little Princess Sonja in Exile*. It was the fur-trimmed hooded cloak from the cast-into-the-cold-cold-snows scene. She had the little red foxfur boots as well.

She stuck out her grey-gloved hand, as if wanting to be escorted across a busy street. He took her paw and led her up through the thronging backstage corridors and out of the theatre. A crowd at the stage door were petitioning the Three Little Clots for autographs on scraps of paper, not caring that none of them could write. Detlef recognised the two disguised aristocrats who were competing for the affections of la Marsillach, eyeing each other from behind domino masks and enormous bouquets of Gris Mere blossoms.

'Old Detlef's taking them younger and younger,' jeered someone.

Detlef reddened. That was not an item he looked forward to appearing in the *Boulevardpresse*.

Melissa kicked the jeerer in the shin.

'How dare you be rude about my dear old uncle!'

'Sorry,' yelped the hopping man.

She kicked him in the other shin.

'So you should be.'

The jeerer fell over and the Three Little Clots laughed at him.

Detlef felt more much kindly towards his 'niece'.

* * *

X

SO LONG AS she kept quiet, Genevieve found it easy to seem like part of the traditional funereal statuary of the Temple of Morr. All around were reminders of the grave she had never found time to lie in: wreaths of black flowers, refectory tables shaped like tombs, marble urn soup tureens, chairs with gravestone backs and seats, mausoleum dormitories with cots like coffins, skullfaced-doorknobs, ossuary skirting boards. She had never seen a place so desperately in need of the cheery touch of an elf interior designer with a passion for bright orange and turquoise cushions and sweet little paintings of happy kittens and fat babies.

Brother Preiss had ordered her to stay always a few arms' lengths from the Temple Father and watch him like the proverbial Warhawk.

Within the Temple of Morr, acolytes were expected to show due deference and not speak unless a superior addressed them directly. She was relieved not to have to keep up the Jenny Godgift voice.

Antiochus Bland, all eyes and smile, had put out his warm, wet hand to be kissed when Preiss presented her to him. Ever since, he had paid her no attention.

Now, after the evening rituals, Bland was in conference. Genevieve had to stand still in an itchy black robe, stacked against the wall of the temple inner sanctum like a mummified grandparent. She was one of several sisters in attendance on Bland and his cadre of cronies. Preiss had told her to act like an ordinary attendant, unless provoked. She was getting lost inside her impostures: she was a Bretonnian vampire pretending to be a live country lass dressed in the robes of Morr to seem like a serving wench while acting as a body-guard. She would have liked to see Eva Savinien pull that little lot off.

With Bland was Sister Liesel, the visionary behind the holding-up-a-severed-vampire-head poster and the skewered-bat-toy arrangement. She was working her way down a long list of petty matters, mostly to do with news items placed with the venerable *Spieler* or the scandalous *Boulevardpresse*.

'As you remember, Temple Father,' said Sister Liesel, 'some concern was expressed that by putting so much weight on the broadsheets we were neglecting the vital illiterate segment of the citizenry. It is still a sad fact that barely three in ten Altdorf households contain someone who can read and write. Our vital message must be delivered to the whole of the city.'

'The masses will follow the elite,' said the freckle-faced but venerable Father Knock, who had a habit of passing his thin fingers through his thinner red hair, constantly trying to rearrange it over his orange-ish expanse of scalp. He had been Temple Father before Bland and seemed to think all this vampire-slaying a distraction from the proper business of the Cult of Morr. 'It has always been that way, and that way it always shall be.'

'Actually, father, it's a misconception that the most influential people are literate,' said Liesel. 'Many aristocratic families actively discourage their sons from learning to read. The finer houses retain a pet scholar to read aloud any letters or papers that might be necessary. In the von Sutin household, my brothers were schooled only in hunting, duelling and wenching. My father graciously permitted my useless female head to be filled with letters so I could perform minor tasks. Reading out the results of wrestling matches upon which he had placed unwise wagers, for instance. As above, so below – only inkies like me can read or care to.'

Genevieve had known straight off that Sister Liesel was the real danger in the temple. She had set Bland down as one of those people who were obsessed with vampires but (literally) wouldn't recognise one if it kissed his hand, but the scribe-proclaimer was cooler and more calculating. Sister Liesel's fingers were permanently ink-stained from all her ledgers and scrolls, but the eyes behind her thick spectacles were clear and clever. It was her job not to miss much, and Genevieve had hung back to avoid coming to her notice.

'How shall we reach these unfortunate – indeed, unenlightened – souls, high and low?' asked Bland.

'I have taken care of that,' said Sister Liesel. 'I have hired criers to proclaim stories of the campaign in the streets, simplified versions of the material we have supplied to the broadsheets. The story of your swift action of last night has been heard in every square and market-place. This direct manner serves us well, but I have given some thought to subtler methods. I understand, Temple Father, that you found Detlef Sierck unsympathetic to our good works?'

Genevieve bit her lip. Detlef had told her about Bland's visit.

Bland shook his head sadly. 'He will come round, sister, but for the moment he is insensible – indeed, blinded – to the danger. A sad, sad case. A man of such talent, burdened by such old-fashioned notions.'

'If the theatre will not serve the temple, then we must have our own theatre.'

'Sister Liesel,' blurted Father Knock, 'The expense, the expense! Our coffers are already depleted, what with the night-patrols and the purchase of extra equipment. Why, our debts to the silversmiths alone run into…'

The sister waited for Bland to dismiss Knock's protest, then continued: 'I agree that the establishment of a conventional theatre is beyond us for the moment, but our grant to the mummers has yielded excellent results. *Vampireslayer* is very popular with the young. It is my proposal that we extend this policy and sponsor a number of puppet-theatre booths. It is a long-established tradition among the masses to leave their children in front of the puppets as they busy themselves drinking or buying groceries. Why should we not take advantage of that neglect, to offer instruction as well as entertainment?'

Liesel produced a very inky bundle of manuscript.

'I might not be Jacopo Tarradasch, but I am in my own small way a playwright. This is my rewritten version of the popular history *Kattarin and Pavel*. Temple Father, you will be pleased to learn that I have given the vampire-slaying Tsarevich several choice speeches extracted from your own recent public pronouncements. Of course, I've told the carver to make the puppet of Pavel an endearing likeness of yourself. You are our public face in this campaign, our sharpest weapon against the night.'

Genevieve remembered the real Pavel as tall, fork-bearded and (thanks to the tsarina's temper) one-armed. She occasionally wondered how he had managed to do the deed, but supposed he got someone to hold the stake against the old monster's heart while he wielded the mallet.

'This is all very encouraging, sister. What do the people think?'

Genevieve understood another of Liesel's innovations was a miniature census, whereby she sent her apprentices into the streets in secular dress and had them ask passersby pointed questions about the Temple of Morr and Antiochus Bland, and vampires and what should be done about them.

'This afternoon's poll is a significant advance on yesterday's. Fully two-thirds of those we approached were of the "ashes or under the ground" persuasion, which means a switch of many from the "mildly troubled by vampires" to the "strongly hate and fear" category. Almost all the "indifferent to vampires" have gone over to "mildly troubled", and all the "nothing against vampires" fools have switched their tune to "indifferent". I venture to think that by next week, the "indifferents" will have vanished like dew in the morning. Our census-takers are calling this the "Ibby the Fish factor".'

'Hardly in keeping with the dignity of the campaign,' said Bland.

'Their enthusiasm is strengthened by occasional levity, Temple Father. And people remember the name "Ibby the Fish" better than… what was it?'

'Ibrabod Furtwingle? Iblochal Fonebonio?'

'I rest my case, Temple Father. In point of fact, it was Ibrahim Fleuchtweig.'

'There, I would have got it eventually.'

'Without a doubt. But most people have not your gifts. Last night, Ibby the Fish was a dead dockyard bully. Then he was a martyr to humankind, preyed upon by the undead. Now, he is a destroyed potential vampire, the first vanquished foe in the campaign.'

'Surely, not everyone who suffers a vampire bite rises from the dead?' said Knock. 'We'd be overrun.'

'The alchemists are still debating the matter,' said Liesel.

'That's something else we must change,' said Bland, eyes alight. 'Wasting – indeed, squandering – treasury funds on trying to *understand* the undead. What we need from alchemists are better, surer ways of killing – indeed, exterminating – the fiends, not airy-fairy theories of how they came to be. Evil is beyond understanding. It should just be burned out or cut away.'

Liesel clapped, and glanced around the room. The other sisters clapped too, and Genevieve joined in. With others carrying the applause, Liesel pulled out a tablet and stylus and wrote down what Bland had said.

'I'll have that in the *Spieler* tomorrow, Temple Father,' she said, scribbling furiously. '"Wasting trees... funds... trying to *understand*... we need from alchies... better, surer ways of exterminating... not airy-fairy theories... evil beyond understanding... should be burned out or cut away." Very well said.'

Genevieve hoped the meeting was over. She was sure her face-paint needed a touch up.

'The other matter,' said Brother Preiss, who hadn't spoken throughout Liesel's report.

'Ah yes,' said Sister Liesel. 'We need to be careful.'

Preiss clapped his hands once and the sisters began to file out of the sanctum. Genevieve wasn't sure whether she should join them, but Preiss caught her eye and kept her back. When the others were gone, Liesel and Knock swivelled in their chairs to look at her.

'Mistress Godgift is our new secret armament,' said Preiss, proudly. 'She has rare qualities.'

Liesel lowered her spectacles to assess Genevieve.

'I suppose a bodyguard who looks like a bodyguard is too much to ask for.'

'They're easy to find, sister,' said Preiss. 'Too easy. Our enemies can smell them streets away. They'll overlook Sister Jenny.'

Liesel didn't seem convinced, but let it drop.

'Do we know more of the plot?' Bland asked. 'I confess I'm almost excited to know that the vampires of the World's Edge have vowed to put an end to me. It shows we're doing the right thing, rattling the proper cages.'

'Some cages should be left alone,' muttered Knock.

Preiss put his big hands on the table.

'A vampire assassin is stalking you, Temple Father,' he said. 'That much we knew, but our spies now tell us she is already in Altdorf. She has been seen.'

'*She?*' Bland's smile stretched almost to his eyes. 'A bitch vampire?'

'And a practiced murderer. By her hand died Wladislaw Blasko, Lord Marshal of the city of Zhufbar, and Graf Rudiger von Unheimlich, Master of the League of Karl-Franz.'

It was all Genevieve could do not to goggle her eyes like an idiot.

'We are up against a cunning and deadly creature, Temple Father,' said Preiss. 'None other than the vampire Genevieve Dieudonné!'

XI

MELISSA LED GENEVIEVE'S pet down the Street of a Hundred Taverns, weaving him carefully in and out of the late-evening crowds. It was late summer (which all vampires hated because of the long light evenings) and the last of the pink still streaked the sky. A lot of convivial drinkers were on the street, outside their chosen hostelries. Only the sotten patrons of the Drunken Bastard preferred to skulk in shadow as they got miserably soused. She happened, from merest chance, to peek into Slut Alley, where Altdorf's cheapest harlots plied their trade standing up with skirts tucked into their belts. Sierck clapped his big hand over her eyes and hurried her on, scolding like a proper responsible adult.

She didn't want to admit it, but she was starting to become fond of the bearish Detlef Sierck – not in a liquid lunch sort of way, since she respected her grand-get's grazing rights, but in the way she had felt about the very best of her foster parents down through the centuries since her 'coach accident'. Not many shortlivers could make her laugh, but Sierck could. She had a shrewd idea that was why Genevieve was so drawn to him, not for his genius or the quality of his blood or the stoutness of his heart. A sense of humour was rare in the higher races, as demonstrated by the Three Little Clots, and Sierck had the knack of being funny in that way which meant she wasn't sure whether he was trying or not. And she was even starting to like being called 'Missy'.

'Disgraceful,' said a thin-nosed cleric of Ulric. 'Look at that old reprobate dragging a poor child into a district like this. Obviously, his devotion to the daemon drink exceeds any responsibility he ought to feel for the moral welfare of the young.'

Melissa noticed the man was standing outside the Crooked Spear, sipping a thin tube of something green.

'And what are you doing in a whoreboy's haunt, father,' she snapped. 'Missionary work?'

The cleric sniffed with dignity, 'Precisely.'

'Pull the other one, Doris,' said a painted halfling lad. 'It's got antlers on.'

Sierck tugged her away.

'Are you getting into trouble again, Missy?'

'Defending your honour, uncle.'

'That can take care of itself.'

In the street outside the Sullen Knight, half a dozen separate brawls were coalescing into one big fight. A watchman blustered and waved his cudgel, but none of the bruisers noticed.

'Evening, Dibble,' said Sierck to the copper.

Dibble saluted with his cudgel.

'Quiet night...?' Sierck commented.

A bitten-off ear was spat into the gutter.

'Seen worse, Mr Sierck,' said Dibble. 'Did you hear about Ibby the Fish? That Tio Bland is an ass's arse, if you ask me. And Sergeant Munch isn't so polite about him. Ibby was no more a vampire than your little girl there. What's your name, missy?'

'Lady Melissa d'Acques,' she said.

'"Missy" will do,' said Sierck, slipping a hand into her hood and ruffling her curls.

'Would you like a candied pear?' asked Dibble.

'I'm not to take sweets from strange men,' she said.

'Very wise.'

A scatter of teeth spread over the cobbles. Melissa felt her own fangs sliding from their gumsheaths.

'Can we go, uncle, all the blood is making me...'

'Sick? Yes, of course. Come along, Missy. Evening, Dibble.'

'Evening, Mr Sierck.'

Sierck steered her around the brawl, shielding her with his body when some unfortunate came flying across the street. At the centre of the fight was a one-eyed sailor with anchor tattoos on his muscle-swollen forearms. Green juice slobbered over his chin, marking him as an addict to some vegetable drug.

Shortlivers had so many bad habits.

'Now where is this place? The Crescent Moon?'

Sierck had been looking up at inn-signs. That wouldn't help him.

'The sign is painted above the door, in black on a blackboard. You have to have sharp eyes like mine to see it.'

'Very clever.'

'In the circumstances, if you ran a tavern for vampires would you want to advertise with letters of green flame?'

'You have a point, Missy.'

'So I do. Several, in fact, uncle. And here we are.'

The door was in a wall across an alley between the Seven Stars and the Crown and Two Chairmen. Anyone not in the know would take it for a blocked-off shortcut to the next street.

Melissa knocked in a complex rhythm on the door. A peephole opened. Red eyes stared out at Sierck, narrowed and hostile. Sierck pointed down at Melissa's head. She smiled up and saw approval.

'Long live the dead,' she recited.

The door was open in a flash. Melissa and Sierck were pulled inside, and the door closed as if it had never been open.

This was the Crescent Moon, Altdorf's famous vampire tavern.

XII

WHEN THE MEETING was concluded, Genevieve almost gave herself away. With Detlef's blood still coursing through her and hours until cockcrow, she was at her most awake. It took moments to realise she was now expected to go to bed. She'd been given her own cell, off the temple's central cloister, near enough the Temple Father's apartments to be on call in case of an emergency.

This alone earned her the enmity of Mother Superior Debora, who believed all novices should sleep in a dormitory and put in months of silent sweeping and prayer before being allowed to light an incense taper, let alone given her own private cell and entrusted with special duties. Debora was an old crony of Father Knock's, part of a grumbling faction within the Cult of Morr dismissively referred to as 'Old Temple'. Genevieve had picked up, from close observation, that a good two-thirds of ordinary clerics were of the Old Temple persuasion. But Bland's Boyos ran the cult: those who expressed no enthusiasm for his vampire-slaying campaign were relegated to menial duties, those who climbed aboard his band-wagon (like the sham Jenny Godgift) were advanced double-time to the inner circle.

Alone in her tiny room, she considered the latest surprise.

So, Genevieve Dieudonné was expected, to come as an assassin. Admittedly, she'd once been blackmailed by former chancellor Mornan Tybalt, now in retirement-cum-exile beyond the Middle Mountains, to assassinate the odious Graf Rudiger von Unheimlich. As things had turned out, she had found cause to kill the graf, but she hadn't done it for Tybalt and she hadn't collected blood-coin on von Unheimlich. As for Wladislaw Blasko, he'd fallen into the Black Water without so much as a push from her. In that messy little business, so tidied up in Detlef's play, she had been trying to *prevent* an assassination.

She'd stopped Oswald killing the Emperor, too.

She did not murder people. Especially not for money.

But the Cult of Morr had serious intelligence that suggested otherwise. Could it even be true? Had Lady Melissa clouded her mind with her elder's powers of fascination, leaving orders in the back of her brain which would catch light when she heard a particular bell and drive her to fetch off Antiochus Bland's head with a single blow?

It wasn't likely.

Brother Preiss and Sister Liesel had spoken of 'deep cover' agents within the camp of the enemy. They knew that Genevieve had been summoned to the city, and had a fair idea that she was the vampire who escaped the mob in the Konigplatz two days ago. Surely, no vampire would collaborate with Bland's Boyos, but many of the undead had living serfs, lovers and human cattle. Those who shunned the light of day needed tombs and coffins guarded. Many of those full humans must seethe with resentment against their ever-thirsty masters.

According to the insurrectionist poet Prince Kloszowski, whom she had met in Tilea, Professor Brustellin – father of the revolutionist movement – likened all aristocrats to the titled vampires of Sylvania, metaphorically draining the blood of their inferiors. It stood to reason that, come the revolution, the undead oppressors would be hunted down in their own lairs by their own minions. If she had to spend her days hauling away bloodless peasant corpses left to rot by Baron Wietzak of Karak Varn, with only the occasional whipping in the way of thanks, she'd sign up with Bland's campaign too.

She started wondering whether another Undead War might not be the answer. It'd thin out the ranks of the truly atrocious, and teach the survivors to mind their manners. Then, she realised she had been swayed by Bland, had started to think like him. She wondered if he had his own power of fascination, an inbuilt knack like scrying or firestarting. That would explain his rapid ascendance, and the sudden appearance of his fanatical following.

Sitting on her cot, she listened out. She could hear clerics washing, using the jakes, undressing, going to bed, snoring. When the temple was silent, she ventured from her cell.

Bland's apartments were guarded by hand-picked men,
closer in ability to Brother Preiss than Willy and Walther.
The general defences of the building were good: nothing
that would keep out a creature who could transform into a
silent mist but generally up to the job. A system of bell-
alarms was set to trip the unwary intruder: it took some care
to get around without setting the things off. She was glad of
the opportunity to practise her night-skills.

She took the opportunity to snoop.

Across the cloister quadrangle, a single candle-flame
burned. Many dramatic situations began with a single candle-flame burning.

Genevieve crept close and saw into a small chapel.

Beneath the spreading wings of a huge stuffed raven –
sacred bird of Morr, of course – a cleric was bowed over an
altar. No, that wasn't it at all. The cleric was Liesel von Sutin.
She was not at her devotions but bent over a desk, scratching at a scroll with a long black quill. She hummed
tunelessly and almost beneath the range of human hearing,
her mouth set in determined concentration. She had taken
off her spectacles and perched them irreverently on the
raven's glassy beak.

Genevieve relaxed. The scribe-proclaimer wasn't likely to
notice her.

The story the cleric had half-told at the meeting struck a
chord of sympathy with Genevieve. Her own father, dead
for centuries, had no sons to favour over his daughters, but
he had distinct ideas on what was becoming for a dutiful
girl of good family. Even Chandagnac had given her the
Dark Kiss expecting a devoted servant for eternity, something between a mistress and a mother. Before becoming a
vampire, Genevieve had considered a clerical life – it was a
traditional path for the daughters of minor aristocracy
'with too much character' (which was to say, too obnox-
ious) to be eased out of the mansion by an arranged
marriage.

Liesel von Sutin was the cleverest person in the temple,
yet she was trapped again – working like a slave, awake
when everyone else was comfortably in bed. All to fulfil the

cracked dreams of a man who wasn't even a father or husband to her.

Did Liesel love Tio Bland? The Temple Father's 'dear wife and three lovely children' were staying in the country at the moment, and he could easily satisfy a passing interest in the worshipful scribe-proclaimer. Genevieve was surprised to find herself believing he was committed enough to his image of self not to take advantage of any female opportunity that came his way in the course of his campaign. Maybe that made it worse: to love someone for their faithfulness to another. That must be a nasty burr under anyone's chemise.

Liesel turned and held up her candle.

'Who's there?' she whispered. Genevieve saw she had reached for an icon – not a raven of Morr, but a dove of Shallya.

'Sister Jenny,' Genevieve said. 'I couldn't sleep.'

Liesel was relieved and dropped the dove.

'I know how you feel,' she said. 'I don't sleep. Haven't for years, except in cat-naps. I work through the night. There's so much to do.'

Genevieve stepped into the chapel.

Sister Liesel unhooked her spectacles from the raven and put them on. They made her eyes seem enormous and watery.

'You're Preiss's pit-fighter?'

'I do what I have to,' Genevieve said.

'You've lost your accent, I hear.'

Genevieve's nails sharpened. She kept her hands in the sleeves of her robe.

'Never let the mask slip around men,' said Liesel. 'Never let them know you're not a foolish girl. Take my example.'

'Everyone knows you're not a fool.'

'Exactly, and look where it's got me. What do you think of this?'

Liesel held up a sketch. A fanged she-creature bearing down on a resolute, scythe-wielding Tio Bland. The sister had used red ink for bloodied eyes and fangs.

'That's our enemy,' she said. 'This Dieudonné creature.'

Genevieve wondered if there was a resemblance.

'I wish she would come and it would be over,' said Liesel.

'She won't get near the Temple Father,' Genevieve said. 'Not on my watch.'

'Commendable spirit, sister. But I've a piece of advice for you. It might shock you. Do you care to hear it?'

Genevieve nodded.

'When the vampire attacks, and she *will* attack... if it comes down to a choice between saving Temple Father Bland or yourself...'

Genevieve tried to peer behind the shield of Liesel von Sutin's spectacles.

'Save yourself.'

XIII

DETLEF FOUND HIMSELF pressed against the wall by Heinrich and Helga, two creatures with the same face. Heinrich wore his hair long for a man, Helga wore hers short for a girl. They dressed in identical costumes: pale blue hose and doublets embroidered with dozens of tiny skulls. The vampires had not started out as twins, but had been together for so long that they had bled into each other, coming to look and think alike, an old married couple with centuries to manage convergence.

As one sniffed around his neck bites and the other stroked his hair with long, lacquered nails, Detlef saw a red flicker in their eyes.

'He's got the marks on him...'

The flicker passed from one to the other.

'He's been bled within the last day.'

'He is the property...'

'...of a lady elder.'

The Crescent Moon wasn't crowded, but Helga and Heinrich were vampires enough to be getting on with. Detlef realised his feet were off the floor, and he was mounted on the wall like a trophy. The vampire couple continued to examine him, as he might assess a horse he was thinking of buying.

'A strong heart...'

'...but past his prime.'

The tavern was a low-ceilinged room, a vaulted space with too few lanterns for human comfort. Behind the bar – where Genevieve had once worked – thin-faced, sharp-fanged women bustled. Above them were arrangements of leather-straps and glass tubes. With business off thanks to Clause 17, only three of these contraptions were filled with warm bodies, spigot-taps stuck into major veins so the blood could be decanted in measures for the customers. Two of the 'barrels' were fat pigs, but one was an ailing youth trussed and hung upside-down, floppy hair dangling, wriggling a little in discomfort.

Detlef understood that in less jittery times, the Crescent Moon had a surplus of applicants for the position of barrel. Some were would-be vampires hoping to meet a patron who would bestow the Dark Kiss upon them, others derived a species of perhaps-unhealthy pleasure from the binding and draining.

According to Genevieve, the latter had to be watched carefully – they would try to come back too many times and let themselves be bled empty. This barrel did not look as if he was in anything like ecstasy, and no one was drinking from him anyway.

'There are kisses enough...'

'...for us all.'

'Helga, Heinrich,' snapped Lady Melissa. 'You have shown off enough. Now let Mr Sierck go, apologise profoundly and get back to playing with yourselves. No one finds your antics charming any more. If you can't treat guests properly, you can go to your crypt and think upon your shortcomings for, oh, eighteen months.'

Gently, the vampires let him down. They brushed off his coat where it had pressed against the slightly-damp brick-work. One pinched his bottom, but he let it pass.

'We respect the lady elder...'

'...and accord you courtesy.'

'That sounds awfully grudging, you two. Do I have to remind you of the circumstances of our last meeting? You were seeking shelter from witchfinders. A certain gracious lady elder obliged you with a carriage. One or other of you would have suffered a nasty beheading. And we all know how long the survivor would have lasted.'

The vampires bowed to Melissa.

'You are an honoured guest, living man…'

'…and you are welcome in the Crescent Moon.'

'That's better. Now, leave us alone.'

Helga and Heinrich faded backwards into the shadows. Their pale, slightly-glowing faces seemed to linger a moment, then went out like candles. Detlef heard them creeping away.

'Some of us regret the loss of the looking glass, and will go to great lengths to provide themselves with reflections.'

'There's a story there, Missy.'

'Oh, I hope not. Couldn't you write something amusing for a change? I always liked *A Farce in the Fog*. Whatever happened to your early, funny plays?'

'The world stopped making me laugh.'

'Gené has a lot to answer for, if you ask me. It is my considered opinion, and I've had a long time to form it, that no work of narrative art can be truly great unless it contains at least one good laugh. All Tarradasch's tragedies have clowns in them.'

Melissa looked comically serious, lecturing him in this mausoleum.

'There, you're smiling again. Let's just blend in with the crowd, and you let me do the talking.'

They made their way past empty tables to the bar.

At the far end, a scarecrow creature wrapped in a tattered black shroud looked down at a bowl of spiced pig-blood. It opened a hole in the cerements around its face and unrolled a long, tubelike tongue into the blood, then proceeded noisily to drain its dinner.

'You don't want to know about the Mosquito Man,' said Melissa.

Detlef silently agreed with her.

Melissa rapped her tiny knuckles on the bar.

'Katya, some service, if you please.'

One of the barmaids came over. Her flat, pretty face was covered with soft, silky hair. She had slit pupils and permanent fangs.

'Lady Melissa, what is your pleasure?'

'Who's the "special"?'

Melissa thumbed at the human barrel.

'A student of the Dark Arts. Making good on a wager he lost. We've had better, but at least he's free of disease. With business down, we take what we can get. The girls have been nipping from him all night and none have dropped dead.'

'Very well, I shall have a glass of the special.'

'Coming right up,' said Katya, holding a goblet under the student's neck and opening the spigot. The barrel shook as the flow filled the goblet to the brim. Detlef saw the straps around his head included a leather-ball gag in his mouth, doubtless to keep him quiet so as not to upset the delicate sensibilities of the customers.

'We've a barrel-place saved for Tio Bland if he ever finds the doorway,' said Katya. When she mentioned the Temple Father's name, her cat-face contorted into a jungle snarl. 'There'd be a queue out onto the street if we could chalk his name up on the bill of fare.'

Detlef nudged Melissa.

'I was forgetting myself,' she said. 'Do you have anything for living people? What is it they drink? Tea, wine, milk?'

Katya looked as if an indecent suggestion had been made.

'We don't usually serve *his kind* in here,' she said, pointedly not looking at Detlef, 'but since you're such a favoured customer, I'll see if we can't scare something up.'

The barmaid called to a junior, a girl-faced woman with snow-white hair and blue bat tattoos on her swanny neck. Katya addressed her in a language Detlef didn't know, which seemed to have miaows in it. The other barmaid replied, without much enthusiasm, but scurried off in little steps. She wore a skirt that was almost immodestly tight (and limiting) from thigh to ankle, but spread out like octopus tentacles around her feet.

'Gela thinks she saw some wine about. We keep a little in the cellar, to top up the barrels.'

Melissa looked at her own goblet.

'It's been a long, dry spell,' she said, then lifted the drink and sucked it down at a single draught, her movement a

blur. With red on her lips, Melissa's eyes burned like flares
and Detlef thought he saw a jewel-faceted skull under sud-
denly-transparent flesh. Then, the elder vampire shook her
head, setting her curls bouncing, and swallowed. She looked
like a little girl again.

'Here,' said Katya, grudging.

A dusty mug of weak wine was shoved across the bar
towards him. It sloshed a bit. Melissa ordered another measure of the special.

'Two is my limit,' she said. 'Must keep a clear head.'

Detlef took a swig of the wine and decided to leave the
rest. It had gone to vinegar years ago.

'Someone in here will know something,' said Melissa. 'It's
just a question of knowing who to ask.'

'A brilliant observation, Missy.'

'Think you could have found this place on your own, Herr
Genius? Or that you'd have fought off the Necksuck Twins?'

'I concede that you are far more fearsome than me.'

'So you should.'

Melissa's second drink came, and she sipped this one,
casting her eyes around the room.

'Anyone unusual been in lately?' she asked Katya.

The cat-vampire shrugged. 'Most of the unusuals have
been staying away. A lot of the regulars have left the city.
Some have gone underground.'

'She means that those with crypts and graves are lying in
them, bloated on their last meals, hoping to sleep for sev-
enty-five years or so and wake up in a world without Bland's
Boyos. It's not a stupid thing to do. I myself snoozed
through the Undead Wars, surrounded by pressed and dried
flowers. I woke up to find a shrine thrown up around me
and a group of outcast dwarf miners worshipping me as
some sort of sleeping martyr princess. They'd somehow got
hold of a handsome prince whose kiss was supposed to
bring me back to life.'

Melissa sipped.

'Does this story have a happy ending?' he asked.

'Oh yes. Well, sort of. I drained the prince and raised him
as my get. He had to be put down, though. The red thirst

made him blood simple. He killed those dear little dwarfs. And all their animal companions. And quite a few other people, actually. These things happen. A lot of vampires can't hold their drink like me. I have learned much in my many, many years.'

She had finished her second special.

'Just one more, I think, Katya. Since it comes after a long fast. And make it a double.'

'Glad to oblige, my lady.'

Melissa was beginning to glow. She was sat cross-legged on a tall stool. She was still wrapped in her furs, which made her face all the tinier.

'Ask the girl if she knows about Ibby the Fish?' Detlef suggested.

'I was getting to it, Mr Genius. Who's in charge of this investigation, eh? Don't hurry me. Shortlivers always hurry too much. Katya, you heard him. Any word on the late Ibrahim Fleuchtweig?'

'He was a Fish,' said Katya. 'Hooks got him. End of story.'

'I thought as much.'

'Vampires don't bother Fish. Or Hooks, come to that. It's one thing to have a cult on a campaign to wipe you out, but it's a lot more serious if one of the dock gangs gets a down on you. Sleeping a century won't be much use then. Those bravos tell their children and their children's children to keep up a feud. Look at the Hooks and Fish, themselves. Been at each other's throats since the time of Sigmar.'

'So all this business with the posters and the proclamations, making out that Tio Bland prevented Ibby from rising as a vampire? That's just...'

'Wormshit,' said Katya. 'Now, if you'll excuse me, I have to drain the pig again. Mosquito Man has finished his appetiser.'

The barmaid moved away. She had a certain lithe, catlike grace, and the back of her dress bustled out suggesting a tail. Detlef wondered how one would manage her without getting seriously clawed.

'You have to stroke the fur the right way.'

He was shocked to be so transparent. 'Missy,' he said, haughtily, 'I don't know what you mean.'

'Liar.'

'Well, yes.'

'I won't tell Gené, but only if you promise to write something about me. Something light and charming. No orphans in the snow, no deaths at the dead of night. Just delights.'

'I shall try.'

Looking across the bar to the entrance archway, Detlef saw a pair of black boots on the stairs. A newcomer had been admitted. A black cloak followed the boots, and then a sallow face.

'Ah-hah,' said Detlef. 'I thought as much.'

He knew the new patron at once. The fellow had the decency to look shifty at being caught out.

'If it isn't the Sylvanian scene-shifter, "Alvdnov Renastic". Or should I say, anagrammatically… Vlad von Carstein!'

The exposed von Carstein raised his cloak to ward off the truth.

'Don't be silly, Mr Genius,' said Melissa. 'He's not a vampire.'

'Then what's he doing here?'

She scrunched up her face, like a very drunk person trying to seem sober, and thought about his question.

'I've no idea. Let's ask him. Avldovn Rascinet, whatever your name is, come here and be grilled severely. Hop to it, scene-shifter.'

She started hiccoughing, which was something he didn't think vampires did.

Renastic, not denying anything, slunk over at them. His long cloak was bulked out, making the scene-shifter look like a hunchback.

Melissa pounded her fists against the bar. She had no breath to hold, but she banished the hiccoughs somehow.

'Must be something in that student,' she said. 'He's probably a secret weirdroot-chewer. I'm tired, Mr Genius. Give me a cuddle.'

She lurched, almost falling from her stool, tumbling into his arms. Gingerly, he held her to him like a baby, patting her back. She laid her head on his shoulder and mumbled about wanting to sleep.

Renastic didn't know how to take this.

Helga and Heinrich, noticing Melissa was *hors de combat*, had crept back, and were paying keen attention.

'So you're not a vampire?' Detlef asked.

'I never said I was,' said the Sylvanian.

'But your name?'

'It's what you said it was. Vlad von Carstein. Count Vlad von Carstein, actually. The fifteenth to hold the title. I prefer not to use it.'

Detlef pointed with his freer hand, shifting Melissa up closer in his grip.

'And you expect us not to suspect you!' she said.

'How would you feel having the same name as a notorious villain? Being a direct descendent of one of the most evil creatures ever to walk the Known World? Who nearly destroyed this city and the Empire? If you were called "Constant Drachenfels" at birth, wouldn't you think up something else as soon as you could?'

That sounded reasonable.

'But you're in a vampire tavern?'

'Family obligations. Nothing I'm happy about. The problem with being the current Count von Carstein isn't just persecution from the likes of Tio Bland, it's all the vampires wanting you to turn into one of them and lead a holy war against the living. That's why I left Sylvania in the first place. I'm here, among the undead of Altdorf, to renounce any claim people might think I have to be considered leader of vampirekind. I just want to get on with my life. I like working in the theatre. I've been practising my own turn, and am hoping you'll give me a spot at the next open-stage night.'

Only now did Detlef notice Renastic lacked fangs.

'What kind of turn?' he asked.

Renastic dramatically threw back his cloak to reveal a miniature version of himself attached to his arm like a parasitic twin, a smiling wooden head with a widow's peak and a sharp goatee, atop a trailing body in a child-sized evening outfit complete with cloak and shiny leather shoes.

'Gentriloquism,' said the dummy, mouth flapping.

'This is Vlad,' said Renastic, from his own mouth.

'Yes, I'm Glad,' said the dummy, with an exaggerated Sylvanian accent, 'the gloodthirsty gampire. Why did the gampire cross the road? Gecause it was suckeeng the glood of the cheecken? Hah hah hah. I got a meellion of 'em. Egeryone a weenner!'

Renastic made a grinning end-of-the-act grimace.

'What do you think, Mr Sierck?' he asked, eagerly.

'It needs work, Renastic.'

'Get me a gottle of glood,' shouted Vlad.

Detlef understood what Genevieve had seen in the darkened dressing room. Renastic practising his act. She would laugh when she heard.

Melissa mumbled into his shoulder, saying the act was terrible, but the stagestruck scene-shifter didn't hear.

'What does he mean, "needs work"?' said Vlad the Dummy, angrily.

'We should practise more. Think of better jokes.'

'Gullshit! What does he know? I theenk I'll suck his glood!'

'Oh don't do that, Vlad,' said Renastic, shaking the dummy angrily. 'I really must apologise, Mr Sierck...'

'Gug off, human!'

'...he gets carried away sometimes. Very temperamental. Like all vampires.'

Renastic put his hand over the dummy's mouth, stifling further protests. Vlad's head shook in fury.

It was a reverse of Helga and Heinrich. Two people in one body, rather than one person in two.

Weird.

He set Melissa on her stool, and shook her. She came awake, showing red eyes and fangs.

'I've got the beginnings of a very bad headache,' she said.

'I know the feeling.'

Helga and Heinrich had slid down the bar. They were standing either side of Renastic, hands slipping in and out of his pockets, tongues darting at his face.

'Fresh blood...'

'...noble blood.'

'He's a von Carstein,' Melissa said. 'You'd best leave him alone. His relatives might not take kindly to you tapping him.'

The twins huffed.

'Does every live cow who comes in here...'

'...have a patron and protector?'

'It's most vexing...'

'...and a true frustration.'

'You can bite the little one,' said Melissa.

Detlef didn't understand, until Helga – or Heinrich, it was hard to tell – darted at Vlad, and bit into wood.

'Watch my wrist,' said Renastic.

Spitting – the face of the twin who hadn't bit as contorted as that of the one who had – Helga and Heinrich withdrew again.

Renastic shrugged his hand out of Vlad and looked at his white cuff.

The skin wasn't broken.

'So you aren't even an interested party in all this?' Detlef asked.

'I wouldn't say that. I don't want to be a vampire, but I'm still a Count von Carstein. I know Bland's Boyos won't make any fine distinctions when they're avenging their Temple Father's murder. I'll be just as likely to get hoisted on a stake as Baron Wietzak himself.'

'You know about the assassination plot?' said Melissa, aghast.

'Oh yes. It's all anyone talks about backstage. Kerreth had it from Antonia, who heard it from Eva's dresser, who...'

Detlef felt that Melissa had got her wish and he was back playing farce again.

'And, of course,' said Renastic, 'tonight's the night. She'll be at the temple, by now. Let's hope for all our sakes that she's not as good an assassin as she is everything else.'

'You know who Wietzak's hired killer is?' asked Detlef.

Renastic nodded.

'Doesn't everyone?'

* * *

XIV

'WHAT WAS THAT?' said Genevieve.

'I didn't hear anything,' said Liesel von Sutin, a little too quickly.

She had forgotten she wasn't supposed to have sensitive-as-a-bat's vampire ears. It hadn't been an obvious disturbance, just a faint clanking – perhaps a stifled groan. Suggestive enough.

'I think I should check on the Temple Father.'

'He has night-guards.'

Sister Liesel held her sleeve. The woman was apprehensive, close to scared.

Genevieve's night-senses were pricking. She stretched her upper lip to cover her sharpening teeth.

'No harm in checking.'

Reluctantly, it seemed, the scribe-proclaimer let her go. Genevieve padded across the quadrangle, towards Bland's apartments. Liesel hesitated a moment, then followed. The sister's footfalls sounded very loud. Genevieve signed to her to be quieter.

Genevieve ducked under a hanging, and knew something was wrong.

The first guards were sprawled at their posts.

Fresh-spilled blood hit Genevieve's nostrils like a snort of daemon dust. Her night-vision grew more acute. She saw the blood on the guards' throats as a vivid scarlet, pooling in the folds of their vestments, pulsing from twin neck-wounds. Something had crept up on these two and struck serpent-fast.

Vampire-swift.

They had been attacked as they took a snack break. Bread and cheese was spread around, soaked in blood – so much *blood!* Broken mugs spilled strong milky tea. With so many smells making her eyes sting, she had to concentrate. Blood, tea, milk, cheese. And something else, something herbal and repulsive.

'Merciful Shallya,' swore Liesel, almost falling over the bodies. 'Are they...'

'No, but they will be if their wounds aren't treated.'

Genevieve, suppressing the red thirst screaming from the savage stem of her brain, checked the wounded guards, feeling for heartbeats.

'Is this a vampire attack?' Liesel asked.

'It looks like it, doesn't it?'

Sister Liesel was suffering from shock, quivering with potential panic. She was demanding attention when Genevieve ought to be following the trail.

'Stay here and see to these men,' Genevieve ordered. 'Press something over the bites. Anything to stop the bleeding.'

'Don't go,' Liesel said. 'Jenny, please.'

'I have to.'

She pushed through the door. Bland's apartments were reachable only by doors at the end of this corridor. There should be two more guards.

The doors were open and the guards lay bleeding on the floor.

The herbal smell was more noticeable. Genevieve almost staggered.

She sprinted silently down the corridor.

Inside Bland's quarters, a small fire burned on a carpet, a dropped lamp in the middle of it. Flames cast shadows on the low ceiling, where a painted Morr presided over the torments and rewards of the beyond.

Genevieve caught the assassin at her work.

The blonde woman held Temple Father Bland in a vampire embrace, bending him over backwards at the knees. The cleric was in his nightshirt and cap, awake but frozen with terror, open eyes twitching, perpetual smile a rictus grin.

Blood on his neck.

'Stop,' said Genevieve.

The assassin raised her bloodied face and looked at her.

It was as if the gift of a reflection had returned. Genevieve was looking into her own face. Rather, at the nightmarish worst she had ever looked – a mask lit by wavering flame, eyes red bursts, finger-length fangs bloodied, streaks of gore in her hair.

'Who dares disturb the feeding of the vampire Genevieve?'

The voice was her own but different, coming from outside her skull.

Dazzled by the firelight and befuddled by all the spilled blood, Genevieve wondered what this creature was. Had her vampire self detached from her own body and set out on its own to kill?

Then, she saw through it.

'Do I really look like that?'

The assassin recognised her.

'You!' she said, startled.

'How inconvenient for you,' said Genevieve.

The assassin dropped Bland, whose head fell dangerously near the fire. He was twitching, still alive.

'Not inconvenient at all,' said the assassin, whom Genevieve saw was taller than her, with a longer reach. 'The vampire Genevieve murders Tio Bland, and is then captured and destroyed at the scene of the crime. It's better than the original plan.'

'Do you really think you can be me, Eva?'

'I've been playing you for years,' said Eva Savinien. 'The critics say I'm much better at it than you were. In the Genevieve Dieudonné business, you're an amateur.'

Genevieve faced herself. The fangs and claws were functional fakes. The hair was a wig.

Only the blood was real.

'How much is Wietzak paying you? Surely you could do better as a royal mistress?'

'Wietzak? He's not the half of it, sister.'

'You're not my sister.'

Genevieve leaped at Eva, but tripped over Bland, whose bulk wrinkled the carpet on the slick stone floor. Eva darted out of the way with something close to vampire swiftness. The actress had been possessed once, by something called the animus – it had emerged from the ruins of the fortress of Drachenfels for revenge. When it quit this host, the animus had left something of itself behind.

The blow came out of the dark, and caught the back of her head as if landed by a mace.

This was not like fighting a living woman.

Genevieve, lifted off the floor, sailed across the room. She hammered against a case of old books, which tumbled around her as the shelves collapsed. A heavy wooden board struck her head like a hammer. She put out her hands to steady herself and her sharpened fingers sank into book-pages. They were all blank, impressive bindings with nothing inside. That said something about their owner.

Still, she was doing her best to save the man's life.

'He won't be grateful,' purred Eva, suddenly close to her face. 'Tio Bland will still hate you. I've just opened his throat a little. You must be *thirsty*. All this blood spilled and none to drink. You must hate him, Genevieve. I'm not a vampire, and I hate him. I'll help you get away. You can have the credit. You'll be a heroine to your kind. You'll be another Kattarin...'

'One was enough, play-actress.'

Genevieve jabbed out with the heel of her hand, smartly clipping Eva's chin. One of the assassin's fangs was jarred loose. Her eyes widened as she nearly choked on it. She spat the thing out, a carved chicken bone.

Eva's clawfingers – steel-and-silver sheaths with curved barbs – came for Genevieve's face. The tips just raked skin, and dreadful black pain slashed across her cheek, eating to the bone.

She was out of the way of the second strike.

From behind, she got a hold on Eva's neck, and wrenched off her wig.

Eva's hands came up and tore off Genevieve's own wig. It had been securely attached and a lot of hair came with it.

They stood with each other's hair in their hands.

The fire spread to the fallen volumes. Flamelight rose. Bland was trying to get up on his hands and knees but kept falling. Blood trickled from his mock-bites.

Eva shredded Genevieve's wig and let the segments fall. She was skilled with her sharp killing-talons. And she'd had the foresight to use silver.

'I can take out your heart, lady leech.'

'You have to find it first.'

Mantis-style would leave her sides open. Too easy to get to the heart under the arms. Genevieve knew she'd have to fight like the bare-knuckles bruisers in Arne's gymnasium, elbows close to her ribs, punching with jabs, concentrating on the head and belly.

She damned Eva for her extra height, her extra inches of reach.

She slammed at Eva's head, with the same left-right-left, hook-jab-jab combination Preiss had tried on her. Eva ducked the hook, but took both the jabs. Her left eye was bruised and bloodied, then her cheek-bone broken. Genevieve stood back and pivoted, arching out her leg, knee loose, foot stretched. She landed her boot-toe in the big eye-cheek wound.

Eva gave out a satisfying yelp.

'Time for a final bow, understudy,' suggested Genevieve.

Eva recovered, faster than Genevieve had expected, and reached, taking a grip on Genevieve's side, on the soft part below the rib-cage.

Four needles of agony cut through her robe and lanced into her body. She opened her mouth in a scream that wouldn't come.

Eva took another hold, on Genevieve's shoulder. A thumb-thorn stuck into her neck. Hot hurt spread, covering her from upper arm to upper ear. Half her vision was fuzzy. Eva's face was half-blur, half-mask-of-hate. Eva held Genevieve pinned, squeezing her side. But the thorn in her neck was the killing tool – it probed, parting veins and stringmeat, and scraped her jaw-bone.

It was agonising.

'The first time I played you,' Eva said, conversationally, 'in the *Treachery of Oswald* revival, I slept with Detlef. When this is over, I'll go back to him. I'll gut him and let you take the blame. You'll be remembered as a monster.'

Genevieve took a firm hold on the talon stuck into her neck. The silver sheath seared her palm, but one more pain among so many could be ignored. She extracted the thorn from her flesh, twisting brutally. With a snap, she broke Eva's thumb.

Then, she hammered her forehead against the bridge of Eva's nose.

Cartilage gave way and a cloud of blood exploded all around.

Some of it went into Genevieve's mouth and she tasted Eva. There was almost nothing there.

Eva's hands went to her face.

Genevieve was free, though two of the fake fingers were still stuck in her side like white-hot arrowheads. With fast fingers and gritted teeth, Genevieve plucked the claws and threw them away.

Eva, horror-struck at the assault on her good looks, held her hands over her squashed nose. Blood poured between her fingers.

The room was on fire now.

Genevieve slung Bland over her shoulder and stepped into the corridor.

That herbal smell hit her again.

Liesel had dragged the two inner guards away. She was surrounded by four bleeding, unconscious men at the end of the corridor.

'Wake up, Brother Preiss,' shouted Genevieve.

Liesel still seemed too horrorstruck to move.

Genevieve set Bland down with the guards. His wounds were shallow, though his nightshirt was on fire. Almost absent-mindedly, Liesel patted out the flames.

'Get Preiss,' Genevieve insisted.

That smell! She knew what it was. Ground sleeprose petal, usually taken in tea. Before Eva came along, the guards had been drugged. The assassin had an ally within the Temple of Morr.

'Liesel,' Genevieve said, 'it's important. The danger isn't over. Snap out of it.'

'This isn't how it was supposed to be,' Liesel muttered. 'I told you to save yourself.'

'I'm fine. So will he be. But we must act fast...'

There was an explosion within Bland's apartments, and a crack shot through the walls. Genevieve half-turned and saw a creature of flame exploding through the doorway. Eva, burning all over, charged down the corridor, screeching, claws reaching.

Genevieve punched her in the heart, knocking her down.

She tried to smother Eva's flames – apart from other considerations, she wanted the actress-assassin alive to explain herself – but the fire kept bursting back wherever it was slapped out. Eva's face was black but for her eyes and teeth. She struggled, scratching at Genevieve though her claws were gone.

Genevieve's own clothes were smouldering.

Fire was less bad for vampires than silver. But enough flame would kill her.

A beam split above and the ceiling fell in. A broken spar plunged, jagged end like a stake, and speared into Eva's heart, stopping her writhing.

The actress died like a vampire.

Genevieve made it out of the collapsing corridor in time.

Liesel was doing her best trying to heave five heavy, insensible men away from danger.

There was other activity in the temple now.

Brother Preiss and Father Knock were here. And other brothers and sisters, half in robes, half in nightwear. The collapse of the corridor had limited the fire to Bland's apartments.

She heard Preiss order Willy and Walther to organise a bucket-passing line from the stables-pump to quell the blaze. Knock had some of his Old Temple cronies see to certain sacred items he wanted removed to a place of safety. Thoughtfully, someone tossed a pail of water over Genevieve, drenching her robes and drowning fire she hadn't noticed.

A chaplain-healer was looking at the guards and the Temple Father.

'They've been bitten,' he said.

Everyone was looking at Genevieve. Her hands, swelling and insensible from silver poisoning, went to her hair. Some of the wig-pins were still there. The last of her healthy country lass's make-up was washed away.

'Sister Jenny,' said Preiss. 'You have fangs.'

* * *

XV

'LADIES, GENTLEMEN, EXCUSE me,' he declared. 'I am Detlef Sierck, genius.'

Certainly, his announcement attracted attention. As a good entrance line should. Melissa gave him a little round of applause.

The central quadrangle of the Temple of Morr was smoky and crowded. A row of bleeding, insensible bodies were being seen to by a chaplain-healer and several sister-nurses. A wrestler-sized cleric – Detlef recognised Lupo Preiss from his epic bouts with Hagedorn a decade ago – had Genevieve, who seemed to be in a sorry state again, pinned to the ground. Several guards held down her arms and legs.

'That lady is Genevieve Dieudonné, my fiancée. She is under the protection of my sword. I call upon you in the name of the Empire and common decency to let her up at once. If you do not comply, I shall be forced to cut you to ribbons.'

He bowed slightly and held up his sword, blade catching the lantern-light.

A brother rushed onto the scene, holding a wooden mallet and a short sharp stake. He caught sight of Detlef's blade and skidded to a halt. He didn't hand the vampire-slaying apparatus to Preiss.

'What is this intrusion?' asked the sister with spectacles.

Detlef spotted her instantly as the one in charge. He recalled her name: Sister Liesel von Sutin.

'A rescue,' Detlef declared.

'And you've brought a *child* with you?'

Melissa smiled, showing fangs.

'Oh,' said the sister. 'That sort of child.'

In the carriage on the way over from the Street of a Hundred Taverns to the Temple of Morr, Detlef had tried to persuade Lady Melissa that it would be best if she didn't accompany him as he forced his way into a nest of vampire-slayers. She'd said she had no intention of missing out on any of the fun and had, at her age, learned to walk into and out of far worse places. When that hadn't impressed him, she just started repeating everything he said word for word in a high-pitched child-voice that scraped his nerves. Finally, he had just given in and told her not to look smug about it.

'The assassin must be destroyed,' said Preiss.

'Genevieve isn't the assassin,' said Detlef. 'She has been defamed by a woman named Eva Savinien, who came here in disguise.'

'This thing came here in disguise.'

Genevieve tried to sit up. She was bleeding from several places, had been set on fire and put out, and her white skin was blotchy with what looked like swollen insect-bites. The last of her make-up was washed away.

'You are not to call my grand-get a "thing",' said Melissa.

The child-shaped vampire walked across the quad and stood over the brothers pinning down Genevieve. Melissa tapped her foot and looked cross.

'Let her go, you bullies.'

Force of personality persuaded the clerics to slink back.

'Genevieve is a heroine,' said Melissa. 'She has saved your horrid Temple Father. I hope you'll learn a lesson about the undead from this. A living woman came to kill Tio Bland but a soulless vampire saved his life.'

Genevieve flung her long arms around Melissa's tiny neck, exhausted and grateful.

'Ugh, child,' said Melissa, 'you'll ruin the furs. How did you get so bedraggled?'

'Lady elder,' Genevieve gasped, 'my apologies.'

Genevieve still hugged her grandmother-in-darkness, face lost in voluminous fur.

Preiss looked to the injured, soliciting further orders from Bland. The Temple Father was alive but unconscious, bandages wrapped around his neck, face pale. Then, the wrestler looked to the woman in charge.

'Sister Liesel?'

The sister was thinking.

'Vampires have come among us,' she said, at last. 'And their human slaves. They must be put to the stake.'

Genevieve's face reappeared. She looked at Liesel, eyes burning.

'But, *Liesel*…'

Detlef recognised a complicated flow of emotions. The set-up within this temple was beyond instant understanding.

'Impostor, betrayer, assassin,' said Liesel, pointing at Genevieve.

Genevieve stood up, setting Melissa aside.

'No,' said Genevieve. 'I'm not the betrayer here. The assassin had help inside the temple, but not from me. Liesel, you swear by Shallya, not Morr. You are a very clever woman in a world that too rarely rewards you. I don't think you're dim enough to subscribe to Tio Bland's vampire prejudice. But you do see opportunities for advancement. After the assassination, what were you to become? The guardian of Bland's memory? Would you relay his wishes from the beyond and take control here? Make up a title like "Temple Mother" or "High Priestess? Everyone is already looking to you for orders. They've got used to it in the last months. Will you have us all killed and get back into your huddle with Baron Wietzak? Cooking up another Undead War so you can both make names for yourself?'

A lot of eyes were on the sister.

'Jenny,' she said, 'I hoped great things for you.'

'There is no Jenny. She was just pretend. Just as there was really no Liesel.'

'Brother Preiss, kill this leech. Now.'

The wrestler looked at Sister Liesel and shrugged. He made no move.

'With the Temple Father injured, I assume command here,' said Knock the elderly priest. 'A sister cannot decree the policy of the temple. Even the lowest novice brother comes in the precedence before the mother superior.'

An elderly woman in robes beamed approval. Sister Liesel fumed.

'To kill, even to kill a vampire, is to usurp the domain of Great Morr,' continued the Father, making devout signs. 'He alone decides when to take a soul. There must be no more blasphemy.'

'Aye, Father Knock,' assented Preiss.

Sister Liesel, frustrated, was still thinking. She knelt by Bland and began to shake him.

'Wake up, Temple Father, the vampires are here!'

'Leave him be,' said Father Knock.

'He's dying,' said the healer. 'Nothing can be done.'

'You see,' said Liesel. 'They're monsters.'

Detlef had not put away his sword. He thought he still might have to fight for Genevieve.

The brother with the stake and mallet held them up, ready for use.

Bland's eyes fluttered open. He was still smiling. His face must just be in the habit. He looked ghastly.

Father Knock muttered last rites and sprinkled incense over the Temple Father, with what Detlef intuited was a certain grim satisfaction.

'They've killed you,' Liesel told Bland.

'I was always prepared,' gasped the Temple Father, 'ready to fall first – indeed, to die – in the conflict, so long as my ending was a greater beginning. Here starts the Last Undead War, which must end with the eradication – indeed, obliteration – of the vampire taint from the world…'

To come so far and fail! Detlef would have killed Bland himself, only that seemed to be what the martyr wanted. The eager vampire-slayer tapped mallet to stake, and looked at Genevieve's chest.

'This is silly,' said Melissa. 'You, sawbones, out of my way.'

The chaplain-healer stepped back. Liesel looked electric hatred at Melissa.

'Don't let her near.'

Brother Preiss had a firm hold on Sister Liesel's shoulders.

Melissa got on her knees and crawled to Bland. She nestled into his lap, and stroked his bandaged neck. He smiled indulgently, until she showed her adorable little fang-teeth, then he cringed, eyes rolling upwards.

'Leech,' he gasped.

'Hush, silly man,' said the vampire.

Melissa raised her wrist to her mouth and bit as if into an apple, pricking her own vein.

Scarlet blood welled. She jammed the spouting wound into Bland's mouth. The Temple Father's eyes widened, and went red with the infusion. Melissa chewed away his bandages and sank her fangs into the red scratches on his neck.

Her whole body bucked as she drank deeply, sucking Bland's blood as he swallowed hers. This was how little leeches were made.

It lasted a while.

When the mutual feeding was over, Melissa dropped Bland and stood up. She was shaky on her feet, having lost as much blood as she'd drunk. Genevieve steadied her.

'He's dead,' said the chaplain-healer, hand on Bland's heart.

'Not for long,' said Melissa. 'Lay him out, and have a goat or something close by. When he wakes up, he's going to be very *thirsty*.'

'And he might want to reconsider his policy on vampires,' suggested Genevieve.

XVI

SHE HAD TRIED to find out what was to become of Liesel von Sutin. According to Temple Father Knock, the sister was on a retreat in the Northern Wastes, devoting herself to the simple duties of cleaning and cooking for an order of ascetic monks who had vowed never to look a woman in the eyes much less talk to one. Genevieve still wasn't sure what she thought of Liesel. She kept hearing Knock's proud statement that 'even the lowest novice brother comes in the precedence before the mother superior'. The only comfort she could take was that, as a vampire, she should live to see that change, in the Cult of Morr and throughout the human world. It would be a long while coming, though. Even Brustellinite anarchists like Prince Kloszowski, who wanted to bring down kings and lords and set peasants on an equal footing with their former masters, treated women like strange combinations of slave, slut and long-suffering mother.

The Temple of Morr wasn't issuing much news about her newest brother-in-darkness – perhaps because the responsibility for issuing any news had formerly laid with the now-closed scribe-proclaimer's office. The *Boulevardpresse* alleged that the cult's goat consumption had risen tenfold and that novices wore silver collars when attending late-night services. Tio Bland's 'dear wife and three lovely children', on an extended tour of the provinces, were not expected to return to the city this season.

The whole vampire campaign had blown over completely. Under Knock and his 'Old Temple' faction, the Cult of Morr announced a 'Back to basics' campaign, and clerics were busying themselves with their former good works and funereal duties. Clause 17 was, by quiet agreement, struck from the Sanitation Act.

Happy hour in the Crescent Moon had lasted a week. Lady Melissa would never have to pay for the special ever again.

The Vargr Breughel was looking for a new leading lady. The surprise success of Renastic and Vlad, the comedy ventriloquist and his vampire dummy, meant that the theatre could play variety to full houses while auditions were held for *Genevieve and Vukotich*. She had sensed that Detlef was working up to asking her to play herself again, and had deftly reasserted her permanent retirement from the stage.

No one had been arrested for the murder of Ibby the Fish, but Watch Sergeant Munch announced that progress was being made on the case. The monthly number of Hooks found floating off the docks was roughly equal to the number of Fish found hooked in back-alleys.

Munch was more concerned with the 'mosquito murders', a series of gruesome deaths among well-connected criminals who had recently bought themselves out of Mundsen Keep but ran into a strange instrument of justice that sucked all the flesh out of their skins through a single puncture-wound over the heart. It was rumoured that 'Filthy Harald' Kleindeinst and his sometime partner Rosanna the Scryer were on the case, which involved a conspiracy reaching from the lowest stews of Wharf Vermin Way to the perfumed palaces of Imperial Row.

Baron Wietzak was truly dead – transfixed with hawthorn, beheaded with silver, burned in a holy fire, ashes scattered in the sunshine. Someone had told the Tsarevich Pavel Society how to penetrate his castle crypts via secret passageways unknown to anyone under a thousand years old. Melissa claimed not to know anything about that.

It turned out that Eva Savinien had been profitably moonlighting as an assassin for years, committing murders for hire during the times when she was 'resting' – though she earned far less as a killer than she did as a star actress, suggesting some compulsion lingering from her old encounter with the animus. The story of her Zhiekhill-and-Chaida life came out in the *Boulevardpresse*. The body recovered from the fire at the temple was impossible to identify and so many of her admirers hoped she was merely missing.

And Genevieve was still here. In the theatre, in the city.

She couldn't remember precisely how it had happened, but she and Detlef seemed to be engaged. Obviously, the traditional silver ring was out of the question but gold was a fair substitute.

Waking at nightfall from a day's lassitude in the divan she had insisted be installed in the office, she saw Detlef at his desk, scratching quill to parchment, a fresh candle burning. He was working on a second sonnet cycle. He was losing weight and the character lines in his face were firming up. When he was writing, he had the concentration of a dedicated schoolboy.

She watched him for several minutes before he noticed her. When he did, he smiled, set aside his pen and blotted the page.

'Tonight,' he said, 'you can read it.'

She had been waiting for that.

At once, she was across the room. She slipped into Detlef's lap, and greedily snatched up the paper. For an instant, she was disappointed to find he had not been working on a poem. He was drafting an announcement to go into the *Spieler*, of their wedding.

The ceremony would be held on stage, with the Arch-Lector of the Cult of Sigmar solemnising the vows of nuptial devotion and Honorio of the Convent of Eternal Night and Solace reading the invocations of fortune and long life. Melissa was monopolising Kerreth the costumier with many refinements of the pattern for the gown she was to wear as maid of honour. Prince Luitpold, heartbroken by the disappearance of Eva Savinien but cheered by a sudden interest in the dance stylings of Antonia Marsillach, had consented to represent the Imperial court at the wedding. He was to become official patron of the Vargr Breughel Memorial Theatre, which ought to make future censorship of Detlef Sierck productions unlikely and was 'one in the eye for the fogeys of the Imperial Tarradasch Players'. The wedding reception was to be at the Crescent Moon, which would consent to admit living people equally with the undead for the occasion and had been instructed to import vintages of quality for the cellar. Rumour had it that virgin lads from the mountains, raised on only fresh beef and purest springwater, were being brought to the city to be on offer as the special for that evening. Genevieve had issued strict instructions to Poppa Fritz and Guglielmo Pentangeli that the Three Little Clots were on no account to be allowed to organise Detlef's stag night – but had few illusions that her wishes would be acceded to in the matter.

Genevieve hummed over the announcement, then approved.

'Missy says I make up too many tragic endings,' Detlef told her. 'Just for a change, let's live happily ever after.'

'It's worth a try,' she said.

Detlef bared his neck to be kissed.

ABOUT THE AUTHOR

Besides his contributions to the Games Workshop
Warhammer and Dark Future series, the seldom-
seen Jack Yeovil is the author of a single novel, *Orgy
of the Blood Parasites*, and used to fill in occasionally
as a film reviewer for Empire and the NME. Kim
Newman seems to have Jack under control at the
moment, but the stubborn beast flesh occasionally
comes creeping back.

More Warhammer from the Black Library

DRACHENFELS
A Genevieve novel
by Kim Newman writing as Jack Yeovil

NOW CONRADIN WAS dead. Sieur Jehan was dead.
Heinroth was dead. Ueli was dead. And before the
night was over, others – maybe all of the party – would
be joining them. Genevieve hadn't thought about
dying for a long time. Perhaps tonight Drachenfels
would finish Chandagnac's Dark Kiss, and push her at
last over the border between life and death.

DETLEF SIERCK, *the self-proclaimed greatest playwright in
the world, has declared that his next production will be a
recreation of the end of the Great Enchanter Drachenfels
– to be staged at the very site of his death, the Fortress of
Drachenfels itself. But the castle's dark walls still hide a
terrible and deadly secret which may make the first night
of Detlef's masterpiece the last of his life.*

More Warhammer from the Black Library

GENEVIEVE UNDEAD
A Genevieve novel
by Kim Newman writing as Jack Yeovil

GENEVIEVE'S MOUTH WAS full of blood. An ancient instinct took over. She fixed her mouth to Schedoni's wound. She sucked, and the old man's blood was pumped into her. Her mind cleared, and she swallowed.

These people were nothing to her. She was a visitor, like Aleksandr and d'Amato and the girl. They had made her play her part, but it wasn't her. She wasn't Genevieve Udolpho, she was Genevieve Dieudonné. She wasn't sixteen, she was six hundred and sixty-nine. She wasn't even human. She was a vampire.

Genevieve drank, and became stronger.

DARK AND TERRIBLE *secrets may be found lurking within the cities of the Old World and the savage wilderness that surrounds them. Genevieve Dieudonné, vampire heroine of* Drachenfels, *battles to outwit adversaries both magical and mundane, human and beast, in this series of three linked novellas:* Stage Blood, The Cold Stark House *and* Unicorn Ivory.

More Warhammer from the Black Library

BEASTS IN VELVET
A Warhammer novel
by Kim Newman writing as Jack Yeovil

'WHEN YOU ARRIVED,' said the baron, 'did you scry anything?'

She thought back beyond the blackness of her fainting spell. She remembered opening the coach door, and setting her foot on the cobbles. Then there were flashes of red in the dark. She heard the ghost of a scream, and received the image of someone in a long, voluminous garment, bent over a shrieking animal, working away inside it. No, it was not an animal. It was – had been – a woman.

THE DARK, CROWDED *streets of Altdorf, greatest city of the Old World, have always teemed with rogues and cut-throats. But now the City Watch is faced with its greatest challenge, a murderer so savage that he is known only as the Beast. Against a background of mounting fear and hysteria, three unlikely allies must work together to track down the killer. A trail of bloody clues leads to the Imperial court – can the Beast be apprehended before the Empire is overwhelmed by the flames of revolution?*

More Warhammer from the Black Library

ZAVANT
By Gordon Rennie

'YOU HAVE EXAMINED the corpse, no doubt?' Graf Otto rasped, looking at Zavant Konniger. 'What are your conclusions?'

Konniger set down his wine glass and composed himself before answering. 'Foul play has been committed, certainly. But it was not a robbery-turned-murder. The victim's killer left a full purse of gold behind him. And Altdorf's footpads and cut-purses may be a bloodthirsty lot, but I have yet to meet one who would make a habit of ripping out his victims' throats with his bare teeth.'

'Surely it is the work of some wild animal, then? Some beast loose within the city walls?'

Konniger paused, sensing that he was being tested. 'Animals kill for food. Whatever killed this poor unfortunate did so only for its own savage pleasure.'

THE OLD WORLD *is a dark and dangerous place, and even the towns and cities offer little shelter, for the evil that stalks their fog-shrouded streets is as deadly as it is elusive. Enter Zavant Konniger, the great sage-detective of Altdorf. Accompanied by his trusty halfling manservant, Vido, this most brilliant scholar must use his incredible powers of deduction to solve the most sinister mysteries of the day.*